MY BEST FRIEND'S LIFE

MY BEST FRIEND'S LIFE

Shari Low

ISIS

LARGE PRINT

Oxford

First published in Great Britain 2008
by
HarperCollinsPublishers

Published in Large Print 2008 by ISIS Publishing Ltd.,
7 Centremead, Osney Mead, Oxford OX2 0ES
by arrangement with
HarperCollins

British Library Cataloguing in Publication Data
Low, Shari
  My best friend's life. – Large print ed.
  1. Lifestyles – Fiction
  2. Women librarians – Fiction
  3. Single women – Fiction
  4. Female friendship – Fiction
  5. Large type books
  I. Title
  823.9'2 [F]

ISBN 978–0–7531–8198–0 (hb)
ISBN 978–0–7531–8199–7 (pb)

Printed and bound in Great Britain by
T. J. International Ltd., Padstow, Cornwall

Thank you first and foremost to Sheila Crowley (at AP Watt) and Maxine Hitchcock (at Avon), the two talented, fabulous women who encourage me, guide me in the right direction and hold my hand when it's all going wrong.

Thanks to Caroline Ridding, Keshini Naidoo, Sammia Rafique and Sara Foster at Avon for their skill, patience and endless good humour.

As always, huge gratitude to Rob Kraitt, Linda Shaughnessy, Teresa Nicholls and the whole team at AP Watt for their belief, optimism and all the work that goes on behind the scenes.

Thanks to Melanie Harvey at the *Daily Record* for always understanding (and to her mum, Maureen, for bringing in the nuns!).

To the lovely Gemma Low for being nothing like the teenagers in this book.

And special thanks to Carmen Reid, Liz Murphy, Sadie Hill, Janice McCallum, Linda Lowery, Anne-Marie Low, Wendy Morton, Pamela McBurnie, Sylvia Lavizani, Frankie Plater, Jan Johnstone and Gillian Armstrong — who dragged me up the mountain of the last year with laughs, support and the promise of a big bucket of Lambrusco at the top.

Shari xx

To Rosina Hill, for your support, your courage
and your huge big heart . . .

To John, just everything, always . . .

And to my gorgeous, incredible boys, Callan
and Brad . . . Now go tidy your rooms.

PROLOGUE

The Daily Globe
22 June 2006

The Prime Minister announced today that, in line with European legislation, the government has decided to ease restrictions currently placed on the operation of brothels within the UK.

In this controversial move, it is proposed that from 1 July this year, local authorities will have the power to license and oversee premises engaged in the business of providing sex for payment.

Announcing the new regulations, the Prime Minister released the following statement:

"It has been clear for some time that current legislation pertaining to the adult entertainment industry is neither realistic nor effective. In recent years we have seen dramatic increases both in the number of arrests for prostitution and in the influx of sex trade workers from other EU countries. This government has concluded that the only progressive, sensible way forward is to legitimise this industry, therefore allowing it to be controlled and regulated.

I'd like to give my firm commitment that I — assisted by a focus group comprised of six cross-party MPs to be called the Adult Entertainment Regulatory

Commission — will personally monitor the success of the new guidelines and be fully involved in the forthcoming months in the evolution of progressive policies to further develop this sector."

The Prime Minister refused to confirm, however, that applications to join the Regulatory Commission reached an unprecedented level, with 91 per cent of government members requesting a position.

CHAPTER
ONE

Tom, Harry, Forget about Dick

Ginny's bedroom, the village of Farnham Hills, near Chipping Sodbury, Autumn 2007

"So you mean, like, a penis embargo?"

"Correct," replied Roxy. "I'm going to be an official willy-free zone. I'm on a twelve-step male-genital detox programme: Step number one, boyfriend is history. Step number two, I quit my job. Step number three, I recruit my best friend to help me get a new job. Er, Ginny, honey, that's you."

There was a pause so pregnant it could have applied to Social Services for free milk vouchers and child benefit.

Roxy waited for a reaction. None. *Nada*. Okay, so this wasn't going to plan. Normally she could rely on Ginny to react in exactly the way she'd been reacting to everything Roxy said since they were sitting side by side in the playpen.

Act one: Rolling of eyes.

Act two: Loud tutting noise.

Act three: Adopts the approximate expression of someone who has just discovered that she is chewing a wasp.

1

Act four: Capitulates, offers sympathy, then digs friend out of big hole.

But no. Ginny was staring mournfully into space, as if she'd slipped into one of those cosmic, out-of-body trances that pass the time while you're waiting in the bank queue or having a smear test.

"Ginny?" she probed, attempting to snap her friend's focus back to the most important thing in life — herself.

"What?"

"Didn't you hear me? I need help! Ginny, I'm single, I'm unemployed, I'm devastated . . . I'm desperate!"

From her cramp-inducing position on a tatty beanbag (circa 1990), Ginny looked over at her clapped-out single bed and the female reclining on it — probably the least desperate-looking woman she had ever set eyes on. Roxy's jet-black hair hung in sleek, shiny slates from her middle parting to her shoulder bones. Her perfect, size twelve, über-toned frame was adorned in her standard uniform of black Prada boot-cut trousers, a black Nicole Farhi cashmere roll-neck and lethal four-inch stiletto Gina boots. Skin: flawless. Nails: perfectly plastic. Make-up: subtle. Breasts: pert. And Ginny just knew without looking that there were no hairs on Roxy's legs, no hard skin on her feet, and her nethers had applied for permanent residence in Brazil.

There was no doubt about it: Roxy Galloway was channelling Angelina Jolie.

Ginny Wallis, meanwhile, was channelling the bag lady who sat outside Superdrug on an inner tube flogging jewellery she'd made out of string and discarded scratchcards.

She sighed wearily, so immune to Roxy's perpetual melodramas that she'd slipped into a moment of reflection instead of enthusiastically participating in the panic. The contrast of her glam, glitzy, cutting-edge friend with the greyness of Ginny's life somehow highlighted the fact that Ginny was twenty-seven and still living at home in a bedroom that hadn't changed since the Nineties. The duvet was a tribute to the golden days when boy bands ruled the world. If the carpet ever revisited its former life it would have been baby pink and orange — now, ten years of spills and wear later, it was a delicate shade of road-kill. Even woodworm would shun the furniture. And the curtains were obviously designed by someone on LSD, bought by someone on crack and then hung by someone on two bottles of cider and a Lambert & Butler that Roxy had stolen from her mother's handbag.

And they had paid for that wild, drunken, smoky, teenage night of fabric-hanging by being grounded for a month and having their Christmas Top Shop vouchers confiscated.

Urgh, it was depressing. Ginny pulled a bit of fluff off her hoodie, and pushed her riot of mousey-brown frizz back off her forehead.

"Roxy, when did I become so old that I thought jogging bottoms and sweatshirts were acceptable as everyday outerwear?"

"Honey, until four o'clock this afternoon when I resigned from my erstwhile employment, I worked with people who thought a crotch-baring French maid's costume, nipple rings and five-inch Perspex platforms were acceptable everyday outerwear." Roxy's bottom lip trembled. "Oh, I miss them," she wailed. "Have I made a mistake? I mean, it was a prestigious career in the hospitality industry . . ."

"Roxy, you worked in a whorehouse," Ginny interjected, with a tut and a roll of the eyes.

Phew. Normal service was almost resumed. All they needed was the wasp-chewing face and they were back on track to Moral Support Central.

"A classy, cosmopolitan, extremely upmarket entertainment club, if you don't mind."

Actually Ginny did mind. It wasn't that she was a prude, it's just that, well, she'd never understood Roxy's career choice. Receptionist at the Seismic Lounge: *guaranteed to make the earth move.* Yep, whatever marketing genius had thought up that slogan was probably now enjoying a fulfilling career flipping burgers. Or making scratchcard jewellery next to the bag lady outside Superdrug.

Roxy had been ecstatic when she got the job. The club had opened the day after the government legalised brothels — definitely some insider information at work there — and it was on one of the most exclusive streets in Mayfair. Four hours of copulation cost the same as a second-hand Corsa, most of the girls spoke with accents that could crack windows, and the sex toys came gold-plated. It oozed class and made no apologies for targeting only the extremely wealthy. It even employed chauffeurs to collect the clients in blacked-out Range Rovers and bring them in through a private underground car park so that the paparazzi never got a recognisable shot. Actually, that wasn't true — Stephen Knight, notorious B-list movie star, usually arrived in his open-top Aston Martin DB7 and parked it right outside the door. *He* was obviously channelling Charlie Sheen.

To Roxy, it was all so decadently glamorous. Short of becoming a fake-tan consultant or adopting a serial football-player-shagging habit, it seemed like the easiest way to hobnob with the rich and/or famous on a daily basis.

Glitz, high rollers, decadence and dosh — it was the life she'd always dreamt of (although, to be honest, she hadn't exactly foreseen that the high life would carry a faint whiff of antibacterial cleaning spray and that she'd witness all the activity from behind a desk).

Roxy had always thought it was an aberration that she'd been born in Farnham Hills. She'd decided at an early age that the stork had obviously been on its way to a four-storey, three-million-pound townhouse in Belgravia when it was cruelly struck down by a shot from an armed robber's rifle (yes, she had a very vivid imagination, even as a child) and forced to drop its precious bundle in an environment in which she clearly didn't belong. When her classmates were splashing their pocket money on *Just Seventeen*, she was buying *Vogue*. When, at sixteen, they were fantasising about a fortnight in Faliraki, she was dreaming of a weekend in St Tropez. And when they were imagining their future husbands, children, and three-bedroom semis on the new housing estate on the edge of the village, she was imagining tunnelling to freedom and spending the rest of her life shagging an obscenely rich bloke, surrounded by walnut panelling in the master suite of his custom-built yacht.

And okay, so she wasn't quite there yet, but when she was offered the job at the Seismic she instinctively knew that she had opened the door to the world she belonged in.

And the bonus was that, as receptionist, she only had to meet, greet and keep the customer records up to date. The money was great, the tips were outstanding and, unlike the rest of the girls, her pay packet didn't come at the expense of cystitis.

She loved it — at least to start with. But over the last couple of months it had all seemed a little too repetitive. The same faces week after week, the endless stream of girls (who invariably quit once they'd earned enough to buy a flat, finished university or received an irresistible offer of marriage from a blue-blooded, upper-class, Eton-educated arms dealer), and the rising scepticism after yet another client did an "At Home with the Happy Family" spread in *Hello!*. Roxy had to admit it — the job was wearing down her trust in men and turning the loving act of sex into a business transaction. Did you enjoy your ejaculation, sir? Oh, lovely — now would that be Visa, MasterCard or American Express?

She just wanted to be like normal people (porn stars and penile-implant specialists aside) and experience a daily life that wasn't controlled or influenced by actions of the male reproductive organ.

She could probably have struggled on for another couple of months, but the latest devastation in her love life had tipped her over the edge. She winced. She still couldn't believe that after two years of devotion Felix was history. Gone. Past tense.

But after spending three days submerged in hysterical mourning she had decided that no man was worth a forty-five per cent increase in wrinkles caused by perpetual sobbing — even if he was the first and — penis-embargo withstanding — last love of her life.

She would never, ever mention his name again.

Ever.

Except in a blatant ploy to get help and sympathy from a bored, indifferent best friend . . .

"God, Ginny, you're so self-absorbed. Since Felix betrayed me I'm experiencing such an overwhelming trauma that I've put off having my roots done, I can't face going out and I'm so bitter that my karma has gone all to fuck. I mean, how would you feel if you were not only unemployed, but you'd caught the love of your life shagging the local florist?" she wailed. "And he didn't even have the decency to send me a bunch of bloody flowers."

Ginny nodded in what she hoped vaguely resembled a sympathetic expression. It lasted about three seconds before the truth made a break for freedom.

"He was a twat anyway."

"He was not!" Roxie protested.

"Was."

"Was not."

Ginny sighed. "You do realise that we're twenty-seven? Apparently we should have given up on childish, petty, pantomime dialogue somewhere around puberty. Remind me again why we're friends?"

She had a point. Almost thirty years of friendship, based on having absolutely nothing in common other than the fact that they were born on the same day and their mothers were distantly related. Speaking of which . . .

"Hellooooooooooo, girlies." The sing-song shriek came from downstairs and was accompanied by a slamming door and the smell of chow mein.

Said girlies groaned. "How can you be related to someone who sounds like that? You know, you really have to move out of your mother's house, Gin — it's obscene that you still live here at your age."

"And is *my* favourite girlie still up there too?" screeched another voice, which to the untrained ear sounded very like the first one.

Roxy sighed. "And how can I be related to someone who sounds like that?"

Then, louder, "Yes, Mum, I'll be down in a minute."

"I've got your favourite here, sweetie — prawn crackers and crispy chicken. We thought we'd all have dinner together."

"Gin, do you think our mothers are having a lesbian affair? I haven't seen them apart since about 1974. Urgh, mental image, my mother muff-diving . . . don't think I can face those prawn crackers now. And I'm not buying that my mother moved in here just for the companionship."

Gin giggled. "You have a sex-obsessed, twisted mind. They're not lovers, they're cousins."

"About third cousins, four times removed. I've met people in public toilets who are closer relations than that. But think about it. Since your dad popped his clogs and my dad popped Mrs Fleming from the fish shop, they've been joined at the hip. Urgh, another mental thought that I could live without."

"They're *cousins*!" shrieked Ginny, smacking Roxy with a threadbare, heart-shaped pink pillow, and *still* her perfect hair didn't move an inch out of place.

"There should be a law against parents having sex. Come on then, let's go join them. But when we're finished you have to help me update my CV and find a new job, Gin — you know I'm hopeless at that kind of stuff."

"And what am I, a careers officer?" Ginny replied indignantly.

"You work in a library! There are loads of job information advice thingies in there."

"There are also several editions of the *Kama Sutra* and a whole bloody shelf on the menopause, but I know sod all about those either."

Objection overruled.

"Come on, hon, *please*. I really need you to help me decide what I'm going to do. Maybe I should take a year out and travel a bit. Or go back to university. I only had one year left to do, before . . . well . . . before . . ."

"Before you got caught giving the philosophy professor a blow job. Under a podium. During a lecture."

"Girlies!!!" came another shriek from downstairs.

Ginny groaned. "You know, Rox, you're right — I have to move out of here. I need to stop wearing clothes with 'sweat' in the title, and I need to shred the apron strings."

Suddenly, a rousing chorus of "Hey Big Spender" filled the room.

"Rox, either your arse is singing or that's the naffest ringtone I've ever heard."

Roxy ignored her and checked the screen.

"Shit. Shit. Bloody shit. It's Sam at the Seismic."

"What did he say when you resigned?"

"Actually I just left a note. Couldn't face them."

To Ginny, this didn't exactly come as a newsflash. It was vintage Roxy. Roxy, who couldn't face up to life's unpleasantries if her Miu Miu mules depended on it. It had been the same their whole lives. Roxy couldn't tell a boy she didn't like him any more so she sent Ginny. Roxy never did her homework, she just copied Ginny's. Roxy didn't want to tell her mother she was leaving home, so she did a midnight flit. Ginny carried the bags. Crazy, impetuous, dramatic, spontaneous, endlessly fucking irritating Roxy.

But then . . .

Wasn't that the same Roxy who had poured a can of Vimto down the front of Kevin Smith trousers in primary school because he'd put chewing gum in Ginny's hair? The poor guy was probably still in therapy trying to eradicate the nightmare of spending the next ten years with the nickname Pisspants.

And wasn't that the same Roxy who'd bought Ginny her very first box of tampons? Actually, she'd stolen them from a fifth-year prefect's gym bag, but the thought was still there.

And that was definitely the same Roxy who had invented the care package that got Ginny through every teenage moment of doubt, insecurity or low self-esteem: two Mars Bars, a packet of Silk Cut, a bottle of Diamond White and the *Dirty Dancing* video.

Ginny's face reverted to pensive-slash-wasp-chewing as she grudgingly conceded that, despite all Roxy's faults, she was more than a friend and general irritation: she was the closest thing Ginny had ever had to a sister. One who was insanely annoying, spoilt, demanding, high maintenance, yet still managed to make Ginny laugh more than anyone else on earth. And, if she was totally honest, sometimes she admired Roxy's spirit. At least Roxy had taken chances in life, she'd broken the mould and experienced a bit of excitement and danger — although that police caution for flashing her baps at a bus full of American tourists travelling down Farnham Hills High Street had been a jolly jape too far.

Nope, at least Roxy would never be boring, Ginny conceded dolefully.

Unlike her chum, no one would ever call *Ginny* spontaneous. Her life's CV could fill one paragraph: *Same job since she left school almost a decade earlier, same boyfriend for twelve years, still lives in the same village she's lived in all her life, with her mother, in a bedroom that she hasn't decorated since before the millennium.* Ginny was so ponderous that she took two weeks to decide to order something out of a catalogue, and that was with the safety net of a money-back guarantee.

Boring? Check. Restrained? Check. Dead? It was pretty close . . .

Ginny pulled at a thread at the bottom of her sleeve and half the cuff unravelled. Fabulous. She hastily shoved the sleeve halfway up her arm to conceal the demise of a sweatshirt that had given her years of loyal service.

She glanced at Roxy and guessed that Roxy probably didn't have a single thing in her wardrobe that was more than six months old. Urgh, sometimes Ginny really felt like the bland, wardrobe-challenged poor relation. But then, this was the life she'd chosen. This is what made her happy. Content. Satisfied with her lot. Condemned to a lifetime of mediocrity. Ouch, where had that come from?

It was just that sometimes . . . Well, just sometimes she'd like to know what it felt like to get dressed up to the nines in designer togs, in a bra and pants that weren't matching shades of grey, in shoes that didn't lace up and come in three different shades of boring, and spend just one day where she couldn't predict — down to the last second — everything that would happen.

She shrugged off her melancholy. It didn't matter if she had the odd moment of regret — she'd already chosen her path, and her ship hadn't so much sailed as sprung a leak, capsized, and plummeted to the bottom of the local pond. And anyway, who was to say that any other life would make her happier than the one she had here with her mother, long-standing boyfriend and steady job, in the village she'd always lived in, with the same people she'd been seeing every single day of her life? This was it. And it was as good as it was going to get. Wasn't it?

Over on the bed, Roxy was blustering into the phone. "But I don't know anyone who can cover it! Okay. Okay. I understand. Okay. I'll get back to you. Sorry, Sam."

She snapped the phone shut.

"Fuck."

Ginny climbed out of the pond and rejoined the drama. "Problem?"

"He says I can't just walk out — something about a one-month notice period, blah, blah, blah. He sounds really pissed off. Apparently Sascha has gone off with herpes and Tilly has been barricaded in a hotel by the *News of the World* because she's doing a kiss-and-tell on some MP this week, so they've got no one to cover for me. He says I'll lose my holiday pay and my salary and, oh, I don't know, a bloody kidney if I'm not at the desk tomorrow. So much for turning over a new leaf."

Roxy looked at her watch. "The new, penis-avoiding me lasted for a whole eight hours . . ."

"I'll do it."

". . . and now Felix will know where to find me and he'll come begging me to take him back."

"I'll do it."

". . . And I tell you, if he pitches up with a bunch of petunias I'll shove them up his . . . What?"

"I'll do it."

"Do what?"

"Cover your shift at the Seismic. Sam's the guy I met at your birthday party, right? The one who helped me fill the vol-au-vents?"

Roxy groaned. "Still can't believe you brought vol-au-vents to my party. Thank God Gordon Ramsay couldn't make it or you'd have had his stroke on your conscience."

"Can we just focus on Sam? He was nice. Your type actually — how come you didn't go for him instead of the dickhead?"

Roxy's lip pouted even further than usual. "Thought about it, he fits all the criteria, but the man works in a brothel — could you imagine the dinner-party conversation? 'Hi, I'm Jeremy, I'm in hedge funds, and you?' 'I'm Sam — vaginas.' "

Ginny shrieked with laughter, but Roxy barely rose from her morose state. "Anyway, Sam, party, so?"

"Well, he was nice. Vaginas aside, obviously. Said if I ever decided to move into the city I should check in with him to see if there were any vacancies. Of course, I was wearing your clothes, your jewellery and your shoes at the time, so he probably thought I was Miss Cosmopolitan Girl about Town. Anyway, if it's only for a month, surely he wouldn't mind?"

"But even if it was okay with Sam, what about your job? Where will you live? You can't commute, the hours are too irregular."

14

"I'll move into your place."

"And I would live . . .?"

"Here."

"You're kidding me."

Ginny's inspiration was gathering speed. Suddenly this seemed like the best idea she'd ever had. *Spontaneous?* She could be spontaneous. Her enthusiasm bubbled. Spontaneous was her middle name. Actually, it was Violet, after her mother, but that wasn't the point.

"I'm not. Come on, Roxy — it totally works! That gives you a month to sort out what you're going to do with your life and heal that devastated soul. Should be ample time. You can live here and you can take my job in the library. You said it yourself, it's the best place to research your future options."

"But they'd never let me."

"Course they would. Hold on, I'll ask the manager." Ginny opened her bedroom door.

"Muuuuum, is it okay if Roxy takes my place at the library for a few days?"

"Course it is, dear. Now, hurry up, or I'll have to microwave your hoisin sauce."

"That's settled then. Come on, you know what to do there, you covered my holidays."

"That was in 1998!"

"Trust me, nothing's changed. What shift are you supposed to be on tomorrow?"

"Er, noon till eight," replied Roxy tentatively. She had a horrible feeling that for the first time in her life she was being outmanoeuvred. The library. One month. God, she could *smell* the boredom.

But then, she couldn't face London again. She needed a break. She needed to be away from the Seismic, away from memories of Felix, away from the constant pressure to be nice to grown men who paid for women half their age to attach probes to their testicles.

"Okay, I'll do it. On one condition . . ."

"Name it," said Ginny.

"I'm changing that duvet. If I'm going to sleep with Westlife, then I want them to have working parts."

Farnham Hills High School: Pupil Report: 1993

Name: Virginia Wallis   Year: S2

Subject	Above Average	Average	Satisfactory	Poor
English	X			
Mathematics	X			
History	X			
Geography	X			
Languages	X			
Science	X			
Religious Education	X			
P.E.				X
Art				X
Music & Drama				X

Summary:

Ginny shows little or no interest in PE, Drama, Art or Music. Her only focus in the arts is in the field of literature, where Ginny shows a voracious appetite for all genres.

This was reflected in her achievement of second place in the county short-story competition with her splendid entry, "The Day My Cousin Stole My Bike".

Ginny should be encouraged, however, to broaden her interests to encompass other disciplines and areas.

Personal Skills:

Ginny's behaviour and conduct within the school this year has, as always, been exemplary. She has achieved a 100 per cent attendance record and a perfect punctuality score.

She is articulate, pleasant, diligent and always keen to help others.

She works well under direction, but is equally capable of using her own initiative.

Ginny has a keen analytical mind and excels in her ability to absorb and process information.

Ginny has now assumed her new role in the school library, where she is responsible for the efficient management of the record systems and the inventory. She is handling this position with efficiency and enthusiasm.

Challenges/Development Needs:

Ginny continues to lack confidence and finds it difficult to assert herself, especially in the presence of authority or stronger characters. As a consequence of this, she can occasionally be easily led — as witnessed by the smoking incident earlier in the year.

Shyness also continues to be a challenge, and this often prevents Ginny from participating in class or group discussions or projects.

It is hoped that as Ginny matures her confidence will improve, allowing her interpersonal skills to develop to the same level as her intellectual abilities.

Signed: *Mrs Farquar — Senior Guidance Teacher S2*

CHAPTER
TWO

I Feel the Earth Move

Ginny. Day One, Sunday, 9p.m.

It was hard to tell what was thumping louder: the wheels of the train, Ginny's heart or the adrenaline that was making her toes tingle. Actually, the latter two may have been caused by the fact that she was wearing Roxy's Gina boots and they were a size and a half too small. But bugger it, she was done with playing it safe, being sensible and pitching camp in her comfort zone — now, for war, hostage situations, life and fabulous footwear, she was adopting the motto of the fearless: Who Dares Wins.

As long as the blisters didn't turn septic and kill her first.

And anyway, she was hardly going to start her windswept glamorous month in the UK's metropolis in a pair of Hush Puppies that she had fished from the Shoerite sale bin.

She spotted the middle-aged woman in the beige padded mac sitting across from her, eyeing up her faux leopardskin trolley-case: flashy, trashy, and guaranteed to make Jackie Collins weak at the knees with lust. She'd had to prise Roxy's fingers off it one by one. It was one thing taking her job, her flat and her life, but apparently her luggage was connected to her soul by an invisible umbilical cord and could only be freed by two hours of persuasion, vast amounts of grovelling and the promise of a blood donation should Roxy ever require it.

This furry suitcase on wheels was the personification of the new Ginny: bold, outrageous, completely out of character with its environment. Her stomach flipped with a surge of excitement, an emotion that up until that afternoon she'd thought twenty-seven years in Farnham Hills had knocked out of her. Ten miles from Chipping Sodbury, almost two hours west of London by train, population 3,453, Farnham Hills should have an official disclaimer at the village gates.

WARNING: Residence in this area can induce feelings of intense lethargy, boredom and, in extreme cases, a sudden and irrevocable fusion of the buttocks to the nearest couch.

Ginny grinned and a giggle escaped her as she allowed herself a moment of self-congratulation. She felt bold! She felt fearless!

The woman opposite, however, just felt mildly disturbed that Ginny was laughing for no evident reason and hatched a plan to pretend to disembark at the next station then jump back on into another carriage. But Ginny was oblivious, too busy revelling in the astonishment that she had finally plucked up the motivation for a long-overdue break from monotony. She was on a mission to walk on the wild side —

although she might want to shop for comfortable footwear first. Never in her life had she behaved in such an irresponsible manner, and she was determined that nothing or no one was going to stop her. Ginny Wallis was finally going to start living!

"S'cuse me, dear, is this your phone under there?"

The woman across from her was bent over, peering under Ginny's seat, her support tights fraying under the strain.

Her congratulatory contemplation interrupted, Ginny got down on her knees and fished under her seat for the stray ringing device. She checked the phone, then the screen — Darren. So much for her new, independent life. She hadn't gone three miles from home and she'd already lost her phone, and only a timely intervention by the dual forces of a disapproving stranger and her boyfriend of twelve years had delivered it back to her. Maybe Roxy was right — maybe years of suburban institutionalisation had rendered her unsafe to leave home without a responsible adult.

She took the call.

"Hi babes, it's me. I'm just on my way over — I was going to bring a DVD — are you in the mood for *Scarface* or *Armageddon?*"

Ginny pondered the question. Brutal violence in the gutter of humanity or a global cremation? Somewhere deep inside her, her happy-go-lucky gene was clutching its heart and screaming for a paramedic.

Suddenly Ginny realised that she couldn't breathe, and not just because Roxy's shocking pink Wonderbra was so tight and uncomfortably bosom-levitating

21

that she could rest her chin on her cleavage. Who was she kidding with the whole "walk on the wild side" nonsense? Ginny wasn't wild, she was sensible. Conservative. Cautious. She was the woman who wouldn't go out after dark without a mobile phone, a first-aid kit and pepper spray. This whole thing was ridiculous. She wasn't some flighty eighteen-year-old, she was a grown woman who should know better. Suddenly, she could think of nothing she wanted more than to get off the train and head back home for a familiar night of companionship, affection and violent DVDs. She could just put this whole thing down to friendship-induced diminished responsibility. People would understand — Roxy had been driving everyone nuts for years. But . . .

But what about excitement? What about adventure? She put her hand up her back and surreptitiously unhooked her bra, allowing her breasts to deflate and her lungs to regain their normal capacity.

She inhaled deeply: breathe, breathe, breathe. Okay, here goes.

"Actually, Darren, something's come up. Can we give tonight a miss?"

There was a deafening silence as his brain tried to compute this information. In Ginny's life, nothing ever just cropped up. It was like saying the world was flat or Nicole Ritchie had a high-grade Bakewell tart habit.

He was stuttering now.

"Sure, babes, so tomorrow night?"

"Can't."

"Tuesday?"

Ginny squeezed her eyes shut. She was going to have to tell him. She was a grown bloody woman. She could do this. She could.

"I'm, erm, working. You know. At work. My work. Work. Working. Shit!"

Okay, maybe she couldn't.

"*What?*"

"Okay! But don't be pissed off. It's just that I'm doing a favour for Roxy . . ."

"Are you on a train?" he blurted.

"And she's on a penis embargo . . ."

Exit one fellow traveller, bustling off at speed with suitcase in tow and a backwards, disapproving glare.

". . . so I'm filling in for her at work for a month. Just a month. No biggie. And it's not as if I'm miles away — only a couple of hours. We can still catch up on my days off. And . . ."

There was a deafening noise as the 10.30 p.m. express to Bristol sped past them in the other direction. She wasn't sure if he'd hung up or the signal had dipped out. A sudden creeping feeling of nausea rose from her stomach. And she hadn't even been to the buffet car.

Was she being crazy? Why was she risking upsetting the one thing in her life that was truly outstanding?

Darren. Darren and Ginny. Ginny and Darren.

It sounded so right, like the perfect couple. Or the kind of act that wears coordinating costumes and gets nil points at the Eurovision Song Contest.

They'd met at school. Two pubescent, hormonal souls intrinsically linked by inherent geekdom and the love of biology, physics and orderly conduct.

Twelve years later they were still together and happy. If you overlooked the whole "bored rigid, fleeing to London" thing.

She'd miss him. She really would. He was one of the good guys — he'd never cheated, betrayed her, let her down or told her that her arse was massive. Actually, since he'd developed his love of science into a degree in anatomy and a career as a personal trainer to Farnham Hills's rich and bored housewives, he could probably nip the fat-arse thing in the bud anyway.

But the firm bottom line was that he was a nice guy. And the six-pack stomach wasn't exactly a hindrance to his desirability either. But lately . . . Well, sometimes nice just wasn't enough. He worked such long hours maintaining the inner thighs of the village that they'd settled into a mind-numbing routine. He'd work all day, then pop over to her house every second night around nine. They'd watch TV, fall asleep on the sofa, and then he'd let himself out when he woke up. At weekends, they'd really live it up and order in a takeaway or nip down to the local pub for a few drinks. Just a few. After all, it would border on criminal to deprive the wedding fund of its weekly income.

The wedding. Or, to give it its official title, "Her Mother's Reason for Living". They'd been planning it for so long that at least a dozen of the original guests would only be attending with the help of Derek Acorah.

Every single iota of her being wanted to marry Darren Jenkins — except the ones that watched *Sex and the City*, realised that there was a big world out there and recoiled at the very thought of only having sex with one bloke for the rest of her life.

What was she, a Fifties throwback? How many women would go through the whole of their lives and only have intimate relations with one male organ?

It was obscene. Prehistoric. Pathetic. Her gravestone would read, "*Here lies Ginny Wallis — woman of morals, traditional values, and the most unadventurous vagina in the free world.*"

The passing of the 10.45p.m. to Bath caused a thunderous noise that snapped her from her discontented musings.

She blew her hair off her face and gave herself a swift reality check. She loved Darren. She was going to marry him. This little adventure was not, repeat NOT, some veiled excuse for infidelity and wanton sexual exploits. It was just a bit of fun. A little injection of high-grade *joie de vivre* to snap her out of the mind-numbingly predictable torpor that she'd slipped into over recent years. One month of new routines, new faces, new sights and new experiences.

As the train pulled into Paddington Station, the bubbles of adrenaline started thumping through her veins again. She pulled up the handle on the leopardskin trolley case, swung her scarf around her neck and applied some lip-gloss. Roxy's lip-gloss. She'd found it in the pocket of Roxy's Zara swing coat, which she'd adopted a few hours before.

Ginny Wallis, visiting London on a one-month sanity visa, wore lip-gloss.

Oh yes, her pucker was going to teach her lady bits a thing or two about adventure.

As she stepped off the train and pulled the trolley behind her, a familiar figure caught her eye. Weird. She was sure that woman had got off the train a few stops back.

Curiosity forced her to crane her neck around. Yep, it was definitely . . . upside-down. The world was upside-down. She'd been in London for approximately thirty seconds and she'd fallen at the first hurdle. Literally. She winced as she took in the damage to her sprawled limbs. Her thighs, knees and ankles were fine but — whoa — her footwear was terminal. Shit, Roxy would kill her.

Ginny's next thought wasn't one she had ever imagined would run through her brain.

So exactly how many shifts would she have to work in a brothel to buy a new pair of Gina boots?

Farnham Hills High School: Pupil Report: 1993

Name: Roxanne Galloway   Year: S2

Subject	Above Average	Average	Below Average	Poor
English		X		
Mathematics		X		
History		X		
Geography		X		
Languages		X		
Science		X		
Religious Education				X
P.E.	X			
Art	X			
Music & Drama	X			

Summary:
Roxanne shows a keen interest in all areas of the expressive arts. She is currently a member of the netball team, the hockey team and the athletics team and is especially committed to her roles in the Lower School Mixed Volleyball Team and the Lower School Mixed Swimming Team. It was regrettable that Roxanne's positions in the latter two teams came under threat due to the breach of school rules that was brought to your attention last month. This has, as advised, been noted on her school record,

and she will in future be supervised when travelling to outside events with male members of any sporting squad.

She continues to excel in Drama and will play the role of Mary Magdalene in the forthcoming production of *Jesus Christ Superstar*.

Personal Skills:

Roxanne continues to be a challenge in areas of discipline, structure and responsiveness to authority. Her attendance score was 72 per cent this year, although that is expected to improve after our joint discussions with the amusement arcade and village café. She is, as agreed, now barred from both within school hours.

She is often resistant to direction and is easily distracted when charged with using her own initiative. She is prone to rambunctious behaviour and often displays a tendency to manipulate her peers and defy school rules and regulations.

However, it should be noted that, as her superior grades demonstrate, Roxanne is capable of achievement, especially in the subjects that she enjoys. It is perhaps unfortunate that she achieves these grades without any discernible effort or endeavour. Needless to say, should Roxanne apply herself to her schoolwork, it is the opinion of the teaching staff that she would excel in all subjects.

Challenges/Development Needs:

As discussed during our frequent contact this year, Roxanne must improve her general conduct and commitment within the school. She continues to flout authority, often initiating forbidden activities — as witnessed by the smoking incident earlier in the year. Her behaviour must improve if she wishes to remain at Farnham Hills High School.

Signed: *Mrs Farquar — Senior Guidance Teacher S2*

CHAPTER
THREE

Don't Go Changing

Roxy. Day One, Sunday, 11p.m.
Tick. Tock. Tick. Tock.

Roxy stared at the ceiling as the hands ticked round on Ginny's alarm clock. Her anxiety levels rose with every sound. It was bloody ridiculous — I mean, who even *had* ticking bloody clocks these days? Hadn't Ginny realised that Europe now imported almost the whole of the national export quota of LCD tat from China? Well, at least now Roxy knew what to buy her for Christmas.

Tick. Tock. Tick. Tock.

Urgh! She put her head under the pillow. After a few seconds she realised that this caused a slight problem with the respiratory functions necessary for maintaining life. She stuffed the alarm clock under the pillow instead. Finally, silence! She heard a creaking coming from further down the hall and her eyes widened. She bloody knew it! Her mother was sneaking into Auntie Violet's room for some naked duvet wrestling. She should have known when her mother joined Weight Watchers that she was up to no good. Why was the thought of middle-aged parents having sex so hard to deal with? Still, she supposed she should be grateful — her mother and Auntie Vi having a tickle she could just about cope with, but the mental image of her mother being rogered over the sofa by some burly, hairy bloke would traumatise her for life.

Her ears strained as she craned to hear the Marks & Spencer's thermal slippers padding along the Axminster.

Nope, it was too much — there were some times in life that oblivion was the preferred option. She needed a diversion and fast. She pulled the clock back out from under the pillow.

Tick. Tock. Tick. Tock.

This was a living hell. Okay, so maybe it wasn't on the same scale as, say, civil war, famine or disease, but then, at least there was official aid for those situations. Who did she have to help her? Bloody no one. Her one stalwart, the only person she could depend on, had buggered off on the last train to London.

If it weren't for the fact that the only things that could make this situation worse were puffy eyes, she'd have cried.

She missed Felix. She'd given him the best two years of her life, and how had he repaid her? With a betrayal that had devastated her to the very soul.

The lying bastard. The cheating, lying, arrogant, cold, condescending, mendacious scumbag. God, how she missed him.

She clenched her teeth to stop the tears. If she succumbed to a full-blown sobbing session she'd have to go to the bathroom for tissues, and the risk of what she'd meet on the way there was enough to quell the waterworks.

She had a sudden feeling of almighty dread. Didn't her mother tell her that she'd been to an Ann Summers party in the village hall last month? A mental picture of two middle-aged women in PVC bondage gear only six inches away through a plasterboard wall flooded into her head. She pulled the alarm clock closer to her ears to drown out any sound effects. If she heard a buzzing noise coming from the next room the therapist bills would leave her bankrupt.

This wasn't supposed to happen to her. She'd had her whole life planned out. Go to London. Fall in love with wealthy bloke. Marry in big castle with Mariah Carey singing "Ave Maria" as she swept up the aisle.

Oh, she knew she was being unrealistic. Mariah didn't do private functions — she'd have to settle for Charlotte Church.

But she'd really thought Felix was the one, because here was the thing: she really had loved him. After a lifetime of dispensing her love and affection towards the opposite sex in direct proportion to their wealth/status/ generosity (if she ever met Bill Gates, he was in for the time of his life), Felix had totally ambushed her in the emotional department. They'd met in the underwear section of the gents' floor in Harvey Nicks. He was stocking up on new Prada pants, while she was searching for trendy boxers for her latest fling: a fifty-five-year-old with a saggy arse and a penchant for thongs that was putting her off her food. Although the fact that he owned half of Buckinghamshire was a huge consolation (and, in all honesty, her very favourite thing about him).

But despite her devotion to her current man's portfolio, she couldn't help but admire Felix's merchandise. He was over six foot (she checked out his shoes — nope, no lifts) and his shoulders were as broad as his hips were narrow. He was wearing cream chinos, moccasins, and the kind of preppy shirt that made him look like he belonged in one of those old black and white films of the Kennedy family playing touch football on the beach in Martha's Vineyard.

The moment they made eye contact and he smiled at her across a Y-Fronts for the Older Man display, she realised to her utter astonishment that all that Mills & Boon "love at first sight" mush that Ginny used to read really did have a basis in fact. If she'd been wearing a corset, she'd have whipped it off and made a dive for his throbbing loins right there and then.

Instead, she smiled back, said hi, and ten minutes later they were having coffee, two hours later they were having sex, and within the month they were talking long-term relationship with the prospect of a city flat and a house in the country, four kids (all at boarding school) and a month every summer in Barbados. She'd absolutely adored him. Her knees went to jelly when he walked into a room. Her stomach flipped when he grinned at her. Okay, so he was sometimes a bit on the arrogant side. And yes, he could be abrasive, self-centred and ruthless. But then, weren't those common attributes in most successful men? She loved his confidence, his strength, his certainty, and from that first orgasm in the fifth-floor toilet of Harvey Nichols, she'd known without a single doubt that he was her soul mate and that she wanted to spend the rest of her life with him — in sickness and in health, till death (or his unfaithful cock) do them part.

Roxy bit her lip and swallowed back a sob as she had a sudden astonishing thought: *She would have loved Felix even if he were poor.*

She let that magnanimous sentiment float in her mind for a second, before taking an imaginary baseball bat and battering it to death. Who was she kidding? She was in love, she wasn't Mother Teresa.

And while Felix wasn't exactly Donald Trump, he did work in the City (something to do with liquid assets) and earned a six-figure salary — enough to provide them with a comfortable future. Sadly, it was also enough to provide some tart from the florist with a second-hand Micra and reduced rental in one of the flats in Felix's property portfolio. Daisy, that was her name. Bloody Daisy, working in a florist — you couldn't make it up. Sometimes, in painful moments (eyebrow plucking, bikini waxing), she took her mind off her agony by torturing herself about how long it had been going on. Days? Weeks? Surely it couldn't have been more than a couple of months without her spotting the signs? After all, it would surely have affected his behaviour. Unless . . . Her heart tightened. Could it be that this wasn't the first time? Was his wandering dick the reason that he'd always blocked her suggestions that they move in together? Had he been shagging everything in sight since the moment they met?

How could he have been? She had never even contemplated being unfaithful to him. Well, apart from the time she'd snogged his brother in the coats cupboard at the family Christmas dinner. Oh, and the time she'd let his mate grope her to orgasm in the back of a taxi. But alcohol was to blame on both those occasions, and anyway, neither of those incidents counted because there was no exchange of body fluids. After all, a girl *had* to have her standards.

His mate had been rather cute, though . . . What was his name again? Nope, it was gone.

But the point was, she had never breached his trust, even when she had really wanted to. Hadn't she had a raging crush on Sam since the minute she had started working in the Seismic? But had she once acted on it? Absolutely not. And that was only partly because a) she realised that he wasn't interested in her in the least, and b) as previously ascertained, the man ran a brothel for God's sake — not exactly the type of career that you'd be happy to disclose on passport applications.

A buzz cut through her thoughts.

Dear God, no. Please no. She clenched her eyes shut and wondered if she could remember the phone number for the Samaritans.

Bzzzzzzzzzz.

Noooooooo. Mental instability beckoned and she saw her future — rocking back and forth in the foetal position and recoiling at the notion of sexual relations.

Bzzzzzzzzzz.

She suddenly realised that the buzzing noise was a bit closer to home. Or, rather, to her single bed and Mark, Kian, Shane, Nicky and Bryan.

Her hand grappled across the bedside table and snatched her vibrating phone.

It would be Felix — well, he could bloody well rot for all she cared. She would never forgive him. Never.

Actually, since her feet were sticking out the bottom of the duvet and hypothermia was slowly setting in, she was beginning to realise that a fortnight at the Sandy Lane Hotel in Barbados would probably heal her shattered heart.

But she'd never tell him that. Let him come begging, the bastard — preferably with Expedia vouchers in hand.

She opened the new text message.

Arvd safe. On way 2 flat. Hope u r ok. Lol, G.

She tossed the phone onto the floor. Typical bloody Ginny, rubbing salt in the wounds. In approximately an hour's time, Ginny would be snuggled down in HER king-size bed, between HER 800-thread-count Egyptian cotton sheets and HER cashmere throw, drinking a decaf mocha choca from HER state-of-the-art coffee machine. Actually, the coffee machine belonged to her flatmate, but that's why it was called communal living.

She pulled the duvet up around her ears. She missed her life. She might only have left it about thirteen hours earlier, but she missed it.

But in the words of the Dalai Lama, as one chapter closes, so another opens. Or was that Oprah?

Maybe this break would be good for her. No city living, no crushing crowds, no five-pound vanilla skinny lattes from the faux American coffee bar at the corner of the street and no cocaine crumbs on her handbag after she'd propped it on top of a toilet cistern while peeing in a nightclub. Ew, she hated it when that happened — why couldn't people clean up after themselves? She really didn't get the whole cocaine thing — why snort up all that cash when it could be used to finance a high-grade Marc Jacobs habit instead?

Maybe she should just view this whole episode as a city detox. She would de-clutter her life and her mind, and get herself back on track to the glorious existence she deserved. She would take bracing walks that would leave her with the complexion of Heidi Klum after a week in a Swiss spa. She would heal her tortured heart and soul by reconnecting with those less fortunate than herself (and, let's face it, in this backward land that time forgot that was just about everyone). She'd embrace the slower pace of life and use it to recharge her batteries and catch up on all those things she didn't have time for in the city: reading, exercising, eating healthily, plotting Felix's death.

She wiped her eyes with Shane's hair. Yep, this was going to be fine. Great. Perhaps not in the same league as a night in Pangaea knocking back champagne with minor (and occasionally major) royals, but she'd cope.

She let her eyes droop and her breathing settle into a steady rhythm.

Roxy Galloway was a survivor and she was going to be okay. It was her last thought as she fell asleep . . . just missing the strange buzzing noise that started in the next room.

Excerpt from an old journal belonging to Daisy Davenport

Daisy's Diary 2006

22 December 2006

Dear Diary,

It finally happened! Six months stuck behind the counter in that bloody florist's shop and finally he noticed me — you know, Ivy League Guy. Except he's not from America — I'd say no further west than Chiswick but that's only a guess. Anyway, I'll find out soon because HE ASKED ME OUT!

Okay, okay, I'm going to start at the beginning because I never, ever want to forget this. I'd just been on the phone to the agency again (STILL no jobs lined up — can't believe I'm over the hill at twenty-five — I could definitely still pass for twenty-one and Yasmin bloody Le Bon is still working and she's so ancient). I was just thinking maybe I'd try Paris (Kelly told me she's getting loads of knicker work over there and she's, like, thirty) when he came in, bang on time (every Friday, three o'clock). He smelled as gorgeous as ever, although I do wonder if Paco Rabanne isn't taking the whole retro thing a bit too far. It was the usual: a dozen red roses for some bird called Roxy, to be delivered to her home Saturday a.m., with a card that says "Endless Love, from Felix". You'd think he'd have used a bit of imagination and varied the message every once in a while, but then when you look like he does you don't have to make much of an effort to get your leg over. So I reach out to take his credit card and bam! Our hands touched, our eyes met and he smiled this adorable smile. Ten minutes later we were in the back having coffee, and one thing led to another and before long we were doing it on top of a pile of hydrangeas that will have to be binned before the boss sees them. I know, I should have held out, done the whole hard-to-get thing, but it was truly love at first sight. Well, about twenty-fourth sight really, but this was the first real meeting of eyes and minds. And other parts. Yeeeeeeeeeeeeee! (And, incidentally, he's built like a horse down there and went at it for ages — thank God I remembered to put the CLOSED sign on the door.)

The important thing, though, is that putting out so quickly wasn't a bad idea because he loved the fact that I was so adventurous. He says that he's never met anyone like me before and it was meant to be, and that's why he just had to have me right there and then. I could definitely tell he's not the kind of guy who normally pulls stunts like that because he was so embarrassed afterwards that he got all shy and left really quickly to get back to work. But — and here's the really great bit — I'm seeing him again tomorrow night. And, even better, he told me to forget sending the flowers to that Roxy girl — says from now on the only girl he'll be sending flowers to is me. Except, I don't really need them since I'm allowed to take home the ones that are about to go on the wilt, but I didn't want to tell him that — thought it might spoil the moment.

This is it. I've got a feeling about him — I finally think I've found the one decent straight bloke left in London . . .

Just hope the girlfriend doesn't take it too hard when he breaks it off with her tonight . . . FOR ME! Yasmin Le Bon, eat my pants! **Dxxx**

CHAPTER
FOUR

Ginny. Day One, Sunday, midnight

Ginny pushed the key into the door, thumped it open with her shoulder, then hobbled through, dragging the trolley case behind her. Style was all very well but you could go off a fashion item really quickly when you had to lug it up a flight of stairs late at night while balancing on one shoe. And, naturally, she'd managed to get the only cab driver in London who didn't want to talk, wasn't in the least bit helpful, and ejected her at such speed that she'd left the broken heel on the seat. That was the superglue plan scuppered then.

None of this would ever happen to Roxy. Roxy could walk a tightrope in six-inch heels, the cab driver would have been falling over himself to help her, and he'd probably have been so enraptured by her divine sodding goddess-ness that he'd have carried her case to her door.

As she stepped into the hall a barrage of sounds accosted her. She vaguely recognised the music — it was that bloke . . . the weird-looking one . . . erm, Beyonce's boyfriend . . . what's-his-name? She racked her brains. Crazee. Lazyee. Note to self: brush up on contemporary music artists — there was more to life than those collections of number-one hits that Woolies sold for a fiver.

She dumped her handbag and the trolley case on the hardwood floor, careful not to scuff the sheen on the cream silk walls. She'd always loved Roxy's place. On the floor were rich, thick planks of glossy solid oak, the walls were lined with a light vanilla suede, and hanging from the ceiling was a stunning, simple crystal and chrome chandelier that struck the perfect balance between class and contemporary. The light, the space, the beautiful pastel prints on the walls, there was something so uncluttered and simple about it — especially when juxtaposed against the chaos that was Roxy's perpetually melodramatic existence.

And it was clean. Spotless. Although that probably had less to do with Roxy's domestic skills and more to do with Bogna, the Polish cleaner who charged fifteen pounds an hour and came complete with an overwhelming aroma of Eau de Domestos.

"Hi. Are you . . . *okay?*"

Ginny snapped her head around to see a blonde with Rachel Hunter's legs and Dolly Parton's mammas staring at her like she didn't know whether to scream or dial the emergency services.

"Erm, yeah, hi. I'm Ginny, Roxy's friend. I'm, erm, staying here tonight," she stuttered, toe-curlingly aware that she was windswept, dishevelled, her hair was sticking to her contraband lip-gloss and she was only wearing one boot.

But at least she had manners, she thought, as she haltingly held out her hand to shake Miss Amazonian Breastfest 2007.

Her action was met with a shrug, and only then did Ginny notice that the blonde's hands were full. One tub of strawberries, one aerosol can of whipped cream, one bottle of champagne, two glasses. Didn't anyone just go to bed with a cuppa and a good book any more?

"Hey, Ginny — what are you doing here?"

She did her best not to gasp out loud as Jude, Roxy's flatmate, appeared from his room with only a towel covering his modesty. He threw his arms around her and lifted her up in a bear hug. Big mistake. When he plonked her back down she lost her balance and folded like a sofabed. "One shoe," she explained weakly, getting back on her feet. "It's a long story — I'd tell you but those strawberries will be past their sell-by date by the time I've finished."

He grinned and Ginny felt her one good knee go weak. God, he was beautiful. His dark blond hair fell down to his shoulders, every muscle was rounded and defined, his square jaw was on the Brad Pitt side of Buzz Lightyear and the green eyes . . . oh, good Lord, they could make a girl swoon, sweat and remove her knickers all at the same time. He was, quite simply, a fine specimen of manhood. But then, most male strippers were. Except the ones who did social-club hen nights and thought *The Full Monty* gave them a lifelong licence to flash milk-white, flabby bodies in the break between the bingo and the buffet.

43

"Ginny, this is my girlfriend, Cheska." He pointed at the Amazonian with the penchant for late-night berries. "Cheska, this is Roxy's friend Ginny."

"We've, erm, just met," Ginny said with a nervous smile. Shit, what was the protocol for this? The only people she ever met in her mother's hallway were the parish priest and the bloke who collected money for the Salvation Army. Oh, and that Ann Summers party planner, who seemed to be popping in regularly.

"Anyway, erm, so, didn't Roxy call to tell you I'd be coming?"

His blank face answered the question. Bugger. Typical bloody Roxy. She'd promised that she'd let Jude know and make sure it was okay with him.

He picked up the apprehension on her face and grinned. "Hey, look, don't worry, it's fine. It'll be great to have you here. Are you just staying the night?"

"Erm, a month?" she announced tentatively.

"Okay, so what have you done with Roxy? The Priory? A rich bloke? Or am I going to see her picture on *Crimewatch*?"

"No, she's staying at mine for a while. You know, to get her head sorted out."

"And there was me thinking she'd never go out of a ten-mile radius of Joseph, Daniel Galvin and Harvey Nicks," he said with a grin.

She'd forgotten about his teeth. He could have a part-time job as a product tester for the Hollywood Smile Company.

Ginny switched her focus back to Cheska. Body like that, legs like those, the waist-length shiny locks . . .

44

She may only have been in the city for an hour but Ginny knew a pole-dancer when she saw one.

"Well, it was nice to meet you," Cheska said with a smile. "I'll just head for bed, early start tomorrow morning. Have to be in Chambers by seven o'clock."

Ginny suddenly had a vague notion that she'd seen Cheska before. Her powers of recall raced to catch up. Of Course! Wasn't she the lawyer who was on the six o'clock news every night, going in and out of court at the side of the soon-to-be-ex-wife of a Sixties band legend? The divorce was proving messy, slanderous and keeping the whole nation entertained. And the tabloids had already made a poster girl of the gorgeous lawyer with the stern "No Comments".

Ginny stopped herself from her habitual tutting and rolling of the eyes. Oh, the injustice. Cheska was a lawyer — those looks and a brain too. That should be illegal.

"Gin, you know where everything is. Roxy's room is in there, if you're hungry help yourself in the kitchen — we share everything." Ginny fleetingly wondered if that included those strawberries, the cream and the champagne . . . licked from his naked torso. Jesus, a couple of hours since she'd left home and already her ovaries were sending filthy thoughts to her brain.

"Great, thanks," she wittered, "I will. Thanks. I'll . . . do that." Jude and Cheska backed into his bedroom, leaving her standing in the hall, sweat patches forming puddles under her arms, her face beaming so brightly it could have guided in ships. Aaargh, she was rubbish at dealing with awkward situations — a great quality for working in a brothel, she thought with a plummeting heart.

She limped into Roxy's room and flopped down on the king-size, elaborately upholstered, cream leather bed, then leaned over to switch on the bedside lamp. No switch near the light bulb. Her fingers traced along the wire. She was halfway to the plug before she gave up on that possibility.

She turned it upside down. Nothing. She gave it a gentle nudge on the bedside table. Nope. She placed it back down and flicked the shade. Nothing.

"Shit!" she exclaimed, and then, like a veritable miracle, it flashed into life.

Ah, she had it now.

"Off!" she commanded. It obeyed.

"Tit!" she declared loudly.

And then there was light.

Ginny lay back on the bed, her illuminating débâcle reinforcing that it was blatantly obvious she didn't belong there.

She looked around her. The white carpet was so thick and fluffy that it looked like it had been knitted from pure angora wool. Mental note: be careful with contact lenses as they'd be lost forever if they landed on it.

The walls were papered with an ivory water-silk fabric that contrasted perfectly with the gold silk bedding. There were four, five, six, seven, *eight* pillows of assorted sizes and shapes, all in metallic shades of copper and bronze, scattered across the bed with haphazard panache. To her right, in front of the huge bay window, was a modern, double-ended chaise longue upholstered in white suede (another mental note to self: no sitting on chaise while eating, drinking, or wearing any fabrics that could possibly transfer dye — in fact, just stay beyond a one-metre radius of chaise at all times).

Against the far wall was a stunning cream gloss dressing table that matched the long row of drawer units next to it and the sleek bedside tables on either side of her.

She decided not to turn around to stare at the life-size nude photo of Roxy that hung above the headboard — a gift from an admirer with a love of both art and porn. Instead, she took in the huge plasma television. The pots of cream on the dressing table that would cost her a month's salary. A stereo system with more buttons than a NASA flight deck. The wall-length wardrobe to her left, bursting at its designer seams.

How the hell did Roxy afford all this? But then, that had been Roxy's gift her whole life: things just came to her. Never did she have to resort to Ginny's Christmas-present tactics (Argos catalogue left open at the appropriate page). No, for years Roxy had had life handed to her on a plate . . . and for the next month, to a tiny degree, Ginny was going to see how it felt.

As she snuggled into the silky bedspread, she mentally bitch-slapped her doubts out of the way. Roxy's life was one of indulgent luxury and, occasional embarrassing sweat patches aside, Ginny had a sneaking suspicion that she was absolutely, definitely going to enjoy it.

Sadly, that wasn't a feeling that was shared by her fiancé. As she drifted off to sleep, strangely blissful despite the fact that she was still sporting a Zara swing coat, one boot and hair like a spider plant, her boyfriend was lying awake wondering what the hell had happened to his future wife.

The Palace Grand Hotel, Mayfair, London
Security Log

Date: 30/09/07

Security Officer: Desmond Taylor

Duty Manager: Robert Hunter

Details of Incident:
At approximately 2.30p.m., Anton LeComber, restaurant manager, requested security attend an altercation in the dining room. On arrival, it was found that the dispute was between one newly arrived female and a couple seated at table six. It became clear that said female had encountered her boyfriend dining with another woman and had become irate. A heated argument ensued which culminated in a bottle of Bollinger being taken from a nearby ice bucket and emptied over the head of said male and female. The offending female was removed from the premises. However, at the request of all parties, the police were not called. No further action will be taken, although the female — Roxanne Galloway, photo attached — has been advised that she is now barred from this hotel. Her abusive reply made it abundantly clear that she agrees with this decision.

CHAPTER
FIVE

We Are Family

Roxy. Day Two, Monday, 8a.m.
"ROXY!!!!!! Come on my darling, your Shreddies are on the table."

Roxy prised open her eyelids. Fuck, what a nightmare. She'd dreamt that she'd chucked her job, caught Felix shagging a florist and spent the night with Westlife. And now she couldn't swear it but she was sure she'd just heard her mother's voice. It was definitely time to cut down on the cocktail consumption.

"Roxy!!!!"

She bolted upright, her eyes wide. Noooooooooooo!

Of course! Her life was in the sewer — how could she have forgotten? Shane, Kian, Nicky, Bryan and Mark looked at her disapprovingly. "And you lot can piss off as well," she muttered. She clambered out of bed and gasped as she caught sight of herself in the teak dressing-table mirror — MFI circa 1976. Her pulse raced. Was she too young to have a heart attack? There, covering her lithe frame, were . . . man-made fibres! She could sense the impending wrath of the gods of Dolce & Gabbana. By fishing pyjamas from Ginny's drawer in the semi-darkness the night before, Roxy Galloway had been catapulted from the House of Prada to the House of Matalan.

It was official: her life was in ruins.

"Roxy!!!!" And now her mother was screaming at her from the bottom of the stairs. It was like she'd been transported back in time and was fifteen years old — actually, that wouldn't be so tragic: she'd be precociously beautiful, the most popular person she knew, and she'd be allowing Mr Kennedy the Physics teacher to feel her up at lunchtime in return for straight-A passes and bottles of Charlie.

"Your Shreddies are getting soggy!"

That was Auntie Violet that time. How, in the name of adult independence, had she come to be living with two middle-aged, potential lesbians? She felt like she'd wandered into a Sixties commune. Next they'd all be chanting mantras about vulvas and having their periods at the same time.

Not for the first time, she considered the theory that females ended up looking like their mothers. In which case, whoever married her had better steel themselves to end up with a peroxide-blonde fifty-five-year-old who had tits like melons, fifty pounds to lose, a fondness for tight pink clothing and who lived by the theory that you could never wear too much lip-liner.

And the weirdest thing was that although her mother and Auntie Vi were only distant cousins, they looked exactly the same — if you didn't count a weight variation of about four stone. It was like Christina Aguilera had gained sixty pounds, aged thirty years, and teamed up with her identical but much skinnier twin.

Roxy slumped back down on the bed.

Why hadn't she gone home last night and packed some clothes? Why didn't she go home right now, reclaim her life, and tell Ginny that this whole thing was bloody ridiculous? Because then . . . The truth was that then she'd remember how much she'd lost. She'd sleep in the bed that Felix had bought her. She'd wear the clothes that she'd shopped for with him. Or, rather, with his American Express card (the red one — he liked the fact that it made the very attractive shop assistants in Armani think he was compassionate and humanitarianly aware). And she'd have to accept the cold, hard fact that the compassionless tosser hadn't called her once since she'd caught him in The Palace Grand with that tart.

No, self-delusion combined with the determination to appear elusive was a much better option. Let him play his little games, and when indeed he did come to beg her for forgiveness he'd realise that she'd moved on, got over him, washed that dick right out of her hair. She felt a wave of resolve return. She was destined to plan a new life, to rewrite her destiny and to spend a few weeks just taking time to find herself.

"Roxy!"

And apparently herself was to be found eating Shreddies at her mother's kitchen table. She pulled open Ginny's wardrobe. She used the term loosely. This cupboard was so dilapidated that she just knew whoever had built it had had loads of unidentified bits left over at the end and had chucked them instead of investigating where they'd gone wrong. One door hung off its hinge, one leg had been replaced by a pile of books, and there were just bare screws where the knobs should be.

So, what to wear to work? As Ginny had borrowed her boots, the only footwear she had with her was a pair of Louboutin peep-toe platforms that she'd shoved in her overnight bag. She flicked through the rail:

— Jeans, from a supermarket — she'd rather take her own life.

— Three gypsy skirts, assorted colours — only useful if she needed an emergency tent while camping, a hobby up there on her enjoyment list somewhere between basket-weaving and piercing her clitoris with a stapler.

— Two cheap denim miniskirts — definitely handy, if she planned on taking up residence in a trailer in a Southern US state.

— Three pairs of black trousers of unidentifiable make or fabric. One of those would have to do. She felt the fabric — pure new wool. Kidding. They were of such high-grade polyester that if she went within twenty yards of any type of incendiary device there was a good chance she'd spontaneously combust.

She pulled a sweater from Ginny's drawer, then immediately tossed it to one side when she realised it had butterflies on it. Dear God. This couldn't get any worse. She pulled out another sweater and inspected it: pink wool with embroidered red reindeers. Reindeers. In October.

She turned back to the wardrobe and dragged a white blouse from the furthest end of the rail. It was probably Gin's old school shirt, but since it was that or the reindeers, it was going on. She'd leave the top couple of buttons open so that her Agent Provocateur slate-grey silk bra peeped out, giving the whole outfit a small but significant edge of style. She pulled her hair back and gripped it in a tortoiseshell clasp. There was no point even looking for a decent pair of straighteners — she knew without even asking that Ginny thought GHD was a violent offence that carried a mandatory two-year sentence.

She plodded down to join Rosie O'Donnell and Martina Navratilova. God, she couldn't even look them in the eye. She knew she was being ridiculous — the chances of middle-aged-woman on middle-aged-woman action even registering on her mother's radar were about as high as Vera having a part-time job as a stripper. Shit, that reminded her. She'd forgotten to phone Jude to let him know Ginny was coming. No matter, she knew he wouldn't mind. He was such a sweetheart. Kind, generous, self-deprecating and built like an Adonis — just a shame that he was such a serial shagger, she wouldn't touch his privates without the protection of antibacterial spray and a pair of marigolds.

She wandered into the kitchen. "Morning, Mum. Morning, Auntie Violet," she grumbled as she pulled out a chair and sat down.

"Morning, darling," said her mother, Vera, kissing her on her head. "Oh, it's so lovely to have you here, dear. Just like the old days."

Roxy tried valiantly to muster a smile as she attempted to masticate soggy Shreddies. The welcome mat at the kitchen door would have tasted better. Urgh, she missed her lightly toasted bagel with organic marmalade.

She sighed as her mother and aunt bustled off to attend to the rest of their morning routine.

As soon as they'd left the room she picked up the phone. Ginny answered on the first ring.

"Your life is officially crap," Roxy announced.

"And this is a newsflash to you?" Ginny laughed. "Anyway, it's not crap. There are loads of nice things about my life."

"Name three without hesitation."

"Darren, my mother and . . . erm . . ."

"Sorry, time's up! And anyway, the joy of having two people you love is outweighed by the fact that you possess a butterfly jumper. Have I taught you nothing?"

"You know, you are so shallow, Roxy. One butterfly jumper doesn't make me a bad person . . ."

"No, but the reindeer one proves you're a fucking lunatic."

Ginny shrieked with laughter. "Don't let my mother hear you swearing — before you know it she'll have the rosary beads out and Father Murphy will be making house calls."

"Jesus, shoot me now," Roxy muttered.

"Not sure that Jesus actually takes requests. Anyway, why aren't you on your way to work?"

"Just going. What are you doing?"

"Oh, I'm still in bed. Jude just brought me an orange juice and a warm bagel. With marmalade."

"I've never liked you."

"Oh, sword through my heart. Now get to work. And remember to keep all my records up to date — it took me months to devise that system and get it up and running."

"Ginny, you really need to get a life. And I don't mean mine. Anyway, how'd Mr Motivator take the news of your thirty-day desertion?"

"Fine."

"Honestly?"

"Yeah, fine."

"You haven't told him yet, have you?"

"Not exactly. Okay, not at all. He got cut off last night and I've not been able to reach him since. So I was thinking, since we're doing this role-reversal thing and I've spent my entire life delivering messages of doom for you, maybe you could break the news. Gently. He's doing a Bums & Tums class in the back room of the library for the Young Catholic Mothers this morning at nine thirty. But please, please, Roxy, promise that you'll say you begged me to help you. I don't want him to be pissed off before I've had a chance to explain it properly to him."

Roxy groaned. "Ginny, it might have escaped your notice, but your boyfriend isn't exactly my biggest fan. He's never liked me since I tried to set you up with Jason Morrison in fourth-year PE. You'd have been much better off with him — he's made it to the first team at Millwall."

"Yep, and the *Sunday Mirror* had two pages of photographs of him snorting coke off some female's nipples at a dogging site last weekend."

"Well, no one's perfect. Okay, I'll break the news gently. Anyway, better go before my mother grounds me for late time-keeping. Oh, and if I die today, tell the doctors it was polyester poisoning — it'll save them doing a post mortem."

She hung up as her mother hurried back into the room. "Come on, dear, if I don't open up the community centre then the Perky Pensioners committee will be loitering on the pavement and those mobile oxygen tanks are such an obstruction to passers-by."

Roxy somehow resisted the urge to stab herself to death with her Shreddies spoon.

"Okay, you go warm up the car and I'll just get my bag."

"Car? Oh, no, dear, Violet's got me on a diet and exercise plan and I think it's starting to work — I've lost two pounds this month! Although that might be something to do with starting *the change*. Anyway, we walk to work. Look, I've got my pedometer — 10,000 steps a day — got to keep the bones strong and the muscles flexible."

Roxy's life flashed before her. Or, rather, the life of her £650 Louboutin shoes. She felt like she'd just been told a family member was on life support and unlikely to make it.

This couldn't get any worse.

"Oh, and Roxy, love, you need to do up your shirt — your button's come loose and you're flashing your underwear."

Half an hour, three blisters and two toes with frostbite later, Roxy hobbled into the community centre through a throng of senior citizens in felt headwear and plastic footwear. But at least they looked comfortable. She contemplated offering one of them fifty quid for a pair of shoes that came from the same kind of catalogue that sold bath chairs and those long rods with the grippers that allowed you to pick things up without bending down.

Her mother kissed her goodbye and toddled twenty yards to the entrance of the doctor's surgery where she'd been the receptionist since dinosaurs roamed the earth.

Roxy moped across the corridor and followed Auntie Violet into the library. Located in an annex off the back of the community centre, it was the book depository that time forgot.

She dumped her bag in the staffroom and readjusted her hair, before snorting at the ridiculousness of it. Who was she trying to impress? Johnny Depp was hardly going to wander into the Farnham Hills library, find himself overcome with wild abandon and an insatiable desire for her before bending her over the gardening section and shagging her senseless. And anyway, wasn't she absolutely, definitely, resolutely *off* men?

She wandered into the main section of the library and marvelled at how nothing, absolutely nothing, had changed in the twenty years she'd been coming here. The walls were still that impossibly depressing shade of inconsequential grey. The plastic flooring, probably manufactured by some seismic shift in the earth's crust before time began, still stuck to your feet as you walked. The overhead fluorescent lighting could still bring on a migraine in under thirty seconds. And the rows and rows of books were still propped on thick hardwood shelves that buckled precariously in the middle.

The reception desk, or rather the four-foot-by-twelve-foot plank of Formica that masqueraded as Mission Control, still had bits peeling off the edges and smelled of Flash. Roxy sank to her knees and peered under the counter. Yep, still there — a carved love heart with "Roxy loves Stevie" engraved in the middle. She'd done it in the summer of '94 when her mother had made her work every day for two weeks as punishment for getting caught smoking a roll-up in the park pavilion. She'd have made her work for six weeks if she'd realised that the roll-up contained a couple of grams of the finest Moroccan weed.

"So what do you think of our new look then? We're all high-tech now and no mistake," boomed Auntie Violet as she joined her behind the desk.

"Oww." Roxy banged her head on the underside of the desk, then prised herself upright.

She glanced along the counter, looking for some signs that the new millennium had actually arrived: a laptop, an MP3 player, a cordless phone — Christ, an electric kettle would be progress — but nothing, just yards of box files, record cards, a blue plastic pen-holder and a phone that still had a circular dial.

"No, over there!" gestured Violet, pointing down the feverishly popular Historical Romance aisle to two archaic-looking computers sitting side by side, each one complete with is very own grey plastic chair. Yep, thought Roxy, the producers of *Gadget* magazine would get a hard-on if they saw this lot.

"They're in such demand that we sometimes have to have a waiting list and limit the use to twenty minutes per person. Imagine! Oh, and remember old Reverend Stewart? Well, he's banned from them — caught him looking at a site called 'Babes with Biggies' and it wasn't referring about their feet. Of course, he said it was an accident but we're not convinced. His eyes are too far apart."

With that, she turned on her heel. "Anyway, I'll get the kettle on. Tea, love? Course you will. Milk and two sugars, I remember," she added with a wink. "It's lovely to have you here, Roxy — we do miss you, you know. I'll just get the tea and then you can tell me everything you've been up to. Dying to hear about all those city boys you've been courting. Back in a min — and since it's a special occasion I'll break out the Penguins!"

Roxy couldn't decide what hurt more — the toes that were curled in excruciating mortification, the teeth that were clenched in horror, the jaw that was fixed into a manic, tortured grin, or the forehead that was thudding repeatedly off the desk.

This. Was. Never. Going. To. Work.

This wasn't a city detox, it was a Saga tour to insanity. She'd never do it. She couldn't. She wanted her old life back. Fuck it, she'd even take Felix back and just threaten to amputate his organ somewhere around the testicles if it was caught in enemy territory again. She wanted her job, she wanted her flat and she wanted Petrov, her bisexual, bilateral thigh trainer.

She let the cool stickiness of the Formica soothe her wrinkled brow. See! Bloody wrinkles! That settled it; she was on the next train out of here.

"S'cuse me."

There was nothing, *nothing* on God's earth that could make her suffer this for a nanosecond longer.

"S'cuse me."

She rolled her head so that her left cheek was now on the Formica, and she squinted to focus.

It couldn't be! She jolted up. Nope, it wasn't. But it was pretty damn close. If she was squinting. In a dark alley. Wearing sunglasses.

So a bloke who, on reflection, had nothing in common with Johnny Depp, except long, brown unbrushed hair and gorgeous hazel eyes, was standing in front of her with an expectant grin on his face.

"Hi," he said.

Okay, not exactly knocking her out with super-smooth chat, but hey, he was male, he was relatively good-looking and he didn't appear, on first impression, to have any psychotic personality disorders — he therefore qualified in the category of "reality distraction." She briefly wondered if he'd just stand at the desk all day and allow her to look at him and perhaps fondle his man parts on an hourly basis to ease the inevitable boredom. If she wasn't off men, that was. And she was. Definitely. Until hell froze over or the real Johnny Depp appeared in front of her wearing nothing but a "Roxy Be Mine" badge.

Farnham Hills Porn Prevention Officer chose that moment to reappear.

"Oh, hello Mitch, love, how are you this morning? Fancy a Penguin?"

"I'm grand, thanks, Mrs Wallis," he burred in a soft Irish accent. "Where's Ginny then? Having a day off today?"

"A few days off, actually. She's gone up to London for a wee bit of excitement. You know how you young things are these days. Anyway, this is our Roxy, Vera from the doctor's surgery's daughter. Her and our Ginny have been best friends since they were still peeing in nappies."

Toes re-curled. Jaw reset into manic grin.

Violet turned to Roxy. "And this is Mitch. Father Murphy's nephew. He's over from Ireland and staying at the chapel house with his uncle while he finishes writing his new novel. Imagine, a real writer in Farnham Hills!"

Roxy was indeed imagining. Mitch. Laptop. Naked.

Mitch held his hand out. With only a slightly embarrassing delay while she attempted to surreptitiously reopen those top two shirt buttons, Roxy reciprocated the gesture.

"Pleasure to meet you," he said. "I usually call in every morning to have a coffee and a read of the papers. Hope that's okay with you?"

Yep, Roxy thought, perhaps this life detox was going to work out fine — just as long as she went with the flow, took the ups with the downs, and managed to nip to the chemist in her lunch hour for a new diaphragm. She re-evaluated her strategy — perhaps the generic term "penis embargo" had been too all-encompassing.

Perhaps what she'd really meant was that she was avoiding *Felix*'s penis. Yep, why should the rest of the world suffer for one man's sins?

An irritated voice cut through her contraceptive/copulation contemplation. "Morning, Violet, morning, Roxy."

Strange, that someone could manage to say the word "Roxy" in such an insidious tone that it sounded like something you'd throw up after eating raw chicken. She'd almost have preferred it if he'd had the balls to be upfront and greet her with, "Morning, have I told you today that I'd prefer you dead? No? Okay, brutal torture, slow demise — lovely."

Roxy sighed as she turned to face her nemesis. Darren Jenkins. She loathed him. She'd always loathed him. Although under the influence of alcohol or physical torture, she might be prepared to concede that this negative emotion was born around the same time as she offered to show him her boobs in second-year Woodwork in return for his Sony Walkman and he knocked her back. She'd been horrified when Ginny had started seeing him a couple of years later, and over the following decade she'd pretty much avoided straying within a hundred yards of his supertoned thighs.

She had never understood what Ginny saw in him. He might be fit, he might be easy on the eye, he might be testosterone fuelled . . . but he was about as exciting as a daytrip to a morgue and just as warm. And he didn't exactly treat Ginny as well as she deserved — last year he'd bought her a steamer for her birthday. A steamer. What the fuck was that about? Who woke up and thought, "D'you know what, I'm going to prove to my fiancée how much I adore her by buying a household item that aids the production of healthy vegetables"?

What. A. Prick.

Roxy suddenly realised that a tiny part of her hoped Ginny would meet someone else in London and dump this bore before he had time to save up for a matching sandwich toaster for Ginny's Christmas present.

She snapped out of her musings when it became clear that they'd all been standing in awkward silence for about ten seconds, Darren staring at her with the type of expression more commonly seen on men who have bodies stored under their kitchen floorboards.

Johnny Depp-ish picked up on the tension and made himself scarce. Brilliant. The first time her hormones had stood to attention in weeks and Darren the Prick had scared him off.

"Darren, love, I've brought in a nice smoothie I made for you last night — mango, kiwi and pineapple. The pineapple was just chunks out of a tin, but I don't suppose it'll matter. I'll just nip back and get it for you."

As Violet disappeared, Roxy contemplated reattaching her head to the desk while waiting for the inevitable explosion.

"So, care to tell me what kind of insanity you've involved Ginny in this time?"

Houston, we have lift-off. And he was just getting warmed up.

"You can't bloody leave her alone, can you? What's the problem, Roxy? What inconsequential, superficial little blip on your horizon have you blown out of all proportion and roped Ginny into sorting out for you this time?"

Roxy bared her teeth with a smile she pitched at "carefree while maintaining an appropriate level of undiluted evil".

"Oh, nothing really. I just decided that she was far too happy so I thought I'd fuck things up for her by selling her body to an Eastern European slave trader."

Darren shook his head as his face cracked with irony. "You know, Roxy, you're priceless. You just use and abuse everyone who has the misfortune to stumble into your screwed-up, pathetic existence."

Roxy very maturely folded her arms, looked heavenward and ignored him, determined not to even dignify his accusations with a reply.

"You're toxic. Always have been."

She stayed silent. He was a grown man who wore Lycra, for God's sake. Who cared what he thought of her? She'd never stoop to his level. She'd just take this on the chin and handle it in a manner Ginny would be proud of. Ginny had made her promise to deal with this in a sensitive manner and she would. After everything Ginny had done for her she deserved it. St Roxy of the Blessed Martyrdom — it had a ring to it.

"And I'm sick of you interfering in Ginny's life. Why can't you just piss off and leave us alone?"

Aw, fuck the sainthood.

"Listen, you twat, if you want a reason that Ginny's not here, go look in a fucking mirror. You take her for granted, you walk all over her and you bore her baps off. Ginny hasn't gone to London to save my ass, she's gone because she was desperate for some excitement, desperate to do something other than sit on a bloody couch night after night waiting for you to honour her with your presence. You have a problem? Take it up with your fiancée and don't shoot the messenger."

Silence. Stunned silence. Until a troop of Young Catholic Mothers marched in to have their buttocks remoulded. As Lycra Man backed off in the manner of an armed robber with a hundred SWAT guns pointing at him, Roxy had a feeling of impending doom.

The 1960s telephone burst into life. Roxy snatched up the receiver to hear an anxious Ginny on the line.

"So did you break it to him gently?"

Roxy bit her lip and then did what all truly good friends do in a crisis — she lied.

"Of course! I told him I begged you to help and that you should be sainted for services to friendship. He was fine about it. Absolutely fine . . ." Roxy closed her eyes. Good Lord, she had to stop. She had to stop. Sod it — in for a penny, in for a huge big whopper that'll prevent risk of blind fury from irate best chum.

"In fact, he said you deserved a break and not to worry about him — you're just to go and enjoy yourself."

"Really? Thank God. See, I've told you a million times, Roxy — he's one of the good guys."

And there it was — the kind of utter blind devotion and unquestioning adoration that a lifetime relationship required.

And that, Roxy thought glumly, is why I'm single.

School Disco, Farnham Hills Hall
Christmas 1993

"Come on, Ginny, let's dance — it's 'Relight My Fire'"!

Ginny shrugged and shook her head. She hated dancing in front of people. She'd memorised every step in the video, but somehow it was easy to do in her bedroom with only her Take That posters as witnesses.

"Forget it then! Honestly, Ginny, how are you ever going to get a boyfriend when you're so boring. Boring. Boring. Boring. Well, I'm sick of boring!"

Roxy stormed off in a strop, leaving Ginny squirming in her chair. Roxy would ignore her all night now as punishment for not doing what she wanted — probably not a bad thing because if she got dragged into another smoking incident her mother would kill her. And no matter what Roxy said, those menthol St Moritz cigarettes were revolting.

She loathed these discos: chairs lined along the walls of the hall, a table outside the toilets selling flat Coke and crisps, and Father Murphy spinning records on a double stereo deck that the local pub had donated after the invention of CDs. And all this was witnessed through the haze caused by the two flashing disco lights attached to the front of the deck. Red. Green. Red. Green. Red. Green.

About a hundred youths had taken hours to plan their big night out, pick an outfit and then get dolled-up to the nines, only to be illuminated to the approximate shade of someone with acute gastroenteritis.

"Move."

Even over the volume of Lulu singing her lungs out, the aggression in the familiar voice was unmistakable. Ginny raised her eyes to see Fanny Brown staring down at her (actually her real name was Felicity, but Roxy had nicknamed her Fanny years ago and it had stuck, although obviously no one, other than the blatantly suicidal, said it to her face), along with her two pals Dora and Dorothy (aka Dopey and Daftarse, again courtesy of Roxy).

"What?" Ginny replied tentatively, trying to disguise the slight tremor in her voice. There was no denying it, Fanny Brown terrified her. She'd been suspended twice for fighting, once for stealing, once for threatening behaviour and once for kicking Mr Wilkinson, the Art teacher, in the goolies. Ginny made it a point to stay out of Fanny's way.

"I said MOVE! Something wrong with your ears?" Fanny was bearing down on her so that her face was only six very scary inches from Ginny's, choking her with the intoxicating fumes from the bottle of Diamond White Fanny had necked before coming to the disco. "We want to sit there, so move."

Ginny's heart was beating so fast that she was starting to feel dizzy — which at least took her mind off her churning stomach and the ever-increasing desire to throw up or faint. Panic overruled her motor skills and she discovered that although her brain was begging her legs to adjust to a standing position they were too busy trembling with fear to respond.

A split second later, Ginny felt a searing pain in her head and a compelling urge to levitate, the result of Fanny's hands gripping on to her hair and wrenching it upwards. She was going to die. She was definitely going to die, right in the middle of Gary Barlow singing about needing her love.

Suddenly, there was a loud scream, a lurch, and Ginny fell back to her seat. Strange, she was pretty sure that fear had paralysed her vocal cords and the scream hadn't come from her. So who . . .?

She pushed her hair back from her face and gasped as she saw Fanny Brown bent so far backwards that her spine looked like it was about to crack, and behind her, clutching her ponytail, was Roxy, who was leaning down, whispering something in her ear.

Fanny went bright red. Green. Red. Green. Aaah — it was hard to tell what colour she was but she definitely didn't look happy. Without releasing her grip, Roxy whispered something else and then gave Fanny's ponytail a sharp tug. Fanny wailed with pain then nodded furiously. Roxy slowly pulled the ponytail upwards, allowing Fanny to stand up again, then released it with a flourish.

Ginny suddenly realised that not only was she about to die, but Roxy was too. Fanny threw back her shoulders, went chin-to-chin with Roxy, and then . . . quickly turned away and made for the door, taking Dopey and Daftarse with her.

Ginny's eyes were bigger than the disco lights as she watched the retreating gang.

"But . . . but . . . what . . . what . . . what . . . did you say to her?" she blustered.

Roxy just shrugged. "Doesn't matter. But I don't think she'll be chatting to us again anytime soon."

Ginny's wave of nausea was swiftly replaced with relief and a massive dose of love. Roxy might be a nightmare, she might be moody, demanding and annoying, but Ginny knew without an iota of a doubt that Roxy would defend her against the world without a moment's hesitation.

Now she had Ginny's hand and was pulling her out of the chair. "Come on, you boring moo, let's dance — or I'll tell Fanny you want to have a chat with her," she added with a mischievous grin.

Just at that moment, Father Murphy's DJing skills came into play and with the resounding screech of a needle being dragged across vinyl, Take That was replaced with the opening bars of Mr Blobby.

"Aw shit, I hate this song," Roxy moaned.

Ginny sighed with sweet relief. Great. She could go back to just sitting in the corner, counting the minutes until it was time to go home.

Or maybe not.

"Bugger it," Roxy continued, "let's go outside until something decent comes on — I'm dying for a fag."

CHAPTER
SIX

The Love Shack

Ginny. Day Two, Monday, 9.30a.m.

Ginny hung up the phone and checked the clock. Nine thirty. Bliss — another two and a half hours before she had to be at work. Or, had to be at Roxy's work, technically speaking. She picked up her mobile and tried Darren's number again, hoping to catch him before the class started — nope, no reply. Never mind, she'd try to catch him later, in between Bums & Tums and his afternoon Tai Bo class with the Perky Pensioners.

She turned the TV volume back up, then burrowed back under the duvet with a smile on her face. Goldie Gilmartin, the glam forty-something darling of *Great Morning TV*, was gliding effortlessly from a feature about the current grooming trends for metrosexual males (new discovery — testicle waxing at breakfast-time puts you right off a marmalade bagel) to her standard superficial waffle as she closed the show. Ginny groaned at the naffness of it. Yes, the nation would have a good day. Yes, we'd be good to one another. And yes, you're a patronising, condescending cow.

Good grief, what was happening to her? She'd been in Roxy's world for one night and already she was adopting bitchy mannerisms and coming over all judgemental.

And she was even enjoying it! Yes, she could definitely get used to this. It was just a shame that Darren wasn't here to share it with her. Maybe a romantic break was exactly what they needed to jolt them out of the rut they'd slipped into. But then, didn't all couples go through this? Wasn't this what love was all about — taking the sickness with the health, the poor with the rich, and the exciting with the bored-so-rigid-you-want-to-weep?

She wondered if he was missing her, and then chided herself — she'd been gone for less than a day! She was beginning to sound like one of those reality-show contestants who crumbled in a heap and wailed about missing their families after twenty-four hours in a psychedelic house in East London. And anyway, didn't Roxy say that he'd taken it well? That he didn't mind? That's what she loved about him — he was so supportive, and if he was rooting for her then she could do this. She could. And she was only a tiny bit scared. Okay, she was bloody terrified. She'd never been on the tube on her own, let alone set foot in a brothel, and she just knew that all the girls at the Seismic would be like Roxy — cosmopolitan, switched on and fearless.

But how hard could it be? *She* could be cosmopolitan, *she* could be switched on, and although fearless might be a stretch, she could probably hit the middle of the apprehension scale, halfway between mildly nervous and hyperventilation.

In the meantime, a bit of shameless pampering would be nice. She padded into Roxy's en suite and marvelled at the opulence. Travertine walls, polished marble floor, a huge vanity unit in natural oak with a square white sink perched on top. And the sink taps — wait for it — were those ones with the infrared beam which came on automatically when you waved your hand in front of the sensor. The glistening porcelain toilet gave the impression that it was floating in midair and the bath came complete with a remote control for the complex computer panel located between the taps. She wasn't sure if she should bathe in it or attempt to contact the *Starship Enterprise*.

The prospect of an hour of glorious relaxation made her opt for the former. No wonder Roxy always looked so bloody gorgeous with all this time in the mornings to prepare. Ginny's normal routine didn't quite hit this level of luxurious self-indulgence — three women plus one bathroom equalled a five-minute shower, deodorant fumes that made your eyes water and a monthly visit from Dyno-Rod to clear the unidentified hairs that were choking the drains.

She turned on the tap on the spa bath. Oh, the decadence. She was thinking candles, she was thinking soft music, she was thinking bubbles, she was thinking . . . strange farting noises! Shit, wrong tap. She spun it back off then opened the other one, letting water cascade into the gleaming ceramic. Note to self — water in first, air in second.

She spotted the candles that were nestled in groups at the top corners of the bath. Jo Malone, grapefruit-scented. She'd never heard of them — she usually went for whatever was on offer in Sainsbury's — but she was sure they'd be lovely. Bugger it, she'd light them all, Roxy wouldn't mind. And if she did, Ginny would pick up some more for her next time she was doing the grocery shopping.

Finally, bubbles. She checked out the bottles on the shelf. Chanel. Bvlgari. La Prairie. So, Body Shop coconut bubble bath was out of the question then.

Ginny added a little of everything then slipped into the warm water before opening the air tap just enough to add a gentle, undulating flow. Monday morning, ten a.m. — Ginny was on the Bliss Highway, heading for Heaven. She took a wild stab in the dark and pressed the ? button on the remote control, and smiled as the intoxicating tones of Usher's "Burn" filled the room.

And as her eyes drooped and she fell into a blissful slumber, the Young Catholic Mothers' arses were the furthest things from her mind.

"Ginny. Ginny! Time to go!"

Glug.

Three things happened at once: Ginny's eyes flew open, her mouth followed suit, and the shock-induced loss of her equilibrium sent her shooting under the water.

As she performed a whole choking/retching/lungs-filling-with-fluid panic, she fleetingly wondered if anyone had ever drowned in Chanel bubble bath. It wasn't an appropriate end for Ginny Wallis from

Farnham Hills. It was the kind of demise more befitting of, say, Brigitte Bardot. Or Anna Wintour. Or Elton John.

Just as she surfaced and regained the use of her cardiovascular system, the door opened and Jude's gorgeous head popped round.

"You okay?"

Ginny shrieked with embarrassment and squeezed her eyes tight shut.

"Can you see any inappropriate naked bits?" she squeaked.

"Only if you're a really strange person who gets their rocks off at the sight of an erotically exposed elbow."

Phew. Gingerly, she opened one eye and checked for herself. What a relief, he was right — the few bubbles that were left had congregated to preserve her modesty so there wasn't a nipple in sight.

Actually, that wasn't exactly true. Jude was wearing nothing but a faded pair of jeans and a smile.

Was that mandatory in this house? Was it a condition of the tenancy?

Clause 1(a): I will pay the rent on time every month.
Clause 1(b): I will refrain from causing damage to the house or contents.
Clause 1(c): I will at all times wander around looking like I belong in a Calvin Klein advert.

"Sorry, I must have . . . erm . . . fallen asleep. What time is it?"

He consulted his TAG Heuer. "Eleven o'clock."

"Noooooo! I'm late, oh shit, Roxy will kill me."

In a blind panic, she levered herself out of the bath.

"Whoa . . . inappropriate naked bits overload." Jude laughed and shut his eyes as Ginny shrieked again, hands flying to cover her vital anatomy.

"Jude, you need to help me! I should have been on the tube fifteen minutes ago. And I don't have anything to wear. And my hair looks like an explosion. And . . . I . . . can't . . . breathe."

She grabbed a towel from the vanity unit and wrapped it around her.

"Okay, you can open them now." Did he ever drop that cute grin? Aaaargh — why was she contemplating the merits of a stripper's dimples when she was late for her first day at work? Roxy's work. Shit. Shit. Shit.

"Don't panic," said dimple man.

"I'm already bloody panicking!" she shrieked, grabbing a can of deodorant and spraying under her arms.

"Stop!" he yelled. The sheer force of his voice made her freeze — apart from her bottom lip, which was trembling, and her tear ducts, which were threatening to burst their dam.

"Okay, here's the plan. First of all, drop the can — that's Glade air-freshener and you now smell of Alpine hills."

Ginny flushed with mortification and placed the can back on the vanity unit.

Jude pressed on, kindly ignoring her beaming face. "Okay. Good. Now, forget the tube — there's a car waiting outside for you. That's why I shouted to you that it was time to leave."

Ginny shook her head. "What car?"

"Roxy came to some arrangement with the local taxi company — think she gets the boss a discount at the Seismic. Anyway, a car comes every morning to collect her and take her to work."

Of course! What had Ginny been thinking? Roxy would rather set fire to her Jimmy Choos than enter the sweaty, over-populated tunnels of the London tube system.

"And he always waits because Roxy's never ready either. So you've got about fifteen minutes to get ready."

Ginny felt the rising panic again. Fifteen minutes? To go from someone with the face of a jalapeño pepper and the hair of Crystal Meth Barbie, to the kind of cool, groomed perfection required at the Seismic? She'd need a fucking miracle.

The dam burst, tears and snot commencing flow. Now Jude was the one with the terrified expression.

"Hello my darling, it's just me!" came a voice from the hallway, followed by a slamming door.

"In here! And we need your help," shouted Jude, his tone one of palpable relief.

Ginny wiped her forearm along her nose to stem the snot.

Clicking heels announced the arrival of a figure in the shadows of the doorway.

"Mmmm. My boyfriend, half-naked, strange woman, completely naked, and yet this doesn't seem in the least strange or awkward. What does that say about our relationship, my sweet?"

Ginny sniffed and sighed at the same time, causing a delay in her brain registering the word "boyfriend". Even in her over-emotional, frantic, ears-filled-with-Chanel-bubble-bath state, she was cognisant of the fact that the voice bore no resemblance to the dulcet tones of Cheska, attorney at law.

Jude turned to the new arrival.

"It says that you trust me implicitly," he replied, teasing gently.

"It says I'm fucking mad," countered the girlfriend, with an unmistakable smile in her tone. "Okay, explain . . ."

"This is Ginny, she's Roxy's friend, she's got fifteen — nope, make that ten — minutes to transform from . . . erm . . ."

"I'd go with 'tragic disaster' ", Ginny offered ruefully.

". . . erm, lovely but fairly tragic disaster to groomed perfection, sitting in the back of that cab out there. Honey, think you can do it?"

The heels clicked forward. And in that split second, Ginny's perception of a national icon changed forever.

"Are you kidding me? I've already waxed some bloke's crack on national television this morning — a ten-minute makeover will be a fucking doddle."

And indeed, ten minutes later, Ginny Wallis, make-up flawless but subtle, hair swept back into an elegant chignon, dressed head to toe in cutting-edge black Prada, emerged from the doorway of a Knightsbridge building and headed towards a waiting cab.

As she pulled the cab door open, she looked back up at the flat's window to see the silhouette of Jude and *Great Morning TV*'s Goldie Gilmartin snogging the faces off each other.

She smiled, turned and tripped into the car, landing spread eagled on the back seat.

Well, there were only so many miracles that Goldie Gilmartin could perform.

Now this was the way to go to work in London — no stress, no hassle, just sit back, relax, and watch the frantic bustle of the metropolis go by . . . Oh, and text your pal while you're doing that.

2 grlfrnds? & 1 is GG. Thnx 4 wrning!

Roxy's reply came back in seconds.

All hail da sex God. PS: re-arrngd ur filing systm.

Ginny felt a flush of anxiety creep up her neck. No! That system was her pride and joy, her baby. She'd planned it meticulously, she'd worked late, she'd even bought coloured card from the stationer's up the High Street with her own money, and now — she couldn't even bear to think about it — now, Roxy had gone and . . .

Her phone bleeped again. Roxy. She opened the text.

Ha! Kidding.

Why? Why were they friends? Ginny sighed, trying to get her heart rate back to a state that didn't suggest cardiac arrest was imminent — a task that was immediately undone when she turned her thoughts to the Seismic.

On the plus side, Sam was obviously okay about her coming, as Roxy had promised to warn her if he had any reservations about it.

On the negative side, her body slipped into a mild panic attack at the very thought of the day ahead. Let's face it, it wasn't even noon and so far that morning living Roxy's life had involved near drowning, indecent exposure, and being dressed by a woman who earned in excess of a million a year. If this was normality then she'd hate to get a taste of crazy.

She tried Darren's mobile again — still no answer. Maybe she should just go home and stop this ridiculous charade before the stress caused permanent damage to her major organs.

Why was she doing this? She could be sitting in the library right now, drinking tea, eating a Penguin and trying to stop the fifth-year study group from the local high school from smoking hash and shagging in the toilets. It wasn't the actual activity she minded so much as the fact that in the last month they'd broken two towel holders and a soap dispenser off the wall. It was just wrong on every level that sixteen-year-olds should be having hot, frantic sex when she was suffering from acute boredom of the genital department.

She frowned — had that thought really come into her head? There was nothing wrong with her and

Darren's sex life! Okay, so it was fairly perfunctory — missionary, doggy, and if they were feeling really wild, a spot of oral sex just to get things going — but at least it was regular: Mondays, Wednesdays, Saturday nights and Sunday mornings (except when Mrs Jones from next door had PMT because then she booked Darren for a Sunday-morning five-mile run to work off the aggression).

No, there was absolutely nothing wrong with their sex life and the only reason she resented Team Delinquent was because the library didn't have a maintenance budget to repair the damage in the loos. That was definitely her only issue. Well, that and the fact that the noise sometimes reached the members of the Perky Pensioners in the poetry corner nearby and she wasn't sure their pacemakers were up to the strain.

Anyway, it was time to push the shenanigans of Farnham Hills out of her head and concentrate on psyching herself up for the shenanigans of Mayfair.

She tried to remember the tips in the best-selling self-help book that had come in the month before: *Stress Overload? Take the Steps to Serenity*. Although she wasn't sure the book was up to much since the author had recently taken the steps to the Priory after a road-rage incident involving a truck, a milk cart and a thirteen-mile police chase.

She shook out her shoulders, exhaled, closed her eyes and took a deep breath.

Okay, step one: Picture the situ —

"Excuse me, love, but we're 'ere."

And that's why self-help books were a load of tosh — if you had the time to read the bloody things then you obviously didn't need them in the first place.

She pulled her purse out of her bag.

"What do I owe you?"

"Nothin' love, it's on account."

She pulled out a fiver and slipped it through the slot in the glass.

"Cheers, darlin'. Same time tomorrow?"

Well, would it be? Would she be coming back? Or would one day in a place where the activities would make Team Junior Delinquent look like spokespeople for conservative values be enough for her?

"Definitely. Same time tomorrow."

Ginny Wallis had come — now she just had to conquer.

Or should she leave that kind of stuff to the sadomasochism department of her new place of employment?

Ginny stood and stared at the tree-lined street, with a row of luxury vehicles bordering each pavement. Porsche. Mercedes. Porsche. Bentley. Another Porsche. Mercedes. BMW. There wasn't even a complementary Corsa thrown in as an ethnic minority. This was where people of serious dosh flashed their cash. And their privates, apparently.

She switched her gaze to the building in front of her — a Georgian terraced townhouse, sandblasted walls, restored windows, petunias in the planters on either side of the entrance, a glossy green door and, beside it, a very subtle gold plaque, announcing in black italics that this was the home of *The Seismic Lounge*.

Class. Sheer class. If you overlooked the whole "get your knockers out for the boys" stuff that took place inside. *Inside.* Ginny took a deep breath and steeled herself for movement. Who. Dares. Wins. If that motto could motivate the SAS to storm foreign embassies then surely it could get her past the front door of a knocking shop.

One foot in front of the other. One foot in front of the other.

Seconds later she was pressing the bell and watching as two cameras swivelled in her direction. "Good morning, can I help you?"

Ginny leaned over to the chrome speaker above the buzzer.

"Er, I'm Ginny. Erm, Ginny Wallis. I'm working here today." She somehow managed to stop short of adding, "Which is a really, really bad idea and I've changed my mind so can you please phone my mum and beg her to come and collect me."

The door swept open and Ginny crossed the line. That was it — no going back. She followed the shiny walnut floor along the hallway, barely registering the striking primary-coloured canvases that punctuated the lush ivory walls.

The end of the corridor opened into a reception area that — wow — was so far from her expectations that she was temporarily stunned. She'd anticipated pink walls, red sofas, porn posters and glass tables dotted with *Playboy* magazines and penis-shaped cigar holders. Where were the girls in red chiffon baby dolls and Perspex platforms the size of Fiat Puntos? Where were the red glass bowls filled with an international selection of condoms?

This room wouldn't be out of place at the HQ of any large corporation. Welcome to Hookersville Inc.

It was an eclectic mix of old and new. The stunning glass and chrome reception desk juxtaposed against beautiful antique lamps. The original wooden flooring was an exquisite contrast to the thick, cream rugs. And the modern-art pieces were the epitome of clean lines, yet somehow didn't clash with the three more traditional large bronze life-form statues — although that may have been because the statues demanded full attention on account of the fact that they were all males with their extremely generous appendages dangling in the breeze. Cancel that last statement. Ginny's eyes widened as she took in the full view of the third statue — which, going by the evidence, was probably called something like *Man in State of Arousal*.

So at least now she knew where to hang her umbrella.

"He has that effect on everyone. What I wouldn't give to get stuck in a lift for two hours with the real thing. I'm Jennifer."

Ginny automatically smiled at the stunning girl sitting on the cream leather chair behind the desk. Flawless skin, two sheets of perfect blonde hair hanging from a middle parting, a cream roll neck and cream crepe trousers. She was Roxy in negative.

"Hi, I'm Ginny".

The muted ring of a telephone cut into the conversation. Jennifer immediately turned her attention to the state-of-the-art switchboard and gesticulated in the direction of a door on the opposite wall.

"Great — go through that door, turn right, along to the end of the corridor and it's the room that says Eden Suite on the door."

Okay, not quite the reception she'd been hoping for, but then at least she'd been expected so Roxy had obviously phoned and cleared everything as promised. Phew. After last night's encounter with Jude and the Amazonian, she'd had visions of arriving to puzzled expressions.

A wave of dizziness overtook her; a sharp reminder that she'd been holding her breath for so long that there was a distinct lack of oxygen reaching the brain. Breathe. Breathe. She could do this. She was Roxy's lifelong friend, she'd been styled by Goldie Gilmartin and she was borderline premenstrual — a combination that should give her enough balls and determination to get through anything.

She followed Jennifer's directions and crossed the reception, then turned right into a sumptuous corridor of pale gold walls and a deep olive carpet so thick that she started to wobble on her heels. She passed several solid wood-panelled doors and a small elevator, and then just as the effort of staying upright was beginning to bring on a tension headache, she reached the door at the very end of the corridor: the Eden Suite.

Human Resources department, perhaps? Or Sam's office? Staffroom? Or where they provided the brown paper bags for her to hyperventilate into?

She tentatively knocked on the door.

"Come in," replied a very posh female voice.

"Confidence, Ginny, *confidence*," she whispered to herself as she made the necessary last-minute adjustments — hair flicked back, bag pulled up onto shoulder, sweaty palms wiped on trousers — then clutched the brass doorknob and turned it.

The door swept open and in the ten seconds it took for Ginny's brain to process the scene in front of her, there was a quizzical look, a muffled groan, a massive gasp, a rush of blood to the ears and paralysis of the limbs. The last three belonged to Ginny — apt, as she was apparently in the right place to receive medical attention, having stumbled onto the set of *Holby City*. Or, rather, the porn version — *Holby Titty*.

The room itself was remarkable only in its luxury. One wall was partially covered by a huge brass mirror that must have been at least six foot square. Directly opposite was a beautifully upholstered gold headboard framing a super-king bed dressed in crisp white sheets. To the side was a rustic Chesterfield sofa in gleaming brown leather, and next to it stood an antique side table topped with a bottle of Krug and two crystal champagne glasses, half-filled with the bubbling liquid.

But that's where any semblance of normality ended, because standing at the foot of the bed, one eyebrow still raised, was a female doctor dressed in a uniform that Ginny was guessing hadn't been passed by any NHS committee: six-inch steel heels on black platform pumps, a white coat that was wide open, revealing a cupless black leather bra, perfectly pert pink nipples, black suspenders and stockings. And Doctor Decadence may have had her auburn locks secured in a very efficient chignon, her black-framed glasses perched on her perfectly formed nose, subtle make-up and an air of authority, but she appeared to have forgotten her knickers.

Not that her patient was in a position to remonstrate about her omission. Lying prone on the bed, his identity concealed by the white bandages that covered him from head to toe, was a groaning man. Yes, definitely male — the only part of his anatomy that appeared to have escaped mummification was the massive erect penis that was pointing at the ceiling. And it appeared a rigorous medical examination was taking place as the doctor was tickling the red, throbbing end of his organ with her stethoscope.

Ginny's jaw dropped so far she was in danger of incurring carpet burns to the chin area.

"Can I help you?" asked the doctor archly, with an edge of amusement in her voice.

It was no use — Ginny couldn't get the words out.

"Is that the consultant here to give a second opinion, Doctor?" The voice came from behind the bandages and, astonishingly, despite the fact that it was muffled and obviously constrained by the lack of jaw movement, it still had a leering intonation.

A barrage of critical questions raced through her mind. Was this some kind of test? Did they put all the new recruits through this? Was she supposed to join in? And did that stethoscope get disinfected between patients?

The doctor (okay, so she obviously wasn't a *real* doctor, but job descriptions seemed to have been temporarily scrubbed from Ginny's mind by the dual forces of mortification and shock) was still eyeing her quizzically, all the while continuing to run the stethoscope over the patient's cock. Ginny did admire women who could multi-task.

Suddenly, Ginny sensed a movement behind her and flinched as she was gently nudged to the side by a new arrival squeezing past her in the doorway. She was scared to look. What next? Naked paramedics? Nympho nurses?

Ginny caught the back view of the new arrival: white coat, high-heeled pink mules, long, glossy red hair that tumbled down almost to her waist. Doctor number one smiled in her colleague's direction. "Ah, here's Doctor Dee now," she announced.

Doctor Dee strutted around to the other side of the bed, allowing Ginny a front view. Stethoscope around neck, white coat fastened, cleavage like two wrestling beach balls spilling over the top two straining buttons. She reached over and took the tip of the patient's exposed anatomy between her thumb and forefinger. "Mmmm, what do we have here, then?" There was a pause as she surveyed the evidence and racked her obviously considerable medical knowledge for the appropriate diagnosis.

"Well now, Doctor," she addressed her partner in vice, "I think I'm going to have to take a much, much closer look . . ."

As she bent forward, the patient's ecstatic groan snapped Ginny out of her fright-induced rigor mortis. There were many things in life that she didn't want to see, and this was one of them. She took a swift step backwards and swiftly pulled the door closed, then staggered backwards until her buttocks hit the opposite wall and she slid down it into a kneeling position. Oh. Dear. God. Oh. Dear. God. In the last few moments she'd been given a snapshot into the adult porn world, a whole new perspective on the emergency services, and had doubled the number of male penises she'd actually seen in the pink flesh.

Why would people even do that kind of stuff? Her idea of the ultimate decadent sexual fantasy was imagining Brad Pitt in his boxers bringing her a high-carbohydrate breakfast in bed.

She had to get out of here. She couldn't do this. She was cut out for a simpler, more innocent environment, where the inhabitants were non-aroused, non-naked and preferably not about to ejaculate in full public view.

She half-walked, half-stumbled back down the corridor and into reception, where she summoned every ounce of self-discipline to force her mouth to form proper sentences.

"I'm . . . I'm so . . . sorry, I think . . . I think there's been a terrible mistake," she stuttered.

Jennifer looked suitably apologetic. "I figured . . . I'm terribly sorry. Roxy just called and explained who you were. I thought you were . . ."

"I know!" Ginny interrupted, determined to cut her off before Jennifer could reveal why or how she could

91

possibly have been mistaken for a hooker who specialised in private healthcare porn.

She shuddered as the mental image of what she'd just seen flashed back into her head and realised that there was a certain irony in the fact that she'd probably now require the NHS to fund a lifetime of counselling for post-traumatic stress.

Jennifer was still in mid-flow. "Anyway, it's good to finally meet Roxy's best friend. Oops, hang on one second."

She spoke into a Kylie Minogue headset thingy with a microphone attachment that followed her jawline. "Yes, Mr Cavendish, your car is waiting at the back door and your payment has cleared. Have a good week, sir."

Ginny wondered what boarding school Jennifer had gone to. The posture, the confidence, the accent . . . it was straight out of some £20K-per-year college with "Lady" in the title. Or at least it was until she removed the headset and became Jenny from the Block. A block that was obviously located somewhere near Toxteth.

"Okay, so do you want the good news or the bad?"

Ginny's stomach flipped over. On the scale of bad days, so far this was up there with her first period and the time she'd stuffed her bra only for the balls of toilet paper to fall out in front of the whole school as she attempted the hundred-metre hurdles on sports day. And that had been bloody Roxy's idea too.

"Give me the bad."

"Roxy hasn't actually told Sam that she's sent you to replace her. She's asked me to pass on the news. God, she's a fucking nightmare, I don't know how you put up with her. Rough break, though — how's that asshole Felix anyway?" Jennifer asked.

"No idea. Roxy hasn't spoken to him since she caught him . . . well . . . you know."

"Urgh, he needs a padlock on his dick. And I don't think for a minute that was the first time he had wandered either. Sorry, hold on, arrival at the back door."

Jennifer switched her headset and Princess Anne's voice back on.

"Good morning, Mr Reid, lovely to see you again. Natalya is waiting for you in your usual suite. Certainly, I'll have that sent right up."

Ginny knew this was her moment. With Jenny distracted she could bolt for the door, dive into a taxi and be home before *Neighbours*. It was Monday — otherwise known as Spaghetti Bolognaise Day, with low-fat tiramisu for pudding. Her mother was very proud of her new talents since she and Vera had gone on a cookery course and learned to conjure up "traditional foreign dishes".

Without turning, she gingerly backed away towards the doorway, when . . . hang on, wasn't that the whole point of this? Didn't she want to get away from predictability, habit and a lifetime of non-eventfulness? Tuesday — ham and chips. Wednesday — shepherd's pie. Thursday — chicken and potato croquettes. It would be the same menu, the same routine, the same mind-numbing repetitiveness interspersed with only very occasional flashes of variety — like last month when her mother and Vera had taken up a new hobby and insisted on bellydancing in the front room.

Two middle-aged women, wearing sequinned bras and belly-dancing during the *Coronation Street* adverts.

One middle-aged man with a mummification fetish.

Rock. Hard place.

Her feet stopped moving. How could she explain to Roxy that she'd bottled out on the very first day? The very first hour? Urgh, she was unbearable enough, but she'd never let her live this down. It would be, "Poor little Ginny — couldn't cope with life in the big, bad world" from now until they were filling out the application forms for Perky Pensioners.

Jennifer pressed another button on her phone. "Hi Harry, Mr Reid in the Thatcher Suite would like strawberries, two bottles of Cristal and — brace yourself — custard. Oh, and better put housekeeping on standby — that stuff gets into places that you just would not *believe*."

Headset off, Scouse back on.

"Twelve suites, all named after prime ministers," she explained. "Churchill is popular with the over-sixties, the sadists love Thatcher, and the Blair Suite is a big hit with the fantasists. We live in a sick world. Okay, you've got a choice. Sam's not here, he'll be back in half an hour, so you can either wait and talk to him first or I can spend the next thirty minutes training you up in the hope that he won't have a seizure when he realises that Roxy has pulled a fast one."

Ginny felt her teeth start to grind. She couldn't do this, could she? *Could she*? This would officially be the most stupid, reckless thing she had done since . . . Actually, since she'd flashed her baps at Jude in the bath that morning.

She bit her bottom lip, still not convinced, and murmured, "Or I could turn around, run out that door and forget this insane idea altogether."

For the first time, Jennifer smiled. "You could . . . but I'd hunt you down and drag you back. I've got a date with a rampant French chef in an hour and I refuse to miss it just because Roxy is having a diva fit."

She held up another headset.

"Now, strap this on and let's get going. Shit, that reminds me . . ."

She pushed the intercom button again.

"Harry, can you send someone to the Clement Atlee with a leather dildo and a gimp mask? They asked about fifteen minutes ago and I totally forgot."

Turns out, Ginny could do it after all. Twenty-nine minutes later, she pretty much had it sussed. In theory. Answer the intercom from the back door, direct the client to the suite if ready; if not, direct him to one of three comfortable waiting rooms. Since it was a rule of the house that clients must never meet each other, it was imperative that no more than three stooges were ever waiting at the same time. If this did indeed happen (an event that had only occurred once before — in that instance inefficient condom disposal had resulted in a plumbing débâcle/flooding situation that put five suites out of action simultaneously) then it was the receptionist's responsibility to contact the limo drivers heading in with clients and ask them to circle. The Seismic Lounge — the Heathrow Airport of prostitution.

The receptionist also logged all requests from the suites for refreshments, contraception, sex aids or reinforcements. Who knew when a cosy twosome would suddenly become a titillating *ménage à trois* (hopefully, without Ginny being *un, deux* or *trois*)? Or *quatre*? Apparently, if Stephen Knight was involved it often stretched to a netball team.

Other tasks on the job description included answering the phones, making appointments and managing the very efficient payment system.

When a client entered he swiped his credit card at the door. While he was showering/bathing after his appointment, his "service provider" would call down to the receptionist with a list of any supplementary charges. There was a standard hourly rate, but optional extras included refreshments, costumes (dry-cleaning bills were extortionate in Central London), additional girls or the extension of the session. It was Ginny's job to finalise the account, charge it to his credit card, and then update the client's personal record file so that his likes/habits/requests/tendencies could be prepared for his next visit.

So far, so clinical and efficient. Not to mention twisted and borderline freaky.

Not that Ginny was judging.

The receptionist then alerted the drivers and ensured that the client's departure was seamless.

"So, under normal circumstances, do I ever actually see these . . . *men?*" Ginny asked, beyond relief that — cases of mistaken hooker identity aside — her new role seemed to be no more sordid than a day at Farnham Hills library. In fact, given that the teenage population of the village were hellbent on giving anatomy lessons in the library toilets, this was actually a step up in the sexual activities department — at least the dual benefits of contraception and soft furnishings were provided.

"Sometimes. If there's someone you particularly want to get a look at, just make sure you're there to open the door personally when they arrive. Or direct them to a waiting room and then pop in to ask if they need anything. Occasionally they'll wander through here but usually they prefer to keep out of sight. There are two butlers, Harry and Fred, so if you're busy just give one of them a bell and they'll do the running around. Got all that?"

Ginny frantically searched her head for any missing links in the sexually deviant chain — nope, she reckoned she just about had everything covered.

"I think I've got all that. But what do I do if anything goes wrong?"

"Just call Sam. And if he's not around then buzz Destiny — that's her real name, her mother took too many drugs in the Sixties. Anyway, she's lovely and during the day she's the most senior of the girls — Sam's right-hand hooker. On the overnight shift it's Charlotte — scary, freaky and only comes out after dark. Yes, there have been rumours but she's massively popular with the men of the cloth and she's never actually punctured a customer's skin yet. Don't worry, you'll get used to her, but I wouldn't turn my back just in case . . ."

The noise of the front door closing travelled down the hall. Jenny switched her gaze in that direction.

"That's if you last long enough to meet her . . ."

Just when Ginny's confidence was edging back up to somewhere near normal, Sam Carvell strutted towards her. The hairs on the back of her neck stood to attention and her knees summoned the spirits of all things Elvis and began to shake. This was ridiculous. It was only a job — and a temporary one at that. What was the worst he could do? Say no? Fine — she'd just head back to the Hills and return to her old life, old habits, old job, old spaghetti bolognaise. Roxy had been at the library for a full morning so she'd probably have been fired by now anyway.

But . . . sod it, her emotional pendulum had swung back in the direction of "excitement and confidence" and she realised she wasn't ready to give up. She. Was. Going. To. Do. This. She just had to keep focusing on the positives. The positives. The positives . . .

Sam was five feet in front of the desk when he stopped reading the papers in his hand and looked up, the puzzlement clear on his face. Ginny decided to jump straight in — after all, what did she have to lose except a gorgeous flat, a designer wardrobe and a flatmate with pectoral muscles like split cantaloupes?

She took a deep breath. This was her chance to impress Sam, to reassure him that she was more than capable of representing his company in a calm and intelligent manner.

"Hi, Sam, I'm Ginny. Roxy's friend. We met at the . . . vol-au-vents . . . and, erm, you said, erm, if I needed a job . . . that, erm . . ."

She clamped her jaws shut. There were some times when silence was the better option and this definitely seemed like one of them.

Sam looked at her searchingly, trying to place her. His brow furrowed above his brown eyes and, as he distractedly ran a hand through his neat black hair, Ginny realised who he reminded her of: Ben Affleck. Just in looks, obviously. As far as she was aware, Ben Affleck hadn't compounded his acting success by putting together a stable of voluptuous beauties that charged by the hour.

"Hi Jenny . . ."

"Ginny!" she interjected instinctively.

Sam turned to look at her, adding gently, "I know, I was saying hello to Jennifer." He gestured to Jenny from the Block. Ginny's stomach flipped. This was fast sailing to the *Titanic* end of the "First Day in New Job" disaster scale.

"Okay, then. Ginny, I do, of course, remember you. Roxy's party, right?"

Ginny nodded.

"And is Roxy okay?" He sounded genuinely concerned. Or perhaps he was just trying to get a grip on whether or not his receptionist had completely lost the plot. Either way, she realised that she had to try to speak in an intelligible fashion.

"She's fine. Well, sort of. Well, not really. She's just kind of upset and . . . upset . . . and . . . you know . . ."

"*Upset.*" He finished the sentence for her, just a touch of teasing in his tone.

She felt a flush burn at the bottom of her neck and then sprint upwards, crashing to a halt at her hair follicles.

"It's nice to see you again. But I'm afraid I'm not looking for any more girls. We're fully staffed at the moment. In fact, two of our former girls have just returned from a six-month sabbatical on a rapper's estate in New York, so we're actually *over* quota at the moment."

A horrible realisation dawned. Bugger, not again!

"Oh, no, you don't understand — I'm here to cover for Roxy. She's, erm, you know, the upset thing, with all the problems she's been having, and you said she couldn't resign, and yes, I know I'm speaking really quickly and I promise I don't always do this, and anyway, Roxy asked me to cover for her and work her notice period because you said if I was ever looking for a job I should . . ."

"Breathe! Please, breathe — you're turning purple," Sam deadpanned.

"Sorry, I'm just nervous."

Jennifer looked at her watch. The date with the French chef was looming large.

"Sam, I've spent the last hour —" she nudged Ginny under the desk "— showing her the ropes and she's picked everything up really quickly. I'm sure she'll be fine. Really good."

Sam subtly tilted his head to one side.

"You'll sign a confidentiality contract and provide ID and references?"

Ginny nodded.

"And you've done similar work before?"

She nodded again.

"Well, since Roxy has left us with little choice and it's only for a few weeks then welcome to the Seismic. I'll be here for the rest of the afternoon, so just yell if you have any problems."

"So I can stay?"

"You can definitely stay."

The bubbles of excitement worked their way from Ginny's stomach to her throat, manifesting themselves as a huge grin and a barely discernible squeak.

This was going to be great. As long as she stayed within the reception area, this was going to be so posh, so cultured, so windswept and so fascinating.

"Oh, and Jenny, before you go, can you show Ginny the staffroom, the kitchen, the condom cupboard and the sex-aids vault."

And so *not* a job she would ever put on her CV.

Farnham Hills Library — Customer Record Card

Name: Mitch O'Donnell
Address: The Church House, FH
Telephone: 897981
Joined: 7 April 2007

Currently on Loan:	Return Due:
Hurling: The Revolution years by Dennis Walsh	31.10.07
Promise me by Harlan Coben	31.10.07
The Last Assassin by Barry Eisler	31.10.07
The Rabbit Factory by Marshall Karp	31.10.07
One Shot by Lee Child	31.10.07
The Irish Farmers' Handbook by Martin O'Sullivan	31.10.07
May Contain Nuts by John O'Farrell	31.10.07

Currently on Request:
Munster Hurling Legends by Eamonn Sweeney.
The Ultimate Encyclopaedia of Gaelic Football and Hurling by Martin Breheny and Donal Keenan
Echo Park by Michael Connelly
The Woods by Harlan Coben
Writer's and Artist's Yearbook 2007

102

Areas of interest:
Crime
Thrillers
Sport
Comedy

Comments/misc:

Newspapers requested: The Irish Times, The Irish Post, The Sun, The Daily Mirror

CHAPTER
SEVEN

Do You Really Want to Hurt Me?

Roxy. Day Six, Friday, 1p.m.
Text, Roxy to Ginny:

> **Please, please swap bck, homicidal urges getting harder 2 ignore.**

Text, Ginny to Roxy:

> **Plead PMT, u wl get off with parole.**

Roxy sighed and decided to use her murderous tendencies for the good of the community. She marched over to Hi-tech Central.

"Excuse me, the computers have a twenty-minute limit and you've been on it for twenty-five — could I ask you to log off so that someone else can use it, please?"

The teenager barely registered Roxy's existence. Or maybe he did. It was hard to tell when all she could see under the baseball cap was a couple of zits, a cold sore and facial hair that looked like the aftermath of a bush fire. Oh, and an aggressive sneer, but that might be a result of playing an online game that involved him eradicating masses of people with the nuclear weapon of his choice.

"I'm busy."

Roxy glanced at the Reverend Stewart on the next computer. Yes, she knew he was banned but there were no kids in the library and Auntie Vi had popped out to get her hard skin seen to, so Roxy had decided there was no harm in it. Just because he was a man of the clergy didn't mean he didn't have the same needs as everyone else. She peeked at his screen — High Street Knockers. And no, it wasn't the official website of a manufacturer of mid-priced door brassware.

But back to the delinquent with the social skills bypass.

"Your time is up."

He turned his head, raising his chin enough for Roxy to see that underneath the mandatory Burberry baseball cap was a fifteen-, possibly sixteen-year-old with dead eyes and a challenging expression.

Jesus, what was it with teenagers these days? It was Friday — only her fifth day at work — and already she'd had to pick three roaches out of the Crime/Thriller section, found a bra and a half-bottle of vodka in Diet & Nutrition, and caught one couple indulging in an anatomical lesson of their own underneath the Science & Nature shelves. To be honest, she didn't know whether to be outraged, horrified, or jealous that the only hot and heavy action around here didn't involve her. In the end, she'd waited until the whole of the fifth-year study group was present then

105

announced to Romeo, Juliet and all their mates that the next time she caught any of them behaving in an inappropriate manner she was getting the nuns from the local convent down to give a talk on the merits of chastity before marriage. They'd reacted with horror, fury, and then resorted to truly rebellious behaviour — studying.

"Look, just piss off. I said I'm busy."

Roxy leaned right in so that the man of God and large mammary compulsion couldn't hear her.

"Listen, you little prick, I'll make a wild guess that you're supposed to be at school, so either fuck off now or I'll phone the headmaster — no, make that the police — and I'll tell them that you're causing a breach of the peace. Which, trust me, you will be when I tip your spotty arse out of that chair."

The teenager turned and stared at her, his hand hovering ominously over his jacket pocket. Roxy rolled her eyes. What was he going to do? Assault her with a deadly packet of sugar-free gum? She gave him the stare of death she normally reserved for lecherous drunk guys with the dual delights of halitosis and a hard-on. Eventually, he stood up, pushed the chair back so violently that it almost took out the A — G shelf in the Self Help section (*ABC of Contentment, Be the Best You Can Be, Clitoral Exploration for Dummies*) and pushed past her as he headed to the exit.

The reverend turned to check out the disturbance and Roxy shrugged.

"Too many E-numbe —"

Halfway through the sentence he refocused on the computer and Roxy realised that she'd lost him to the High Street Knockers. She sighed. What did it say about her that she was in her early twenties (it only became late twenties after 28), attractive, witty and chic and yet she couldn't even hold the attention of a man who was paid to be a professional listener?

She sat down and reached for her mobile again.

We regret 2 inform u that Roxy Galloway died from boredomitus.

Ginny's reply was swift.

Condolences. So can I have her Prada bags?

Roxy tossed her phone across the desk in disgust and then logged on to her Hotmail account. Fifteen emails. Three adverts for cheap cosmetics, one announcement that she'd won the national lottery of Zimbabwe, one request from her bank to log in and update her security details (made somewhat dubious by the fact that it was spelt "seceurity detaels", five offers to improve her girth and erectile stamina, three prescriptions for weight-loss pills, a voucher allowing her to purchase shares in a Colombian diamond mine and an online shopping survey from Boots.

Messages from Felix? None. Not bloody one. Not even one of those crap jokes or filthy personal emails that got hijacked and spread around the globe ruining some poor sod's life in five minutes flat. Nothing. Nada.

Roxy's shoulders slumped and a little part of her wished that the cyber scum she'd just ejected from the building would reappear so she'd have someone to vent her irritation on. What the fuck was wrong with Felix? Why wasn't he grovelling? Didn't he realise that she was the best thing (other than the six-figure salary, the yacht and the Ferrari) that had ever happened to him?

Let's face it: she was at least one league above him in the looks department, she wasn't clingy, needy or whiny, and her blow jobs were legendary — he should by lying prostrate in front of her, begging for forgiveness. He was an arse. A completely self-absorbed, narcissistic, delusional arse. And she was glad to be shot of him. Really glad.

But why wasn't the bastard calling?

She shuffled back over to the reception desk by the windows and immediately spotted Auntie Vi on approach. She was difficult to miss. If the psychedelic anorak wasn't enough to grab your attention, the glare from the yellow legwarmers and bright pink wellies could cause temporary blindness.

"Reverend, the Porn Prevention Officer is just about to walk in the door — get over to the Natural History section or she'll be on the phone to the archbishop before the hour's out."

Five. Four. Three. Two. One.

"Hello, dear, sorry I was so long — had a bunion you could've skied down. Morning, Reverend." The reverend flicked over a page of *The Official Guide to Prehistoric Habitation* then gave Vi a wave.

She returned the gesture, while whispering to Roxy, "Has he been on that computer?"

"Nowhere near it, Auntie Vi."

Violet smiled. She couldn't deny she'd been a bit apprehensive about taking Roxy on — you never knew what that girl was going to do next — but she had to admit that it had worked out wonderfully. The customers seemed to like her, she kept on top of the paperwork and, strangely, there had been no damage to the toilets for days. Just a shame she seemed to be, well, a bit subdued.

Roxy, meanwhile, was waiting for nature to take its course. There was a silence for a few seconds and then,

"Cup of tea, love?"

And there it was. The Nobel Prize for Services to PG Tips goes to Violet Wallis. Tea. And another tea. "Like a cuppa, love?" "Time for a brew?" At least twenty times a day. Violet Wallis was single-handedly keeping the entire tea-producing industry of the Indian subcontinent afloat.

Roxy needed comfortable shoes, the patience of a saint and the water-retention skills of a camel to work here. Auntie Vi might mean well, but in the name of reinforced bladders she wasn't sure she could take it much longer.

Five days she had been there. Five days of no phone calls, no emails, no flowers, almost no conversation with anyone over sixteen or under sixty and — argh!!!!!!

— no contact from the prick who had betrayed her. Just lots and lots of tea.

Friday. The end of the week. Usually she'd have her weekend planned and, depending on her shifts, it would invariably involve some combination of back-to-back working/shopping/eating/drinking/sex. Her glance flicked to the Self Help section — if she'd written a book in her former life it'd be called *Hedonism Rules . . . And If You Don't Agree, Grab a Drink and Dance While You Think about It.*

Now the closest thing she got to adrenalin-fuelled decadence was when Vi surprised her with a HobNob. Things were getting so wild around here that she might soon go really crazy and hit the baker's for a strawberry tart.

She had to find something to do. The prospect of a weekend in Farnham Hills was up there on her desirability scale with public transport and herpes. The four weeknights she'd already endured had been bad enough. Roxy felt her buttocks clench in horror as the memory of her first night came flooding back . . .

A fabulous night out, they'd said, so Roxy had even dressed up for the occasion (although obviously she'd had to work within the constraints she'd been dealt). In the end, she unpicked the reindeers and was left with a plain jumper, her black trousers and her Louboutin heels. Not bad for an emergency fashion situation.

She even tried not to object too strongly when she realised that once again they were walking to their destination. Bloody hell, she'd have a four-figure chiropodist bill after a month here. But at least she'd have thighs of steel.

It was a ten-minute walk and Vera and Vi had talked up their surprise destination the whole way there. Fun. Excitement. A great laugh. Really gets the adrenalin going. Gets a bit rowdy. You can't help but join in. Oh, the suspense. By the time Roxy arrived at the village hall she was expecting an audience with Billy Connolly. Instead . . .

"Two little ducks!" yelled the eighty-year-old man with the wig that stayed facing the front even when he turned his head ninety degrees to snatch a ball out of a Perspex drum.

"Twenty-two!" chorused the crowd.

Meanwhile, Roxy contemplated how long she'd take to die if she mutilated herself with a bright purple dabber.

And just when she thought it couldn't get any worse, her mother and Vi had roped her into their weekly yoga class, French for Beginners, and she could now yee-har any cowboy into a frenzy on the line-dancing floor. That's when she wasn't developing the skills she'd picked up at the seminar in the church hall on "Finding Your Inner Woman." Although it seemed that Roxy's inner woman had buggered off on the same bus as her will to live.

She fleetingly considered hopping on a train and heading back to London but the truth was she couldn't face that either. For a start she'd have to share a bed with Ginny. Secondly, there was no way she was showing her face in London until she'd had her eyebrows done. And she didn't think that Anastasia, the resident eyebrow guru at Harvey Nicks, did house calls to Loserville, No. 1 Dead End Street, The Back of Beyond. And thirdly . . . if she was really honest, she just couldn't be bothered.

What was wrong with her? It was as if she'd gone to sleep as a fabulous, adventurous, exotic creature and woken up as an extra in *Dawn of the Dead*. Was twenty-seven too young for a midlife crisis?

She picked up the book in front of her — a rip-roaring romp through job options entitled *Choosing the Right Career*. She'd limited herself to three pages an hour because any more than that caused her eyelids to shut. It was an excruciatingly tedious dictionary of employment that proved beyond reasonable doubt that Roxy Galloway was not cut out for bog-standard work. The As were mildly interesting: airline director, architect, aviation instructor. Bs bordered on mind-numbing: baker, billboard erector, butcher. By the time she got to the Cs she realised that not one job appealed to her. Not one. Actually, that wasn't strictly true — "costume mistress" had potential, but only if she was guaranteed major movie work and got to examine Kiefer Sutherland's inside leg measurement at close quarters.

She slammed the book shut. Boring. Boring. Boring. She contemplated texting Ginny again, but changed her mind. She'd already sent her approximately thirteen texts that week begging her to swap their lives back, and all she'd accomplished was a repetitive strain injury in her thumb.

How had Ginny survived here all these years? No wonder she'd slumped into apathy and dejection — if the boredom didn't kill you then it just rotted your brain cells until you lost the power to speak using words of more than one syllable. And since you never saw anyone remotely interesting (kinky reverends aside), grooming and presentation inevitably slid down the slippery slope that ended with Flokati leg hair and eyebrows you could crochet.

Tuesday — she hadn't bothered with make-up.

Wednesday — grimy hair in a ponytail.

Thursday — she wore a pair of her mother's trainers to work.

Friday — she borrowed Auntie Vi's lilac velour tracksuit and in a certain light it actually didn't look too bad on her. Okay, it looked like crap, but she didn't care.

"Nice tracksuit." Mitch slapped a pile of books on the reception desk. She was wondering where he'd got to today — the early morning had been even more excruciating than normal without his predictable presence.

"Don't you Catholics believe telling lies is a sin?"

He did a shrug/nod thing that indicated an affirmative response.

"Then if you don't mind standing back . . . that way the bolt of lightning may kill you but I should escape with minor scorch wounds."

Mitch grinned. 'Have you always been this self-absorbed?' he teased.

113

"And by self-absorbed, you do of course mean gorgeous and fascinating?" she fired back.

"Self-centred and obnoxious," he countered.

"Witty yet smart."

"Spoiled and arrogant."

Roxy leaned forward on the counter, eyes twinkling, their noses almost touching.

"But you still think I'm fabulous, don't you?"

"Absolutely."

"Good. Now stop staring at me, because if you're the type of bloke who gets excited about velour then our lives are even further apart than I realised."

And the truth, Roxy had discovered, was that if you put them in their natural positions on life's big playing field, they'd need a telescope and a satellite navigation system to find each other.

She may have experienced a small surge of cervical interest when she first set eyes on him, but she soon learned that Mitch was the personification of her six-inch Manolo stilettos: initially appealing, but obvious that they were a bad fit, uncomfortable and didn't gel with her lifestyle. Turns out that far from being an erudite, angst-ridden, tortured writer who was working on a future classic, he was actually penning a sequel to his surprise début hit, a lad-lit tale of frolics among the hurling community in his home town on the outskirts of Dublin.

Er, fab. Three hundred and fifty pages of in-depth fluff about men with sticks and irreverent dicks. And no, she hadn't confessed to him that she'd had to look up "hurling" in the dictionary.

114

Other own goals? He was from a family of farmers and priests — which meant he woke early, dressed badly and would never agree with Roxy's theory that Sundays were for breakfast in bed, lunch in bed and dinner in bed.

Oh, and he could talk until her hooters were literally dropping off with boredom about the merits of small-town life. And how did she know all this? Because it seemed that in Mitchland the definition of "writing a novel" was "spend an inordinate amount of time lounging around the library".

Roxy picked up a piece of paper from the desk — preparation for today's round of a new game she'd dreamt up after a conversation on Monday when she realised that he had absolutely no concept of fashion, technology or current trends.

"Okay," she announced, "here we have today's puzzlers."

Mitch laughed. "Noooo, haven't you humiliated me enough?"

"Probably, but it's the only pleasure I've had all week so go with it unless you want to see a grown woman cry."

He exhaled deeply, pushed up his sleeves and stretched his head from side to side. Then he closed his eyes and made beckoning gestures with his hands.

"Okay then, give me your best shot."

Roxy checked the array of scribbles in front of her and selected her first blow.

"Roberto Cavalli is famous for making what?"

Mitch's brow furrowed as he racked his brain.

"Er . . . Tyres?"

"Fuck, you're useless."

"I'm fairly sure it states in the rules that the compere isn't actually allowed to abuse the contestants," he replied, in his very best serious tone.

"Sorry, sorry . . . I'll award you one point as compensation for my unprofessional conduct. Okay, next question. A Blackberry is a famous . . .?"

"Pie."

She shook her head mournfully.

"Mark Anthony famously married . . .?"

"Cleopatra."

"A Bluetooth is a . . .?"

"Dental problem."

"And finally, a true or false. A metrosexual is someone who is fond of a fumble on the tube."

"False!" he blurted instantly.

Roxy was astonished. "Correct! Yaaaay! So what is it then?" she grinned. Maybe she'd underestimated him after all.

"No idea, but I figured it was a fifty/fifty shot."

Roxy couldn't suppress a giggle. Mitch, she mused, was the kind of guy who would never, ever understand why she wanted to be cremated after death and have her ashes placed in her beloved Marc Jacobs Stam Bag and buried under a floor tile in Tramp.

The penis embargo was definitely safe. His presence might make an hour or two in the library equivalent of death row pass a little quicker, but the chances of him getting her knickers off were up there with discovering that he was the secret love child of Alan Sugar and Jerry Hall.

He just *so* wasn't her type. But if she didn't break the monotony of her life then she was going to be the first official casualty of terminal boredom, so that's why it was so easy to say,

"Mitch, do you have plans for tonight?"

"Well, I'm still waiting for Cameron Diaz to confirm, but I could probably squeeze something else in."

Roxy groaned. "You do realise that you're not funny, don't you?"

His eyes widened and he clutched his chest. "Oh, dear Lord, the shock! The pain!"

"Yep, I'm feeling it too . . . somewhere around the arse region. Anyway, presuming Cameron doesn't call, fancy going out tonight? Thought I could dig out my tiara and slip into a little taffeta number and we could go for oysters, champagne, and then you could spin me around a dance floor before whisking me home in a chauffeured limo."

He shook his head dolefully before shooting her down. "Sorry, can't. I need twenty-four hours' notice to get my tiara out of the bank vault and I'm not going out without it."

The edges of Roxy's mouth crept up.

"Oh, fine — we'll skip the tiaras. So how about you pick up a bird in a lilac tracksuit, take her to the nearest pub and ply her with alcohol until she forgets she's stumbled into the seventh circle of hell?"

"How did you know? That's my idea of the perfect night out. Did the same thing to Drew Barrymore last week and she's been stalking me ever since. I'm sure that's why Cameron hasn't called — doesn't want to upset her pal."

"Understandably. Oh, and just so we're clear, I'm only doing this because you're the only person I've met all week who doesn't qualify for school dinners or a bus pass. This is what's called 'desperation'."

"Fine, but just so my ego doesn't top itself, can you at least pretend that it's wanton desire for my body?"

She looked him up and down. Grey T-shirt that screamed "Asda." Jeans that screamed "High Street". And boots that screamed, "I should have been at that line-dancing class too."

He obviously didn't realise that the only defence for wearing cowboy boots this season was if you planned to pass the time between lunch and dinner rustling sheep up the High Street.

"No," she replied, deadpan.

"Great — pick you up at five then."

The door banged behind him just as Vi reappeared with two steaming mugs and a box from the baker's.

"Thought you looked a little down in the mouth when I left, my love. So I brought you a little treat."

She opened the box with a flourish.

"Strawberry tart!"

"Yep, you really know how to show a girl a good time. Could you stand a little to the left?"

"Then I'd be in the direct line of the dartboard," Mitch objected.

"That would be the general idea."

Darts. In a pub. On a Friday night. If she were a horse someone would have put her out of her misery by now.

How did other people stand this?

She looked around her, her eyes only slightly blurred by the alcohol that was slowly taking effect. It was a typical rustic pub found in typical rustic villages all over Britain. The carpet was a fraying collision of pink and purple fleur-de-lis. The walls were decorated in a shade of peach that she believed Dulux called "Crappy Pub Walls". There were several shelves dotted about, all decorated with small brass jug things and plates with blue designs on them. And dried flowers everywhere. They were in huge pots in the corners. They hung upside-down over the five-foot-wide fireplace. They dangled from every corner of the room. The sixty-something, loud, drunk woman at the bar who had obviously yet to be informed that the Seventies had actually ended had even shoved some dried flowers down her silver lamé-encased, abundant cleavage. This wasn't just a pub — it was where dried flowers came to die. Of suffocation, apparently.

Roxy wiped the palm of her right hand on her tracksuit, then pointed her first dart towards the board on the opposite wall.

"Ginny!" she spat as she threw the first one. It caught the wire grid and ricocheted off to the side. Six feet away, eight senior citizens playing dominoes ducked in unison.

"Felix!" she spat as she threw number two. Triple nineteen. Half-pissed, yet she was still a natural.

119

"Men!" The third dart hit the bull's-eye. Eight senior citizens moved to another table and several members of the pub's ladies' darts team eyed her with newfound interest.

Roxy pulled her two darts out of the board, retrieved the third from the leg of a nearby chair, and then grabbed her purse from the ring-stained table. "I'll get the drinks. And don't even think about cheating when I'm clutching three instruments of death. By the way, are you having a good time?"

Mitch laughed. "Absolutely — how could I not when I have such great company in such salubrious surroundings? I'd come help you at the bar but my feet have stuck to the floor."

A few minutes later she was back, slamming a pint of Guinness and a Cosmopolitan (also in a pint glass — eat yer heart out, Carrie Bradshaw) down on the table. "If that barmaid draws me one more evil look I'm going to deck her," she muttered. "It seems that ordering cocktails makes me about as popular as genital warts around here."

She slumped into the burgundy, faux-velvet banquette and put her head on the table. When she eventually straightened back up, almost swaying off the chair in the process, the tears were welling.

"Sorry, Mitch, but I'm just pissed and pissed off. How did I get here? This has been the worst week of my life, and Felix . . ."

"The boyfriend?"

"The bastard — he hasn't even tried to get in touch. Two years! Two years we were together and he can't

120

even phone me! And I'm only telling you this because after this month is over I'll never see you again. Hopefully," she added dolefully.

"Thanks," said Mitch, raising his glass to her.

She pushed him playfully. "You know what I mean. I am never, ever going to set foot in this hellhole again. It's nothing to do with you. I'm actually beginning to think that you're quite . . . nice."

"Nice?"

"Nice."

"Hold on, I just want to rustle up some witnesses so that they can remind you that you said that when you sober up."

"But other than you, nice man, my life couldn't get any worse."

Roxy felt a slight breeze behind her. It could have been her imagination but she was sure the temperature in the pub just dropped by a few degrees.

"So, still here then? I'd have thought you'd have moved on to your next lot of victims by now. Hi, Mitch, how're you doing, mate?"

"Grand, Darren, grand."

Roxy sighed. "Forget what I said about life not getting any worse. Mitch, can you see from there if I've left my darts on the bar? Why do I never have a lethal weapon when I need one?"

She briefly scanned Darren up and down. Brown boots. Khaki combat trousers. A white T-shirt. She wasn't sure if he was going to have a few drinks in a relaxed atmosphere or invade a small country.

"How's Ginny doing?" she asked sweetly. It was so far below the belt it was trailing on the fleur-de-lis carpet, but hell, he deserved it.

Darren shrugged his shoulders, doing his best to adopt an air of windswept nonchalance.

"I've no idea. I thought that when it came to my fiancée you had all the answers."

Ouch. His tone couldn't have been deadlier if it came with a side order of anthrax.

He turned to face Mitch, blanking Roxy out completely.

"See you later, mate. Good luck with Cruella."

His firmly toned thighs retreated into the blur of villagers and desiccated hydrangeas.

"A fan, obviously," Mitch laughed.

"One of many," replied Roxy. A pain had started to work its way from her temple to the crown of her head. She should go home, but she'd forgotten her house keys and her mother and Auntie Vi had said they wouldn't be back from their Art class at the local college until after eleven. And that was . . . She squinted at her watch but it was no use, the numbers swirled before her. Time for another Cosmo then.

She was scoping the bar to see how busy it was when she spotted two familiar faces in the corner just outside the ladies' loos. They looked around furtively, then ducked inside. No! What the hell were they doing here? It was ridiculous! It was outrageous! It was . . . too good an opportunity to miss!

"S'cuse me a sec." She pushed herself up and followed the retreating forms into the ladies' loos. They were so busted! They wouldn't know what had hit them! Oh, the cheek . . .

By the time she got into the toilets, they'd already locked themselves in the loo together and were giggling merrily. Did they have no shame?

She battered on the door. "Open up right now." Silence.

She kicked the door loudly enough to show she meant business.

"Open up. I saw you come in, I know it's you and I'm not bloody leaving until you open this door," she repeated, this time with an extra pinch of menace.

Silence.

Eventually the door catch clicked and it slowly opened, exposing two nervous, shamed faces.

Roxy folded her arms and put on her very best stern face — the one she usually reserved for traffic wardens and sales assistants who tried to refuse her a refund.

"I don't believe you two! Did you honestly think you wouldn't get caught? Urgh, I'm disgusted!"

She slapped her hands onto her hips and her eyebrows jumped half an inch to a position of "Don't even think about arguing with me."

"Right, here's the deal. I can go and shop you to the guy who owns this place and you can persuade him not to phone the police . . ."

They stared at her with barely disguised contempt.

"Or you can hand over that stuff and I'll say no more about it."

Romeo and Juliet from the fifth-year study group stared at their shoes for a few seconds then surrendered. They knew when they were beaten.

And that's how, three minutes later, Roxy Galloway, aged twenty-seven, came to be hanging out of a pub window, in the village she'd grown up in, inhaling some of Morocco's finest. She made a mental note to make a new carving under the library desk first thing Monday morning. "Roxy loves under-age drinkers with weed."

Ten minutes later, a very relaxed Roxy slid back into her chair. Mitch pointed to the two fresh drinks on the table.

"I got you another."

Roxy picked it up and downed it in one go.

"Are you okay? You look, erm, weird."

Roxy very fastidiously put her empty glass back down on the table.

"You know, your chat-up lines really need work. I'm fine. I'm absolutely fine. I'm . . ."

Thump. Crash.

The noise was so loud that the domino team even took their eyes from the game.

One of the ladies' darts team, in mid-throw, missed the board and speared a poster advertising the forthcoming karaoke night.

And two pissed-off teenagers took advantage of the diversion to steal ten pounds from a kitty in the middle of a table near the door.

And Mitch . . . Mitch wondered just how he was going to get an unconscious woman home to bed.

Client Record — Classification Code 1

Stephen Knight
Credit card: 2045 4512 2367 0134
Contact No: 06767 667434
Client Since: June 2006

History: Most Recent Visits (21+ archived).		
25.06.07	Camilla	Pref. Explicit language, sex toys
01.07.07	Antoinette	Domination, explicit language
04.07.07	Mimi, Georgina	Viewing only — no participation
14.07.07	Coco	Film-set fantasy — business suit/clipboard
23.07.07	Natalya	Film-set fantasy — business suit/clipboard
02.08.07	Mimi, Coco	Viewing and participation, edible enhancement
12.08.07	Destiny, Mimi, Coco	Batman fantasy/Catgirl suit (Destiny)
15.08.07	Destiny	Batman fantasy/Catgirl suit
16.08.07	Deedee	Submission, restraints
23.08.07	Mimi, Georgina, Megan	Full participation, edible enhancement
01.09.07	Deedee	Submission, restraints

08.09.07	Angelina	Role play — George Clooney
10.09.07	Destiny	Batman fantasy/Catgirl suit
12.09.07	Mimi, Deedee, Ceecee, Coco, Destiny, Camilla	Master/harem
19.09.07	Destiny	No sex — client meltdown — age crisis
24.09.07	Mimi, Camilla	Kidnap fantasy — Charlie's Angels
08.10.07	Camilla	Role play — Brad Pitt, submission

Props/Costumes:

Business Suit/clipboard	Restraints/handcuffs
Catgirl suit	Leather whip (no visible marks)
Porn (preference for girl/girl)	

Refreshments:
Jack Daniels, Champagne (Bollinger)
Edible enhancements: cream, honey, grapes, peanut butter

Preparations:
Edible enhancements available, superhero costumes on standby.

Additional Info:
Birthday: 12 September
Make no references to age, ageing process, success of other A-list stars (esp: Christian Bale, George Clooney, Brad Pitt, Orlando Bloom) and reassure regularly that he does not need hair transplant.
Own transport provided.
If credit card rejected, call management immediately for reimbursement.

CHAPTER
EIGHT

These Boots are Made for Walking

Ginny. Day 6, Friday, 9p.m.

"Careful that tassel doesn't end up in your soup." Ginny casually gestured to the collection of six-inch-long silver and gold threads — one end attached to a perfectly formed rosebud nipple, the other end dangling precariously over the edge of a bowl of Heinz minestrone.

"Thanks, hon. I'd take them off but they're a bugger to get back on again and my next client is due in ten minutes."

Destiny stood up, picked up her bowl and teetered over to the sink. Ginny marvelled at how she could walk in shoes so high: two-inch platforms rising to six-inch heels of translucent silver Perspex, with an inch-wide strip of clear plastic holding the shoe onto the foot.

Plastic and rubber products, Ginny had discovered, were big in Hookersville. There were the PVC outfits, the plastic shoes, the masks, the vibrators, the dildos, the whips, the clamps and the condoms. Oh, and the plastic sheeting that was used when the "golden shower" clients were in attendance, but Ginny

128

preferred to push that whole scenario to the furthest recesses of her mind.

And then there was the plastic surgery.

Charlotte, Deedee, Camilla, Antoinette, Mimi and Georgina: breasts.

Camilla, Antoinette, Angelina, Megan and Coco: lips. And hopefully the swelling from Coco's latest treatment would go down soon because at the moment she looked like she could plunge sinks.

Camilla, Ceecee and Natalya: nose jobs.

Camilla: vaginal rejuvenation. Her favourite, most regular client was a very famous, innovative cosmetic surgeon so she'd had no hesitation in putting her crotch in his dexterous hands. Made a change from the other way around. Apparently her lady-garden now had a grip like a vice and could shoot ping-pong balls for fifty feet.

Destiny, however, was purely as the gods of Physical Perfection had intended. Her naked body looked like it had been intricately carved from the smoothest marble. Or at least it would do if it wasn't currently adorned with a sparkly thong, two swinging tassels and a pair of bright yellow fur-topped marigolds. Five feet, eight inches tall, Halle Berry elfin-cut hair, and caramel skin that was a genetic gift from a white mother and a Jamaican father. She was truly, truly beautiful. And naked.

Destiny had pretty much taken Ginny under her wing from the minute they met (Ginny: black Armani shift dress. Destiny: black rubber catsuit, three-foot tail and holes cut for protruding breasts) and they'd become, well, friends. In fact, with the exception of

Charlotte, who hadn't cast more than an irritated glance in her direction since their tense encounter on Ginny's first afternoon, all of the girls had been very open and sweet. And, of course, naked. She had never seen so many nude body parts in her life. The staffroom was female-only, so nobody gave a second thought to modesty or inhibitions.

Ginny took a bite of her tuna mayonnaise sandwich and marvelled at how quickly she'd become attuned to her new environment. She realised that in a strange way her baptism of fire had been the best thing that could possibly have happened. Or rather, her baptism by two fake medics, forty feet of white crepe bandages and a ten-inch appendage that was pointing at the chandelier. It seemed to have got the shock out of her system, and after that, well . . . it was kind of like chickenpox — once you've dealt with it once, you build up an immunity.

Since then, the challenges and surprises she'd faced were easier to deal with, although for the first couple of days everyone did think she had a skin complaint because her face permanently beamed red with embarrassment . . .

Embarrassment that she didn't know what she was doing.

Embarrassment that she was dealing with men who, five minutes later, would be wearing short trousers and begging to be spanked.

Embarrassment that she spent all her breaktime staring at the floor because every other line of sight included naked anatomy.

Meeting most of the staff for the first time hadn't quite matched that first encounter on the Richter scale, but could definitely be classed as a significant aftershock. She'd been sitting at the desk for a couple of hours on, thankfully, that relatively slow Monday afternoon, when Sam had come out and announced she could take a break.

She'd shaken her head nervously. "That's okay, I'm fine here, really I am," she'd replied nervously.

Sam hadn't budged.

"Ginny, you have to take a break — I don't want a reputation as an employer of slave labour."

She'd searched his features to see if he was joking. Hard to tell. Words implied jolly camaraderie, but tone and mask-like facial expression implied matter-of-fact moodiness. Strange, because she definitely remembered him being on the sunny side of brooding hunk when she'd met him at Roxy's party. Now he was emanating that whole Bruce Willis/José Mourinho broodiness that some females found irresistible. Ginny just found it deeply unsettling and more than a little scary.

"Ginny . . .?"

Shit, he was still standing there, anticipation obvious.

She'd jumped up and nervously looked around her. "Sorry, can't remember which way the staffroom is."

His face had softened a little, either in sympathy or pity, as he'd gestured towards the door into the back corridor. "Through there, turn left, first door on the right."

She'd tentatively smiled as she'd stood up, then tripped over the leg of her chair and was only saved from possible fracture and definite indignity by Sam's lightning reflexes as he grabbed her flailing hand and pulled her back up onto her feet. Her face could have doubled as an incendiary device.

"Sorry," she'd blustered, gesturing to her feet. "New shoes, bit of a learning curve."

There'd definitely been a hint of a smile on his face as he'd spoken this time. "Just try not to kill yourself between here and the staffroom — this is already Health and Safety's favourite place to inspect."

She'd followed his directions and breathed a sigh of relief when she reached the staffroom door. Ten minutes. Rest and relaxation. And hopefully a stash of Paracetamol for her headache.

She'd swung open the door and been greeted by new sight number two of the day — a completely naked female, her short, bobbed black hair tucked behind her ears, her white make-up and dramatically lined black eyes reminiscent of ancient Egypt. She had been balancing on one leg, while spreading what looked like chocolate sauce on her other leg, which was in a perpendicular position with her foot halfway up a wall.

"Just in time!" the strange but very flexible woman had announced in a mildly irritated tone. "Can you do my back and my bottom — I'm going to pull something if I try to do it myself."

Ginny had racked her brain for the appropriate response. Was it:

a) Of course, no problem, please bend over.

b) Sorry, but it'll put me right off my afternoon snack and I hate to miss my Jaffa Cakes.

c) Ermwellpffftermcanermermsure.

Naturally, Ginny had gone for the obvious choice of c). She'd picked up the tube of thick gunge, squeezed a large dollop onto her hands and proceeded to rub it tentatively across the female's back.

"I'm, erm, Ginny, by the way," she'd stuttered, anxious to detract in some way from the most excruciating thing that had happened in her life since, well, two and a half hours before.

"Charlotte," had come the brusque reply. "And can you make sure you get right in under the butt cheeks because I don't want lines."

Ginny had raised her eyes heavenwards, offering up a silent, "God, you have got to be kidding me!"

Apparently not.

There had been no bolt of lightning. No sudden intervention by a crowd of jolly japers jumping out of a cupboard shouting, "Gotcha!" No sniggering camera crew behind a plant pot.

Just a naturally grumpy, rude woman demanding that a virtual stranger apply fake tan to her buttocks.

Baptism of fire number two. And this one had left its mark. Tanning session over, Charlotte had impatiently snatched back the fake-tan tube and with a barely audible "Thanks" stomped out of the room, leaving Ginny red-faced, sweating, with hands the colour of Tango, having received a fast-track lesson in "Modesty is a wasted virtue: discuss".

It had taken a couple more days of extreme exposure for her "embarrassment in the face of nudity" gene to fully desensitise, but now?

"Nice thong," Ginny commented nonchalantly as Destiny washed up her dishes. "Don't the sequins come off in the machine though?"

"Handwash only. Want me to get one for you? I'm shopping tomorrow, I could pick one up."

Ginny laughed as loudly as the mouthful of tuna mayonnaise would allow.

"Thanks, D, but I'll pass. Don't think I'd ever have the opportunity to wear it."

"What? Not even for that boyfriend you're always talking about?"

The tuna caught a giggle on the way up from her throat. "Definitely not for that man I'm always talking about — the shock would probably kill him."

"Then, honey, you need to find yourself a *new* man."

Destiny pulled off her marigolds and checked her watch. "Better go. The next one likes to be locked in the cupboard and I haven't cleared it out yet. Are you coming out with us tonight?"

Ginny shook her head.

"No, think I'll pass. I'm on again at ten tomorrow morning and I didn't bring a change of clothes with me."

"Aw, come on. You look great," Destiny cajoled her.

And that, Ginny accepted with only a mild flush of the cheeks, was the truth.

She'd lost a couple of pounds — no doubt due to chronic tea and HobNob deprivation. Then, a couple of days before, Destiny had taken her to an über-trendy hairdressing salon in Knightsbridge for a sharp new hairstyle. It had been like saying a traumatic goodbye to

134

an old friend — albeit one with split ends, a tendency to frizz and more than a few premature signs of greyness.

Actually, just walking into the salon had been terrifying. It was a veritable explosion of chrome, glass and crystal, with chic, black-clad stylists at every chair, cutting and drying the crowning glories of champagne-sipping, impeccably groomed clients. Her normal hairdressing experience was absolutely nothing like this — but then, having a cup of tea while her mother gave her a quick trim with the pruning shears in the kitchen was never going to be in the same league as the ultimate in cutting-edge coiffures.

Andre, her personal consultant, had managed to hide his horror well as he attempted to run his fingers through her mane.

"And vot product do you normally use, my dahling?" he'd asked with more than an undertone of astonished dubiety.

"Product?"

Destiny to the rescue.

"Shampoo, conditioner, gel, mousse, that kind of thing," she'd prompted encouragingly.

"Oh . . . er, none of those. I just use some of that all-in-one-shampoo-and-conditioner stuff."

Andre's eyes had widened and he'd gasped so dramatically that for a few horrifying moments Ginny wondered if he'd swallowed his tongue and would require the administration of the Heimlich manoeuvre.

"Just do your stuff, Andre," Destiny had cajoled him. "Make her fabulous."

135

And fabulous she now was.

He'd started by doing some kind of reverse perm thing that had beaten her mane of frizz into submission and rendered it straight and pliable. Then he'd highlighted the area around her face with a soft blonde that made her green eyes pop out and her skin glow. And finally, he'd put her hair into a middle parting and cut in some long chunky layers to add beautiful movement and texture (his effusive words, not hers). Afterwards, on Destiny's instructions, a beautician had shaped her eyebrows (borderline sadism), applied eyelash extensions (two caterpillars on her eyelids), sprayed her with an all-over fake tan and given her a French manicure so gorgeous she'd been overcome with the urge to wave to passing strangers. In the space of four hours she'd been transformed from an unremarkable-looking woman with hair that closely resembled a welcome mat to Reese Witherspoon's cute sister.

Cognisant of the fact that she'd have to replicate the new hairstyle on a daily basis, she'd spent hours practising styling her new locks with those GHB things.

She was definitely getting the hang of them — by this morning she'd managed to get it down to forty minutes and only three burns requiring treatment with antiseptic cream.

As for the face, Goldie Gilmartin, national treasure, had shown her how to take five minutes to apply make-up that made her look like she'd spent an hour being beautified by Elizabeth Arden.

But of course, it was Roxy's clothes that should take a large chunk of the credit for the transformation. Today she was in a slate-grey Roland Mouret Galaxy dress — not this season, but who cared when it made her look like Jessica Rabbit from the neck down — and Christian Louboutin black patent leather platforms with peep-toes and fishnet tights. Her feet were going to resemble a string vest when she took them off, but it was worth it.

Even Sam had complimented her that morning. He'd nodded as he passed her, broken into a barely discernible smile, and said, "You look good today," in a quiet, understated tone.

Okay, so it wasn't exactly gushing praise, but she'd come to realise that for Sam that was damn well close to a drum roll and trumpets. He was always very sweet, very polite, very civil. He always seemed patient when he was training her on something new. He regularly asked how Roxy was getting on. He was never irritable, or angry, or moody — yet she had a real feeling that he was definitely on the Prozac side of the happy scale.

Her phone started to vibrate and she checked the screen, expecting another hysterical text from Roxy. She'd already decided to ignore it. Cruel — but this whole thing had come about because Roxy was being her usual impetuous, petulant self and Ginny had decided that a wee taste of normality and account-ability would be character-building. Okay, so she was making that up. The truth was that she was having a blast and she'd be buggered if Roxy's perpetual fits of dramatic, self-indulgent pique were going to cut it short. For once in their lives, Ginny was calling the shots. She was in charge, feeling fearless, and could handle anything life threw at her. Except . . . DARREN.

One word written along a mobile-phone screen; one stomach doing a flip, and two hands starting to tremble.

Crap.

She contemplated letting it go to voicemail but she knew he'd just keep calling back until she answered. He was persistent that way. Some might say "stubborn," but she preferred "tenacious." Now that he'd finally, *finally*, deemed to call her, she knew she had to speak to him. Just as soon as she managed to shift from "speechless apprehension" to "capable of conversation."

As the days had gone on, Ginny had realised Roxy had been lying when she had initially claimed that Darren had taken the news of her Houdini act well — a hunch backed up by the absence of any contact for the rest of the week. She'd texted him — no reply. She'd called his mobile phone — no answer. She'd called his home — his mother said he was out.

She was definitely in the relationship equivalent of Siberia and he was obviously intent on a prolonged stew while contemplating how he should react to her crime of grievous bodily spontaneity.

This was classic Darren. Throughout their whole relationship they'd had very few falling outs, but when they did it was always Ginny who had to make the first move to reconciliation. The longest she'd ever lasted was thirty-six hours after she found condoms in his sports holdall. Not a crime in itself, but taken in conjunction with her monthly prescription for contraceptive pills, it did look a bit suspicious. In the end, though, her gut told her he was telling the truth when he said they'd been part of a goodie bag given to everyone who attended a health and fitness exhibition.

So she'd called him and apologised, and he'd loved her enough to put it behind them. She could trust Darren, she knew that. After twelve years together you just knew a person. And that's why, as she pressed the green button on her phone, she knew he was going to be a little on the irritated side.

"Hi."

"Have you lost your mind? What the hell are you doing?"

Make that incandescent.

"Babe, I'm sorry, but . . ."

"Sorry! Ginny, you upped sticks and left without even telling me! How could you do that?"

"I'm sorry, but . . ."

"I mean, how would you feel if I did that to you?"

"You're right, Darren, I'm sorry, but . . ."

"And it's even worse that I have to look at the smug fucking face of that smug fucking pal of yours . . ."

Oh, this was bad. Twelve years and she could count on the fingers of one trembling hand how many times he'd sworn at her.

"Darren, I'm sorry, but . . ."

"So come home and stop being so bloody ridiculous. I'm booked solid all day tomorrow so just get a taxi from the station."

"No."

It took her a few moments to realise that the word had actually come from her mouth — she'd been on such a good roll with the "sorry"s.

"What?"

"I'm sorry, but . . . no."

Her heart knew that it was time for the truth — time to own up, be honest and admit to him what was really going on. However, her mouth went for subterfuge and duplicity.

"Darren, I can't. Roxy would be in so much trouble if I left. I've promised that I'll stay here for the rest of the month, and even though I'm hating every minute of it I have to stay. I promised."

"You promised lots of things to me too, but that doesn't seem to count."

"Oh, for God's sake, Darren, it's only for three more weeks. Stop being so dramatic — you're starting to sound like Roxy."

Light. Blue. Touch. Paper.

"What? How can you compare me to that self-centred, spoiled brat?"

And that's when it hit her. Darren and Roxy were so similar they could have shared a womb. Both Alpha personalities. Both self-centred. Both expected everyone else to fit into their world. And because Ginny was by nature such a laid-back, acquiescent person, it had always just seemed like the easiest option to go along with them.

The eternal engagement, the excruciatingly uneventful relationship, the blind acceptance of everything he said — she'd been dancing to Darren's tune for years.

When it came to both Roxy and Darren, she honestly couldn't remember ever having refused them anything.

And even her mother . . . She'd never left the library because the truth was that her mother liked having her there and she didn't want to upset her by leaving. She was planning a huge wedding because her mother wanted one. And she'd never left home because her mother didn't see the point. And, frankly, Ginny didn't feel strongly enough about anything to fight her own corner — as long as everyone else was happy she was content to be the poster girl for non-confrontation.

She was, she realised, a doormat. A spineless doormat.

Well, no more. This was the first time she'd ever done anything for herself and she'd be damned if she was cutting it short to please Darren. Didn't she have the rest of her life to spend with him?

"Ginny, if you don't come home you can forget it. Forget the engagement, forget the wedding, forget everything."

"*What*? You can't be serious," she replied with a nervous laugh.

His voice dropped a few notches, from blind fury to tired and irritated.

"I am, Gin. I'm serious."

Strangely, and for the first time ever, Ginny was heading in the other direction on the pissed-off-o-meter.

"Wait a minute — so you can go to week-long sports camps, you can go for golfing weekends with your buddies, you can cycle across Uzbeki-bloody-stan just because you feel like it, you can nip over to La Manga with clients, you can go anywhere and do anything you bloody well like, and I never complain, but the first time I do anything, ANYTHING, by myself you practically call out the National bloody Guard to drag me back! You're right, Darren, you're absolutely right — let's forget it!"

Ginny disconnected the call and slammed the phone down on the table, causing the battery cover to fly off, ricochet off the sex-aids cupboard, shatter and crumble over the top of one of the costume boxes. Shit, it'd take her ages to fish all the bits out of the feather boas.

Argh! She could feel her heart pumping sheer bloody fury around her veins and the hairs on her arms were standing on end in protest. Her first instinct was to call Roxy. She had to talk to her. Roxy would know what to do — although given that this situation involved Darren, chances were Roxy's solution would include suggestions involving male genitalia and electric currents.

Perhaps it was just as well the phone was trashed — wasn't it time for her to stand on her own two feet? Even if they were encased in her best friend's shoes.

And anyway, Ginny realised that if she called Roxy it might just give her an excuse to charge to the rescue, reclaiming her flat, her job and her life in the process. And even in her emotional turmoil, Ginny wasn't sure that she was ready for that.

No, she had to face this, embrace her feelings and deal with it — and right now she was dealing with a feeling of utter fury.

And, weirdly, it felt great.

"Are you okay? Sorry, couldn't help overhearing." Sam's shoulders filled the open doorway.

She leapt to her feet.

"I'm sorry, Sam, I'm just coming back to the desk now, I'm really sorry, I'm just, I mean, coming, I'll just, the desk, shit, no one's at the desk . . ."

"Do you ever breathe? In. Out. Come on, do it with me. Government employment regulations state that breathing in the workplace is mandatory."

Ginny attempted a smile, terrified that Sam's sympathetic face would give her that last little push from "barely holding it together" to "crumble". She couldn't cry in front of her boss. Not even her only-for-another-three-weeks-temporary-boss. He'd have her out of the door before she got halfway down the Kleenex box.

She sniffed her first sniff as a single woman in twelve years.

"Sorry, Sam, it's just . . ."

"Boyfriend stuff?"

"Apparently that's ex. Ex-boyfriend stuff."

Oh. My. God. Darren was her ex. Another first — she'd never had an ex before. But then, she'd never had chickenpox, tripe or a sexually transmitted disease before, and she wasn't keen on embracing any of those either.

Okay, two choices — go and jump on the first train home or stay here and finish out the month.

"Do you need to go home? The *News of the World* has cancelled Tilly's story — the MP she was shagging

143

pulled some strings — so I could call her in to cover. Or maybe even Roxy . . ."

"No, no, it's fine. I'm absolutely fine."

"You're sure?"

"Positive. I'll just, er . . ."

A familiar bleep sound emitted from the intercom on the desk.

". . . go and answer that phone."

To hell with tears, to hell with Darren, to hell with pleasing everyone else — she was a confident, together woman with a six-foot-tall government minister who liked to wear nappies at the door. Ginny Wallis had a job to do.

"One. Two. Three. Shoot."

The girls licked the salt off their hands, knocked back the tequila and slammed the empty shot glasses on the bar. At least that was the plan. Since Ginny had raised her normal evening alcohol consumption from two white-wine spritzers to three glasses of Bollinger and six tequila shots, she licked her glass, missed her mouth and tipped the alcohol over the bar, from where it promptly ran into the lap of her Roland Mouret. She now looked like she had really good fashion sense and a really bad incontinence problem.

After Darren's Oscar-winning performance in the category of "Severely Pissed Off Fiancé", it hadn't taken much persuasion for her to join the others for that night on the town. And apart from the tequila incontinence she was having a great time.

144

She had to admit there was a thrill about it. They'd headed for their regular haunt in Soho, a fabulously trendy club called Nude. The whole "naked" thing had definitely become a theme in her life lately.

There were twelve of them — all girls, all gorgeous, all dressed to kill. Imagine the Pussycat Dolls, without the vocal talent, then multiply it by two. As they bypassed the queuing masses and headed straight to the front door, Ginny couldn't help but notice thirty metres of "irritated but curious" craning their necks to see who they were. Somehow she thought they'd be a bit disappointed if they realised they were being usurped by the librarian from the Farnham Hills Community Centre.

As the bouncers on the door offered familiar smiles, greetings, then swiftly parted to let them through, she felt a little surge of adrenaline. Tonight she was one of the in-crowd and it felt great.

Inside, they made their way straight to the far side of the futuristic steel and glass bar, where a thick red velvet rope drew a line between the anonymous clubbers and the VIP section. On the left-hand side of the barrier was the equivalent of airline economy class — everyone packed in, slightly sweaty and pretending they didn't mind that they hadn't managed to blag an upgrade. On the right-hand side of the barrier, first class: space, great service, and huge comfy seats. Ginny and her tequila partners had their finely toned posteriors on the firm upholstery of half a dozen cowhide barstools, while the rest of the group mingled around them.

Ginny did a spin on her stool just to check out the rest of the room. Weird. When they'd first come in she hadn't noticed anyone that particularly floated her boat, but strangely, as the night went on, several of the guys nearby were starting to look fairly attractive. Another few tequila shots and there was every chance that she'd be surrounded by fine specimens of manhood.

Not that she'd be interested, of course — but that didn't mean she was immune to the thrill of being "in demand". She'd lost count of the number of bottles of champagne that had been sent over. And she'd already been chatted up twice, air-kissed by a fit hunk from a jeans commercial and asked if she wanted to go for a spin in some bloke's Ferrari.

It seemed the Seismic girls were top of every horny, red-blooded male's "Want List", courtesy of the fact that they were smart, stunning, and spent eight hours a day perfecting their sex techniques.

The whole scene was shallower than her shot glass. The old Ginny — engaged, grounded, disciplined Ginny — would have been uncomfortable, intimidated and disdainful about the utter superficiality of it all. That, of course, was presuming she somehow managed to persuade the bouncers that tracksuit bottoms and a bobbled hoodie was the kind of dress code that every trendy club wanted to encourage. The new, single, impulsive, swanky-hair-do Ginny was bravely putting her heartache aside (what was her ex-fiancé's name again?) and relishing every fabulous, hedonistic, decadent, tequila-soaked moment of it.

146

"I'm glad you came with us," Destiny grinned.

"Me too!" Actually, that's what Ginny meant to say — what came out was "Meeeeshooo."

Destiny threw her head back and laughed, then hopped off her stool.

"Come on, let's dance."

Ginny looked around her — the place was mobbed. Or was that just the very confusing positioning of mirrors on every wall? Nope, it was definitely chock-a-block and she couldn't see the dance floor so it must be over the other side of the club. She wasn't sure that she wanted to move — getting off the stool would be tricky, navigating the throng of clubbers would be a nightmare, and then shuffling on the spot on a crowded dance floor was a one-way ticket to bruised ribs and crushed toes.

"I think I'll just sit it out," she yelled back.

Destiny smiled as she shrugged and repeated the suggestion to Ceecee, a breathtaking, tall Arctic blonde who spoke five languages, carried herself like royalty, and liked to whip her customers until they needed TCP and a cold compress to numb the pain.

Ginny watched, expecting them to slip off their stools and disappear into the sea of faces. Suddenly, there was a movement, everything went dark, and then there was the extreme discomfort of a heavy pressure on the top of her head.

Shit, she was having a blackout. Too much alcohol? Salt overload? Or maybe her drink had been spiked. Her stomach churned — hadn't her mother warned her about this? She'd be sold for fifty quid and locked in

147

the basement of a psychotic Eastern European madman by the end of the week.

"Sorry, hon, just be a minute."

Suddenly the darkness cleared and Ginny realised that she'd just been used as a prop so that Destiny and Ceecee could lever themselves up onto the bar.

There was a deafening roar from the crowd as the girls strutted to either end of the steel surface, each stopping at a silver pole on opposite corners of the bar top.

Ginny groaned. Crap — they were going to get thrown out. The last time anyone climbed on the bar in her local (actually it was the *only* time anyone had ever climbed on the bar in her local) it had ended with thirty-six smashed glasses, a broken ankle and a caution for breach of the peace.

Ginny waited for the bouncers to descend. So much for her glamorous night out — not only had she been dumped by the love of her life, but now her arse was about to hit the pavement. If her Mouret dress got damaged there'd be hell to pay.

So it was a bit of a surprise that the DJ suddenly turned the spotlights towards the bar and demanded that everyone give him a "Hell yeah!"

"Hell yeah!" yelled the crowd, drowning out Ginny's "What the hell . . .?"

And as the throbbing beat of Justin Timberlake's "SexyBack" filled the room, the girls made eye contact, winked at each other, then slowly, seductively, peeled off their dresses in time to the beat, revealing nothing but sheer, sexy, elaborate shiny underwear. And for the rest of her life, Ginny would always remember that her first thought wasn't horror shock, or embarrassment — it was "wow, the sparkly thong has a bra to match".

As Destiny grabbed onto the pole with both hands and used every single perfectly formed muscle to shimmy up to the top of it, it was obvious that many in the room felt two other things rising. One was their temperature . . .

Now Destiny was clutching the pole between her thighs, while arching her back so far that her head almost touched her feet.

Over on the other pole, Ceecee was performing exactly the same movement in perfect synchronisation. They curled their heads back up, and then used their arms for support and leverage as they stretched their legs out so that their bodies were almost at ninety degrees to the pole.

Ginny was entranced, and thankfully the shock had cleared her vision so she was no longer seeing everything in duplicate. This was the strangest day of her life. How had she managed to go to work this morning, get chucked, get drunk, and now transport herself to the set of *Coyote Ugly*?

As she slowly moved to the throb of the music, she was, however, experiencing some new sensations of an entirely different kind. Something felt . . . well, *weird*. Strange. Unusual.

The girls had dismounted and were now strutting boldly towards each other, every movement oozing pure sex and lust.

Ginny adjusted her posture. Mmm, definitely a strange kind of sensation going on.

As the girls met in the middle, they slowly, provocatively, removed their bra tops. The place erupted as the crowd split into four camps: straight guys cheering with excitement at the sheer sexiness of it; gays guys cheering with excitement at the sheer theatre of it; some women loving the sheer celebration of female sexuality; and the feminists searching for a lighter to burn their bras then torch the poles in sheer disgust.

And Ginny? Sheer . . . *surprise*. Surprise that another new sensation had suddenly come to the party. And what a party. It took her tequila-soaked brain a little while to catch up with the rest of her anatomy, but finally Ginny realised that she was experiencing the same feeling she used to get for a couple of minutes roughly four times a week, and only then if she really concentrated. She was . . . horny!

Yep, her drink had definitely been spiked. She was Ginny Wallis — she didn't do lust, desire and uncontrollable urges. She did conservative, sensible and control-top tights.

She slid off the bar stool and made her way to the door. Fresh air. She needed some cool fresh air to clear her head and give her nipples a physical reason to be standing out like her mother's bunions.

Just as she stepped outside the door into a chaotic throng of Friday-night revellers, a black cab pulled up and three merry Scotsmen, all kilts and hairy legs, poured out of it. They had about as much chance of getting into the über-chic club as she had of waking up tomorrow morning and discovering that she could speak five languages and whip posh blokes into sumission, but she decided not to rain on their tartan parade.

"You need a taxi, love?"

The taxi driver hung out of his window, eyeing her expectantly. She must look like she'd had enough for one night. And even in her befuddled state, she recognised that she probably had. She clambered in and gave him Roxy's address. Fifteen slightly sobering minutes later, as they pulled up outside the door, she did a mental inventory:

Bag? Check.

Two shoes? Check.

Tequila-stained dress? Check.

Nipples like fighter-pilot's thumbs? Check.

Lord, what was going on with her? She fumbled in her purse for some money, ended up grabbing two twenties, and thrust them in the general direction of the driver, before making it to the door with only a slight stagger.

Key in lock. Key in lock. Drunk. Horny. Key in . . . Why the hell wouldn't the key go in the lock?

She was just about to commit her first forced entry by Louboutin platforms when the door swung open and there he was . . .

Yep, for a moment she thought it was Darren too. Then she realised that he was built like an Adonis, smiling, and wearing his normal "at home" attire.

Jude. Gorgeous, sexy, half-naked Jude. This time his battered, fraying Levis were so tight she feared for his testicular health.

"Oh, great, I have a topless butler," she grinned. Smooth. Clever. And it might have been impressive if she hadn't chosen that moment to step forward, catch her heel on the thin strip of wood that ran along the floor under the door, and enter the hallway in the manner of a scud missile.

Jude lurched down and grabbed her in the manner of Superman rescuing Lois Lane. Without the pants over the trousers, obviously.

"You're making a habit of falling at my feet. Good night?"

"Great night." And, she realised, it had been. Drinks, laughs, fun, sexy stuff, and now the best-looking man she'd ever seen in her life was carrying her into her bedroom.

"Where are the girlfriends tonight then, stud man?" she teased.

"Night off. Goldie's in Spain presenting a house to a couple who won it in a phone-in and Cheska's working all weekend because she's summing-up on Monday."

He plonked her down on the raw-silk duvet cover.

"Can I ask you something?"

He winced as he rubbed one molehill-shaped bicep, then sat down next to her.

"As long as it doesn't involve carrying you anywhere else. I must be out of practice."

"Do they know about each other? Goldie and Cheska?"

He shrugged his shoulders, his expression suddenly bashful, embarrassed. "They don't ask. It's just the way it is with us. We're exclusively non-exclusive. I know Goldie sees another guy, a cameraman on the show, and Cheska — not sure. She was having a thing with the head of her chambers when we met, but I don't know if that's still on."

Ginny's face was pure puzzlement.

"It's what works for us — no expectations, no promises. And let's face it — with my job I couldn't exactly be with someone in possession of a jealousy gene, could I?"

"So you could —" Shit, her mouth was still talking. Why? The rest of her was on normal time, but her gob was on tequila time.

"— sleep with anyone at all and they wouldn't mind?"

What? Where did that come from?

Her nerves would have been stretched to pinging point if it wasn't for the fact that she picked that very moment to kick off a shoe and then watched with horror as it flew across the room and knocked Roxy's DVD player off its shelf and onto the shagpile carpet.

Jude didn't notice. He shrugged those intricately carved deltoids.

"They wouldn't know. Or care to know. It's just . . . aaaaw!"

Ginny gasped. How the hell had she managed that? She'd flicked off the other shoe and it had somehow managed to fire straight up in the air, then come down and hit Jude on the back of his beautifully conditioned, glossy head.

153

His laughter was contagious. "You are dangerous to know, Ginny. And I always thought you were the innocent, harmless type."

Argh, his eyes were doing that crinkling-up, twinkly thing that she thought was irresistible. And so, it seemed, did her fighter-pilot nipples, which had reappeared in anticipation of a new mission.

A kamikaze one.

"You know what, Jude — I'm sick of being the innocent type. Look where it's got me so far: I've had to steal someone else's life just to get a bit of excitement and my boyfriend has just checked me!"

His eyes widened with surprise. "He chucked you? Ginny, I'm sorry." And, bless him, even though he probably couldn't care less, Ginny could swear that right in that moment he was looking at her with eyes that were full of concern.

She pushed herself up on one elbow and traced her finger down his cheek. She wasn't sure if his new expression was surprise, shock or horror, so she did the only intelligent, decent thing.

She shut her eyes, put her hand around the back of his neck and pulled him towards her. Her hormones had just taken her brain hostage and demanded a ransom of one nipple erection, one amazingly long, sensual snog, and one . . . holy crap, her hand was undoing the top button of his jeans.

He gently pushed her back down on the bed and pulled back from the kiss, his nose six inches from hers, their eyes locked, their breathing in perfect unison.

"We shouldn't do this," he whispered.

154

Ginny stayed mute. The tequila, however, was staging a full-scale protest.

"We should. We definitely should," it replied. Out loud.

He leaned down and kissed her again, the delicious smell of his body assaulting her senses. And just when she thought, no, *knew*, that she was going to rip a bloke's kegs off for the first time in her life, he pulled back again.

"Ginny, this is a really bad idea. You're hurt, you're drunk, and you're a friend."

"Jude . . ."

He stopped her by pressing his lips to hers again, this time not with passion, but with a slow, tender movement.

They stayed like that for what seemed like ages. Until her pulse slowed down from manic to just slightly rapid, until her brain absorbed what he was trying to tell her, and until tequila could be trusted not to interfere.

Eventually, he lifted his head, still staring into her eyes. He pushed back a strand of hair from her forehead and ran a finger along her brow.

"You are beautiful."

She snorted. Okay, not the sexiest thing she'd ever done, but it was a reflex action.

"You are," he insisted. "And you've no idea how much I want to take that dress off and make love to you."

He looked so sincere that she almost believed him. Until . . .

"But it would be such a bad idea. You're vulnerable, Ginny."

"I'm not vulnerable, I'm horny."

He smiled, and kissed her again. "And if you're still horny in the morning, then knock on my door. But not tonight . . . The last thing you need tonight is another complication."

He kissed her one more time . . . slowly . . . sensually . . . then pulled her close to him and held her tight.

He was right. As a rogue tear squeezed from the corner of her eye, she knew that he was right. She had only had sex with one man in her entire life, and if that man arrived at her door tomorrow morning, full of remorse and begging her to come back to him, how could she look him in the eye if she'd been unfaithful? Did she want Darren back? Was it really over? Did he mean what he'd said or was that just a furious outburst fuelled by ego and rejection?

There were too many questions. She'd loved no one but Darren — and until she understood where they were, she wasn't sure that she was ready to replace lifelong commitment with random lust.

Was she?

Jude was lying behind her now, spooning her, his breathing heavy on her neck. And her last solemn thought, before her eyes closed and she drifted off to sleep in the arms of an incredibly sweet, gentle, caring sex god was . . . that she must be fucking mad.

And that's why she smiled lazily when a hand gently cupped her breast, stirring her out of her slumbers. It could have been minutes later, or hours. The room was

156

in darkness so it was definitely still night-time. His finger was slowly, teasingly circling her nipple, his breath on the back of her neck as he playfully, sensually licked that soft spot at the top of her spine.

The hand was moving now, kneading the whole of her breast before creeping slowly, inch by erotically incredible inch, down over her ribcage, her stomach, her hip bones . . .

Oh, she wanted him. She wanted him so badly that nothing, nothing was going to stop her this time.

"Oh baby," he whispered.

The tingling feeling was radiating out from the very core of her, working its way through her body. This was truly sublime: every pore, every crevice wanted him. Wanted him to . . .

"Oh, Roxy, baby, you are so incredible."

The steel shutters of her libido came crashing down. *Roxy?* Roxy!? So that's why he hadn't wanted to make love to her — he was in love with Roxy. Fabulous, gorgeous, infinitely more phenomenal bloody Roxy. Argh, did her life never change?

She bolted upright. Oh, bad move, her stomach lurched as the tequila sloshed around inside it. She tried to breathe deeply to fight off the combination of a spinning head and nausea.

"Hey, what's wrong? For fuck's sake, Rox, you nearly took my teeth out there."

Hold on . . . Even through the haze of the woozy head and the outraged emotions, she realised that something wasn't right. It was the tone, it was just wrong, it was . . .

"Lights!!" she yelled, and the bedside lamp immediately kicked into action. Two sets of eyes squinted and as their vision cleared the screams were simultaneous.

"*GINNY!!!*" from the male.

"*FELIX!!!*" from the female.

And then there was darkness.

Farnham Hills Library — Customer Record Card

Name: *Reverend Stewart*
Address: *The Old Manse, FH*
Telephone: *895698*
Joined: *24 October 1972*

Currently on Loan:	Return Due:
The God Delusion by Richard Dawkins	20.10.07
Angels and Demons by Dan Brown	20.10.07
Online Dating for Dummies by Judith Silverstein and Michael Lasky	20.10.07
What is the Point of being a Christian? by Timothy Radcliffe	20.10.07
Misquoting Jesus: The Story Behind Who changed The Bible and Why by Bart D. Ehrman	20.10.07
Living the Celibate Life: A Search for Models and Ministry by A.W. Richard Sipe	20.10.07

Currently on Request:
Sex God: Exploring the Endless Connections Between Sexuality and Spirituality (Hardcover) — by Rob Bell
A History of God by Karen Armstrong
Common Worship: Services and Prayers for the Church of England: Times and Seasons (Common Worship)

The Art of Tantric sex (Paperback) by Nitya LaCroix and Mark Harwood

Areas of interest:

Religion

Psychology

Nature

Anatomy

Comments/misc:

DO NOT ALLOW USE OF COMPUTERS UNLESS SUPERVISED — ON THIRD WARNING FOR VIEWING OF INAPPROPRIATE MATERIAL

CHAPTER
NINE

Doctor Feelgood

Roxy. Day 7, Saturday morning, 11 a.m.

Dum-dum. Dum-dum. Dum-dum. Her heart was beating like an amp at a heavy-metal gig as the doctor stood over her. Actually, it wasn't just any doctor, it was that Luca bloke from *ER*. Dum-dum. Dum-dum. Oh, yes, he definitely warrants a little acceleration there. Dum-dum-dum-dum . . . "Nurse!" he yells. "She's crashing!"

"Noooooo," thinks the patient, "I'm a-lusting. Lusting. Go on, listen to my heart and you'll see I'm . . ."

Beeeeeeeeeeeeeeeeeeeeeeeeeeeepppppppppppppppppp.

"One, two, three, CLEAR!"

Beeeeeeeeeeeeeeeeeeeeeeeeeeeepppppppppppppppppp.

"Again — shock her again!"

"One, two, three, CLEAR!"

Beeeeeeeeeeeeeeeeeeeeeeeeeeeepppppppppppppppppp.

"It's no use, Doctor, she's gone. She's gone, I tell you! You have to let her go, Doctor. You did everything you could. Please, Doctor, let her go. Let her go . . ."

Beeeeeeeeeeeeeeeeeeeeeeeeeeeepppppppppppppppppp.

"Roxy. Roxy!"

The white sheet was over her head and she was fighting it. They had to see she wasn't dead, they had to! They had to! It was a mistake! She wasn't . . .

"Roxy!"

Suddenly the sheet was pulled back and there was light. Light and . . .

"Roxy!" Light and the voice of the bloke from the library — whom she could say with fair certainty had never had a starring role in *ER*.

"Roxy, your phone is beeping. Either answer it or batter it to death — just make it stop."

"Mmmmm. Sorry. I was dreaming. I didn't realise." She stuck her right hand out from under the duvet and felt around for the offending object and . . . nothing. That's when it struck her.

An icy chill swept like a tsunami from her toes up to her matted locks. Shit! Where was she?

She gently opened both eyes. Whoa, bad move. Perhaps start with one and work up to it. Straight above — ceiling: cream, swirly pattern. On top: sheets, white, blue stripes. In front: bookcases, a whole wall of them, crammed full to overflowing. The floor littered with so many books and papers that the nondescript brown cord carpet was barely visible. A chair, draped with clothes. Her clothes? Then . . . Dear. God. No. To the left: sleeping on the next pillow, the bloke from the library, who *definitely* wasn't in *ER*.

Dum-dum, dum-dum, dum-dum . . .

Slowly, tentatively, she lifted up the sheet, peeked underneath and, phew . . . Never in her life did she ever

162

think that she'd be grateful to see her toned, nubile body bedecked in a screaming-lilac velour tracksuit.

"I put pillows down the middle — just in case you woke up during the night and got a bit freaked out. I would have slept on the sofa but I didn't want the housekeeper to wonder why I was there. And then I tried to sleep on the floor but it was minus three degrees and I thought you might find it unpleasant to wake up next to a hypothermic corpse."

"Good point," Roxy whispered, almost managing a smile. Giddy relief. Mixed with a voracious thirst, a thumping head, and a rampant desire for anything containing Paracetamol.

"How did I get here?" she asked, turning to face him. But before he could answer there was the unmistakable thump of footsteps outside.

"Sssshhhh!" His eyes flared with panic as he clapped a hand over her mouth.

Wow — what was with the gagging action? Had she been kidnapped? Was Mitch one of those *CSI Las Vegas* psychos who kept body parts in his pickle jars? What if . . . what if the local police were already scouring the countryside for her body while her mother gave a tearful plea for her safe return on national telly?

"Mrs Donald is outside in the hallway. My uncle is away but if she finds you here we'll have the wrath of God, the most righteous woman on earth, and half the village to contend with."

As she eyed the general disarray around her, Roxy had a sudden moment of clarity, and with it came shock, surprise and one burgeoning question.

163

"You have a housekeeper, yet your room looks like this?"

The footsteps retreated until they were once again enveloped in total silence.

Roxy still couldn't take in the chaos of the room. How could people live like this? It was the kind of bedroom that belonged to students who were in the first throes of independence and cannabis discovery.

"I asked Mrs Donald not to clean in here. Felt a bit weird being picked up after by an elderly woman with a dodgy hip — especially when I'm perfectly capable of doing it myself." He glanced around the room, seeing it through Roxy's eyes, and added, "In theory."

"So let me get this straight — you refuse menial help? You are a very, very strange man. And I'm in bed with you. Whoo-fucking-hoo. Okay, while I'm at the lowest point in living memory . . . last night — give me the bullet points but don't miss out any vital revelations. And by the way, I don't suppose you've got anything liquid over your side — my mouth feels like a landfill site."

He reached down and produced a bottle of Lucozade, much to her amusement.

"Impressive. Okay, now I'd like a bacon roll, next week's lottery numbers and Matt Damon's phone number."

"So do you want the good news or the bad news?" he asked, ignoring her witterings.

There was more bad news? She was suffering from amnesia, lying in a bed, in a church house, in lilac velour, with a man she barely knew and under threat of a cataclysmic discovery by a woman with a dodgy hip. And there was more?

"You fainted at the pub, so I took you home, but there was no one there to let you in, so I snuck you in here and put you to bed."

She absorbed the facts — so far, so acceptable.

"Did we have sex?" she asked bluntly.

"No!" replied Mitch, his face contorted with horror as he pulled the sheet up a little tighter around his neck.

"Kiss?"

"No!"

"Fumble?"

"Absolutely not! What do you take me for? I brought you home, I put you to bed, I put pillows down the middle and you snored all night."

"So what's the bad news?"

"Mrs Donald doesn't finish until noon, so we have to stay in here for another hour before the coast is clear. Oh, and your phone has been beeping constantly — it's in your bag down by your side there. I think it's your mother trying to establish that you're not dead."

Trying to avoid the crushing pain of moving her head, she groped around, located the bag, retrieved the phone and fired off a quick message to her mother.

All ok, slept on friend's couch, b home soon.

As she snapped her phone closed, the battery gave one last indignant beep and then died. She must remember to pick up a new charger from somewhere.

Presuming that she ever managed to regain the powers of standing upright and clear thoughts. Her head hadn't hurt this badly since the time she drank too much Cristal and persuaded Peter Stringfellow to let her display her gymnastic skills by doing a somersault off the bar top in his club. She'd have landed perfectly if that rogue paparazzo hadn't picked that precise moment to pull out his hidden camera and start flashing pics of Robbie Williams with his face buried in some woman's cleavage.

Still, at least the x-ray had ruled out permanent damage to her skull.

"Thank you," she whispered.

"For what?"

"For taking care of me. That was . . . nice."

He gave her a languid, teasing grin.

"When your memory comes back I think you'll find that we already established my 'nice' credentials. Feel free to promote me to gorgeous, fit, funny, hunky and irresistible whenever you like."

She took in his lazy grin, his crazy bed-head, the adolescent, naff, politically incorrect T-shirt that proudly announced he was a "Male God in Training".

Then the realisation came.

Winning the prize for "Strangest Emotion in Weirdest Circumstances," it came to her that, potentially fatal hangover aside, and despite the prospect of being run out of town by Mrs Donald (at a very slow speed, obviously), for the first time in ages she was waking up with a man and she actually — and astonishingly — felt, well, *happy*. She definitely wasn't

166

anxious, bored titless, or desperate to leave. Whoa, that was so weird. She double-checked. Yes, she was absolutely almost bubbly.

"I think for now we'll stick with nice."

A feeling of dread crowbarred into her wee basket of bliss. Roxy Galloway was lying in bed with a "nice" guy and she wasn't hatching an urgent plan for escape.

And that could only mean one thing . . .

She'd definitely been back in Farnham Hills for too long.

Roxy mentally summed up her sad excuse for a life. Farnham Hills: Day 11. Location: Hell's library. Velour tracksuit: pink. Hair: pony tail. Scrunchie: purple.

She had a vision of her obituary: *Suddenly, behind the Formica reception desk at the Farnham Hills Community Library, Miss Roxy Galloway died of mortification.*

A scrunchie. It didn't get much more undignified than this. If Daniel Galvin could see her now she'd be banned from his opulent hallows of shiny, healthy hair for life.

She picked up a pile of record cards that she'd meticulously updated, detailing the transactions from the day before. At home she had a computer to do everything from making the coffee to running a bath. Here she'd been reintroduced to the giddy joys of a world that ran like clockwork as long as you were accomplished in the cerebral task of filing bits of card in alphabetical order.

The doors swung open and in marched the fifth-year study group. Romeo and Juliet avoided eye contact.

"Good morning, my favourite customers!" she offered in the sing-song grating melody normally espoused by really condescending weather girls. They looked at her like her natural habitat should be nine foot by five foot and padded. Roxy gave them a deranged grin in return, and they swaggered off to the back of the room in a flurry of sneers and mutterings of "She's like, you know, totally fucked up, man."

Roxy laughed loudly, making them walk even faster. Whey hey, she'd discovered a great new sport — teenager baiting.

"What are you looking so smug about?"

She splurted her tea across the desk, some droplets dripping onto her hoodie top and spreading like ripples in a pool of water.

"Do you always sneak up on people?"

"Do you always slip into these little trances that stop you from hearing swinging doors and footsteps?"

She shrugged her shoulders. "Must be some kind of self-preservation mechanism kicking in — the one that stops me from lying down in the middle of the road out there and waiting for a lorry to put me out of my misery."

Mitch leaned towards her, his folded arms on top of the desk.

"Aw, come on now, you don't really hate it here that much, do you? There are worse places than this."

"Only those where there's a high probability of contracting Ebola."

168

As she picked up another pile of cards, she caught a movement in her peripheral vision.

"Sit!" she yelled. Romeo and Juliet stopped in their tracks at the door to the ladies' toilets, then turned and skulked back to their seats.

"Jesus, they're rampant around here. This is like a day at my normal job but without the posh accents."

Mitch was intrigued. "Really? And what kind of office do you normally work in then?"

It suddenly occurred to Roxy that she'd never enlightened him as to her usual mode of employment. She'd just kind of presumed that he knew; that Ginny would have passed on that little salacious nugget of information. Time for confession . . .

"It's a . . . staff agency. For the upper classes. You know, matching up wealthy people with the right people to fulfil their needs."

She was getting into the swing of the lie now. She had a flashing image of the last time she saw Ceecee. "Things like maids . . ." Then there were the blokes with the rampant Oedipus tendencies. ". . . nannies . . ." And the gents who had obviously developed strange habits at public school. ". . . private tutors . . ." And not forgetting the food fetishists. ". . . and catering staff. Never a dull moment with that lot. You know, all that *Upstairs, Downstairs*, illicit mingling with the hired help."

"Sounds really interesting."

"More than you know," she agreed, as a pang of longing consumed her. What she wouldn't give to be in a room right now with an espresso machine, a sex-aids cupboard and twelve high-class hookers. But in the meantime, Mitch would have to do. "So anyway, thanks for saving my arse on Friday night. And for smuggling me out of the church house — it's reassuring to know that I'm not the talk of the God-fearing people of Farnham Hills."

Over Mitch's shoulder she caught two of the fifth-year girls very obviously bitching about her, complete with whispers, gesticulating fingers and barbed looks.

"It seems that I'm just persona non grata among the shy, innocent youth of the village. Do you think they're bad-mouthing me on MySpace yet?"

"What's your space?" Mitch asked, his face a picture of puzzlement.

"No, *MySpace*. It's an internet site, where you have your own homepage and . . ."

He burst into fits of laughter.

"I'm kidding, I know what MySpace is."

"I'll never like you," she huffed indignantly, face flushing slightly as she feigned concentration on the record cards. Davidson. Davies. Dickson. Doherty. How dare he take the piss out of her? Didn't he know that she was desperate, dejected and . . . and . . . only pretending to ignore him.

He leaned over and ruffled her hair. Great, now she'd have to readjust the cutting-edge scrunchie.

"I know, but I'm the best company on offer and I hereby vow to protect you from rampaging sixteen-year-olds, so how about grabbing something to eat tonight?"

170

Argh, he was irritating. But then she did owe him a favour for being her knight in shining high-street clothing the other night. She considered the options: inedible grub in a manky pub with a nice-but-smugly-irritating guy, or pulling her legs into unnatural positions with her mother and aunt at the church-hall yoga group. Incidentally, why had no one ever warned her about the flatulence issues of yoga? No wonder Gwyneth Paltrow always looked sour-faced, the poor girl must be in a permanent state of drowsiness caused by toxic emissions.

"Meet you at five thirty. But don't let me drink anything with alcohol — removes every iota of sense and I end up in inappropriate situations with undesirables."

And as he chortled his way over to the sporting section, Roxy contemplated the back of his broad shoulders, narrow hips, and ridiculous boots. She might have said it in bantering jest but she meant every word. She wouldn't find Mitch desirable if he stripped bollock naked and dangled diamonds on his dick.

He must have felt her stare boring into his back, as he turned, grinned and winked at her, causing the study group to burst into fits of giggles.

Definitely not desirable. Absolutely not. No way.

But maybe she would just nip home at lunchtime and wash her hair so she could lose the scrunchie.

"Ta-da!"

It was six hours, one hair-wash and a phone call later and now she was standing at the doorway of a darkened library, holding up two bags in front of a perplexed Mitch.

"I'm cooking you dinner. Actually that's a lie — I'm taking already-prepared food out of foil containers and putting it on a plate."

"Nigella Lawson must be shitting herself."

He spotted the name on the side of the bags — The Mill House. He may have only been around for a few months, but he'd already heard of the three-star Michelin restaurant a few villages away that attracted an A-list crowd even though there wasn't a landing strip, a five-star hotel or a rehab centre within fifty miles. A meal for two must have easily cost a hundred quid.

"How did you get that here — I didn't realise that they had a delivery service?"

"Taxi, it just arrived two minutes ago," Roxy replied glibly.

Mitch struggled to stifle a splutter.

"Look, I know it's a bit of an indulgence for a Wednesday night but it was Felix's treat."

"So you're talking to him again?" Mitch's right eyebrow raised in surprise.

"Not exactly," she shrugged. There were a few quizzical seconds of silence before she caved. "Oh, okay. I was going to pay for it myself, honestly, but I thought I'd try all the credit cards Felix gave me just to see if the heartless bastard had cancelled them all, and then I discovered that one of them was still active and I couldn't help myself. Anyway, it's just a meal. And a taxi."

"And what else did you buy?"

"Nothing!" Even the noise of a bin wagon trundling by didn't drown out her indignant screech.

"What else?" he repeated.

"Nothing!"

He drifted back half a step behind her and playfully grabbed her hood. "Confess all or the velour gets it."

"Don't you dare, my mother would kill me."

He put both hands on the edge of the hood, poised to rip.

She knew when she was beaten.

"Okay! Three pairs of Jimmy Choos, a Lulu Guinness bag, a Marc Jacobs jacket, two tickets for my mother to see *The Vagina Monologues* — don't say a word — and I also treated Reverend Stewart to a subscription to *Big Girls Are Easy* — well, he was at the computer next to me while I was on the spree and I didn't want him to feel left out."

They crossed the High Street and headed left, past the bank, the post office, the chemist and the funeral parlour.

"Won't he go crazy when he finds out?"

Roxy just shrugged. "And I would care *why*? Let's just call it severance pay."

"Wow, you're vicious. I swear if you ever show the slightest sign of violent tendencies I'm buying a mace spray."

"Shit!"

Several things happened at once. Roxy spat the expletive, then he felt the full force of her body against his, knocking the wind out of him as she propelled him into the doorway of the Help the Aged office. Then her hand went over his mouth and he felt a burning sensation in his ribcage. They stayed like that for a few seconds, startled, enveloped in the darkness, the searing heat on the right side of his torso making him bite his bottom lip to refrain from doing something really butch like whimpering pathetically.

His teeth were starting to draw blood when he heard running footsteps and then Darren jogged past the doorway, deep in conversation with his running partner, who, if Mitch wasn't mistaken, was Cecilia Dupree, the recently divorced wife of a London billionaire who'd secured their Farnham Hills country house as part of the settlement. She'd then promptly decanted her whole life to the house that she'd only previously used for the occasional weekend soiree, and taken to wearing Barbour jackets and growing an organic vegetable patch. The locals had a sweepstake running as to how long she'd last before hightailing it back to the city, bored of her little *Country Life* adventure when she realised that she wasn't in fact living in a Jilly Cooper novel of lust and glamour among the welly brigade.

"I think they've gone." Roxy took her hand off his mouth. "Sorry about that — couldn't face running into that twat. You okay?"

He nodded gingerly, acutely aware that she was still pressed up against him, her face upturned to his. Her hips were pressed against his, her chest rising and falling against his, one hand now resting on his shoulder, her mouth inches from his.

174

Their eyes locked as his heart began to beat faster, faster, faster, fuelled by what was going on in the near vicinity.

"Roxy," he gasped.

"What?" she answered breathlessly.

"Can you move the bags away from my side because I think those foil trays have just given me third-degree burns."

"So how's Ginny getting on in London?"

"To be honest I'm not sure. It hurts too much to ask."

"Why? Because you're missing her?"

"No. Because the cushy cow is living my life, in my fabulous flat, with my fabulous clothes and my general fabulous fabulousness, and I'm stuck here in a backwards hovel where they think frappuccino is a destination in an Airtours summer-sun brochure."

Mitch laughed. "You mean it isn't?"

"See — my work here would never be done."

Roxy was delicately trying to manoeuvre two eight-inch-high slices of mille-feuille out of a cardboard cake box and onto two mismatched plates dragged from the back of her mother's crockery cupboard. Mitch was getting one engraved with the lofty banner "My Friend Went to Clacton-on-Sea and All She Brought Me Was This Lousy Plate" while Roxy's was a memento of Charles and Di's big day.

The conversation over dinner had been easy. This, Roxy had decided, must be what having a brother was like — warm, comforting, and handy to have someone who could reach high shelves.

"Mmmm. Must remember to send Felix a thank-you card for dinner," she declared, popping a glob of cream into her mouth with her index finger.

The food had been truly sublime. Intricate little baskets of seafood — crab, lobster and chunks of delicate soy-marinated hake — to start. The main course had been the tenderest slivers of fillet mignon, nestled on a bed of shiitake mushrooms and surrounded by thick-cut potatoes, then doused in a tangy red-wine jus. And now dessert — thick cream, iced top, and a dozen layers of paper-thin pastry. It was an orgasm in a bowl.

"Anyway, enough about my woeful existence. I've just realised that I know practically nothing about you."

And what's more, Roxy realised as she slid his plate over to him, she was actually quite interested. Normally when someone was giving her the history of their life she glazed over and scouted the room for the exits, but she had to admit this time she was intrigued.

He hadn't replied, mainly due to the fact that he was chewing on two inches of French pastry.

"So spill. Seeing someone? Married? Divorced? Stalkers?"

"Would you hang on a minute?" he said, still chewing. "I've got about thirty quid's worth of your boyfriend's cake in my mouth and I just want to savour it."

"Ex."

"Ex. Sorry." After a few seconds he finally swallowed. "Okay, no ex-wives. Never been married, therefore never been divorced, no kids, and — although I would occasionally welcome one — I'm afraid there's no stalker either. I'm officially the most romantically barren man on the face of the earth."

Roxy got up and flicked on the kettle — screaming-pink, retro, matching the screaming-pink retro toaster, the screaming-pink retro sandwich-maker and her screaming-pink tracksuit. It was like living in a little bubble of oestrogen. She reached up to grab a jar of instant decaf out of the pastel-pink cupboard, when a question bypassed her brain and came straight out of her gob.

"Are you gay?"

A lump of cake shot from his mouth, flew across the room and adhered itself to the back of her hoodie.

"Erm. No. I'm not. Why would you think I was?"

"I didn't," she shrugged, turning back round, a jar of Mellow Birds in hand. "I was just double-checking. You could *never* be a gay guy."

Mitch was now sitting up a little straighter, with his chest puffed out just a little more, and speaking in a voice that was just a little deeper.

"Why's that then?" he asked, reassured in his masculinity.

"Because you dress like crap, you live in a tip, and that hair has never seen a deep-conditioning treatment. So how come you're single then? And if you answer that using clichés I'm eating the rest of your cake."

"Oh, I don't know. Never met the right girl. Waiting for 'The One'. Sowing my wild oats. Not settling for second best."

She raised her spoon in a threatening manner. "Okay, hand it over."

He curled his arm around his plate so that she couldn't even see it any more. "Never — you can take my body, soul and worldly goods but get your hands off my pudding."

Roxy groaned. "Oh, if I had a pound for every time a bloke has said that to me . . . Anyway, you're not getting off that easily. Telly is crap tonight, we're living in the social equivalent of the Gobi, I haven't been able to get *Vogue, Vanity Fair* or even *Cosmo*, and the video shop was frozen in time somewhere around *Pretty Woman* — so whether you like it or not we have to pass the rest of the night with meaningless chat. So . . ." she ran her finger along the edge of her plate, scooping up cream ". . . relationships? Lasted how long? How many? Heartbroken? In love?"

His slumped shoulders revealed that he realised that resistance was futile — whether he liked it or not he was going to be spending the next couple of hours in the testosterone equivalent of living hell: emotional revelation time. "Two main relationships — one lasted two years, the other nine."

Roxy choked. "Nine years? What — after the first five you wanted to wait a while just to be sure?" she teased.

He tried his best not to rise to the bait, replying casually, "Something like that. You know, these things shouldn't be rushed. That's why there are so many divorces these days."

"Wow. Mitch O'Donnell, anthropologist, social commentator and moral conscience."

"Clutching a sharp object," he warned, picking up the cake slice.

"Okay, okay. God, you country boys are so touchy. So you didn't answer the last one — in love?"

She caught his eye; a mischievous smile playing across her lips, a big dollop of cream perched on her chin.

There was a definite pause as he flushed and shrugged his shoulders.

"Jackpot!" Roxy grinned. "Okay, come on then — who is she? I want to know everything and don't spare the details. If we can drag this out until about eleven o'clock I'll have survived another night without succumbing to lethal boredom. Right, on you go."

He squirmed in his chair. Pause. Cleared his throat. Pause. Another squirm. Pause. Roxy observed the whole "uncomfortable/playing for time" routine while wearing an expectant expression that refused to disappear without some kind of response.

"She's just someone I met not too long ago — kind of love at first sight, you know?" he stuttered.

"And it didn't work out?"

He shook his head and busied himself with the task of scraping his plate with a spoon.

Roxy was on her feet now, her back to him, spooning coffee into two mugs and reaching for the kettle.

"I never actually got around to telling her. She — erm — has other things going on so we haven't, erm, had that conversation. Yet."

She shrieked as she spun around, her face emitting a beam of pure glee at the delicious new revelation. But as she twisted, her hand somehow caught the top of the boiled kettle, tipping it over, sending boiling water cascading towards her.

She screamed as she jumped back, missing the worst of the torrent but feeling the pain as some of the water splashed onto her. Mitch shot up, grabbed her, spun her round and wrenched the zip down on her sweatshirt before instinctively tearing the soaked fabric from her body, so panicked that he honestly, hand on heart, didn't notice that she wasn't wearing a bra and was therefore displaying her assets in all their remarkably pert glory.

At least, not at first.

Because, like the very worst scene in the very worst soap opera about the unluckiest woman in man-made fibres, that was the very moment that the door swung open, and there, in front of her, was the man she'd been waiting to see for what seemed like months. She took in his beautifully cut suit, his impeccably groomed hair and his five-hundred-quid shoes. She chose to ignore his homicidal expression, the two astonished blonde women standing behind him, and the fact that she was standing in a puddle.

Half-naked. Two inches away from an Irish bloke clutching a pink velour sweatshirt.

"Felix!"

He was standing in front of her, top lip curling in anger, having obviously put two and two together and got a severe dose of the hump.

"I won't ask if you missed me then," he said with the kind of accompanying cackle that the really bad guys always emit in horror movies right before they decapitate their next victim.

"But, but . . ." She didn't even know where to begin.

"Save it, love," he sneered, turning to leave. Suddenly, he stopped, turned back, and then looked her up and down.

"You know, I've just realised something. You look great . . ."

Roxy's spirits momentarily soared.

". . . but to be honest, after the other night I actually think Ginny has better tits."

Farnham Hills, the alley behind the youth club, May 1994

"Okay, okay, it's my turn," slurred Roxy. "What do you want, truth or dare?"

Ginny took a huge slug from the bottle of Diamond White. She couldn't believe the man in the off-licence had allowed Roxy to buy it. But then, he hadn't stopped staring at her boobs for long enough to check her face and realise that there was no way she was eighteen. She did look at least sixteen, though — a whole two years older than she actually was and about four years older than Ginny looked. It wasn't fair — how come Roxy had got all the premature development genes?

As always, their outfits were matching but the effect was totally different. Ginny was wearing a black cropped vest top, black Lycra leggings, pink leg-warmers and flat suede boots. With her ironing-board chest, boyish figure and her mass of frizz pulled back into a low pony tail, she looked like she was about to go and audition for an under-twelves' tap dancing class. Roxy was wearing the same outfit, but with her 32C chest, waist-length black curls and hourglass torso she looked like Madonna's more controversial little sister — Jailbait Ciccone.

Ginny swallowed the sweet, fizzy liquid and tried not to retch. She hated the stuff but Roxy got really annoyed if she refused to join in. She inhaled deeply, waiting for the wave of nausea to pass.

"Truth," she eventually replied.

Roxy thought for a few minutes. "If you could kiss any boy at the disco tonight, who would it be?"

Ginny flushed so brightly she could double as a disco light. She hated these questions. Fourteen and she'd never kissed a boy, whereas Roxy had snogged every decent-looking guy in the school. Except . . . except . . .

"Josh Tressor," Ginny finally admitted bashfully.

Roxy giggled, an unfortunate move as she had a mouthful of cider. Some of it escaped and sprayed Ginny's hair. Great. Like she needed more reasons for her mane to frizz.

"Yeah, you and every other female with a pulse — me included," said Roxy. "God, he's so gorgeous — I had a dream once that I lost my virginity to him and it was so incredible. He had a donger the size of . . ."

"Roxy! Shut up!!!"

Roxy roared with laughter. "Okay, okay, but it was huge! And should he ever want my virginity I'd definitely make it available. Oh, I wish!" she paused, savouring the thought, then snapped out of it. "Anyway, I didn't know you fancied him too. You should tell him. Definitely. I'll tell him for you."

"DON'T YOU DARE!" Ginny screeched, mortified at the very thought. It was one thing having a secret crush on someone, but she'd have to leave school, change her identity and emigrate to another country if he ever found out. Oh, she'd die!

And anyway, she knew he'd never, ever look twice at her. Josh Tressor was by far the best-looking guy in the school: captain of the football team, top in athletics, smart, and so handsome he could get any girl he wanted. And Ginny knew with absolute certainty that he'd never want her. He was way, way out of her league — two years they'd been in the same chemistry class, sitting in the same group, and she'd bet her last Take That album that he didn't even know her name. It was partly because she never spoke in class and partly because he was always occupied with the dual pastimes of class work and fending off the affections of the endless stream of girls who wanted to go out with him — one of them being Roxy.

Still, she was allowed to dream . . .

Roxy took a huge gulp of the cider and then passed it back to Ginny to finish, before pulling a packet of Juicy Fruit from her bag and opening a stick for each of them. "Right, come on then, let's go. I've promised Jack Symms I'll get off with him — he's no Josh Tressor but his dad's got a BMW and he's promised to sneak the keys out so we can sit in it."

"Roxy, you promised you wouldn't leave me on my own again!"

"I won't! I'll wait until the end of the night before I even talk to him, honest!"

And for once she was true to her word. For three hours they danced, laughed and made frequent trips to the toilet — courtesy of the diuretic effects of Diamond White. Ginny was returning from her twelfth pee of the evening just as she heard the last record start. Groan — she hated this bit. This was the slow dance, where all the guys picked the girl they fancied most and smooched for three long romantic minutes on the dance floor, trying to avoid letting Father Murphy spot that their pelvises were actually touching and that they were kissing with tongues. Ginny never, ever got picked.

As she left the loos, she turned right and was walking towards the swing doors leading to the main hall when she heard voices coming from the fire-exit recess just ahead of her on the left-hand wall of the corridor.

Oh crap, crap, crap, it was Josh Tressor and he was talking to . . .

"Come on, Roxy, just one dance. I've been wanting to ask you for ages."

Ginny's stomach flipped and her knees turned to Angel Delight. Typical. Totally typical. Okay, so Josh would never ask her out in this lifetime, but now Roxy would be his girlfriend and Ginny would have to listen to her drooling his praises night and day for the rest of their lives. It was just so, so pants! She leaned against the wall, frozen to the spot by her legs' sudden refusal to cooperate. Urgh, now she'd hear them getting it together. In fact, if she knew Roxy then they were already kissing and Josh Tressor's hand had been guided into her bra.

"Josh . . ." Roxy started to speak.

Here we go, thought Ginny. This is the part where Roxy says yes and they boogie off into the sunset, leaving her, as usual, to help Father Murphy pack up his records and then pick up all the crisp packets and empty Coke cans.

"I'd love to . . ."

Ginny tutted, rolled her eyes and adopted the approximate expression of a bulldog chewing a wasp (thereby proving that some mannerisms originate in childhood). She was just about to head back to the toilets and seek refuge in a locked cubicle when she realised what Roxy was saying.

". . . but I can't."

Ginny almost gasped out loud in astonishment. Like the entire female population of the school, Roxy had worshipped Josh for years, and yet now she was rejecting his advances. Just how much of that cider had she drunk?

Josh's voice conveyed his surprise. "Why not? Come on, Rox."

"Look, I said no," Roxy replied firmly. "I really like you but . . . well, one of my friends does too and it wouldn't be fair."

"Who?" Josh probed.

"Can't tell you or she'd kill me."

"But I don't want to go out with any of your friends, Roxy; I want to go out with you."

Roxy sounded doleful. "Sorry, Josh, but I couldn't do that to her — not even for you. Aaaagh, I bloody hate being nice."

Ginny's eyes widened. Oh. My. God. Roxy had rejected the most amazing, totally cool boy in the school, a guy who was the best catch in the village — no, make that the whole world — because . . . because of her. It was incredible. And so, so lovely.

Suddenly Roxy alighted from the recess, her back to Ginny, still talking to Josh. "I have to go, something to do. Don't suppose you know if Jack brought the keys for his dad's BMW?"

Ginny couldn't help but grin. That was Roxy: crazy, wild, shallow, and utterly superficial . . . and the best friend a girl could ever have.

CHAPTER
TEN

Many Rivers to Cross

Ginny. Day 11, Wednesday, 10.49p.m.

"I didn't! Okay, I suppose technically I did, but I swear it's not in the way you think. Roxy! Roxy! ROXY!!!!"

Ginny realised that she was now shrieking like a banshee to the accompanying sound of a dialling tone. She quickly punched in Roxy's mobile number — straight to answering machine. She speed-dialled her mother's house — engaged.

Jude came storming through into the kitchen. "What's wrong? What's happened? Are you okay? Is Roxy? What's going on?"

Amazing — the man was capable of grasping the severity of a situation, reacting to it at blinding speed and asking all the pertinent questions, yet he was, apparently, incapable of putting on a T-shirt.

And it was even more disconcerting because he was so tall his nipples were in Ginny's eye-line. For a brief moment she didn't know whether to speak or take her mind off her crisis by latching on and hoping for the best. And she couldn't believe she was having impure thoughts at a time like this.

"I'm fine! No, I'm not. I'm not sure how, but Roxy somehow thinks that I slept with Felix and she's gone into orbit. Oh my God, how could she think that? How? Why?"

"*What?* It wasn't your fault he ambushed you in the middle of the night. I'm just glad I'd left or it could have been one of those scenes that I'd have relived until I die."

He grabbed a bagel from the worktop and broke a bit off. "Phone her back, explain what happened and tell her she's being ridiculous. I'll speak to her too, if you want."

"I tried, but her mobile is off and the house phone is engaged. Shit, I have to go home and explain. Shit, I can't, I'm on early shift tomorrow. Shit. Shit. How could she think that?"

The astonishment and horror were very gradually being replaced by indignation and anger.

"I mean, for God's sake, we've been best friends our whole lives — how could she ever think that I'd do something like that to her? Does she give me no credit at all?"

Her hands were on her hips now, ire in full flow.

"She knows me much better than that! How could she!"

"Ssshhh, ssshhh." Jude tried to diffuse the situation by wrapping his arms around her and shushing her into serenity.

It was several moments before Ginny realised that she was nestled in the best set of pecs she'd ever fantasised about licking. Only Brad Pitt came close and

189

even then Jude's gained the edge because they didn't come with the threat of certain death at the hands of Angelina Jolie.

Come to think of it, she didn't think taking on Goldie Gilmartin would be conducive to the retention of limbs either. Where *was* Goldie these days? She hadn't seen her all week. Or Cheska, for that matter. Actually, if she was being totally honest, that might have been something to do with the fact that she'd been avoiding Jude too.

Mortification often had that effect.

Mortification arising from the last time he had charged into a room, ostensibly to her rescue, to find her sitting bolt upright in bed with her best friend's ex-boyfriend dangling from her left mammary.

"What the fu—?" had been his initial take on the situation. Then, thankfully, Felix had regained the power of speech and in a flurry of apologies and explanations had climbed out of bed and pulled his clothes back on. He'd had the cheek to ask her to turn away to protect his modesty. Marvellous. The man had almost performed a gynaecological procedure on her and now *he* was making *her* look away to save *his* blushes.

In the end, they'd all calmed down, sobered up and re-clothed enough to clarify the situation.

"But why has she gone back to live at her mother's house?" Felix had asked, dumbfounded. "She always said that your life was like slow suffocation by boredom."

Ginny gave a rueful shrug. "She isn't even here and yet still she manages to insult me. But to go back to

190

your question, it may have something to do with her catching you — er . . ."

She couldn't say it. She might now work in a brothel. She might give the illusion of being cosmopolitan and worldly wise. She might be single. She might fantasise about lewd acts with unsuitable men. But she still couldn't have an upfront discussion about sex.

"Banging someone else," Jude contributed to the silence.

Ginny gestured a thanks to him for filling in the blanks.

"Oh, come on, that was just a fling. It's over. Roxy knew that would never last. A bloke has to have the odd dalliance, ain't that right, mate?" Felix addressed the question to Jude, who found it difficult to answer from his position midway between a rock and a hard place.

Ten minutes later, Felix was out of the door, armed with Roxy's mother's number and address, the latter being given in case he found it preferable to soften Roxy up by sending gifts. Anything except flowers.

After he'd gone, there was a brief instant of discomfort as Jude and Ginny stood facing each other in the hall. She'd checked Roxy's Cartier Tank — 5a.m. "I'd better get to bed. Early rise in the morning." A whole week and she still hadn't had a day off. Jennifer's romance with the French chef had bypassed casual courting and occasional overnight stays and gone straight to a week-long love-in at The Langham.

Ginny had been only too happy to cover for her, figuring that more work meant more money, busier days and less temptation.

Jude had given her his trademark languid, easy smile and kissed her goodnight. On the cheek.

They'd only had a few brief meetings as they passed each other in the hallway since then.

Until now.

Now he was holding her, shushing her, and all she could think of was that her best friend was devastated. Okay, that was a blatant lie. The old Ginny would have been consumed by desperation about her friend's pain; the new Ginny was busily engaged in the lofty pursuit of surreptitiously, almost discernibly counting the grooves on a stripper's six-pack.

But in her defence there was part of her brain that was disturbingly puzzled by this latest twist in events.

Almost as puzzled as she was about Darren's behaviour.

She'd called him a dozen times since he'd unceremoniously binned her and, like those initial few days when she'd come to London, he was refusing to answer the phone again. She'd stopped calling his mother's house because she was sure that all those trips to the phone must be playing havoc with the old dear's gallstones. Travelling home from work that night she'd decided that she wasn't going to try to contact him again. Game over. If he wanted to be so childish and petty then that was up to him, but she wasn't calling him again. So there.

She would, however, call Roxy again in a minute — just as soon as she'd disentangled herself from Jude. Make that two minutes. Maybe three.

Right on cue, he lifted his head from the top of hers, allowing her to look up into those sea-green eyes. He'd break off any minute now. She knew it. So she waited . . . and waited . . . and . . .

"Are you okay?"

She shrugged her shoulders. "Honestly?"

"Honestly."

The truth was that sometimes she thought this new life was fabulous, and other times she felt, well, like she'd do anything to be back at the library drinking tea and spending all morning chatting to Mitch. There was no denying Roxy's world was more glam, more dramatic, sexier, and sure, it was a perpetual tornado of excitement, but sometimes it felt a little, well, hollow. And exhausting. She absolutely loved the girls at the Seismic but it seemed like they never really talked about anything other than the next party. She had the distinct feeling that she could work there for years, socialise with them on a daily basis, yet never really find out anything about them other than who they were sleeping with, where they shopped and where they were spending their next night out. There was definitely something to be said for zero stress and nothing to do all day except keep an eye on wayward teenagers and chat to people who had all the time in the world to chat back.

The truth was that somewhere among the last couple of weeks of grooming demands, the sexual tension at home, the emotional tension with Darren and the witnessing of more naked body parts than an overworked porn star, she was starting to see that her old life did have some advantages. However, she put that thought to the furthest recesses of her mind for the time being, since her old life didn't come with the added perk of being able to snuggle into the torso of a man who, despite the fact he originated from Hackney, had somehow been gifted the body of your common or garden Greek god — one who was still waiting for her reply.

"I honestly have absolutely no idea. I seem to have stumbled into this crazy world where there's a drama every five minutes, a crisis every ten, and loads of outrageous things happen in between. I've had more bizarre experiences in the last ten days than I've had in the rest of my life. Either the world's gone mad or I have."

"It's the world — Roxy's world. It's always like this."

"Yeah? Well, how come she doesn't look fifty because I swear all this drama is ageing me by the minute."

They locked eyes and Ginny realised that they were holding a perfectly normal, buddy-type conversation while there were still arms clutching opposite anatomies.

And they were still staring . . . still staring . . . and — breathe, breathe, breathe — his face was coming down closer to hers.

When their lips locked she could have sworn blind that the earth moved, but that may have been caused by him lifting her from the ground and moving her back against the huge American-style fridge freezer. They kissed slowly, seductively, devouring each other, and thankfully — Ginny realised with a wave of relief — they didn't bang teeth once.

He took her hands and pushed them up above her head, all the while kissing and licking and nibbling at her neck, her face, her ears. And then back to her mouth, his lips pressed hard against hers now, his breathing deep, his tongue embracing hers in a frantic tonsil dance. One of his hands held both of hers above her head, while the other one came back down, gently opening the buttons on her aquamarine silk Chanel blouse to reveal a balconette bra that made her normally insignificant cleavage look like two bald men caught in a hammock. She gasped with something between desire and relief.

Suddenly, he stopped. Noooooo, not again! No more stopping!

He pulled back and looked at her searchingly, tenderly. "Are you sure? Really sure?"

"Don't. Ever. Stop." She replied with unequivocal assertiveness. "Ever."

He leaned in and kissed her again, his free hand moving around to the back of her bra and unhooking it. He clasped her hands over the top of the fridge freezer.

"Leave them up there," he whispered, and she had no intention of arguing.

Both of his hands in action now, he moved down her body, caressing her as he took one nipple in his mouth and then moved over to the other. She clenched her teeth to stop the screams that were desperate to escape. Never, *never* had she felt anything like this in her life before. It was indescribable, it was the ultimate rush, it was . . . *orgasmic.*

Her legs shook as the first waves ripped through her. Fuck! Normally with Darren it took twenty minutes of grinding and the intervention of manual stimulation —

195

now she was climaxing before she even got the rest of her kit off.

A point that Jude seemed to have taken upon himself to rectify.

He was kneeling in front of her now, his glorious blond head licking the soft skin just below her waist as his hands reached around and unzipped her skirt. He pulled it down, his lips tracing the top of the fabric as it passed over her hips. She made a mental note to thank Destiny for the gift — the translucent red thong and suspender set that matched the bra that was now dangling from the top of the banana rack on the opposite worktop.

He slipped the thong off, leaving her naked, except for the red suspender belt, holding up sheer black stockings.

He opened her legs and then moved in, licking every inch of the inside of one thigh, then the other. She was trembling, gasping, and she could no longer feel her arms, but who cared? His head was buried in her now, his tongue tracing its way round the inside of her before focusing on her clitoris, gently but quickly darting back and forward. He pulled one of her legs over his left shoulder, then another over his right, so that she was sitting on him, allowing him to angle her pelvis and let his tongue go even deeper, harder. As he brought her to another climax, the screams wouldn't stop. And neither, it seemed, would he.

He pulled his head back as he moved downwards, allowing her to put her feet back on the floor. Then he

196

rose up, his hands pulling off his jeans before he got to a standing position.

"You're still okay?" he asked tenderly. Ginny reached up, put her hands into his hair and pulled his face down to hers, surprising herself with her urgency. She kissed him, their tongues probing around each other's mouths, their hands pulling and kneading each other's skin. She tore her mouth away, pulled his head down further until her lips were devouring his earlobe. Then Ginny Wallis did something she thought she'd only ever encounter in novels: she removed a stripper's earlobe from her mouth, reached down and grabbed his gorgeous, huge dick, pulled it towards her and whispered, "Fuck me now. Hard."

And after reaching to a nearby cupboard to extract a condom (yes, it would later cross her mind to wonder at the generous dispersion and location of condoms around the apartment) he pushed inside her. And just when she thought he couldn't have any more, he pushed in even further. Her legs came up around his waist, her hands were now tangled in his hair, as he thrust inside her again . . . and again . . . and again . . . until . . . when the liquid came there was so much that it splashed on the floor, soaking everything within distance.

Ginny wasn't sure who was more surprised — Jude or her. She'd been so immersed in her own bliss, so high on the best ride of her life, that she hadn't even realised that he was getting to that point. But hold on . . . the condom. The condom meant that there shouldn't have been any . . .

"Ginny! Ginny, stop!"

She opened her eyes, confused at the levity in his voice. Surely he should be panicking and making a beeline to the nearest chemist for the morning-after pill?

But instead he seemed to find the whole situation highly amusing.

"Ginny!" he repeated. "You're pressing against the water dispenser."

She turned around to see that, yes, sure enough, in the midst of passion she hadn't noticed that one of her buttocks was wedged against the dispenser on the front of the fridge door, causing rivers of ice-cold Evian to flood the kitchen.

The two of them dissolved into fits of giggles, until Ginny realised the most important conclusion to be drawn from this — he wasn't finished yet.

She grinned as she pushed his hair back off his stunning face. "Then get me over to that dishwasher and finish what you started," she ordered.

"Are you always this demanding?" he teased, as he lifted her, his magnificent penis still tucked inside her, and walked across the kitchen and deposited her on the requested electrical appliance.

"Never! But I think it's working for me — what do you think?"

His left hand moved round behind her neck, his right hand moved down to tickle her overworked and ecstatic clitoris, and his dick resumed its exploration.

"Honey, it is definitely working for you. And for me."

WHAT CAREER?

INDEX — L Page 234

CHAPTER
ELEVEN

Blowing in the Wind

Roxy. Day 12, Thursday, 8.14a.m.
"Indeed you will not take the day off, young lady. Now get your clothes on and be downstairs in ten minutes or you're grounded."

Vera Galloway was a fearsome sight. Black patent court shoes, the only token elegant item in an outfit that included a purple calf-length floaty linen skirt and a wrap top so kaleidoscopic that the local primary school could use it for their next production of *Joseph*. Added to that, her hands were on her hips, her face was flushed, and she looked about as happy as George Bush on a two-week package tour to Kabul.

"Mother, stop being ridiculous. I'm twenty-seven years old — you haven't been able to ground me for the last eleven years."

Roxy pulled the duvet up around her neck a little tighter, giving her mother her very best defiant stare. "I feel ill, my head is pounding, and I'm not going to spend all day standing in a library surrounded by deadbeats."

"You're letting Vi down, you know."

Roxy could feel her blood pressure rising by the second. "Oh, for Christ's sake, Mum, stop being so dramatic. All I'm doing is taking the day off! The way you're acting you'd think I'd been stopped at customs with ten pounds of coke up my jacksy. I'll be back tomorrow — I'm sorry — okay?"

Vera sniffed the air. "Roxy, have you been *smoking* in here?" she asked, astonished.

Roxy looked at her like she was crazy. "Mother, if you'd even been remotely paying attention to my life you'd have noticed that I don't smoke. You're making my headache even worse, so can you just go now, please?"

Vera's face contorted and it was all Roxy could do not to pull the duvet right over her head in horror. She knew that look. It was the first sign that Vera was about to . . .

3-2-1 . . . Houston, Space Shuttle Ranting-Vera has lift-off.

"Roxy Galloway, God knows why I love you because you haven't been the easiest of children: spoiled, demanding, self-centred, all traits that you did, of course, inherit from your father. And that whole mortifying episode the other night — well, I didn't know where to look. I'd never have let that Felix one in if I'd known that you . . . well, good riddance, anyway. I never did take to him. If there's one thing I know about it's unfaithful men and that Felix had all the trademarks: flash clothes, flash car, and he wore aftershave that could suffocate you at ten yards. Oh yes, if ever there was a man who would go through life being directed by his willy, he was it."

Vera then performed her unique and brilliantly co-ordinated master talent: ranting while reversing out of a doorway and plodding several steps downstairs. By this time Roxy had conceded defeat and disappeared under the duvet, an action that caused her to miss Vera's dramatic encore.

"Well, all I can say is Thank God you've found a nice boy now — you and Mitch make a lovely couple. Oh, don't think you can kid me, young lady. Spilt water? Huh, do you think I'm buttoned up the back?"

Back in the bedroom, Roxy counted to a hundred, checked the coast was clear and emerged from under the covers with her Marlboro Lights. She lit one, then reached under again and pulled out a dish in the shape of a hand that Ginny had made in fifth-year art. The memory brought a pang of sadness. Art was one of the subjects that Roxy and Ginny had done together and they'd laughed so much when the dishes came out of the kiln, when Mr Stevens, the doddery old Art teacher, had finally realised that Roxy had deviated from the standard cupped-hand and made hers a fist with a defiantly raised middle finger.

She felt a tingling sensation across her sinuses. No, she would not bloody cry. She wouldn't. Even if she felt like her heart had been pummelled to death by a Jimmy Choo in the hands of the one person she never, ever thought would betray her.

Not Ginny. Never. A lifetime of friendship and now . . . How could that nasty, two-faced slapper have done this to her?

202

She flicked the ash from the end of her ciggie into the palm of the hand and gritted her teeth as another burst of anger replaced the sadness. This was hell. Unadulterated, bloody hell. Her best friend had committed the ultimate betrayal, her career was shite, her love life was shite, her mother was driving her nuts, she had absolutely no idea what she wanted to do with her future, she hadn't had sex for weeks, and now she was sneaking ciggies behind her mother's back. This wasn't just one of life's little blips, it was a full-scale regression back to some time around 1997.

She heard a door slamming downstairs and the unmistakable sound of four heels clicking their way down the path. She stubbed out the cigarette and got out of bed, pulled Westlife around her shoulders and went downstairs. In the living room, she flicked on the television, only for Fiona Phillips's cackles to permeate the silence. She snapped it back off again. She was already feeling suicidal — ten minutes of Fiona's grating witterings and she'd be heading for the nearest high-rise.

The phone rang but she ignored it — unless that was Fiona phoning to tell her she'd won a fortnight in Antigua, there was honestly not a single person she could think of that she wanted to speak to.

Could life get any worse? Felix and Ginny. Ginny and Felix. The thought of them kept turning over in her mind, again and again, making her stomach turn and the veins in her neck pop. Thank fuck her Botox was holding up or there'd be a permanent ridge in the space between her brows.

Why? Why would Ginny do this to her? Felix, she could understand — after all, he had previous convictions, but sweet, angelic, innocent little Ginny? What. A. Cow.

She'd never forgive her — never. Not that her former best friend even seemed to care — about half an hour after she'd hung up on Ginny she'd called her back and no one answered. She'd even tried the mobile but it just diverted to the answering service. Ginny had probably been on the phone to Felix, planning their next sordid little rendezvous and having a good old laugh behind Roxy's back. Bastards.

She flicked the telly on again — Jeremy Kyle now — and marvelled at the dregs of society sitting there in their tracksuits, full of attitude and malice.

Then she caught the tagline running along the bottom of the screen.

"*My best friend stole my boyfriend and I want him back.*"

Well, forget that — Ginny was welcome to him. She hoped they had a long and happy relationship, punctuated by weekly episodes where he shagged everything in sight.

She lit up another cigarette, but stubbed it out after two drags. She couldn't stand this. Her anxiety and anger levels were rising by the minute. This wasn't the way her life was supposed to turn out. She should have tracked down her perfect man by now, the one who would love her, cherish her and take her to a Sandals resort at least three times a year — not one whose cock deserved an ASBO.

She closed her eyes and let her head fall back on the couch. She should go and pack, head back to London and toss Ginny out on her arse. She should call Felix and abuse him in every way imaginable. She should kick-start her life by spending the rest of the day online looking for a new job. She should blow the cobwebs out of her pounding head by going for a long walk, perhaps down along the riverbank where she and Ginny had played as kids. She should call Jeremy Kyle.

But she didn't feel like doing any of those things. She would not be a victim. Kate Moss would have middle-aged spread before Roxy Galloway would ever, ever let those two see how devastated she was.

It suddenly came to her that there was only one thing that would make her feel better, one person she wanted to call, wanted to speak to, wanted to see.

She reached over to the phone table for her mother's address book and flicked through the pages, desperately hoping that the number would be there. Bingo. She picked up the phone and dialled.

"Hi, it's me, Roxy. Look, I know this might be a bit weird, but something awful has happened and I need to talk to someone. No, I don't want to explain on the phone — would you come over? I'm at home. Okay, erm, thanks, I'll see you then."

Half an hour later the doorbell rang and a showered, made-up Roxy with long, flowing locks, a gleam in her eye and minty-fresh breath opened the red-gloss door.

She took a deep breath, psyching herself up. She was ready. Step one: open door. Step two: adopt suitably sweet and grateful expression.

"Hi," she said tentatively. "Thanks for coming. I'm really glad you did."

He pushed back the sleeve on his Nike sweatshirt and checked his watch.

"Yeah, well, I had a spare half an hour — although I can think of a million places I'd rather spend it. So what's so important that you wanted to speak to me — is Ginny okay?"

"Oh, Ginny's fine. In fact, that's what I wanted to talk to you about — just how absolutely, spectacularly fine your little darling really is."

Roxy took a step back, and motioned for him to come in. Darren Jenkins, surprised, intrigued, and in the presence of the closest thing in his mind to the Antichrist, walked straight past her.

On the discomfort scale it was somewhere around the level of being caught naked while shoplifting in Tesco's and having the whole scene played to the nation on *Crimewatch*.

He hadn't said a word for a whole ten seconds, since right around the moment that he'd finally accepted the evidence was irrefutable.

Roxy hadn't been sure how to break it to him so in the end she'd gone for the approach that she'd have appreciated most: blunt-force trauma.

And she'd done it right in between giving him a coffee and offering him a Garibaldi.

"*She's what?*" he'd gasped, before immediately reverting to his standard default setting whenever Roxy was around: unadulterated hatred.

"You're lying. It's another of your fucked-up little games, isn't it? Another classic Roxy attempt to sabotage lives and wreak havoc on everyone around her."

"I swear I'm not! Look, Felix told me, I called her and she admitted it. Not at first, but then her answer went something along the lines of 'Okay, I suppose I did . . .' And I'm not telling you this to hurt you, Darren, I swear, I just thought you should know." Her voice had softened, and for the first time since second-year woodwork she'd spoken to him with compassion. She'd even managed to force out a tear, and this action had a double advantage, as not only did it make her look vulnerable but she'd had to squeeze her buttocks to do it, giving her a killer arse.

"Look, I know how it feels to be treated like this — when I found out about Felix I thought I'd die. But at least I know. I couldn't bear *not* knowing, everyone laughing behind my back, gossiping about me, relishing the scandal. And much as we've had our differences . . ."

"Understatement of the millennium," he'd interjected with a hint of resignation.

"Okay, our huge differences, I couldn't live with myself if I did something intentionally cruel like leaving you in the dark about this. Let's face it, Darren, they've fucked us over. And if I'm going to be in the 'Rejected Twat' boat then it would be nice to have some company."

And now he'd been staring into his cup, struck mute, for ages. She was just about to call on the therapeutic values of those Garibaldis when he gave a long sigh and lifted his head to face her.

"S'pose I don't have any right to complain — I called off the engagement last Friday."

Wow, *this* was news.

"You what? Why the hell would you do that? You two have been joined at the hip since before Ginny even had hips!"

He shrugged. "Thought it might make her come home. Or not. Or at least force one of us to make a decision. You know, twelve years is a long time to be with someone, and I know it's a cliché but sometimes I wonder if it wasn't more out of habit than anything else."

Roxy was gob-smacked. For the first time since he arrived, she felt a pang of uncertainty. Darren was the love of Ginny's life — she must have been devastated when he binned her. Why hadn't she called? Oh, that's right — she'd been too busy straddling Felix. Fury swiftly returned to kick the crap out of any notion of sympathy. She quickly refocused. Okay, this wasn't going to plan. Darren was supposed to fly into a rage, phone Ginny, call her a tart and then head off to London to beat the crap out of Roxy's scumbag of an ex-boyfriend.

Revenge. That's what this was all about. Letting those two shits know that they'd been well and truly caught, and that forgiveness wasn't an option.

But now, instead of blind fury and a rage that might possibly result in six months for grievous bodily harm, Darren was standing across from her emanating a vibe somewhere between mildly upset and pragmatic acceptance. And if she wasn't mistaken there might even have been a pinch of relief.

She felt her eyes well up. No! She would not cry for real! She wouldn't! She sniffed and wiped the back of her hand across her cheek. It was bad enough that she'd actually contacted Darren Jenkins, but her humiliation would be complete if he saw her crumble.

She pulled back her shoulders, took a deep breath and repeated her vow — she would not be a victim in this. She was tired of playing the martyr, of moping around feeling sorry for herself. It was time to look deep inside and rediscover her true self — her strength and her spirit. And as she did so, she discovered that her sex drive came as an added bonus.

As Darren put his cup down on the draining board and checked his watch again, Roxy realised that she was staring at the front of his jeans — jeans that covered an absolutely incredible pair of thighs. And as she saw Darren Jenkins in a new, single, unembittered light, she decided it was time to reclaim her power. Roxy Galloway's power — the one that had brought her happiness, joy, and the eradication of millions of calories.

"Darren . . ." she began in her most endearing voice, the one that once earned her thirty quid an hour on a chat-line service called "Wild Babes and Whack It". Well, she'd been young, poor, horny . . . "Erm, since things have gone pretty much tits-up for both of us, how about calling a ceasefire? You know, trying to be civil to each other."

There was a protracted pause.

When he finally spoke, his voice was loaded with something Roxy didn't think was scientifically possible while she and Darren were in the same room: humour.

"Really? But bickering with you for all these years has been so much fun. Kind of like taking part in an extreme sport — one that could cost you your bollocks at any second."

That comment took her glance straight back to the front of his jeans — there was no going back now.

"Fun?" she asked archly, straightening her back, going into attack position: head up, lips pouted, nipples aimed.

He locked eyes with her, daring her to challenge him.

She did. But granted, it probably wasn't in the way he expected.

She pulled her T-shirt over her head and shrugged it off, revealing the most incredible tits not created with the aid of anaesthetic and a scalpel.

And that's the point where Darren Jenkins decided to repeat the actions of his teenage years and reject her crude advances.

And perhaps he would have, if Roxy hadn't sauntered across the room, pressed those amazing tits against his torso and slowly, teasingly, licked his lips, before sinking to her knees in front of him.

In seconds his button was open, his zip was down, his dick was in her mouth and her hand was slowly, excruciatingly, massaging his balls.

He gasped and threw his head back, all notions of refusal cancelled the minute his brain had relinquished power of attorney to his penis.

Roxy pulled back so only the tip of his cock was between her teeth, her tongue slowly circling the very end, her hand now moving up and down the shaft. She continued to work him as she slipped further underneath, taking one of his balls in her mouth, sucking it gently before moving onto the other. She felt his legs start to tremble, his hands went into her hair, his fingers massaging her scalp to the steady beat of his whispered, "Oh fuck, oh fuck, oh fuck."

She swallowed him again, loving every delicious moment of this. His dick was perfect — thick, strong, and not so big that she feared for her lungs.

She let him gain a bit of control now, her mouth a willing receptacle for his thrusts, sucking hard every time he retracted, making him gasp as he struggled to rationalise the pleasure/pain ratio. He was gone now, lost to what Roxy knew was probably the best blow job he had ever experienced in his life, given by a woman who had picked up this technique from experts who would charge him more than a month's wages.

For Roxy, it was the ultimate rush — knowing without question that she might be the one on her knees, but he was most definitely at her mercy. As she let her teeth squeeze just a little on his undulating dick, she had to admire his stamina; most guys would have been finished, cleaned up and smoking a ciggie by now.

The frequency of the thrusts became faster now, faster, faster . . .

And, as always, her timing was perfect. At the very second he began to come, she pulled back and raised herself further up on her knees, pushing his exploding penis between her breasts and massaging it as every last drop of him covered her naked chest.

She grinned as she raised her eyes to see his face, his expression a combination of astonishment, confusion, joy, and, yes, admiration.

As she rose up, the adrenaline still pumping, the hormones colliding with more than a little rush of victory, she welcomed back that feeling of all-consuming excitement that had been posted missing the minute she'd stepped foot back into the rural equivalent of Mogadon.

To hell with good intentions and conservative behaviour — there was nothing like falling off the wagon and landing on your knees in spectacular style.

Yes, the penis embargo had been broken. And Darren Jenkins's glorious, forbidden dick had been the one to cross the picket line.

"It's time to put the family back at the centre of British culture," thundered Donald Davies in an address to Parliament this week. "And as elected representatives of the people we must lead this campaign by example."

At *Family Values* we've long been supporters of Mr Davies's principles and priorities, so we were thrilled to be invited to join Mr Davies and Clarissa, his delightful wife of forty years, at their Cotswolds home this week.

We were welcomed at the door by Clarissa, resplendent in riding clothes, fresh from a canter in a nearby field on her horse, Major. Sadly, her husband no longer rides, since a recent bout of gout resulted in the loss of two toes, impairing his capacity for physical exercise.

Entering their home, the hallway lined with jolly photographs of their four children and seven grandchildren, it's clear that this is a house not for business or show, but a house for family.

"It's about balance," Mr Davies reveals as we chat over a cup of tea and a delicious platter of homemade sandwiches. "I've never understood people who put their careers or personal pursuits before the most important thing in the world: their family. My lovely wife and my children always come first and in my opinion that is the key to restoring the standards of British culture that once made this country great.

"That's why I've put progressive, family-centric policies at the very heart of my campaign. In this country we have lost sight of the nuclear family, of the importance of nurturing our children within the stable bounds of a secure marriage."

Some of the more, shall we say, *left of centre* politicians have voiced their rejection of Mr Davies's views as "redundant" and "outdated". How does he view this opposition to principles that are clearly dear to his heart?

Ever the gentleman, he offers us another delectable sandwich before proceeding.

"I did not enter politics expecting to be unchallenged in my views. My answer to my detractors is, 'Look around you.' Haven't the last ten years demonstrated that the methods of the liberal majority are causing cataclysmic damage to the very fabric of British life? There is more crime, a lower standard of education, less respect for authority, and our religious institutions are reporting record low attendances. The country is, quite simply, failing to give its children a grounded, disciplined, moral upbringing. And it has to change."

Mr Davies has a clear view of the steps that must be put in place to make those changes.

"It's quite simple — we need mothers to be back in their homes. We need tax breaks and benefits that encourage marriage and, conversely, we need penalties for those who divorce. And we must make it perfectly clear that this moral stance is supported and adhered to from the highest echelons of the government. We need, quite frankly, to restore pride, dignity and a sense of decency to government and to the people."

And with that, Donald and Clarissa show us out and bid us farewell. Turning back, we see a couple with integrity, who have built a life based on the foundations of love, respect and togetherness.

Mr Davies, we salute you!

CHAPTER
TWELVE

Man, I Feel Like a Woman

Ginny. Day 13, Friday, 9p.m.

"Mr Davies, Mimi is ready for you now."

She breathed a sigh of relief as Donald Davies managed to push his lumbering frame out of the leather bucket-chair. Another few pounds and they'd need a JCB and a hoist. Davies panted with the exertion, his face mildly flushed, and then turned on that old public-school charm as he thanked her and waddled towards the elevator. Most customers used the stairs instead of the small service lift, but Davies had neither the inclination nor the lung capacity. As he puffed along, Ginny hoped that Mimi was planning on sticking to her preferred position on top, because otherwise there was every chance of a highly embarrassing encounter involving a team of paramedics and a defibrillator. And if that didn't go well, a shocked widow would have to live the rest of her life knowing that her husband died exhausted and erect.

Ginny smiled as the doors closed behind him and marvelled at how much this job was teaching her. If she hadn't come to London she'd never have learned that Donald Davies, her local MP, rounded off his week at

216

Westminster by paying a prostitute to scream, "You're the General, oh, baby, I want your cannon!" while she rode him into submission in the (thankfully) soundproofed Churchill Suite.

Ginny sat back down at reception and pressed a button on the intercom. Harry answered immediately.

"Harry, Mr Davies has just gone into the Churchill — so can you take up a Glenmorangie on ice, a Havana cigar and two ice packs for his knees in an hour. Oh, and keep anyone in the building with first-aid experience on standby," she added.

She checked her (Roxy's) Piaget watch: 9.15p.m. Forty-five minutes until knocking-off time, a phrase that took on a whole new meaning in this establishment. She checked the appointment book: no more clients due until 11p.m., an hour after she went off shift. Bliss.

She plumped down onto the cream leather desk chair, pulled off her (Roxy's) shoes, and rubbed the excruciatingly painful balls of her (definitely her) feet. Expensive shoes might be the epitome of chic, but the four-inch heels were murder on her arches. What she wouldn't give right now for the analgesic properties of a big glass of wine and a foot spa. Oh, and both of those could be administered while Jude was doing deliciously filthy things to her body. Her stomach bubbled at the memory. Jude. And her. She was still in shock after the sweaty events of last night and had been replaying snatched moments in her head all day, each one accompanied by a huge grin, pink cheeks and a tingling sensation in her chest. All those years with Darren and she could honestly say that only now did she understand why people risked their careers, reputations, marriages and (in the case of certain well-known MPs) parliamentary seats for incredible mind-blowing sex.

After the kitchen sex there had been the bathroom sex, the hall sex, and finally, when her legs were buckling with muscle fatigue, the bedroom sex. But not on the bed. The fourth frantic coupling had taken place with her bent over the dressing table and Jude standing behind her, his hands clutching her hips as they watched themselves in the mirror. Oh good Lord, her cervix was contracting at the memory. Who knew that she could be that horny? Or uninhibited? Or filthy? She'd never talked dirty in her life and yet things had come out of her mouth that night that she hadn't even realised she was capable of saying.

"Sore feet?"

No, that wasn't Ginny's idea of erotic mumblings, it was Sam, who had silently appeared from the back corridor and was now looking at her quizzically as she mentally replayed her own personal porn movie, *Ginny Does the Gigolo*.

Startled, Ginny spun round to face him, then relaxed slightly when she realised that:

a) As far as she was aware he couldn't read minds and therefore was blissfully oblivious to the fact that when he spoke to her the image in her mind was one of her bent double, her nipples pointing at the floor while a perfectly formed bloke rogered her senseless.

218

b) He was smiling and therefore apparently not upset by the fact that one of his employees had her tootsies on a three-thousand-pound, architecturally designed, state-of-the-art reception desk.

She swiftly returned them to the floor.

"Sorry, Sam, but high heels — what sick person invented them? I bet it was a male — and probably the same guy who invented miniskirts, corsets and the thong."

Sam bowed his head in reverence. "God bless him."

He was looking good tonight. He was wearing a beautifully cut black suit, and if you looked closely you could see the very subtle Medusa stamped into the buttons, indicating that it was Versace. His white shirt was open at the collar and his five o'clock shadow had developed into a fairly sexy stubble. Sexy only to look at, obviously, because snogging that would undoubtedly be like undergoing a skin peel by dermabrasion.

She pulled her shoes back on — red Kurt Geiger four-inch stilettos that coordinated beautifully with her (Roxy's) black Escada split-thigh jersey wrap dress and (Roxy's) Butler & Wilson ruby earrings the size of pebbles — and waited for instructions.

"I'm just going to make a coffee — would you like one?"

"Isn't it my job to make you a coffee?" she asked. This was a first. Sam normally either had one of the butlers bring his drinks up from the kitchen downstairs or asked her to fetch him one from the staffroom.

"It's okay, I'll get them. You've been on all day and in those heels another trip to the coffee machine could end in Casualty. Anyway, I just checked and the staff room is empty so I can sneak in free of danger from what Roxy calls the 'Muff Mafia'."

Two minutes later he was back with two mugs of coffee. He handed her one, and then, just as Ginny was expecting him to retreat back into his office, leaving her to contemplate the X-rated memory of the stimulating and frankly unexpected things that Jude had done with the shower gel during the bathroom segment, he sat down on one of the overstuffed cream leather sofas.

She took a sip and then tried not to show that the coffee was so hot it had removed the top layer of skin from her lips.

"Careful, it's a bit hot — I used one of those sachet things instead of real milk."

"Got that," she gasped, wondering if Harry had any more ice packs that could save her from waking up tomorrow morning looking like a puffer fish.

"So, how's Roxy doing?"

Okay, this was confusing. Sam was her boss and in almost two weeks (with the exception of the whole "Darren's chucked me — sob" débâcle) their conversations had consisted purely of work conversations and general pleasantries.

Was he easing into a difficult conversation? Was he about to fire her? Did he want her to consider providing extras à la the girls upstairs?

Was this how it worked? Today: reception duties, booking systems and general admin. Tomorrow: dressed in a maid's outfit and sucking the upper-class

220

appendage of a member of the House of Lords who insisted you called him "Uncle Charles"?

Or, hang on . . . Had Roxy called him? Had she come straight off the phone to Ginny and speed-dialled Sam to spread the misconceived story that Ginny was in some way participant in sexual relations with Felix? She wouldn't! Would she? Of course she would, Ginny realised with a sinking heart — it was Roxy. She'd probably already notified everyone she'd ever met, contacted the national press, and put an announcement on Facebook.

Shit, now he was going to think she was immoral, cheap and easy — and definitely working on the wrong floor.

"Why, what did she tell you?" she replied, flustered.

Was it Ginny's imagination or did he look a bit uncomfortable?

"Nothing. I haven't spoken to her. I've left a couple of messages on her mobile, you know, just checking how she's doing and what her plans are and stuff, but she hasn't got back to me. Probably enjoying herself too much in the peace and tranquillity of the countryside."

Phew, relief!

"So do you know — has she decided whether she's coming back? I mean, I know she resigned but then she's resigned about a dozen times and always arrived back the next day — not that she's volatile, of course," he finished with a really cute grin.

Why hadn't she noticed his really cute grin before? Hang on, what was going on with her? Did you have mind-blowing nookie and all of a sudden you became this highly sexed being who viewed everyone around you as a potential conquest? And, she wondered with just a touch of flippancy, would that really be so bad?

She inhaled deeply. There was no escaping it — twenty-seven years old and she was finally experiencing a sexual awakening. And it was more than a gentle rousing of her sexuality — her libido was jumping up and down on the end of the bed, dressed in crotchless knickers and a peephole bra, clutching a condom while screaming "Rise and shine and let me at 'em".

Mmm, crotchless knickers, peep hole bra . . .

"Ginny?"

"Sorry, sorry, I was just thinking about your question. Which was . . . Roxy. Coming back. That's right. I'm not sure, to be honest. You know what she's like — she likes to be spontaneous and, erm . . ."

"Totally irresponsible, erratic and unreliable?" he added, with the grin that was getting cuter by the second.

"I was going for 'dynamic'."

"Okay, we'll call it dynamic. In an irresponsibly unreliable kind of way."

Silence, while they both sat there looking at each other, wondering what came next. She still wasn't quite sure whether this was a social chat or a loaded conversation that would end with her removal from the premises. Sam was obviously struggling here — he seemed a little edgy, nervous, not at all his usual together, controlled self. This chat was pole-vaulting

222

across the line from "mildly uncomfortable" to "buttock-clenchingly excruciating."

She was absolutely no use at this. It suddenly occurred to her that when it came to long, in-depth verbal interaction with the opposite sex, she was out of practice. Or maybe she'd never actually been "in practice". Ridiculous as it now seemed, she couldn't remember the last time she and Darren had actually just spent some time really talking. And the vocabulary and sentence structure that she volunteered in the presence of Jude was hardly going to win a debating prize. Unless it was at the Porn Olympics. In fact, the only bloke she really, *really* spoke to was Mitch. A smile played on her lips as an image of his bedraggled hair and mismatched clothes came into her head. She missed him. She missed his easy chat and his rubbish jokes and the way nothing — not even her mother on a HobNob and HRT-fuelled rampage — ever flustered him. Maybe she'd give him a call and see if he wanted to come up to London for the weekend. They could see the sights, catch a show, get naked and filthy . . . Wow — she abruptly snapped out of it. Mother of God, what had happened to her?

Thankfully, Sam finally spoke. "The thing is . . . erm . . . actually, we'd still love to have her back here. The clients liked her, and although she was pretty scatty she actually did a fairly good job. So what about the boyfriend — are they back together? Only, I guess that would affect her decisions, wouldn't it?"

Ah, Ginny understood now. He felt awkward talking to her because he was trying to work out whether or not Roxy had definitely left for good so that he could start the recruitment process to find a replacement — and Ginny obviously wasn't in the running for the job. She couldn't deny she felt a twinge of sadness — not that she'd even considered staying there after the month was done, but it would have been nice to have been asked.

"No, she's definitely not back together with Felix. To be honest, I wouldn't bet on that one having a happy ending. He was a bit of a, erm —"

"Prick?"

"That time you got it spot on."

Destiny appeared at the doorway, wearing thigh-high black leather boots, a rubber catsuit and a Batgirl mask. "Stephen Knight is going to have to get over the whole 'Batman rejection/Christian Bale stole my role' thing before I have chafe marks that will never heal. Sam, all the girls are busy upstairs — can I borrow Ginny to help me get out of this garb before the prickly heat sets in?"

"Sure, on you go. Jenny will be here in five minutes and I'll cover until she arrives."

"Thanks, Sam. By the way, are you coming out with us tonight?"

"No, I've got some stuff I need to catch up on."

"What about you, Ginny? Fancy swinging your bits with me and the girls?"

Ginny thought about it: the sore feet, the aching bones, the fact that she was walking like she'd just given birth to quads — of course she wasn't going out. But then, Jude *was* staying overnight in Leeds after a

224

personal appearance as the star attraction at a WAGs hen night. She hoped he'd survive it intact.

Meanwhile, did she really want to go home to an empty flat?

Much as she was currently orbiting Planet Ecstasy, she knew that an empty flat would catapult her crashing to earth, where she'd land on her backside and be forced to confront the questions that her current euphoria was currently suppressing.

1. What did last night mean for her and Jude?

2. Was this the start of a new relationship or just a one-night fling?

3. Did she want a new relationship?

4. Or another one-night fling?

5. Shouldn't she feel some kind of remorse, regret or jealousy that he was probably right now revealing his dick to the most expensively accessorised group of women in the country?

6. Shouldn't she still be mourning the loss of Darren?

7. Why had Darren never licked cream from her nipples or drunk champagne from her cu — nope, unlike her sexual Tourette's of the night before, she couldn't even think or say that word while fully clothed and in a public place — from her *flower*.

8. How did Jude feel?

9. Did he have feelings for her or was this just another shag to him?

10. What was his surname?

11. And did it go with Ginny?

12. Aaaargh, why was she thinking such pathetic, needy, conventional thoughts?

13. Had Roxy calmed down and realised that she was being ridiculous yet?

14. And would Roxy ever take her calls so that she could enlighten her to the truth?

15. How would she feel when this month was over?

16. Could she go back to her old life?

17. Would Jude want her to?

18. If his surname didn't match hers could she just keep her maiden name?

19. Aaaargh! Again — why was she thinking such ridiculous thoughts?

20. And why, oh why, when all this drama was swirling like a tornado around her, did she feel giddy, warm and bubbly every time she thought of the master class in genital stimulation from the night before?

Ginny nodded as she gingerly stood up — not too fast for fear that her muscles would snap like overstretched elastic bands.

"You know, I think I'll come for a little while."

"Great. Right, come help me change then — you get the talc, I'll get the crowbar."

In the empty staffroom, Destiny turned her back to Ginny and leaned over the table, a position that triggered Ginny's four hundred and fifty-sixth flashback of the day.

"Okay, unzip it — but do it slowly, especially when you get near the bottom or I'll have welts on my arse for weeks."

226

Ginny contemplated the sight in front of her and was suddenly curious as to how Sam would phrase the requirements for this job in a situations-vacant ad. To her recollection, she'd never read an advert in the *Times* that included "Must be open-minded, discreet and proficient in the ancient art of stripping rubber from the buttocks of fetish experts."

She reached over to the top of the industrial-strength zipper, and as her body mirrored Destiny's she tried not to dwell on the fact that she was the skinniest she'd ever been in her life, yet Destiny's hips were still a good two inches narrower.

Slowly, gently, she eased the zip down, vertebra by vertebra, watching the back of Destiny's ribcage expand with every inch that the opening widened. She slowed even further when she reached the small of her back, easing the zipper very gently down to its resting place at the bottom of the buttocks — right above a thick black nylon square gusset that stretched from front to back and was held on by Velcro for easy removal.

It was a strange, strange world. And what was even stranger was that none of this seemed in the least bit strange any more. In an incredibly short space of time, the Farnham Hills librarian had, she realised, become so desensitised that she would find it odd returning to a workplace that didn't require the lubrication cupboard to be restocked on a daily basis.

Destiny stood up straight and turned to face her. "This is the worst bit. I swear if we had a union I'd demand danger money for this job. Okay, help me peel it down and don't stop even if I scream. It's like taking a plaster off — better to just bite the bullet and get it over with."

"Don't worry, I'm an expert — you've no idea how often I have to do this after the Holy Union of Dominatrix Christmas Dance in the community centre."

Destiny shrieked with laughter as Ginny started to pull the rubber down from her neck, over her shoulders, to just above her tits now. She moved to one side and released an arm, then moved to the other and did the same again. Back to the front now, she eased it down over Destiny's breasts, each one springing up as it escaped captivity.

Actually, come to think of it, her face was now two inches away from another woman's breasts — perhaps this was still just a *little* strange.

She rolled the suit down further, over ribs, waist, abdomen, and now pelvis, going down over her . . . her . . . hang on, there was something missing here. It was only when she got to the top of the thighs that it was confirmed — another lady garden that was no stranger to the Brazilian Flymo.

A few seconds later, one leg was finally released, followed by the other, then Ginny (not without some considerable strain on her poor, pummelled thigh muscles) retraced the path she'd just taken as she stretched back up to a standing position.

And when she reached the top, *nothing*. No movement, barely a breath, just an incredible realisation that she was once again experiencing the same hormonal rush that she'd had when Destiny was pole-dancing on the bar top.

She was in front of a naked woman, with only six inches separating them, and she was definitely, absolutely, feeling turned on. What the hell was Jude putting in her morning bagel? Two weeks before she'd been Ginny Wallis, sexually reticent, and now she had somehow morphed into Madonna in her experimental years.

Of course, she'd occasionally given the odd passing thought as to whether or not she could ever be attracted to a woman — usually when reading the endless surveys in the kind of farcical, conservative newspapers that claimed a huge percentage of the population were closet bisexuals but as long as they didn't infiltrate the Royal Family we'd still prevail as a nation.

Oh, and while watching documentaries about Angelina Jolie.

But she'd honestly never contemplated being personally physical with a member of the same sex. Then again, until recently she'd never contemplated shagging a male stripper while hanging from the top of a Smeg fridge freezer.

Weird how life turned out sometimes.

"Ginny, honey, do you know you're staring at me?" Destiny asked with a distinct tone of teasing amusement.

"Oh, God, I'm sorry. I'm really sorry. It's just . . . erm . . . just . . ."

Destiny was laughing now as she grabbed a pink silk robe from a coat peg behind the door and pulled it on.

"S'okay honey, you don't have to explain. But if you ever want to do anything about that thought you were having there, just you let me know."

And with that, Destiny turned and strutted out of the room, the noise of her laughter audible long after she'd gone.

Ginny sank down onto a seat and placed her arms on the table, then let her head fall on top of them.

This was too much. Mentally, physically, sexually, this was all too much. She didn't know if she was coming, going, or just hanging around choosing random people on which to foist her new-found sexual liberation.

Too, too much. And it had to stop.

"Ginny, are you ready to go, sweetie? The limo will be here in five minutes."

That was Mimi, who'd politely escorted Mr Davies to the door, kissed him on the cheek, waved politely as his car had driven him out of view, then turned around, pulled his hundred-quid tip out of her scarlet corset and high-fived a passing Deedee.

Ginny gently lifted her weary, exhausted head and tried to get her facial muscles to contort into something resembling a smile.

"Of course I am, just a couple of things to sort out — I don't suppose anyone has a couple of Paracetamol and a spare set of flat shoes, size six?"

Excerpt from Mitch's journal — present day . . .

And so the education in *Life According to a Certain Miss Galloway* continues (note to self — great title for next book?). I now know that an iPod isn't a suspicious growth in the optical area, a Slow Comfortable Screw won't make the earth move unless you consume a dozen of them, and blokes called Dolce, Gabbana, Galliano and Lagerfeld are more important than God.

And I've laughed more than I've ever done in my life. Jesus, she's mental. Last night we got caught sneaking out of her bedroom window by her mother and her Auntie Vi. I did point out to her that she was twenty-seven and therefore quite entitled to leave via the front door, even after dark, but she was on a nostalgia trip that seemed to necessitate hiding a bottle of vino under her bed, smoking while hanging out of the window and then leaving via a twenty-foot drop without the aid of a parachute.

Why? No idea. This is the third night in a row that she's dragged me down her memory lane and every trip seems to involve cigarettes, alcohol and the risk of fractures, hypothermia and/or arrest.

I can't decide whether she's on some kind of crazed mission to take her mind off that eejit who trashed her, or considering a career in stunt work, or borderline certifiable.

Or maybe all three.

But here's the thing . . . For all her bravado and outrageousness, there's vulnerability under there that just makes you want to hold her and make everything better for her. Of course, she'd kick you in the bollocks if you even tried.

The whole Ginny situation sums it up. Roxy is spitting hell and damnation on Ginny's head to anyone who will listen, but yet . . . well, three times now I've caught her with tears in her eyes, and I don't care what she says, no one has that kind of reaction to polyester.

And the thing is, it's difficult to reason with her. Maybe I'm being a gullible sap but I'm pretty sure that she hasn't got the full story about what went on there so it could be that all this drama is unnecessary. I've tried telling her this a dozen times but she gets so pissed off that I'm not risking it again without full body armour and a riot shield.

Hang on — phone's ringing . . .

Right, must go . . . That was Roxy and she says I've to meet her in an alley behind the youth club and come armed with a two-litre bottle of cider. Just struck me that if she's crazy then what does it say about me that I'm going along with her?

White jacket, big buckles . . .

The End.

PS: The not-so-insignificant matter of the heart/declarations/I've-loved-you-since-the-first-minute-I-saw-you situation? Still on hold. Still working up to it.

Maybe that body armour will come in handy on more than one occasion . . .

CHAPTER
THIRTEEN

Have I Told You Lately?

Roxy. Day 14, Saturday, 8 p.m.
  "Am I a female?"
  "Yes."
  "Am I alive?"
  "Yes."
  "Am I a superhero?"
  "No."
  "Am I in movies?"
  "No."
  "Television?"
  "No."
  "Cartoons?"
  "No."
  "Politics?"
  "No."
  "Music?"
  "No."
  "Am I rich?"
  "Yes."
  "Am I married?"
  Pause. "Yes."
  "Am I Victoria Beckham?"

Mitch leaned over and pulled the Post-It note from Roxy's forehead, then turned it around to show her that "Posh" was written on it in blue biro.

"How did you get it so quickly?" he asked, suitably impressed with her powers of perception.

"The 'famous for nothing' thing. It was a toss-up between Vicky B and Paris Hilton — and Paris is single."

"God, you're good," he teased.

"Ah, that's what they all tell me," she replied. And if Mitch hadn't been too busy throwing chips in the air then trying to catch them in his mouth, he'd have detected the subtle tone of poignancy in her voice.

Actually, what Darren had told her was, "[*gasp*] Roxy, [*gasp*] you are sen . . . [*gasp*] . . . fucking . . . [*gasp*] . . . sational."

A strange sensation rose from her toes, flipped her stomach and gave her goose bumps. She couldn't be sure but she had a horrible feeling that it was called guilt. Shit, there it was again. In fact, it had been arriving on schedule every time she conjured up a mental picture of the goings-on on the kitchen linoleum.

But then, didn't that fall under "justifiable revenge"? It did. Definitely. Ginny was the one person she loved more than anyone else and she'd destroyed a lifetime of friendship for what? A quick fuck with a florist's ex-boyfriend. Well, she deserved to know just how it felt when the tables were turned. It was tit for tat. Or rather, tits for . . . Oh bloody, bloody bugger, there was that feeling again.

She knocked out both the guilt and the memory with a right hook from the Pathetically Indulgent School of Self-defence.

"In fact, Felix used to tell me that regularly until he fucked off with a florist then shagged my best friend," she spat, the bitterness in her voice so sharp that if the Post-It notes had the powers of emotional intelligence they'd be trembling and curling up at the edges.

Mitch froze, causing a chip to fly past his face and land in his lap.

"Do not even go there again. How many times do I have to tell you that you're wrong? He was lying."

"But she admitted it!"

"She did not admit it! Roxy, you didn't even give her the chance to speak or explain before you jumped down her throat and hung up. And have you spoken to her since?"

She popped a chip into her mouth and then held up her plastic cutlery.

"I'd rather amputate my nipples with this fork."

Mitch shook his head in despair, but Roxy didn't notice, given that she was too busy tobogganing down the slippery slope to anger, homicidal urges and calorific excess.

This was bad. Negative emotions put years on your face and now she was eating items of food that had come into contact with a deep-fat fryer. She wasn't sure what was worse: the overwhelming urge to murder her erstwhile best friend or the increasing desire to steal a local ned's souped-up Corsa and ramraid the local chippy for a battered saveloy.

But hey, if she did either of those things it would take her away from the sheer joy and delight she felt about the inescapable reality that she was lying on the floor in the lounge of a church-house on a Saturday night, eating carbohydrates and playing inane games with a grown man who was slouched on a nearby couch wearing the chichi combination of a Flintstones T-shirt and Birkenstocks. In winter.

She wondered how long it would take her to bleed out if she pointed the fork towards her heart then plunged it in really hard.

"So where's your uncle tonight then?"

"Usual. Saturday-night mass down at the remand centre, followed by marriage counselling over in the church hall."

"No difference there then — they're both serving custodial sentences. He'd be better just giving the marriage lot the number of a good divorce lawyer and telling them to run for their lives. Relationships are shit."

Mitch nodded solemnly in mock acquiescence. "You know, you should definitely consider a career as a therapist, because those people skills of yours are going to waste."

There were a few moments of silence while Mitch caught three more chips and Roxy tortured herself with the mental image of Felix and Ginny, toasting each other with Bollinger while travelling first class to Barbados for a five-star break of sun, sea and other activities that necessitated leg-waxing. That excruciating snapshot then slid into such a vivid, realistic daydream that she almost felt a twinge of sadness when Ginny was swallowed whole by a great white shark and Felix consoled himself with a three-day binge of debauchery that left him destitute, lost and suffering from several sexually transmitted diseases.

"You're smiling — what are you thinking about?"

"Making amends with Felix by sending him on holiday. What brochure has those special activity trips, the ones where the plane gets hijacked on the way there, then there's a bird flu outbreak and you end up quarantined in a disease-ridden prison cell with two lepers, three blokes with bagpipes and Paul Burrell?"

"Are you always this happy-go-lucky?" he asked with mock concern.

Roxy rolled onto her back and stared at the ceiling. "Nooooo! That's the whole point! Mitch, do you know what I'd normally be doing right now? I'd be wearing Dolce & Gabbana, having dinner in an exclusive, Michelin-starred restaurant before being whisked by limo to a members-only VIP club where I'd fend off the Arsenal squad and David Hasselhoff before Felix and I left to spend the night in his squillion-quid penthouse flat overlooking the Thames. Look around you — are you getting what's wrong with this picture?"

"Can I just remind you that two weeks ago you'd had enough of London?"

"Yeah, well, I understand now that that was a temporary blip with a sound scientific reason behind it."

"And what was that?"

"PMT."

She stuck another chip in her mouth. It was true that she still missed her life . . . but the truth was she missed Ginny more. The old Ginny, that was — not new slut Ginny who had apparently lost control of her values, her morals and her vagina.

And sure, she did miss the excitement and little luxuries of her London life, but yet . . . Well, somehow she didn't quite feel compelled to go back there yet. Best-friend betrayal plus murderous urges should have had her on the first train back to Shaggerville Central, but for some reason she couldn't quite fathom, she couldn't face it. Could it be that fresh air and the heady country fumes of pesticide and cow dung had addled her brain? After all, weren't those the very things that were responsible for beating the crap out of the ozone layer?

"Okay, that's it, Miss Prissy-Arse, moping over. Come on, we're going out."

"Unless Gordon Ramsay and luxury transportation are involved, I'm not interested."

"Move!"

The ferocity of his tone made her take notice — for a whole three seconds before she plunged back into lethargy. *Purleeze.* This was a bloke who trapped spiders and released them into the wild without harming them; did he honestly think he could bully her into action?

"Move right now or I'm calling Ginny and telling her that you're desperate to speak to her."

On the other hand, he did put up a good argument.

"You wouldn't," she dared him in her deadliest voice, the one she normally kept for telephone sales people and the legendary theatre actor who liked to be dominated and requested that he be treated with contempt from the moment he arrived at the Seismic. Oh, pang of homesickness — perhaps the cow-dung sensory overload wasn't permanent after all. She missed the girls, she missed Sam, she even missed the legendary crooner who kept overdosing on Viagra and poppers and trying to dry-hump the vacuum cleaner.

Mitch got up, crossed the room to the huge black circle-dial telephone that was perched on a rickety tripod side table and picked up the receiver.

"Watch me."

"Okay, okay, but this had better be good and there had better be a drink at the end of it. My new plan of escape from this hellhole involves excessive alcohol and rehab."

As they passed the front door, she lifted her cardigan from the coat rack, and as she pulled it on she caught her reflection in the vestibule mirror: pink mohair, ankle-length, size eighteen, borrowed from her mother's wardrobe. She looked like a cross between a furry beach ball and Elton John in his flamboyant phase.

They walked down the path and she pulled her collar tight around her neck as the cold air snapped against her skin, then pushed her arm through Mitch's in the hope that some extra body heat might stave off a slow and painful death from hypothermia. She hated the cold almost as much as she hated Farnham Hills,

Ginny, and any pursuit that resulted in perspiration. Other than sex, of course. Sex. Oh, don't even go there.

As she and Mitch walked in silence, the mental image of Darren, dick dangling, flashed in front of her. She couldn't deny she'd enjoyed their little encounter but the remorse had started to set in before she'd even climbed off her knees. Unfortunately, the initial remorse had been all his.

Was there kissing? No. Sweet words? No. Cuddles? Actually, given the destination of his ejaculation that one would have been decidedly unhygienic.

But there was absolutely nothing except a panicked expression (his), some stuttering (him) and then an excuse about having to go (his) before he pulled up his kegs and bolted, leaving her stunned, surprised and urgently in need of a shower.

She didn't relish the prospect of meeting him again. Number one on her Things To Do List had gone from being "Take Contract Out On Felix" to "Avoid Darren Jenkins".

They were fifty yards away from the pub now, thank God. If ever she was in dire need of a cocktail it was now. She could almost taste the Cosmopolitan when Mitch suddenly steered her to the left and they crossed the road towards the community centre. Lights were flickering in the windows, and as they got halfway across the road she realised she could hear music.

She groaned and stopped dead, causing a pensioner in a Fiat Punto to swerve, take out three road cones and narrowly avoid a fatal collision with a give-way sign.

240

"Mitch, if you're taking me line dancing you're going to have to kill me first."

"I promise it isn't line dancing. Come on . . ."

He pulled her towards the door, and gestured to the hand-made sign beside it.

Oh no. This was worse than line dancing. It was worse than the pub. This was as bad as it got. It was probably on a par with watching Felix and Ginny stage a live sex show in the middle of Primark while Celine Dion's *Greatest Hits* blared in the background.

She stared at the sign.

> *Farnham Hills Youth Club* —
> *Here 2 Nite* — *£3 entry*
> *Free Soft Drink and Crisps*
> *NO ALCOHOL, VANDALISM OR*
> *ROWDY BEHAVIOUR*

"Mitch, do you really, really hate me?" she whined pitifully.

He leaned over and kissed her on the cheek. "Nope, I think you're deceptively lovely. Now come on, it's not so bad, I promise. I've been helping out every fortnight since I got here and I haven't been seriously injured even once. And at least it'll take your mind of all that other stuff. I'll make them promise to be gentle with you."

"Are you taking the piss out of me again?"

"Absolutely. Come on, hurry up before the frost gets to my extremities."

And with that and an unceremonious push he cannoned her inside. Right on cue, the banging of the

241

door coincided with the record ending and forty teenagers turned to stare. There was a mixed reaction: disinterest, curiosity, and from some familiar faces in the corner there came the distinct vibe of hostility. Lip-reading might not have been a talent that Roxy listed on her CV, but she knew enough to recognise several pouting *Aw, fucks* when she saw them.

Roxy inhaled sharply, pushed her shoulders back and rearranged her face into "defiant and hard". She knew that teenagers worked on the same principle as aggressive dogs — they could smell fear.

She tried to find the positives. First, at least there was no chance of an awkward meeting with Darren here, and second, she realised as she scanned the crowd, there had to be at least one reprobate with a stash of contraband alcohol. Or maybe some weed.

Her eyes fell on the fifth-year study group, four boys and four girls, sitting huddled around a table in the corner, all of them still giving her a look that indicated she was about as welcome as headlice and gainful employment.

"Hey, Mitch, how're you doing?"

And thanks to the gods of Embarrassing Situations and Shit Social Events for the latest contribution to the evening. Yes, the voice came from Darren Jenkins as he appeared from a side room and spotted Mitch.

The startled body language and horrified expression came straight after when he realised that Roxy was there too.

"Roxy," he mumbled in the voice of doom with an accompanying nod.

Roxy just raised her eyes in disdain, causing Mitch to completely misinterpret the situation.

"Come on, you two," he interjected. "Can't you just put your differences aside and play nice for just one night?"

Cornered, trapped, a siege situation, there was only one way to handle this: Roxy's inner child decided to come to the party.

She smiled her sweetest, most innocent smile. "You're right, Mitch. Well, what do you think, Darren, babe — would you like to play nice?"

He stared at her for a second, then turned and walked off without saying a word. Roxy shrugged as she turned to Mitch.

"Right then, Kofi Annan, shall we take that as a 'no'?"

"You know, I don't understand why you two have to be so hard on one another."

Roxy grimaced at the irony. "Yep, he's definitely been far too hard on me. Okay, might as well go mingle with my public."

She discarded the neon cardigan on a nearby chair and strutted over to her favourite fan club. They all tried to avoid eye contact, hoping that if they ignored her she'd divert over to the thirteen-year-olds applying temporary tattoos at the next table.

"Hello, chums! Don't worry about lavishing me with overly affectionate greetings, I know you're choked and thrilled that I'm here," she baited. Her gaze rested on Romeo and Juliet, whose intertwined limbs could prove to be fatal should there be the requirement to move quickly in the case of a fire or flood.

It was strange to see the gang out of school uniform. The boys were all in similar baggy jeans, topped with an assortment of sports T-shirts and zip-up sweaters. The girls, however, were definitely channelling Girls Aloud — casually waved, long glossy hair, the kind of natural no-make-up look that required an hour of make-up application, false nails manicured into square white tips, skinny jeans, platform shoes and strappy smock tops that flowed over their size-eight hips. Although she'd rather eat her pink cardi than say it out loud, Roxy was actually pretty impressed at how well they scrubbed up — which was a sign that either they weren't such country hicks after all or she was suffering from some kind of carbohydrate-induced delusional disorder.

Either way, she needed medicinal intervention.

She leaned in so that only they could hear her. "Okay, who's got the booze stash?"

There was a ten-second silence, until Juliet finally spoke. "Is this so that you can confiscate it again, same as you did in the pub?"

"Absolutely."

Like the underage-drinking equivalent of an Olympic synchronised swimming team, their jaws all set into identical grim lines at exactly the same instant and stayed that way until Roxy spoke again.

"But I'll give it back right after I've sampled it and a tenner has found its way into your back pocket. Toilets?"

The four girls looked at each other, and then announced, "Twenty and it's a deal."

Roxy rolled her eyes. "Bloody hell, that's scandalous. What's happened to the youth of today?"

They pushed their chairs back, picked up their clinking handbags, and motioned to Roxy to follow them. Ten minutes and many swigs of vodka and ginger beer later, and with Roxy's back pocket twenty quid lighter, they returned to the table. The boys had all shifted off to bring each other to a premature and gruesome death on the Xboxes set up in the far corner, so it was girls only, and despite their little illegal transaction they were still decidedly uncomfortable and eyeing Roxy with suspicion.

"Look, peace, okay? I'm about as happy to be here as you lot are to have me, but since it's here or freezing your hooters off outside, you're as well making the most of it. So, come on then, let's, er, chat. What were you talking about when I arrived?"

Glances shot between them again before one finally said, "Our physics prelim. It's next week."

This was met with a groan of derision. "Physics? Are you taking the piss? It's Saturday night and you're talking about physics? Aren't you lot supposed to be in the middle of a teenage rebellion that involves hard drugs, violence, sex and shoplifting?"

One of the girls raised her eyebrow and sneered, "Could you be more, like, snide? You have, like, no idea what you're talking about."

Roxy matched the glare. "So go on then, educate me about the wonders of teenage life. Start with your names."

They answered one by one. "Lindsay." "Carrie." "Saffron." Then it was the turn of Roxy's arch nemesis — the girl whose antics were responsible for the unusually high condom sales in the village. "Juliet."

"You're kidding me!"

"Why? What's so strange about that?"

"Nothing. It's a . . . lovely name. And what about lover-boy over there? Don't tell me his name's Romeo," Roxy shrieked, trying unsuccessfully to contain her mirth.

Juliet stared at her, her face blank, her voice deadpan, obviously aggrieved at being the butt of the joke. "It is."

Roxy quickly stopped laughing. The atmosphere at the table had plummeted back to Arctic level and she could sense that the natives were getting restless. Okay, plan B was . . . nope, she didn't have a plan B.

Suddenly all four girls dissolved into fits of giggles. It took a while until Juliet could stutter through the hilarity, "Kidding — it's Ben. But your face was, like, so lame."

Roxy slumped back in her chair. These creatures were one hundred per cent pure evil, and worse, they were laughing at her. She'd gone from being Miss Cool, Chic and Utterly Enviable to being target practice for Satan's spawn.

She pulled her bag onto her lap and pulled out her cigarettes. Juliet took a sharp intake of breath when she spotted the familiar crest. "Wow, is that a Fendi Spy?" she exclaimed, visibly awestruck as her eyes locked on the butter-soft nappa bag with the distinctive handles and the strange cylindrical bit at the top for holding your money/lippy/tampon.

With three excited gasps, her chums followed suit.

And that was the moment Roxy knew she had them.

Forty-five minutes of fashion talk later, with a quick five-minute break to hang out the bathroom windows clutching Marlboros, they were her new very best friends.

"No way, the Paddington is, like, *soooo* over," Roxy declared in what she reckoned was her very best teenage-icon lingo. The girls were now hanging on her every word, giving her ego its first boost since she'd disembarked from that train a fortnight before. They'd done the pros and cons of every on-trend bag for the last two years, the merits of the new Dolce & Gabbana winter collection and discussed the moral and physical consequences of the size zero — a topical debate that would have been highly impressive if it hadn't included Lindsay's insightful, highbrow viewpoint that catwalk models were, "Eeeeew, totally skanky, man — must be like shagging a stick."

Roxy took that as a clue that they'd exhausted that particular line of conversation. "Okay, enough superficial stuff — let's talk serious stuff." She scanned the room. "Who's hot and who's not?"

Her gaze went to the Xbox corner and she nudged Juliet.

"Ben?"

"Hot!" Juliet replied indignantly.

"Not!" chorused her pals. Juliet rewarded them with a bird's-eye view of her middle finger.

"Okay, who's next?"

The girls got there before her.

"Darren," leered Saffron.

"Hot!" A unanimous decision among the girls. Roxy watched him as he handed out cans of Coke to a group of guys who were huddled around TV monitors, all engrossed in saving the planet from invasion, nuclear attack or a four—nil defeat at intergalactic football.

"He's totally lush! Just a shame he's so ancient."

"He's twenty-seven!" Roxy exclaimed.

The other three nodded dolefully in agreement. "Exactly — totally ancient. Probably needs Viagra to get it up," Saffron added to the amusement of the others.

Ancient?! Roxy put her hand to her forehead. Bad idea — she was sure she felt a new wrinkle. There she was thinking she was still in the prime of her youth and these three had her down as approaching end of shelf-life.

And although it was a cast-iron rebuttal of their misconceptions, she thought it probably best that she didn't enlighten them on Darren's capacity for drug-free erectile function.

She watched the girls checking out the other talent on offer. Juliet was actually quite sweet when she wasn't attached to her boyfriend and commando-crawling into public toilets. Lindsay seemed pretty switched-on and sharp. Carrie was shyer, a little more reserved than the other three. And Saffron was definitely the gob of the group: Lily Allen on E-numbers.

248

Roxy was developing a sense of dislike there, but then implications that you should be researching the pros and cons of burial, cremation or cryogenic preservation could have that effect.

"What about Mitch?" suggested Juliet.

"Hot!" her ageist coven crowed.

Okay, so now Roxy knew they were officially insane. She looked over at Mitch, strumming an Arctic Monkeys' song on a guitar while about twelve youngsters sat around him nodding their heads in time to the beat.

He was cute. He was sweet. He was funny.

He also looked like he'd got dressed by wrapping himself in double-sided tape then streaking through Ashton Kutcher's wardrobe — the one he hadn't opened since 1999.

"Definitely hot. He's, like, totally channelling Orlando Bloom."

"And that's a good thing?" asked Roxy. Frankly she'd never seen the appeal of Mr Bloom — too young, too baby-faced, too named after a holiday resort. She preferred men who looked like they were old enough to shave.

"Like, duh!" offered Carrie. Right then. Nods all round.

Mitch must have sensed their stares because he chose that moment to turn around and meet her gaze. He grinned and gave her a wink, invoking an amused chorus of "Ooooooooooooohhhhhhh"'s from her new VBFs.

"Uh-oh, uh-oh, I think he likes you," Juliet chanted, with accompanying drum-rolls on the table.

"Piss off," Roxy replied, then realised to her absolute horror that her face was turning a mild shade of Johansson. Ooh, get her — she was making up her own slang now. Although that happy thought didn't detract from her general pissed-off disposition. "He does not!" she muttered. "I mean, he does, but not in that way. We're friends."

All four were now thumping their hands on the table and joining in the chorus of, "Uh-oh, uh-oh, I think he likes you. Uh-oh, uh-oh, I think he likes you. Uh-oh, uh-oh . . ."

"Very mature," said Roxy dryly, an insult that had the perverse effect of making them sing even louder.

"Shut up," she hissed as she simultaneously snatched off her shoes and grabbed Juliet's handbag. She held the heel above it in a threatening manner. "One more word and the vodka gets it."

The music changed now, the smoky tones of Paolo Nutini's "Last Request" filled the room. Obviously the youth-club funds still only stretched to new records on a biannual basis. The title was definitely apt, though. She briefly wondered if the judge would show leniency if she could demonstrate that she'd been subjected to undue provocation.

"Okay, okay," Juliet capitulated, fighting valiantly to rein in her ear-to-ear grin. She eased the bag out of Roxy's hands and placed it in a safe position beyond breaking distance. "We won't say another word. We promise."

250

It was an official ceasefire. Roxy's hackles slowly returned to their normal position, until . . . "Not another thing about him *luuuuuurvin* you!" teased Juliet in the voice of a *Clueless* character, while swinging her arms from side to side in some kind of teenage victory ritual. The other three creased into laughter again, and it was so contagious that Roxy's ire gradually melted.

A memory of herself and Ginny, dressed in off-the-shoulder mini-dresses (although the effect of Ginny's outfit was somewhat spoiled by the jeans that she refused to remove), shaking their bits to Oasis's "Roll With It" in this very building twelve years before flitted into her mind. They'd been inseparable then, in a time before distance, diverse lives and her boyfriend's wayward penis had forced them apart.

"So what joke did I miss then?"

She'd been so distracted that she hadn't noticed that Mitch had broken away from his worshipping audience and wandered over to their table.

"Oh, Juliet here was just saying how she thinks that you are absolutely adorable and you're her very first crush on a male whose voice has broken."

"I did not!" screeched Juliet, outraged and mortified.

Roxy winked at her as her girlfriends swapped any trace of loyalty for uncontrollable hilarity.

"She did," continued Roxy deadpan. "She said she plans to wait until she's twenty-one and then track you down and tell you she — what was it again? — she *luuuuuuuuurves you!*"

251

Mitch looked suitably abashed as he bowed in front of a teenager so excruciatingly embarrassed that she now had her handbag in front of her face, screams of outrage wailing from behind it.

"Juliet, I think you're lovely, and I can of course understand that you find me irresistible — if I was a girl I'd adore me too," he joked. "But I'm afraid I have a golden rule." He turned to look at Ben, all six foot two inches of him.

"If the boyfriend is big enough to cause life-threatening injuries then it's probably not a good idea. Forgive me?"

The sight of four swooning teenagers — well, three swoons and an "Oh my fuck, I'm mortified" — made Roxy strangely exhilarated. Either there was something dodgy in that vodka or she was actually warming to this lot. Freaky.

Mitch switched focus back in her direction. "Come on you, breaktime and you're on burger duty. I've already put the hospital admissions desk on standby."

He took her hand and pulled her out of her seat. In fact, she realised, she was warming to a few things around here.

She pondered the back of Mitch's head as she followed him across the hall. Okay, so his dress sense was tragic. And yes, he needed a haircut. And no, they had nothing in common. And yes, she'd rather chew off her own arm than take him on a night out in London with her usual circle of friends.

But there was no denying that he made her smile.

She could hear a drumroll starting up behind her as the girls restarted their chant of, "Uh-oh, uh-oh, I think he likes you. Uh-oh, uh-oh, I think he likes you. Uh-oh, uh-oh . . ."

Putting her hand up behind her back, she flicked them the V-sign, making them sing even louder.

Bloody teenagers. But as he opened the kitchen door and stood back to let her go in first, she realised that maybe they had a point. He'd been so lovely, so supportive since she'd got here. She'd only known him two weeks, yet it felt like months. He was always popping in to see her for a chat. And making suggestions for things they could do at night. She had never, ever made such a good friend this quickly. At least, not one who didn't have a trust fund, a discount card for Selfridges or a great line in Moroccan weed.

He was holding up a large packet and a grill pan. "This is a grill — it's a cooking implement commonly used in modern-day Britain. And this mysterious package contains burgers, the nutritional staple of the teenager. Do you think you'll cope or shall I send in reinforcements?"

She took the grill and returned it to the cooker, then snatched the packet.

"Okay, but you're buttering the rolls."

"Deal," he laughed. "Anyway, I don't want to leave in case you go into some kind of cooking-induced catatonic shock. I'm qualified in First Aid, so you're safe with me."

Safe with me. The phrase resonated in her head as she sliced open the packet and began the danger-fraught task of separating frozen burgers using nothing but a knife and brute force. Why had no one ever invented a way to freeze food without it sticking together?

Safe with him. That was so true, Roxy suddenly realised. She did feel, well, kind of *safe* with him. Bang! One burger flew off the counter and landed on the floor. She picked it up and put it on the grill pan, confident that any germs would be annihilated in the cooking process.

Safe with him. And he liked her. Was this . . . Was there something here that she hadn't noticed? She thought back to the night they'd had dinner at her house, what was it he'd been saying? Argh, she couldn't remember it — the shock of the whole tits out/Felix fiasco was blanking out everything that went before. Think. Think. Something about a . . . Okay, it was coming back now. He was in love with someone. Someone new. "Love at first sight," he'd said. And he hadn't told her yet, because . . . because . . . The astonishment took her mind right off the fact that she was making such an arse of the cooking prep that they had every chance of boarding the gravy train to Botulism Central.

"Mitch, can I ask you something?" she stuttered.

"Sure," he said, while continuing to work his way through buttering an Everest of rolls.

How had she not seen this? Of course, it made total sense! She'd been so wrapped up in her own life and her own problems that she hadn't spotted the thing that was blatantly, bloody obvious.

"The other night, when you were at my place . . ."

254

"Yes?"

"And we were talking . . ."

"Yes?"

"And you said that you've met someone . . ."

Pause. "Yes."

He put the knife down and turned to face her.

"Recently . . ."

"Yes."

"And it was love at first sight."

Another pause. "Yes."

"Do you still feel the same?"

"Yes."

"So you love someone?"

"Yes."

"Someone special?"

"Yes."

"And are you going to tell her?"

"Yes."

"Mitch . . .?"

"Yes?"

"Are you in love with me?"

Mr Donald Davies, MP for Chippenham West, was today admitted to London's Priory Clinic as rumours of alleged infidelities gathered pace.

The outspoken politician has built his political career on his controversial views espousing the importance of marriage, religion and moral fortitude within society. However, it would appear that the sanctimonious Davies has not been practising what he preaches.

A source close to Davies revealed today, "It's been known in certain circles for many years that Donald has been living a lifestyle that is in direct contradiction to his public stance. It wasn't a matter of 'if' he'd get caught out, only a matter of 'when'."

It seems that time has come, with reports that a downmarket tabloid will tomorrow be publishing the memoirs of a celebrated London madam. Among her many high-profile clients there are rumoured to be celebrities, high-ranking police officers and politicians, among them one Donald Davies.

While the legalisation of brothels last year removes any criminal consequences of these revelations, it is clear that Davies — if he is indeed implicated — will become yet another elected representative whose career has fallen on the sword of hypocrisy.

Representatives of Mr Davies were contacted but refused to comment.

CHAPTER
FOURTEEN

Do That to Me One More Time

Ginny. Day 18, Wednesday, 2p.m.

The sweet musky smell of sweat permeated throughout the room as the two breathless figures caressed each other. Ginny's hand, having apparently disconnected the synapse that led to the area of the brain marked "inhibitions and restraint", had developed the power to work autonomously and was tracing a circle around Destiny's nipple. She leaned over and licked the delicious peak, her fingers moving downwards now, delicately touching, probing every curve and valley. She found Destiny's pussy and slipped her fingers inside those warm, soft lips. A thrill bubbled up inside her as Destiny arched her back, panting, wanting more. Ginny pushed herself off her side and moved on top of her lover, their lips touching, their hips touching, their breasts touching. Destiny's hands weaved their way into her hair as Ginny lowered herself downwards, her hand still gently kneading the delicious softness. Her tongue found Destiny's other nipple and flicked it gently, then circled it. She let her lips fall on it, sucking it while Destiny whispered, "Harder, harder."

As their breathing deepened even further, Ginny bit softly down, causing Destiny to moan in ecstasy.

"Go down," Destiny begged. "Baby, go down."

Ginny released the nipple from her mouth and, balancing on her free hand, she raised herself above the most glorious sight she'd ever seen: Destiny, her every curve illuminated by the dim light that was seeping through the window, the heat of her body causing her skin to glisten like ice on a dark winter's morning.

She gently eased Destiny's legs apart and moved between them, pulling up her own knees so that she was on all fours, head down, like a leopard devouring its prey. With her tongue, she traced a line from the centre of Destiny's breasts down, down towards a place that she never thought she'd ever go. And as she moved backwards on her knees, every inch taking her closer, closer, she knew this was it. She was finally going to go there, to . . .

"Earth calling Ginny, come in please. Earth calling Ginny."

The shock intrusion made Ginny lurch up, knocking her glass of fresh orange juice flying across the granite worktop and sending it crashing to the floor. She jumped off her stool and grabbed some kitchen roll, hoping the frantic dabbing would give her some excuse for having a flushed face and pupils the size of olives.

Jude watched her with both concern and amusement.

"Hey, hi," she stuttered — dab, dab, dab — "I, er, didn't hear you come in. And I'm, er, sorry, about the

258

juice, and the, er, glass, and I'll . . ." — dab, dab, dab
— "replace the glass and . . ."

"Stop."

Her eyes closed as she froze, mentally chiding herself
for being caught out daydreaming yet again. The only
bonus was that the interruptions generally came from
either Jude or Sam — and neither of them were too
shabby on the eyes.

Jude sighed mournfully. "Oh, Gin, I was worried that
this would happen. The other night was amazing, but I
told you it would make things complicated. And the
thing is, I don't want it to. I don't want you to feel
jumpy around me, or nervous, or anxious, or jealous, or
all those other things that happen when you bring sex
into a friendship. I don't want you sitting here, wound
up, waiting for me to come home. I'm sorry, Ginny, I'm
really sorry, but we shouldn't have done it and I never
would have if I'd known you'd react like this,
because . . ."

Ginny bit her lip to stop herself smiling. The
gorgeous man was so sweet, so sincere, and she could
see that his concern was absolutely genuine.

"Jude, I wasn't thinking about you . . ." she blurted.

He folded her into his arms. "That's okay, honey, you
don't have to say that. It's okay. We'll work it out.
We'll . . ."

"No, really! Jude, I really wasn't thinking about you.
Or waiting for you to come home. I just sat here to have
a glass of juice and then found myself daydreaming
and, and . . . that's when you came in and you startled
me."

He was perplexed now.

"And the daydream was about . . . ?"

She grimaced and shrugged her shoulders.

"Er . . . not you. Sorry."

He took a step back, finally putting down the holdall that was slung over one shoulder. This was the first time she'd seen him since their lustfest the week before, and, despite the embarrassment and mortification thing, her stomach gave a little lurch of delight. He was wearing his standard uniform of vintage Levis and a white Calvin Klein T-shirt. His hair was loosely pulled back and tied at the nape of his neck. His skin was tanned (St Tropez), buffed (Dermalogica) and plucked to perfection, yet he'd still fit in just as well on a building site as he would on the pages of *Playgirl*.

And his voice, husky, sexy, would definitely fit in on those chat lines that began with 0870. Although it would be ludicrous to suggest that she'd repeatedly played back the message he'd left on the answering machine saying that something had come up and he was going to stay in Leeds for a few days. She had, of course, deleted it. Oh, okay, maybe she had listened to it a few times, but not many — definitely not triple figures.

He was grinning now as he pulled up another bar stool and sat facing her across the kitchen island.

"Ah, well. Ego crushed." He paused for a second. "Okay, I'm over it. So tell me all about it — who is he and what were you doing?"

She tutted indignantly. "Who said it was about anybody? It was just a harmless, innocent daydream

260

about . . . er . . ." She glanced around her, searching frantically for inspiration. She spotted the vase of tulips on the opposite counter. "About Amsterdam. Going to Amsterdam. For a holiday. Yep, I was dreaming about taking a weekend break."

He nodded thoughtfully. "Uh-huh. Well, babe, I'm guessing that you were at the red-light district because your shoes have been kicked across the room, your blouse is open, you're wearing very sexy underwear, and unless I'm pretty much mistaken, vital parts of your womanly charms are, er, *prominent*."

She glanced down and gasped when she realised that he was right — her headlights were definitely on full beam. She groaned as she re-buttoned her blouse over her, yep, curl those toes, peephole bra. No wonder he'd got the wrong impression.

"Oh, okay, but Jude, promise me that if I tell you, you won't judge, laugh or ever remind me that I said any of this."

He nodded as he reached down, grabbed a glass from the cupboard underneath him and poured himself some juice from the carton Ginny had left on the countertop. "Shoot."

She alerted her vocal cords that speech would be the best way forward but her gob refused to cooperate. Oh, for God's sake. She was a grown woman. She had done more wild things in the last fortnight than she'd ever done in her life. She'd had sex, she'd dreamt about sex, she worked in the sex industry, now at least she should be able to talk about sex. And relationships. And feelings. And all the things that she'd spent the last dozen years suppressing. It was time, *finally*, to grow up.

"Okay, first of all, the other night was, erm, amazing."

Jude nodded. "It was. Do you know your face is beaming?"

"Shut up or I'll cry and make you feel bad," she warned him, dipping her fingers into his juice and then flicking him with orange. Well, she couldn't expect to grow up *too* quickly.

She steeled herself. "As I was saying, it was amazing, but don't worry because I'm not going to get all clingy and needy. I know exactly what it was and it was great sex."

"Great?" he asked.

"Sorry, fantastic, mind-blowing — very, very best ever."

He was chuckling as he nodded. "Better. Okay, you can carry on now."

"But, trust me, I realise it's not the beginning of a love, hearts and flowers romance and I don't want it to be. I'm still not sure how I feel about Darren, or about home. Or whether I want to be back there, or here, or somewhere else. It's like I've reached a crossroads and I've no idea which way to go."

"Is it getting you down?"

"Are you kidding? Jude, it's *great*. Sorry, *fantastic*. I've spent so long living under the boredom threshold that this feels like some kind of euphoric liberation. But it's one that's come with strange side-effects."

"Like . . . ?"

"I can't stop thinking about sex."

He held up a hand to high-five her. Despite it being on the *Simpsons* side of immature gestures, she reciprocated. "Welcome to my world," he congratulated her.

She was gushing now, relieved to finally be able to share her innermost doubts, fears and orgasmic ambitions.

"And I know it's crazy, but I just want to put normal life on hold while I indulge in all the fantasies I didn't even know that I had. Is this getting too weird yet?"

He shook his head. "Nope, you're fine. Horny, but not weird."

Ginny laughed and put her face in her hands. "Aaargh! This is so embarrassing. I can't believe I'm saying this stuff. And I'm only telling you because, well, you've seen me naked."

"And I thought it was for my empathetic listening skills."

She pulled her shoulders up straight. "So. Erm. Right. So when you came in, I was having a daydream about . . ." Her hands flew to her reddened face again. "Sex," she squeaked from behind her fingers, "with . . . another woman!"

"Nooooo!" He was laughing again, delicious, joyous bursts of laughter. He looked heavenward, talking to some celestial being. "God, I love my life." He refocused on Ginny. "Anyone I know?"

"Destiny. From the Seismic. Have you met her?"

He raised his eyes to heaven again. "God, I really, *really* love my life."

263

She picked up a satsuma from the fruit bowl and threw it at him. "Hey, stripper-boy, pay attention to your confused friend. I'm having a life crisis and a sexuality meltdown. What's going on with me? I've never in my life wanted to share anything more than a bottle of wine with a female and now I'm thinking sweat and tonsils. What's going on with me? I'm becoming obsessed."

"You're becoming bi-curious," he corrected her. "It's normal, especially when you work in our industry. Last time Roxy and Felix broke up for a few weeks she went to Lanzarote for a fortnight with Mimi — double room."

"*Really?*" Ginny was gob-smacked. Roxy had told her she'd gone on that holiday alone, for two weeks of rest, reading and reflection. Damn, she should have spotted that lie a mile off — Roxy had spent a lifetime avoiding all three of those activities.

"Absolutely. But she went back to Felix as soon as she got back because she said she couldn't live without it."

"What — his thingy?" she asked, her eyes gesturing below his waistline.

"Nope, his credit card. And Ginny, if you're going to embrace this whole sexuality thing you're going to have to stop calling it a 'thingy'."

"I know! God, I'm so rubbish at this."

He reached over and stroked the side of her face, his mood switching back to concern. "Are you sure you're okay about all this? I mean, it's a lot to take in, all the

264

changes and the new stuff. I don't want you to get hurt."

She took his hand and kissed it, then released it with a firm pat. "I'm fine, I promise. It's . . . kind of exciting. In a crazy, unbelievable kind of way. I've spent my whole life behaving myself so this is my adolescent rebellion, just a little later than normal."

"Cool. As long as you're okay. And if you're not, you know that you can always talk to me."

"Thanks, Jude."

There were a few seconds of silence as she contemplated how much she liked this man in front of her. Other than Darren, she'd never felt this comfortable talking to anyone. Hold on, that wasn't true — she'd always felt really comfortable with Mitch. She felt a sudden pang of longing for home.

"So are you going to tell Destiny about the fantasies?"

"I don't know. It's one thing thinking these things but another saying them out loud."

"Well, you know you can always practise on me?" he offered, with a glint in his eye that told her he wasn't doing this purely in the capacity of a good listener.

Their eyes locked and she knew he was teasing her again, daring her to step up and be bolder than she'd ever been. She took a deep breath.

"Okay, so Destiny and I are on my bed. And we're naked. And I'm kissing her and feeling her . . . Jude, why are you taking your top off?"

He tossed his T-shirt to one side, pushed himself off the stool and walked towards her.

"Oh, I don't know. Probably the same reason that you're taking yours off."

Her shirt had careered through the air and landed in the sink. Shit, it was dry-clean only.

She reached out and grabbed his waistband and pulled him to her, his torso pressing against hers, her mouth coming to rest by his ear.

"So then I kiss her ears . . . and her neck . . . and move down to her . . ."

"Rrrrrrrrrrrrriiiiiiiiiiiiiiiiinnnnnnnnnnnnnnnng."

The noise of the telephone cut through.

Jude gasped in her ear. "Just leave it. So you were saying . . ."

"Rrrrrrrrrrrrriiiiiiiiiiiiiiiiinnnnnnnnnnnnnnnng."

"And then I . . ."

"Rrrrrrrrrrrrriiiiiiiiiiiiiiiiinnnnnnnnnnnnnnnng."

The clicking noise indicated it had switched to the answering machine and then came the sound of Roxy, provocatively announcing their absence and encouraging the caller to hang up, leave a message or send indecent cosmic thoughts. Even protests from her mother hadn't forced her to change that bit.

Beeeeep.

"Ginny? Ginny, this is Darren."

Ginny's reflex knee-jerk devastated the mood, the ambiance and Jude's testicular health.

"Shit, sorry, sorry!" she stammered as he buckled in two. The next actions were purely reflex: his hands instinctively went to his vital naked bits, as if checking for amputation, while her hands instinctively went to her vital naked bits as if Darren had just walked into the room.

"I'm in London and I wanted to see you. We need to talk, Gin. Can you meet me in an hour? I'll be in the coffee house, the one we went to that time we came to visit Roxy. The one across . . ."

"Bollocks! Across the street!"

Despite the fact that said street was at the opposite side of the apartment, she dived over and pulled the cord on the blinds, sending them crashing downwards.

"I hope you get this in time, Gin. If not, call me on my mobile and maybe we can meet up later."

The line went dead, leaving only silence and the noise of Jude groaning in pain. "Jude, I'm sorry, I'm really sorry."

"Don't worry, I'll be fine. Once they return to the position they're meant to be in."

His voice came out somewhere on the wrong side of helium. He took a few deep breaths then gently eased himself upright, before he did that bloke thing of puffing out his chest and pretending that he wasn't in the least bit of discomfort.

Oh, he was adorable. But, shit, Darren! Focus. Focus.

"Are you going to go?"

She nodded hesitantly. "I think I have to. It's time I faced him. To be honest, I want to see how he makes me feel now. You never know, I might tell him everything I've told you and see whether or not the shock kills him."

Jude reached over and took her hand again, his face a mask of solemnity.

"I think you're right to meet him. But, Ginny, do you want my advice?"

Her heart swelled at the generosity of this man who was so caring even though he'd just suffered the dual indignities of coitus interruptus and bruised bollocks. She nodded once again, preparing to take his suggestions on board, knowing that he was speaking from the heart.

"Probably best lose the peephole bra — might put him off his train of thought."

It had taken her ten minutes to get ready. The first time. Then ten minutes the second time, and the third, and the fourth, and . . . It was exactly fifty-eight minutes later when, dressed in white Versace boot-cut jeans and a cream skinny-rib polo neck, she walked through the door of the coffee house. It was of the incredibly naff but comfy *Friends* variety — huge squashy sofas in varying shades of terracotta and orange, stripped wooden floors, dark oak coffee tables with smaller tables and matching chairs for those who preferred a more formal seating environment. Two identical waitresses, both tall, blonde, with perfect pouts and pert breasts, stood chatting behind a glass counter loaded with pastries and other fancies that contained at least a thousand calories per square inch.

Ginny cast an anxious glance around the room. Immediately to her left was a group of what could only be called yummy mummies, complete with expensive highlights, Fake Bake tans, Ugg boots, the new-season Juicy Couture tracksuits and a menagerie of designer-dressed babies and toddlers. At the next table were two businessmen locked in conversation as they studied their laptop screens. On the couch were four teenage girls sipping smoothies, one of them gesticulating wildly while her arms jangled under the weight of dozens of silver bangles. For a split second Ginny had a flashback to the fifth-year study group and briefly wondered if Juliet was knocked-up yet.

At the next table were two nuns and a priest. Although in this neighbourhood they could either be evangelists for the work of God or three striprograms waiting to scare the crap out of someone.

Next to them, sitting in a battered leather two-seater sofa in the corner, cunningly semi-concealed by two large cacti and a coat stand, was Darren, watching her with an expression that could be anxiety, anger, confusion, or none of the above. God, had she ever really known this man? He certainly looked the same: wide shoulders, the cropped hair, the skin-tight khaki T-shirt and the camouflage combats. He could have been the prototype for a life-size GI Joe doll. Now *there* would be an Ann Summers product with potential.

She was back on illicit thoughts again. Focus, Ginny, focus.

She attempted a smile that probably came across as a demented grimace as she walked towards him, the sweat beads popping up on her palms.

He stood up, and she couldn't swear to it, but she sensed he was as nervous as she was. Luckily, a three-year-old boy with a handful of chocolate fudge cake chose that moment to streak across the room, smearing the walls, the chairs and a nun with brown goo.

"Gaston, come back here this minute!" his mother shrieked, before losing interest and turning back to a scandalous conversation about the president of the PTA who'd just been caught splashing the proceeds of the fundraising dinner dance on a fortnight in Bora Bora. Even their fraudsters were flash.

Little Gaston stopped in his tracks directly in front of Ginny. She perused her white jeans, then his dirty fingers, and then bent down and whispered, "Don't even think about it, shorty."

As he went shrieking back to his mother, Ginny suddenly wondered if sleeping in Roxy's bed, wearing her clothes and shagging her flatmate had turned her by some freaky power of osmosis into Roxy. Then she realised that the fact she was sweating like a marathon runner and almost frozen with fear at the prospect of talking to her ex meant it probably hadn't.

"Hi." He spoke first, motioning her to sit next to him on the sofa. When she sat down there was eighteen inches of space between them — great, plenty of room for her to rock backwards and forwards in the foetal position if it turned nasty. In the meantime, she pulled her feet up, tucked them under her and swivelled her body around to face him.

"You look great," he offered.

270

"So do you." And he did. In fact, given her recent state of mind, if Darren was a stranger she'd be fantasising about shagging him by now. As it was . . .

"This is really weird," she blustered. "Okay, I need to say this first — I'm really sorry, Darren, I know that I should have talked to you before I came here and I'm sorry that I didn't and . . ."

"No, I'm sorry I reacted the way I did — I hadn't realised how controlling I'd become and . . ."

"No, that's okay. That was my fault too for allowing you to take charge and for just going along with everything and . . ."

"What can I get you?" A Croatian accent cut through their mutual-apology session.

Darren shook his head. "I'm fine, thanks — still got my wheatgrass."

"Black decaf, please," replied Ginny, figuring it was best to avoid caffeine — any more stress on her nervous system could possibly be fatal.

A few moments' silence followed, as if the interruption had wiped their conversational slates clean, neither of them sure of where to go next.

Ginny decided to re-break the ice. After all, she owed him that after he'd come all this way to see her.

"I'm here for the Health and Fitness Exhibition at Earls Court," he blurted.

Or maybe not. Bugger it, let him stew. Hadn't the git chucked her first?

"And I thought it would be good for us to talk. I've got stuff I really want to tell you so I'm just going to say it all, and don't freak out, okay?"

She nodded her head, her insides churning, her head racing. Oh crap, was this when he went ballistic, told her he hated her and that he never wanted to see her again? Or, worse, that he *did* want to see her again? Did she want that? Could it ever work again? Did he know she'd had sex with someone else? Would she have to tell him? Would keeping it a secret fill her with so much guilt and turmoil that she'd end up on *Trisha*, on a show entitled, "I'm a Mad Slapper and I Want to 'Fess Up"?

He took a deep breath and then released it slowly, like he was trying to get enough oxygen into his lungs to bench-press three hundred pounds.

"I'm really sorry about breaking things off the way I did . . ."

Oh, shit, he wanted her back.

"It was crap, Ginny, I just flew off the handle and lost the plot."

Yep, definitely wanted her back.

"But, you know, I think it was kind of indicative of how unhealthy our relationship has been lately."

Er, maybe not. And had he been watching Dr Phil because he was coming over all "new man with emotional intelligence", and it was, quite frankly, very strange.

"I think we both know that we'd got into some kind of weird habit thing . . ."

And now he realised that he wanted them to start again?

"And I suppose it was so familiar, so comfortable, that neither of us could bring ourselves to break out of the lethargy . . ."

272

But now he had? And that meant?

"So you leaving was probably the jolt we needed . . ."

To make us realise how much we love each other? Or don't? And why am I having all these thoughts when I should just be paying attention to what he's saying? And has he taken a breath since he started speaking? Oh, shite, his mouth is still moving and I missed that last bit.

"Sorry?"

"Don't be sorry, we had twelve great years together, Ginny."

"No, I mean 'Sorry?' I didn't hear that last bit."

He squirmed in his chair.

"I think it was probably for the best, Ginny. I'm so sorry if that's not how you feel, but to be honest, I really think that it's time for both of us to move on. And I just wanted to see you today to say that properly, so that it didn't end with an angry phone call."

A waitress put her coffee down and glided away. Ginny didn't even notice, too busy staring at the man she'd loved since she was practically a child, absorbing and acknowledging the truth: that she didn't love him any more. She wasn't sure when that had changed, but it definitely had. Now there was sadness, but there was even more relief. She nodded slowly, her voice even and surprisingly strong — the old Ginny would have used Gaston for cover as she fled in terror from such a scene of emotional confrontation.

"I feel the same, Darren. It was time. And it wasn't your fault; it was just as much mine. But thanks for coming today — I'm glad we're both thinking the same things and we can move on with no hard feelings."

In a funny way she had never been more proud of him than she was right now. She smiled tenderly. How sweet that he'd gone to all this trouble to make their parting on good terms, without negativity or remorse. She knew that now she'd always remember him fondly. He was a good guy, Darren Jenkins, and she'd never think otherwise. Shit, he was talking again.

"Sorry, I missed that — what did you say?" she asked.

He stopped short, a vein on the side of his jaw pumping. Strange, that only normally happened when he was furious or really anxious. What had she missed?

"I said I've got something to tell you that's really going to make you hate me, and I'm so, so sorry. So sorry. And I need to tell you because I don't want you to hear it from anyone else, so please, just let me get all this out, okay?"

Had he always controlled their conversations like this?

He did the bench-press breathing thing again. A rising wave of fear was sweeping up from the pit of her stomach.

"I let someone kiss me."

Okay, that's not so bad. Compared to, say, shagging your flatmate under water in a bath for two.

"Okay, it's actually worse than that — I, erm, I, erm, let them . . . go . . . erm . . ." He was pointing vaguely at his nether regions, his mouth unable to formulate the words.

274

"Darren, did someone give you a blow job?"

Four things happened at once:

1. Darren almost fainted at hearing his shy, sexually repressed ex-girlfriend talking out loud, during daylight hours, in a public place, about anything pertaining to sexual relations.

2. Ginny felt a twinge of pride and mentally congratulated herself for her mature, intelligent handling of this situation. Wait till she told Jude about this!

3. One wee boy called Gaston peeked his head out from his hidden position behind a cactus and shouted, "Mum, what's a blow bob?"

4. Two nuns and a priest choked on their skinny latte mocha choccas.

Ginny gestured an apology to the irate yummy mummy who was now dragging one protesting child back to the non-X-rated side of the coffee house.

Darren, meanwhile, was still resting his chin on his combats in shock. Eventually, he tentatively nodded.

Okay, think mature, think mature, Ginny reminded herself. She was a cosmopolitan woman of the sexually emancipated world.

"And was this after I'd come here and you'd told me it was over?"

Okay, he was still nodding. This was good. Definitely good.

"Then forget about it, there's nothing to apologise for. Darren, if I'd wanted to save our relationship then I should have been on the first train back after you'd called it off, and I wasn't. What does that tell us? We

275

both know it was over and in truth I'm really grateful that you were brave enough to end it. I wasn't — at least not then. But anything that's happened since is nothing to do with me. I don't need to know. Actually, I'm happy that you've found someone new."

And that, she realised, was the truth. They were both free agents, they were both starting new lives and they both deserved to find happiness. Oh, it was great being a sensible, mature adult!

The vein was throbbing in his jaw again.

"Actually, that's the thing, it wasn't actually someone *new*."

He stopped. He couldn't say it. And if there was one small mercy in this situation it was that both of them were so engrossed they didn't notice that six mothers, two businessmen, two Eastern European waitresses, four teenagers, two nuns and a priest had all gone deathly quiet and were straining to hear every word.

Ginny's brow furrowed in confusion as he mumbled something.

"What?"

He mumbled again.

"Foxy who?"

Bench-press, bench-press. "Ginny, it was Roxy!"

The whole room gasped, even though they probably didn't know Roxy from the Avon lady. Actually, the waitresses did — she was the stroppy one from across the road who never left a tip.

Ginny didn't say a word as an explosion of conflicting thoughts ricocheted around her head. Roxy! And Darren! Bastards! How could he put his dick in her best friend's mouth? And why had she had her gob open in the first place? They didn't even bloody like each other! She'd spent years shouting, "Ding, ding, round six" as they slugged it out at birthdays, Christmas, and other miscellaneous family occasions. She couldn't have been more surprised than if he'd said her Auntie Vera had flashed him and offered a quickie. Okay, maybe she would have been a little more surprised then. But Roxy? Roxy! Why? And why was he telling her this?

"Darren, are you telling me this to unburden your soul or to hurt me?"

His eyes locked onto hers and the answer was in what she saw there: sadness, regret, honesty. Eventually he spoke, slowly, almost mournfully.

"To be honest, it's partly the unburdening thing — you don't deserve that, Ginny, you really don't, and I was an utter cunt for doing it."

Correct. But then she'd been no angel with the whole her/Jude/exchange-of-body-fluids thing either. But hey, she wasn't going to put him out of his misery by telling them they were equally as lewd — she was Ginny, not Mother Teresa.

"But the main reason is that I know Roxy will tell you. You know what she's like. And I'd always have been waiting for the moment that she put the boot in — so I thought it would be better if I told you first."

Silence. For the longest thirty seconds in history. Then Ginny did something that Mother Teresa (not to mention the two sisters at the next table) would have been proud of — she wrapped her arms around him.

277

And not in an attempt to choke him until his eyes popped and he met his end on a coffee-shop floor smeared in chocolate fudge cake. Although it didn't make her a bad person that she hung on to that image for just a moment.

But back to the hugging thing — it was strange that it should seem so familiar and yet somehow awkward, almost uncomfortable. Most of all, it just felt like the last time.

He pulled back, then, with a sad smile, he ruffled her hair. "I loved you, you know."

"And I loved you too."

He pulled out a twenty-pound note and put it on the table, then leaned over and kissed her cheek.

"Thanks, Ginny. For everything. I'd better get back."

As he walked away, Ginny felt a bittersweet combination of sadness and relief. However, both of those were having the crap kicked out of them by the stampede of sheer bloody rage that was heading in one direction.

If recent events had taught her anything it was that she had to stand up for herself and fight her own battles. She knew she had to act. It had to be direct, it had to be sudden, and it had to really hurt when it hit the target.

She picked up her mobile phone and dialled a number, her fury bubbling over as she barked into the mouthpiece, "That's it, you lying, nasty, evil tart, you've gone too far this time. I'm coming back there and I'm going to fucking kill you."

From: Saffronsastar@farnhamhills.com
To: julietrocks@farnhamhills.com
Subject: Hey ma buddy . . .

Yep, you're right — she's not such a mad old minge after all. So I'm totally up for the sleepover. Her ma — that big blonde one from the doctor's surgery — said she'd phone round all our parents and let them know that we could all stay. Empty house — waaaaaaaaaaaaaay! Roxy said she'll make the drinks and rent the videos. (By the way, what's *Top Gun* when it's at home? Think it's something to do with Tom Cruise — eeeeeeeew, he's, like, so over.) We've got to bring the food — I'm thinking popcorn, chocolate and a few portions of special fried rice out from the takeaway — a tenner each but I can loan you it if you're skint.

BTW — no Ben, no moping about missing him and no weed — Roxy says she's searching us and if she finds some she's smoking it.

Lol, Sxx

CHAPTER
FIFTEEN

Stop, in the Name of Love

Roxy. Day 19, Thursday, 4p.m.

"Yes, yes, that's right — a Stannah stairlift. I'd like it delivered and installed to Apartment 25a, The Thames View, London, W1."

She gave her credit-card details and then hung up, happy in the knowledge that she, the new, benevolent Roxy, was doing something for someone else. Sadly for him, that someone else was Felix, and the stairlift would prove rather unnecessary in a flat with no stairs. No matter, he could store it with the two crates of kippers, three boxes of incontinence pads and "*Areola, the Blow-up Doll Who Never Says No*", all of which she'd also had sent to him that morning. Courtesy of his credit card, of course.

Yes, it was petty, it was immature and it was probably cause for an injunction, but if he was going to be so stupid as to forget to cancel her American Express card then he deserved all he got. She wondered if he'd given an expense account to Ginny yet. Argh, the very thought made her blood boil.

She pushed aside the careers directory. This morning she'd realised that she was eminently qualified to spend the rest of her life in the fields of Waste Management, Water Testing or Window Cleaning.

Woo-hoo.

She put her head on the desk. What the fuck was she going to do with her life? After she got out of jail for credit-card fraud and harassment, that was.

Two and a half weeks in the Slow Death capital of the world and she was still no further forward. Actually, if anything, she was veering backwards, back to London, back to the Seismic. She missed the variety of it, the fact that every day was different and you never knew what was going to happen next. She missed the gossip, the fun, the unpredictability of dealing with a group of people who put pleasure and adventure above all else. She missed Destiny. She missed Sam. Hell, in the last few barren weeks she'd even considered giving Mimi a call, and not just for a chat.

"Tea, love?" asked her aunt, placing down a mug with Camilla, Duchess of Cornwall's grinning face on it. Ah, of course. It had been a whole half an hour since she'd had a cup of tea.

"And here's a ginger slice, love — great for nausea and you're looking a bit peaky these days. Oh, and Ginny just called on the office phone. Said she's left a message on your mobile . . ."

"Battery is dead and I don't have my charge."

"And she tried calling on this line . . ." She gestured to the phone in front of Roxy.

"Had to order some . . . supplies."

"Great, love, glad you're keeping on top of the stock — you've taken to this job like a duck to water. Anyway,

Ginny wants you to call her back as soon as possible. Sounded a bit strange, to be honest. Probably homesickness. Or the pollution. Or . . ."

"Tea deprivation?"

Violet chuckled.

"Still coming to transcendental meditation with us tonight, then?"

Roxy surreptitiously lifted a ballpoint pen, jagged it into her palm and twisted.

"Wouldn't miss it for the world."

Violet rewarded her with a huge grin. "Lovely. You know, it's great having you here, love."

Twist. Twist.

"Even if you can't make a decent cuppa," Violet chuckled as she waddled off back into the office, with just a cursory glance to check that Reverend Stewart wasn't within ten feet of the computers.

"Pollution, my arse," muttered Roxy. More likely she's calling to find out why her afternoon sex session with Felix had been disrupted by the delivery of twenty-five maternity bras (various colours), three candidates for the post of overnight nanny, and a phone call from the production team behind *Wife Swap* to discuss their application to be on the show. She'd thought that was a particularly inventive one. Although it would cause a conflict with Felix's recent application to join the Airtours Summer Sun Team as a tour rep.

And as for calling her back, she could forget it. She had no interest whatsoever in letting that traitorous slut: a) apologise, b) gloat, c) arrange to transfer her name off the joint membership for the spa at the Dorchester.

In her peripheral vision she caught a movement in the corner of the room.

"Stop! Get back to your seat and don't make me have to come over there and act like I give a toss about your educational development. It's called 'Study Period' for a reason and the clue is in the title!"

Juliet and Ben released the toilet door, watched dolefully as it swung shut and then skulked back to their seats. Damn, she was good — they hadn't got past her once this week.

She winked at Juliet as the teenager slumped back in her seat and was rewarded with a one-fingered gesture. Roxy dissolved into giggles and reciprocated. Wow, mutual hand-profanity and matching grins — they were practically very best friends. Which would come in handy since she appeared to be minus one of those right now.

Roxy cast a glance around the rest of the misfits in the room. The reverend was deep in contemplation with a Mills & Boon-style book called *For Whom the Loins Throbbed*. She had real fears for his flock. The fifth-year study group was twittering at their usual table. She still couldn't believe that she'd let them talk her into the sleepover at her place — or that they'd made it through the night without sneaking off to meet their boyfriends, calling her old or vomiting up her fruit punch.

Her eyes continued scanning, falling on the collection of strays that'd shown up for the Young

Catholic Mothers' Yoga Class, unaware that it was cancelled today because Action Man Darren was away at some exhibition in London. Ouch, the very thought of him made her eyes roll involuntarily in their sockets. He hadn't said one word, not one word to her since their blow-by-blow session in the kitchen. When they did bump into each other he just looked right through her like she didn't exist. Score one for the ego — not. Where were the flowers? Where were the declarations of undying love? Or, at the very least, where was the errant dick that should be begging for a rematch? She must be losing her touch.

Cancel that, she was *definitely* losing her touch — why else would she have . . . nope, she still couldn't think about it without cringing. She now understood the intricacies of the concept of denial — if she blocked out her conversation with Mitch then it was just like it had never happened. But no matter how much she tried to forget it, that one question, that one little sentence, kept reverberating in her head.

"Are you in love with me?"

She groaned aloud, causing her VBFs to look over then crease into a fit of giggles.

She held up the biro. "Stabbed myself with a pen. And if you lot don't cut out the snide gestures you're next." A very intimidating threat that was, apparently, the cue for even more giggles.

Nope, she wasn't even going to think about it again. Who could have seen that coming? She would NOT think about it. She wouldn't. That scene never happened — it had been erased from the hard drive of her life.

"No."

Okay, so she hadn't quite managed to delete it.

One word. One final, devastating, deadly word.

Thankfully, unlike her boyfriend, best friend and emotional antennae, her wits hadn't deserted her and she'd immediately slipped into a whole, "Phew, thank goodness, thought for a minute there it was me. I mean, actually, I didn't think that at all, it was the girls, you know, Juliet and the gang, they said that you had a thing for me and I thought I'd better check because I don't, absolutely not, I don't have a thing for you, but I thought I should check because if you did think of me that way then we'd have to nip it in the bud because I don't, don't have a thing for you, not at all, and I just wanted you to know that, that I don't . . ."

Apparently her punctuation had deserted her, though.

While she'd ranted like her mother on two litres of Blue Nun and a vial of crack, Mitch's expression gradually slid down the astonished scale via horror, shock, surprise, intrigue, interest, and landed at humour.

"I know, I know, I get it . . . You don't feel that way about me."

"That's right, I don't," she agreed, her tone one of unequivocal, absolute, complete certainty.

Where was that bloody delete button?

They'd then carried on making the burgers in silence, the grill rendered unnecessary as the meat was now cooking nicely from the heat emanating from Roxy's face. At the end of the night he'd walked her home, their journey shrouded in uncharacteristic silence. On the last three mornings he'd popped in for his usual morning coffee and read of the papers, but there had definitely been a tension, a discernible shift that had manifested itself in uneasy conversation and awkward silences. Evening activities? None. Witty repartee? Gone. Curling toes? Many.

Just another mind-numbing day in Guantánamo Hills.

The double doors swooshed and Saffron strutted in. She was far too cocky, that girl, too sure of herself, too confident, too pronounced in her sexuality. Ah, a girl after Roxy's own heart. If she could travel back in time ten years it would be like looking in a mirror.

Fuck that, if she could travel back in time she'd be on a plane, headed for the US, determined to track down a struggling actor called Ben Affleck and dupe him into marriage before he hit the A-list.

Ben Affleck . . . He always made her think about Sam. She wondered if Sam was still pissed off with her for quitting. Or had he too fallen under Ginny's spell and forgotten Roxy even existed? If he'd given Ginny a pay rise she'd have to kill him.

The ringing of the phone interrupted her thoughts.

"Farnham Hills Library, can I help you?" she droned lethargically.

"Roxy?"

The hairs on the back of her neck jumped to attention. How dare she call again? Couldn't she take a hint? If she thought she could apologise and just forget about it, well, she was wrong. Another image of Ginny and Felix, this time shopping in the — oh, God, the pain — the Dolce & Gabbana aisles in Harvey Nicks flashed into her head.

Her tone was solid ice.

"Sorry, I think you have the wrong number. There used to be a Roxy here but she was brutally murdered when her former best friend stabbed her in the back."

She slammed the receiver down so hard that it bounced back off the cradle, then banged into her cup of tea, knocking it over and causing it to flood into the box of Ginny's meticulously kept record cards that were lying at Roxy's feet waiting for the latest updates.

The screams were simultaneous. Because over at the Study Group table Juliet had jumped to her feet and hit Ben with a right hook that sent him careering into the Arts, Crafts and Hobbies shelf. And Violet had wandered out of the office and spotted that the Reverend Stewart had sneaked onto the computer, causing her to shriek, "Reverend Stewart, you filthy man!"

This wail had woken up the baby that was being carted out by one of the Catholic mothers, and who was now taking the opportunity to demonstrate that it had the most developed lungs in the northern hemisphere.

And then Juliet had charged in the direction of the door, tears streaming, with an elegant and artfully delivered, "Don't ever speak to me again, you fuckers!" directed behind her towards the table of her peers.

Yep, Roxy mused, as she picked up a pile of goo formerly known as efficient record-keeping, it would be great if something exciting ever happened around here.

Several hours later she was on her four hundred and thirty-seventh "Oooooooohhhhhmmmmmm" when she realised that if she didn't get out of there then Mrs Robinson-Smith, the woman who'd spent a fortnight trekking in Nepal and now considered herself on the same spiritual plane as the Dalai Llama, was going to get a Nike Cortez up her arse.

She glanced over at her mother and Violet, both sitting crossed-legged on the floor wearing the fabric of this and every other season in Farnham Hills: velour. Both of them had their eyes closed, their thumbs clenched against their middle fingers, and were making a sound that fell somewhere between a fart in a wind tunnel and the mating call of Moby Dick.

"*Mum*," she hissed. Mrs Robinson-Smith opened her eyes and puffed in outrage. Roxy shrugged an apology. "*Feel ill, I'm going home.*"

The lemon-velour Buddha gave her a concerned look.

"*Time of the month*," Roxy explained, scrambling to her feet.

It was only when she was out of the door and the cold air hit her that she realised the time-of-the-month excuse might not be entirely manufactured. When exactly *was* her period due? She tried to count backwards. She remembered coming on when she and Felix were travelling back from that weekend in Paris.

Was that last month? Seemed so long ago. They'd held hands as they walked along the Seine. Okay, that wasn't strictly true. They'd held hands as they walked along the fifty-foot balcony of a very posh hotel overlooking the Seine. She'd been naked and wearing five-inch stripper shoes so exposure to the general public would probably have resulted in community service and an entry on the sex-offenders register.

She detoured into the village general store for medicinal supplies. Mrs Baxter, the woman who'd stood behind the counter every day in living memory (rumours had it she was approximately one hundred and twenty-six years old), acknowledged her presence with gushing indifference. She'd definitely been off on the days that they taught customer services at Shop School.

"S'cuse me, Mrs B, where will I find Ben & Jerry's?" Roxy asked in the cheeriest tone she could muster.

Mrs Baxter dragged her eyes away from her *Reader's Digest*.

"Is that those gay blokes who moved into the farmhouse?"

"Yep, that must be them." Only here, thought Roxy with a sigh. Only here. "Oh, and can you tell me where you keep the ice cream?"

"Back freezer, right-hand side, behind the Yorkshire puddings. Of course, in my day we made our Yorkshire puddings ourselves — none of that frozen muck."

Apparently Mrs Baxter had also been off on the day they taught effective sales techniques.

Roxy bought a tub of raspberry ripple — not smart when it was freezing outside, she wasn't wearing gloves,

289

and Mrs Baxter only provided carrier bags if you had more than three items. Apparently, her grandson was an environmentalist and she was personally going to save a continent by reducing her plastic-bag output.

By the end of the street, the ice cream had been under Roxy's arm, under the other arm, held in one hand, then the other, then rested on top of a street bin while she blew into her cupped palms and rubbed them together to restore circulation. She now knew how Scott of the bloody Antarctic felt. It was no use. She couldn't go on. It was one small step for man, one giant case of chilblains if she didn't get out of the cold quickly.

There was only one thing for it — she did what people in jeopardy have done since Mrs Baxter was in pigtails: she sought refuge in the house of God.

The church-house door was barely opened when she burst in and dropped the ice cream in the hallway.

"Thank fuck, another five minutes and my hands would have dropped off."

"Good evening, Roxy, my dear, and how are you tonight?"

The bits of her that weren't already frozen now promptly followed suit. God had a mighty sick sense of humour sometimes. She turned to see Father Murphy standing behind the door with an enigmatic smile on his face. To her left, Mitch appeared through the door that led to the kitchen. At least she thought it was Mitch — it was hard to see his face behind a sandwich so tall it could be used to jack up cars.

"Sorry, Father. About the language, I mean. I thought it was Mitch who had answered the door. Not that it's okay to swear at Mitch because it's not. And I wouldn't. It was just . . ."

"I was just on my way out. Don't you worry about a thing, Roxy, I'm sure the Lord will be quite prepared to forgive you after you've sought redemption at confession on Saturday evening — say eight o'clock?"

Cornered. She could either blast her way out and risk eternal damnation or surrender quietly.

"Erm . . . definitely, Father. Eight o'clock. Saturday, confession. I'll be there."

Father Murphy reached over and lifted his hat from the hat stand, before leaving her with a nod as he passed.

"See you then, my child."

As the door closed behind him she turned to a smirking Mitch. "He does realise that if he wants to sit through my confession he should probably bring sandwiches, water, a duvet and some kind of portable toilet system?"

"I'll give him the heads-up."

There was an awkward pause for a few seconds while both worked out the best thing to say next. Roxy caved first.

"Okay, I'm really sorry if I embarrassed you the other night — and I still reserve the right to blame Juliet and her posse and the vodka we'd tanked in the toilets — so I say we never talk about it again and just go back to being pals. I promise you, Mitch, I do not find you attractive in any way whatsoever. Not at all. Definitely not . . ."

"Okay, okay, I get it. Now stop before your reassuring words make me go and sign up for a place on *Extreme Makeover*."

She eyed him up and down — three-quarter-length denim cut-offs with frayed edges, a U2 tour T-shirt circa 1998, flip-flops and Chaka Khan's hair.

"Honey, that wouldn't be your worst ever idea."

"I think I preferred it when you were weird and acting strange around me."

"I was not acting strange."

"Were so."

"Was not."

"Roxy, the last three mornings you've barely said a word to me. Do you know what that does to a guy? I've come to count on your unique brand of abusive friendship to get my creativity flowing in the mornings, and this week? Nothing. Haven't written a decent word since Sunday. Oh, and vodka with teenagers? You want to tell me about that?"

"Nope, I'll add it to the confession on Saturday."

He picked up the ice cream and she followed him into the kitchen and watched as he took two bowls out of the crockery cupboard.

"Sorry I've been a bit off the wall — emotions are all over the place just now. Think my hormones are either late hitting puberty or early on the menopause."

"Hey, look, it's understandable, there've been a lot of changes, upheaval, and it's perfectly normal that you're a bit strung out."

"A bit strung out? I sent twelve space-hoppers, four pizzas and a tribe of African dancers — with bongos — to my ex-boyfriend's apartment today. That's not strung out, it's Care in the Community. I don't know, Mitch — I think being here is driving me nuts. It's almost like I had so much going on in London that I never stopped to question whether or not I was actually happy inside, and now that I'm here there's *too much* time to think. And commit credit-card fraud."

He handed her a bowl that runneth over with raspberry ripple.

"Look, I know it's not been easy, but it's not all bad here. And sometimes you just have to take time out to evaluate where you are and where you're going."

"Wish I was in Prada and going to the Embassy Club."

She licked some dripping ice cream from her spoon. "But then, to be honest, I'm not certain I want to go back there either. I really miss a couple of my friends, but I'm not sure that's enough of a reason to go back. I've no idea what I want to do. None. I just know that I can't stay here. Apart from a glorious five minutes of chaos in the library this afternoon, I've been bored rigid since I got here. Nothing ever happens. Nothing. I mean . . . What's that noise?"

Mitch was already in his flip-flops and dashing out to the vestibule, where a red light was flashing like a beacon on the alarm panel by the door.

"There's someone in the church. I'm sure I locked it before I set the alarm. Bloody vandals have broken in again."

He snatched a set of keys from a nearby hook and tore out of the door, Roxy rushing after him. She would have loved to have said that she was having a *Charlie's Angels* moment and was fuelled by notions of catching the bad guys and bringing them to justice, but the truth

293

was that if there were petty criminals in the vicinity then she wanted a big burly bloke by her side. Even if he was wearing a U2 T-shirt and had Chaka Khan's hair. The alarm could be a decoy to get Mitch out of the house so that they could kidnap her and kill her using Japanese martial arts and cling film. That episode of *CSI Miami* would never leave her.

She jumped over the privet hedge that bordered the path, and then sprinted in Mitch's wake across the lawn to the church. When they reached it, the front door was six inches ajar.

"You stay here, I'll check inside. If you hear me scream like a girl then call the police."

"I was impressed right up until that last bit. And anyway, you're not leaving me here. Come on."

She pushed past him, then froze when she realised that the church was in total darkness. Thankfully, somewhere behind her, Mitch flicked on a switch and the Lord said *Let there be light*.

As soon as their pupils had reacted to the change, they scanned the church. Nothing. No vandals. No damage. No sound.

They stood for several seconds, barely breathing, waiting for a serial killer with a religious obsession to ambush them, slaughter them, and then dangle them from the giant cross on the wall behind the altar. *CSI Las Vegas* that time.

Mitch audibly exhaled behind her. "Must have been the wind. Or an animal, maybe. I obviously left it unlocked earlier, because there are no signs of forced entry."

"Okay, then, Sherlock Holmes, can we go back to the nice warm church house now?"

"Sure. Just let me check that a cat or dog hasn't sneaked in. Don't want to give Mrs Dodds a nasty surprise in the morning."

He walked up the aisle like an air-hostess on seatbelt duty, checking every pew as he passed. Roxy started tapping her feet, partly out of impatience, partly because her toes were icing up, and partly because the adrenaline was charging around her body with nowhere to go.

"Roxy! Roxy!"

That adrenaline diverted to her legs as she charged up the aisle in the direction of Mitch's panicked shouts. She could just see the top of his hair now; the rest of him was crouched down between two pews near the front.

She saw the blonde head first, then the rest of the limp body lying along the ancient wooden bench. Her eyes were closed, her face serene, peaceful. It could have been a breathtakingly stunning image if it wasn't for the empty bottle and packet of pills lying on the floor next to her.

Roxy flew to Mitch's side, pushing him out of the way while taking the familiar head and cradling it in her arms.

"Mitch, go and phone an ambulance. Now!"

She turned back and gently swept the hair off the beautiful face, willing her to wake up.

"Oh, Juliet, honey, what have you done?"

The Seismic Lounge
Thursday Evening, 11p.m.

The phone rang for so long that he'd almost given up hope of even hearing her voice on the answering machine. Just as he was about to replace the handset, he heard the click and then her playful, throaty tones as she invited the caller to leave a message.

It was simple. He missed her. He hadn't expected to, he certainly didn't want to, but the truth was that he'd realised he was living in limbo — and it was time to move on. And he couldn't do that without her.

He frowned as he realised that he should have done this long ago. Better late than never, he supposed. He just hoped that she'd react to his plea and come back. Because until she did . . . Well, how could he find out the answers to the river of questions that were rising in his mind? For weeks now he'd been going through the motions, existing on autopilot, numbed by the frustration of the situation.

No longer. She had to come back . . . she just had to.

The beep finished and there was a brief pause as he tried to formulate his words.

Then . . .

"Hey, it's Sam. I was hoping to catch you because we need to talk. The thing is, I need you to come back. I'm sorry, but I do. As soon as possible. Call me."

He put the phone down with a heavy heart. If there was one thing he was sure of, it was that she didn't respond well to being told what to do. He just hoped that this one time her heart would hear him and she would know that she had to come home.

CHAPTER
SIXTEEN

Easy

Ginny. Day 20, Friday, 8p.m.

The nurse took a long drag on her cigarette, relieved to be finally getting a break after the exhaustive task of working her way through patient after patient after patient. And she still had so many more to get to.

"So is Sam single?"

"What?" Destiny took another drag on her cig. Urgh, these PVC uniforms always stuck to her like Sellotape after an afternoon orgy. It was a specialist service that had to be booked weeks in advance and was especially popular with young-buck bankers who'd just pocketed huge bonuses.

This time there were four of them, all in their late twenties, all strikingly handsome and all happy to spend an obscene amount of their cash on a couple of hours of utter hedonism with half a dozen of the girls. They were Destiny's favourite kind of clients, but she definitely needed a sit-down and a nicotine infusion after they left.

"Sam. Is he single?"

Destiny gave out a sexy, purring chuckle. "Lord, I've created a monster. Don't tell me you're thinking about banging him too?"

"No! Don't be ridiculous!" Ginny declared indignantly.

"Ridiculous? Tell me again about that little fantasy of yours. What did I do to you with the strap-on and the whipped cream after you'd spent ten minutes with your head in my nethers?"

Ginny groaned. "I can't believe I told you about that."

Destiny giggled. "Just tell me again how good I was."

"The best ever, okay? And if you're going to mock then I'm never telling you anything again. I need to stop drinking. Half a dozen drinks and suddenly my deepest fantasies go from being my dirty secret to an appropriate topic of conversation. Another night on the town and I'll be requiring the services of a nurse who has actually had some training in the medical field."

She opened a compact mirror, removed the sponge and patted some foundation onto her face. "I mean, look at me. Under this fine veneer of expensive slap there's a grey face and thread veins popping by the second. I haven't seen sunlight for days. I've forgotten what nutritious food actually looks like."

"But . . ."

"No, don't say it. The garnish on a cocktail does not constitute one of the five portions of fresh fruit and vegetables as recommended by Government Healthy Eating Guidelines."

Destiny held up her cigarette packet. "Here, have a cigarette — it'll take your mind off your unhealthy diet."

Ginny stuck her tongue out at her, before continuing in a more serious vein. "Do you know what I miss most?"

Destiny racked her brain. "Your anal boyfriend? And not anal in a good way, incidentally."

"I miss books. I miss the smell of them. I miss reading them. I miss losing myself in the pages."

Destiny viewed her with genuine concern.

"Babe, you need help."

Ginny couldn't stifle the laugh. "You're right. You're sitting there wearing a plastic nurse's uniform and thigh-high boots, yet I'm the one that needs help."

Destiny feigned outrage as she tossed a fag packet in Ginny's direction. "Remind me again when you're leaving?"

"One week. Seven days. I keep telling my liver that we're on the home stretch."

Of course, now that Roxy was on Ginny's *Five People I'd Like to Kill in Heaven* list, she could walk out at any time. What did it matter if Roxy lost her wages? Or her bonus? Or the guarantee of a good reference?

Ginny, quite frankly, couldn't give a toss. However, the truth was that she didn't *want* to leave yet. Health issues and visits from ex-boyfriends aside, she was still finding this whole adventure absolutely exhilarating. Her only regret was that she hadn't done it sooner. Perhaps if she'd come to university here as planned then her life would have turned out so differently. She would have moved in different circles, experienced different things, developed different dreams. Or perhaps if she'd done this when she was younger she'd have got homesick after the first week and fled back to the life that she left behind. Still, it would have been good to have taken the chance.

"Single."

"What?"

"Sam, he's single. Has been since I started here."

"And does he . . . does he . . . you know?"

"Take advantage of his employer's perks? No. Never. And it isn't for the lack of offers — Ceecee and Deedee have been practically stalking him for months. When Deedee came back from having her St Tropez and her Brazilian done last week, she lay across his desk in the buff and asked him to inspect the merchandise . . ."

"Nooooo! What did he say?"

"Said it was lovely and could she pass the stapler."

In a moment of supreme elegance, Ginny spat a mouthful of milky tea across the table.

"Hey, watch the outfit!"

"D, it's plastic, it'll wipe clean. Anyway, so why do you think he refused then? Gay? Secretly married? Just seems to me that the type of bloke who runs a place like this should be shagging everything in sight. I mean, I think he's lovely, but people tend to go into a field of employment that they plan on enjoying. Just seems strange that he doesn't, you know, live it up a little."

Destiny checked the watch that was pinned to her lapel. "I know, go figure. Anyway, better go. Joe Cave's in next and he'll have popped a Viagra on the way here. If I keep him waiting he'll do himself an injury."

"Joe Cave, the actor? Oh my God, I loved him in that thing about the killer snake let loose in the underground."

Destiny got up, stubbed out her cigarette and took a final sip of her coffee.

"Okay, since it's you and I don't want to fuel your rampant fantasies any more than I have already, I'm not going to make a joke about what I'll be doing to his killer snake in about five minutes." She kissed Ginny on the cheek. "Now go back to that desk and dream about all the other things you want me to do to you. Tell me later."

"Nope, I'm over you. I'm going on to Portia de Rossi next — think I'm entering a blonde phase."

Their joviality resonated down the hallway as they left the staffroom and went in different directions: Destiny off to work with an endangered and potentially hazardous species, Ginny back to her position at the front desk. And as they went, neither of them spotted that their boss was standing against the wall just outside the staffroom door — in the same position he'd been in for the last five minutes.

Ginny had barely sat down when the front-door buzzer rang. Strange — Jennifer wasn't due on shift for another two hours and clients tended to stick to the back door, far from the prying lenses of any persistent paparazzi.

She pressed the intercom. "Good evening, may I help you?"

The voice on the other end surprised her for three reasons: it was as sharp as a scalpel, it oozed confidence, and it was female. Well, she'd heard that they did have the occasional female client but she'd yet to meet one. And, given the target gender of her newfound fantasy world, that was probably a good thing.

"Yes, I'm here to see Samuel Carvell, and since it's raining like Niagara out here I'd be very grateful if you would expedite my entry."

Ginny felt a mild tremble of panic in the pit of her stomach. This sounded like one scary lady. She shouldn't let her in without clearance, but it went against her instincts and manners to leave her standing in the rain. She quickly pressed the entry button that opened the door. If this was a journalist using a ruse to get a look inside London's most unusual service industry, Sam would fire her for letting the woman in. He'd warned her about these kinds of tricks on her first day. Brothels might be legal now but that didn't mean the press were any less fascinated about who was indulging a bit of extramarital, extra-expensive nookie.

Ginny watched with apprehension as the mystery caller came into view. If the woman was clutching a notepad and a Pentax then she might have to rugby tackle her and wrestle her back out the door again — an act that she'd struggle with under any circumstances, but which would be near impossible in her John Galliano skin-tight, calf-skimming pencil skirt and Fifties-style slingback peep-toe platforms.

The minute she set eyes on the guest, she knew that she could never take her. To start with, this woman had a good six inches on Ginny. Her black, glossy hair fell in waves that skimmed past her shoulder blades. Her caramel sallow skin was flawless, her eyes were the shape of almonds, and every feature was perfectly defined by expertly applied make-up. She was wearing a dark, beautifully cut trouser suit that Ginny, fashion dunce that she was, still knew had cost more than she earned in a month. The light glistened off a rock the size of a grape on her index finger. And under her arm was a crocodile Hermes Kelly bag that Ginny was guessing didn't come with a free bottle of Eau de Patpong Market. It was difficult to pinpoint her age. She had that supermodel gait and posture that was so deceptive she could be anywhere between Cindy Crawford and Jerry Hall.

It wasn't just the accoutrements of wealth that gave this woman the veneer of invincibility. It was the way she walked, the way she carried herself, every step taken with the confidence and certainty that she would have exactly what she wanted whenever she wanted it.

Okay, so the rugby tackle was out of the question. Suddenly Ginny had another thought — what if this was someone's wife? If Miss Glossy Veneer made a dash for the stairs then the rugby tackle might just have to be back on the agenda.

"Good evening," the visitor purred, "as I said, I'd like to see Sam Carvell, please."

"Certainly, I'll just check if he's free. Who shall I say is calling?"

"That's okay, Ginny, I know who's calling."

Both women's heads whipped round to see Sam, coffee in one hand, coming through from the staffroom area.

Ginny spotted immediately that his voice was quite different from normal — garrulous, sweet, almost —

304

good grief — sunny. Although (and it could either be blamed on the obvious shock or the dodgy reception lighting) he suddenly had the same pale complexion as Ginny did before she piled the slap on. To the trained eye it was obvious that this visit was completely unexpected, shocking, but definitely welcome.

"Hey, Carmella, long time no see," he drawled.

Ginny was mesmerised. This was like being a spectator on the set of a major soap opera, a really flash one where everyone wore diamonds and transported the kids to school in their Gulfstream jets.

Glossy Veneer smiled, revealing perfect, blinding teeth, and then glided over towards Sam, arms outstretched. Oh. My. God. Ginny suddenly wondered if there was any way she could surreptitiously buzz Destiny and get her down here to watch this. She had no idea what was going on, but going by Sam's demeanour it was obviously something pretty special. He was hugging her now, tightly, with a huge grin and his eyes closed.

"I thought you were never coming back."

"Darling, didn't I say I would?"

"That was over a year ago," he replied, with just a hint of a reprimand.

"Oh, darling, you know how time flies." Her hand flicked away his comment. She wrapped her arms around him again. "But I'm back now."

Sam pulled back, their faces inches from each other, their eyes locked.

"For good?"

"For good."

★ ★ ★

"Son of a bitch!" Deedee spat, and then took a huge gulp of her Bollinger.

"Down, girl," Mimi warned. "If your naked muff didn't grab his interest then I think you have to accept that it's never going to happen."

Ginny marvelled, yet again, how somehow this exchange now seemed perfectly normal to her.

"So then what happened?" Destiny probed eagerly.

"No idea. They went into the office and they were still in there when Jenny came on shift and I left. It was so weird — I swear at one point I thought Sam was about to burst into tears."

"At least it explains one thing, though," Ginny declared.

"That he's got crap taste in women," Deedee muttered bitterly.

"It explains why he's single . . ."

Deedee gave her the glare of death so Ginny quickly performed a defensive move.

". . . and why he, incredibly, refused the stunningly beautiful Deedee's very generous offer . . ."

Deedee's mood visibly softened from premeditated homicide to malicious wounding.

". . . he's obviously in love with this woman and he's been waiting all this time for her to return to him. Quite sweet, really."

Deedee kicked her ankle, causing a swift retraction.

"I mean nauseating. Quite nauseating. And stupid. Obviously. Daft. When he could have you, Deedee."

Deedee pushed herself off the barstool and strutted off in the direction of the nearest millionaire — a

306

simple task since she knew every single man in London with an income of over £500K per annum.

"Wow, I can't believe we never knew. We've spent months trying to work out his story. More Bolly?"

Ginny held her glass up for a refill. So much for cleansing her liver. She hadn't planned to come out with the girls tonight but she was so desperate to tell them the gossip that she hadn't been able to stop herself.

A thought suddenly struck her — when had she ever been interested in gossip? Hadn't she always prided herself on the fact that she never bitched or moaned about other people? Except Roxy, of course, but then she was only human.

A few weeks ago she hadn't known any of these girls and Sam was a virtual stranger, yet now she'd somehow integrated herself into their lives, and vice versa.

She'd changed so much so quickly, and yet she still felt, well, like herself. Just a new, improved self, with better clothes and the occasional desire to sleep with one of her new chums.

She held up her glass. "Here's to Sam. Who got the girl back."

They all clinked glasses as Ceecee added, "And to friends — friends who will post Deedee's bail after she gets her hands on Sam's new woman."

Everyone in the group raised their glasses then downed the contents in one. Ginny felt herself sway — she definitely shouldn't have done that.

She should probably head home — it might be fun to find out what it felt like when your head hit your pillow before 4a.m. It had been so long she couldn't remember.

Yep, she should definitely go. Definitely.

"Excuse me, ladies, the gentleman over there sent this over with his regards."

Four bottles of Cristal were plonked in front of them. Ginny and the girls turned to see who had just become their very favourite person of the evening.

Standing in the corner of the room, surrounded by a huge entourage, Joe Cave answered their curiosity with a subtle salute.

Well, perhaps she'd have one more glass.

Four hours, five glasses of obscenely expensive champagne, too many dances to count, and one surreptitious snog with the son of a football legend in the queue outside the unisex toilets later, Ginny stumbled out of the door. It had been a good move to alternate her alcohol with water because as a result she'd drunk enough champers to feel merry but not enough to feel completely squished. Normally the next destination would be an all-night café for coffee and perhaps and early breakfast, but Ginny could definitely feel her bed calling her back to the Mothership.

"Sure you don't want to go for coffee or come back to mine?" Destiny asked.

Ginny kissed her on the cheek. "Thanks — but I'm trying to get over you, remember?"

Several doormen watched the exchange and spent the next ten minutes immune from the cold as endorphins charged around their systems, fuelled by what they'd like to imagine came next. The stunningly beautiful dark girl with the perfect body and the look of lust versus the blonde girl-next-door who wasn't as innocent as she looked. Carlsberg didn't make women, but if they did . . .

Ginny watched Destiny jump into the black cab at the front of the queue, before taking the one behind her. It was almost 4a.m, so she reckoned she'd be in her bed by half past, and, since she was off the next day, she could stay there for as long as she wanted. Bliss.

Twenty minutes later she let herself into the darkened flat. Jude obviously wasn't home yet, because if he was the lights would be on in every room and the music would be gently throbbing from the sound system that piped music throughout the flat. And anyway, she was sure he'd said something about seeing Goldie after work tonight. Or was it Cheska? Nope, Cheska's court case was coming into its final days and she hadn't been around much lately, so it was definitely Goldie.

Ginny kicked off her shoes in the hallway and then wandered through to the kitchen. She pulled a bottle of water out of the fridge and grabbed a handful of grapes from the fruit bowl, chiding herself that this was the first healthy thing she'd eaten in days. She really must get back to some semblance of normality, at least in the food stakes.

She replaced the bottle of water and closed the fridge door with a little smile. She doubted she'd ever be able to see an American-style fridge freezer without having a flashback to the first time . . . the first time that . . . oh, it was such a shame that Jude wasn't here because she'd definitely come over all . . . *friendly*. Yep, there was definitely something in the water in this flat.

Bed. She needed to be in bed. And no, she wasn't going to touch the battery-operated friend that Destiny had persuaded her to buy on their last shopping expedition. She was going to sleep. Sleep. And tomorrow morning she was going to go and find the nearest bookshop, buy a few new reads and then return to bed with three litres of water, a fruit basket and a historical drama that definitely didn't feature scenes of wild sexual abandon. It was time for a detox of body, mind and libido.

In her bedroom she clicked her fingers and the bedside lamps flickered on. She loved that. She took off her silk halter-neck top then dropped her skirt, before unclipping the sheer taupe bra and sliding off the matching thong. She caught her reflection in the mirror: she'd definitely lost some weight, and perhaps it was just the complimentary lighting but her legs looked a little more toned — probably all that walking around in high heels. Her calf muscles had been tighter than banjo strings since she'd got here.

As she wandered through to the bathroom to brush her teeth, she realised that she was dragging out the whole process in the hope that Jude would be home before she fell asleep. She opened the bathroom door, then stopped dead. It took her eyes a few moments to adjust to the dim candlelight and her brain a few moments to catch up. There, in Roxy's bath, illuminated by a dozen candles, was a very naked Jude. A very gorgeous, naked Jude.

And, lying in front of him, with her back pressed against his chest, her eyes closed while his hands cupped her breasts, was a very naked and very blissful Goldie.

Jude was the first to speak — and he had the good manners to remove his palms from his girlfriend's nipples. "Sorry, Ginny, didn't expect you home so early. We came in here because this is the biggest bath. For two. And . . . okay, I'm going to stop talking now and we'll get out of here."

As soon as he'd started to speak, Goldie's eyes had flipped open. She carried on where Jude left off, with not a shred of embarrassment or awkwardness. "Hey, honey, how are you?" she asked, in the kind of breezy manner that suggested they'd just bumped into each other in the frozen-food aisle at Asda.

"Er . . . naked?" Ginny replied, snatching a towel from the nearby hook and holding it in front of her. Just when she'd thought that life couldn't get any more crazy, she was having a casual, everyday conversation with one of the stars of British television — complete with full-frontal nudity.

Goldie threw back her head and emitted the very same laugh that most of the nation heard as they munched on their cornflakes.

"Babe, you'll have to move first to let me up," Jude prompted her.

Ginny started to retreat. "I'll just wait out here while you . . ."

"Don't."

She had taken a few steps backwards when the command stopped her.

"Unless, of course, you want to," Goldie continued. "But it's okay with me if you stay."

Goldie's voice was suddenly low, seductive, and Ginny's eyes had gone from darting around the room in a desperate bid to find something to focus on other than Goldie's nipples, to staring straight at her.

Her heart began to race. Oh, God. Oh, God. This was another one of those moments. Another one of those crazy bloody moments that had been coming thick and fast since the moment she'd stepped into the parallel universe of Shagville.

"In fact, it's okay with me . . ." Goldie was purring again. Purring. At her. The woman who interviewed pensioners about their talking budgies, who raised money for the sick and poor, who lunched with Cherie Blair, was purring at her.

". . . it's okay with me if you join us."

Ginny's lungs had now stopped functioning and she was struggling to breathe. This was outrageous. It was like discovering Fiona Phillips was a closet dominatrix and used willy clamps on Darren Castle during the commercial breaks.

Her eyes flicked from Goldie's to Jude's. Surprise was etched in his gorgeous features, but he gave her an easy, languid smile. "Only if you want to, babe. If not we'll get out of here."

Right then. So the way Ginny saw it she had choices here:

312

a) Let the nerves that were making her tremble escalate until she threw up — possibly a passion killer and definitely messy.

b) Ask them to leave and spend the rest of the night imagining what they were going to be doing in the next room.

c) Retreat gracefully, throw on some clothes and go spend the night at the nearest Travel Inn.

d) Joi — joi — join — holy crap, she could hardly even bring herself to think it . . . Join in. In which case she would never again be able to watch morning telly without a beaming face and crossed legs.

"Ginny?" It was Jude again, gently probing for an answer.

She couldn't do it. She couldn't. She might have come a long way in the last month but this was a fondle too far. She couldn't do it. She . . . She'd just dropped the towel to the floor and was now standing there once again completely naked.

Goldie held out her hand, and after a moment that seemed to last for longer than a breakfast-telly news bulletin, Ginny walked towards them.

At the edge of the bath, she paused. What was the procedure here? Should she climb in the other end? Climb on top? Don a scuba set and go straight to the underwater exploration bit?

Goldie helped her out. "Sit here," she ordered softly, motioning to a spot on the rim of the bath, about ten inches from Goldie's shoulders.

Ginny climbed onto the edge and swung her legs into the bath, the warm, frothy water reaching up to

313

just above her calves. Okay, what next? Because she didn't like to be pushy but she was still feeling like a bit of a spare tit. Or, rather, two spare tits.

Goldie reached over to the back of the bath and lifted the shower hose from its cradle. She turned on the mixer tap and tested the water jet as it shot out of the chrome head. When it was at the perfect temperature, she manoeuvred round so that she was directly in front of Ginny's (faintly trembling) knees. Ginny gasped as the water bounced off her thighs, slowly tracing a path from her knees, along her thighs, to her hips, then up over her stomach and breasts.

She closed her eyes, blocking out the astonishment at the scene in front of her, allowing her senses to take over and drown in what was proving to be an incredible sensation of utter ecstasy.

She felt Goldie's hand gently slide between her knees, softly prising them apart, wider, wider, then she gasped as the hot jets moved along her inner thighs and found her clitoris, pounding against it. She moaned as every nerve ending in her body reacted to the sheer bloody magnificence of the candlelit cleansing ritual.

Suddenly, she felt the shower jets subside and a very different texture was caressing the soft skin on the inside of her thighs. Slowly, almost excruciatingly slowly, Goldie's tongue moved in small, teasing circles towards the water droplets that still dripped from the little landing strip left after her inaugural Hollywood wax.

And when it reached her tingling mound, Ginny finally opened her eyelids and saw Jude, behind his lover, watching the scene with playful eyes. Then she turned her stare downwards, to the head that was between her legs. Her hands clenched even more tightly onto the edge of the bath rim, her legs opened even wider, and Goldie's tongue went even deeper as Ginny's orgasm built to the most exquisite crescendo.

And Ginny Wallis would forever reflect on the irony . . . She now knew what the woman she'd shared her mornings with for many years *really* liked to have for breakfast.

To: Felix DeMille
From: Mr C. Clacton — Dunhill, Clacton & Smythe Chartered Accountants
Date: 31.10.07 — 10.47a.m.
Subject: American Express Card — R. Galloway

Dear Mr DeMille,

We have received a communication this morning from American Express Card Services regarding the American Express card held on your account in the name of Roxanne Galloway.

As you know, it is a condition of this account that extreme variables in spending patterns be recorded and reported to you as principal cardholder. Over recent weeks, the expenditure on this account has increased dramatically; with an eighty per cent increase in average daily spend. More worrying, it seems, are the nature of the purchases on the account, which do seem to be rather unusual. An example of this follows:

Services of African Steel Drum Band: £10,000
One combine harvester (second-hand): £6,500

Please confirm that this card is still under your control, as we have obvious concerns that it has been stolen/cloned and is being used illegally.

We have been unable to contact you by telephone

to discuss this matter and would be grateful if you would confirm your current contact numbers.

We await your instruction,
Charles Clacton Esq.

To: Mr C. Clacton — Dunhill, Clacton & Smythe Chartered Accountants
From: Felix DeMille
Date: 31.10.07 – 10.48a.m.
Subject: OUT OF OFFICE REPLY American Express Card — R. Galloway

---

I will be out of my office from 26.10.07 until 11.11.07 inclusive. During this time I can be contacted on my mobile number. However, as I will be travelling throughout South America on a research trip, I cannot guarantee that I will always be within range. If you are therefore unable to reach me by phone, I will respond to your email on my return.
Felix DeMille

CHAPTER
SEVENTEEN

Baby Love

Roxy. Day 21, Saturday, noon

"Are you, like, my mother or something?"

"No, I'm Florence Fucking Nightingale, now eat the soup that I lovingly extracted from a tin or I'm putting on my Barry Manilow *Greatest Hits* CD."

"You are, like, more than evil."

Roxy winked and gave Juliet a cheesy thumbs-up. "Sweet of you to say."

Juliet pouted as she dunked a huge wedge of wholemeal bread into the bowl of chicken soup.

Roxy carried on hanging up knickers on a clothes rack that clipped over the one radiator in the living room. The unlikelihood of the situation didn't escape her — she hadn't washed her own clothes since, well, *ever*, and now here she was washing, drying and — God forbid — she might even suss out how to use the iron before the end of the day.

Even in a life that generally ricocheted from one crisis/drama/adventure to another, this had been a truly eventful week. More out of character than the fortnight in Lanzarote with Mimi. More enlightening than the time she paid five hundred quid for the world-famous psychic to tell her she was going to have Felix's babies (the big fat fake — she fleetingly wondered if she could sue under the Trade Descriptions Act).

Finding Juliet in the church that night was a scene that would be etched in her mind forever.

That *ER* box set Sam had sent her last time she'd had the flu hadn't been wasted. In between using scenes of that gorgeous Luca bloke as foreplay for personal relief, she'd picked up on what to do in the case of unconscious patients — apparently she should look beautiful yet fearful, and shout in a dramatic manner.

"Juliet, Juliet, wake up, honey, wake up!"

At which point the patient should wake up, groggily thank Roxy for saving her life, and promise to name her first child Roxy . . . a tad unfortunate if it was a boy.

Sadly it seemed that Juliet had a different perspective on the situation, because her reaction had been to twitch, groan, then throw up all over her rescuer.

It seemed they didn't need the ambulance after all — just treatment for post-traumatic stress disorder. Oh, and Juliet might need some help too.

Supporting her on both sides they'd half-walked/half-carried her into the church house and laid her on the couch, agreeing not to call the doctor after she'd vehemently reassured them that although she'd drunk her body weight in Jack Daniels, she'd only taken two Paracetamol.

Roxy wasn't sure if it had been a misinformed suicide attempt or a sensible measure to prevent a hangover the next morning.

After Roxy had wrenched off her sick-sodden sweatshirt and replaced it with the first thing that came to hand (and no, it didn't escape her notice that Father Murphy's ecumenical robe clashed with her trainers) she'd sent Mitch into the kitchen with an urgent, "Coffee, Chaka Khan, make coffee!" She'd pulled a blanket over Juliet, watching as the teenager clenched her jaw and slipped back into her usual abrasive, sullen demeanour.

"Don't you dare go all huffy on me, Vomit Girl — it'll take fucking weeks for me to get this smell out of my hair," she'd warned, her tone softer than her words. "So do you want to tell me what happened?"

Juliet shook her head and spat a resounding, very definite, "No."

Okay, this wasn't going to any kind of plan. Roxy instinctively knew that she had to tread gently, using the subtle probing techniques that she'd picked up over the years of getting great gossip out of people. Then she'd decided that since vomit was currently hardening on her hair, she didn't have time to beat around the bush. "Tell me or I'm calling the doctor, the police and your parents."

Juliet had caved like a reformed criminal on *Oprah*.

"Saffron and Ben — they've been seeing each other behind my back. Bastards."

Roxy gasped. She hadn't seen that coming at all. "So that's what all the commotion was about this afternoon?"

Juliet had nodded. "Saffron just walked in and announced it. Says she's been shagging him for months and she was fed up of waiting for him to chuck me."

"But she's your best mate!" Roxy had exclaimed. A sudden vision of Darren's dick had come into her head. Pot. Kettle. She'd shrugged the image away. That wasn't the same as this at all. She was the victim in that whole situation and so she knew just how Juliet was feeling. Empathise, Roxy, empathise in a mature yet insightful manner.

"What a bitch! Oh, I could slap the tramp. And he's no bloody better. But, honey, topping yourself isn't the answer."

Juliet had shrugged. "I wasn't trying to top myself."

Roxy gave her a cynical look.

"I wasn't, I promise! I just didn't want to think about them any more. So I started drinking and . . . I suppose I drank too much." She'd shrugged apologetically. "I'm sorry."

"What?"

"I'm sorry," Juliet had repeated.

"What?"

"I'M SORRY!"

Roxy shrugged. "S'okay, I heard you the first time — I was just milking it to make up for the fact that I'm sitting here dressed like a vicar and smelling like a cross-channel ferry toilet. And I can't promise I won't find other ways to make you pay over the coming week."

For the first time, Juliet had managed just a hint of a smile.

Mitch, still in panic mode, had barged in a few seconds later clutching a hot cup of black sweet coffee.

"Urgh, are you trying to kill me?" Juliet groaned. "I hate coffee. Any Lucozade? This is, like, so lame."

"Juliet, honey," Roxy had laughed. "I think you're on the mend."

And that's the point when the titles should have rolled on this happy little scene and they should all have gone back to their lives, sharing forever the secret bond of this emotional experience.

In make-believe land.

In reality, they'd given Juliet a lift home in the church car (a canary-yellow Volvo Estate, circa 1982, that some old bloke had generously bequeathed to the church on his deathbed — although as Father Murphy had been giving him last rites at the time there were accusations of coercion) and made an astonishing discovery.

Roxy had helped her out of the back seat and insisted on coming in with her.

"I'm fine, I don't need any more help!" Juliet had protested adamantly. She might have got away with it if she hadn't immediately wobbled and slammed into the miniature conifer that sat in a chipped terracotta pot at the front door of her tiny terraced house, sending chards of pottery careering along the street.

"Look, I promise I won't tell your mum or dad what happened — but I'm not leaving you here until I know that you've got someone to look after you. If you choke on your own vomit and die my karma will be fucked forever."

"My mum's out."

"So I'll wait until she gets home."

"You can't."

"I can."

"You can't."

"I can. Juliet, face it — you won't win this. When it comes to being determined, obstinate and immature, I'm the master. So I'm coming in whether you like it or not. And anyway, that dickhead Ben might come round and you're in no condition to deal with him."

She'd turned to Mitch, sitting at the wheel of the Volvo and unable to resist a smile as he witnessed the exchange. "Mitch, you go on home, I'll call you tomorrow."

"You sure?"

"Jesus! Can someone just do what I bloody tell them around here?"

He'd gone zero to thirty in about a minute and a half.

Juliet knew when she was beaten. She'd grudgingly opened the door and let Roxy follow her, flicking on a table lamp just inside the hallway. It was a typical two-up two-down, part of a picturesque little terrace that used to house the staff of the big estate back in the early 1900s. The inside was sparse but neat: magnolia walls, beech laminate flooring, two navy Ikea sofas, and a light wood coffee table that matched the TV unit in the corner.

A hallway, made narrow by the flight of stairs that ran up one wall, led through to the kitchen, small enough that the pine units and cork floor tiles added to the cosy feel, but big enough for a tiny wrought-iron table and two chairs to sit in the centre of the room.

Every surface was clean, every corner tidy, so much so that it almost looked uninhabited.

Roxy caught sight of the pictures on the wall — a blonde woman not much older than herself, arms around a slightly younger Juliet, both of them laughing at something off camera. Pictures of Juliet, aged around four, around eight, around twelve.

"So, no brothers or sisters then?"

Juliet shook her head as she went on through to the kitchen, only a slight wobble in her walk now. She returned a moment later clutching two cans of Diet Coke, one of which she held out to Roxy. "Sorry, I don't have any tea or coffee."

"Then don't ever invite my aunt here because the shock would kill her."

Juliet attempted a smile as she sat down on one of the sofas and pulled her feet up underneath her, the dim light of the lamp making her look much younger than her age.

"And Dad?"

Juliet shrugged. "Lives in Manchester. He and Mum split up when I was eight. Haven't seen him for years."

Roxy sat down on the opposite couch. There was a prolonged silence as she tried to make eye contact with her young emergency case and Juliet tried to avoid it.

"So . . . erm . . . what time will your mum be home?"

Juliet shrugged. "You don't have to wait, I've told you I'm fine," she protested again.

Roxy was having none of it. "Okay, let's skip the argument and go straight to the bit where I win — I'm not going anywhere until someone else is here with you."

And that's when it had finally happened — the most unexpected thing of all. Miss Hard-Arse Teenager, the girl who, it seemed, had gone directly from puberty to her mid-twenties, had burst into tears.

"You're going to have a long wait then, because she's in Tunisia."

"What? When's she coming back?"

Juliet shrugged, much to Roxy's despair. For goodness' sake, bloody teenagers these days, they were so self-absorbed they took no interest in other people's lives at all, especially their parents'. But given that Juliet was sobbing and such stressful activity might encourage a repeat of the whole vomit situation, she tried to remain patient.

"Concentrate, honey, concentrate. Did she go for a week or a fortnight?"

Juliet sniffed so hard she started to choke.

"A fo — fo — fortnight," she spluttered.

"Okaaaay. And when did she leave?"

"A year and a half ago."

Roxy choked back her surprise. "You're kidding! So you've been living here on your own since you were —"

"Fifteen."

Roxy was gob-smacked. Fifteen. Alone. "No grandparents, no family around here?"

Juliet shook her head. "She'll come back soon. She said she would. She met this guy, a waiter in her hotel, and that's why she stayed, but they're going to get married and then they'll come back here. They're just trying to sort out visas and jobs and stuff. Promise you won't tell anyone. Promise. I don't want her getting into trouble." She was wailing now.

Roxy sprang to Juliet's side and cradled her head, having a mild panic herself at the prospect of comforting someone. What had she been thinking coming here? She was no good at this. She hated other people's problems. This was exactly why she had a golden rule only to care about her own crap — the minute you got involved with someone else's you ended up with snot on your shoulder and sick in your hair.

She put her arms awkwardly round the snivelling wreck, doing her best to minimise the transfer of even more body fluids to her clothing, hands, face or hair.

"Didn't the neighbours notice? Or school? Or your friends?"

Juliet shook her head. "The neighbours are really old — bed-ridden on both sides. They think Mum just works long hours in two jobs. That's what she did before she left here. They don't get suspicious cos I take them in some biscuits every couple of weeks and tell them Mum asked me to drop them in while she was at work."

Next she'd be saying she rescued puppies and did meals-on-wheels in her spare time. Roxy felt a strange sensation and mentally gave herself a kicking. Do not let this tug on your heartstrings, Roxy, do not! Put the teenager down, back away gently, then run for your life.

Hold on . . . some other things didn't make sense.

"What about money?"

"The CSA make my dad pay up every month — I pay the rent and live off that. It's not much, but it's enough."

"Fair enough. But if you've got a permanent empty house, why are you always shagging in the library toilets? Why not bring prick-head back here?"

Well, at least that one stopped the snivelling. Juliet wiped her eyes, staring at the floor, her voice flat now.

"Because I didn't want him to know Mum wasn't here. Didn't want anyone to know. And anyway, what if she came back, unexpected like, and he was here? She'd go mental."

"Yep, because she's a paragon of virtue and responsibility," Roxy drawled.

The switch on the post-pubescent hormonal roller coaster flicked to "FURY".

"Don't say that! She's . . . she's nice, my mum. She just . . . she hated it here, always working and no life, and now she's met someone and they'll be back soon, they will. Now, please, just go. I'm fine, I'll be fine. Fine!"

"Okay, Okay." Roxy was holding up her hands in surrender. Time for the exit strategy to be activated. As far as she could see, Juliet was no longer in danger of a lethal choking incident or death due to Jack Daniels intoxication. Although, if extreme gobbiness was a life-threatening condition then she was still critical.

But it wasn't Roxy's problem. She rose to her feet. "I get it, you're fine." She picked up her bag from the sofa and grabbed her cardi. She'd walk home — it was only ten minutes and if she rushed then there was a chance she'd get there before hypothermia necessitated the intervention of a St Bernard.

She was almost at the door when another thought came to her.

"So why did you go to the church tonight then? I mean, if no one was here, why didn't you just get wellied here on your own?"

The pre-pubescent hormone switch flicked to "SAD".

"I just . . . I just go there sometimes. When I . . . need someone to talk to."

Roxy's emotional barometer flicked to "AW, FUCK".

She'd almost made it. Almost. Like the prison escapee who gets to the perimeter fence before the floodlights flash on and a hoard of guard dogs attach themselves to his bollocks. Like the comedic marathon runner who gets to twenty-five and a half miles before the heat of his badger suit causes him to faint on national telly. Like the gigolo who avoids an unexpected meeting with a homicidal husband by climbing out the bathroom window. Of a forty-fourth-floor penthouse.

Yep, she'd almost got away.

She let her bag slump to the floor and shrugged her cardi back off.

"Do you know what you need, Juliet? Apart from a bath and some really strong mouthwash?"

She was met with a questioning stare.

"You need me — your fairy fucking godmother."

Two days later and she was still there. In fact, she'd moved in now, lock, stock and Fendi Spy, after making a trip home for clothes, toiletries and essential supplies, which — according to her mother — consisted of three packets of chocolate digestives and a crate of PG Tips. She'd spun them a story about Juliet's mum being called away on a medical emergency for a few weeks and asking Roxy to keep an eye on her daughter.

Juliet slurped her soup and flicked the telly onto the *Hollyoaks* omnibus on Channel Four.

"By the way, I had a new one this morning: combine harvester, a total, like, bloodbath, with the leftover body-parts squashed by cows."

"Oh, I've taught you well, Luke Skywalker."

"Luke who?"

Roxy chuckled as she draped another G-string on the radiator's temperature knob.

"Never mind. But I still think I prefer the parachute that doesn't open, followed by the fatal landing in a sewage plant. Thought that one was a bit classier."

"Probably right." Slurp.

It was their favourite game — slow and painful death scenarios for erstwhile friends and boyfriends. Ben had phoned twice — once to beg forgiveness and the second time to find out if Roxy really did intend to put posters all over the village saying he was a two-timing twat.

Saffron hadn't even had the decency to grovel yet. The devious slut: aeroplane, thirty thousand feet, flushes the toilet and is sucked out, arse first, and scattered over Slough.

The doorbell rang, and Juliet's immediate reaction was to look at Roxy with a panicked expression. She'd spent so long living there on her own that she was

329

finding it strange adjusting to having other people in her space. In saying that, it wasn't all bad. Roxy had pretended to be her aunt (her second fictional relative of the week) and had phoned the school yesterday to say she was laid up with a stomach bug (semi-true — her digestive system was still half-pissed) and they'd spent the whole day slouched in front of the telly watching old *Friends* videos. And somewhere between series three and four, they'd agreed a solemn pact that Juliet would not touch another drop of alcohol until her eighteenth birthday.

"Keep your knickers on, it's just Mitch," Roxy chided her. "I asked him pick us up some food that doesn't come in a package with a list of E-numbers on the front. Shit, shoot me now before I turn into Gwyneth Paltrow."

"Who?"

"Never mind."

Mitch staggered in the door, struggling to carry eight plastic bags, a large box of wine and a multi-pack of six-litre bottles of Evian.

"Oh, and the wine's for me, Oliver Reed," she reminded Juliet.

"Who?"

Mitch laughed as he rushed through to the kitchen, the weight causing his legs to buckle so that he was almost walking on his knees by the time he got there.

Roxy followed behind him. "Oooh, I love it when you flex your muscles," she teased.

"And that's exactly the kind of insincere, sarcastic disparagement that will have me at your beck and call," he jibed back light-heartedly.

Roxy thought again about how much she liked him. He was absolutely, positively the most easy-going, good-natured bloke she'd ever met in her life. If he was a food he'd be chocolate. If he was a drink he'd be Irish coffee. If he was in love with her he'd be . . . Doh! Why did that one keep creeping back in?

After shaking out his arms so the blood started to flow through the hands that had been strangled by plastic-bag handles, he kissed her on the cheek. "How's the patient?"

"She's moody, sullen and bitter, interjected with moments of sarcastic brilliance. I think she's fabulous."

"It's like a meeting of soul mates. Back in a minute, need to pee."

"Okay, I'll unpack this lot. And Mitch? Too much information there, pet."

He was still chuckling when he went into the loo. He wasn't chuckling when he came out five minutes later.

Roxy and Juliet were both in the kitchen, surrounded by open cupboards.

"Do you know the toilet is blocked?"

"Noooo," wailed Roxy. "Oh, crap!"

"Thank you for that summary of the situation. Juliet, have you got a plunger?"

"Dunno. There might be one under the sink — I think that's where the DIY stuff is kept. I've never had to use it."

"And it definitely wasn't me who blocked it. Definitely not," Roxy protested. Too much. The others rounded on her, eyebrows raised, looking at her questioningly.

"I mean," she blustered, "it definitely wasn't me who used four baby wipes to take my make-up off last night and then flushed them down the toilet, even though it says on the packet that you shouldn't. I'd never do that. Never. Okay, okay, it was me — I'm really sorry."

Mitch located the plunger and pulled it out, playfully brandishing it six inches from Roxy's face and moving it from side to side in a pendulous manner.

"Toilet. Your gob. Toilet. Your gob. God, sometimes life's big decisions are really hard. Right, if I'm not back out in ten minutes, call the coastguard. And after this there'd better be a whole lot of lovin' and chocolate biscuits coming in my direction. After I've washed my hands, that is."

And off Plumber Pat went, plunger thrown over his shoulder in a laissez-faire fashion.

Roxy tried to conjure up an image of Felix, dressed in work boots and a very fetching boiler suit, doing the same. Nope, not happening. However, several other scenarios involving him and the plunger did come to mind, although they were rapidly followed by a custodial sentence at Her Majesty's pleasure.

Over the next few minutes there was banging, several expletives and much swooshing of water.

Then there was silence. And more silence.

And just when Roxy was considering checking the *Yellow Pages* for the coastguard's number, they finally heard footsteps.

Mitch appeared in the doorway, looking like a man with a dilemma on his mind.

332

"So did you find the blockage then, or am I going to have to call the trading standards office and report your substandard plumbing skills?"

He hesitated. Then, realising that there was no way out of the drama he was about to cause, he ploughed on nervously.

"Er . . . I did. And it wasn't the baby wipes."

Silence.

"Okay, we're talking about toilet functions here and I'd like to eat soon, so can we hurry this one up?" Roxy heckled.

"Erm, well, I think it was caused by this."

And there, in the doorway, was the nicest man in the world, clutching a plunger in one hand, and in the other, the very unmistakable long white stick of a pregnancy test — one that he'd already ascertained had a little blue line on both windows.

Roxy froze, Juliet froze, both of them unable to tear their eyes away from the stick in front of them.

After a few moments of deathly, incredibly tense silence, Mitch was the first to speak. "So . . . who should I congratulate?"

The Sunday Globe — Lifestyle Supplement
28 October 2007

WHY I'M HAPPY ALONE — GOLDIE GILMARTIN ON LIFE, HEALTH AND WHY SHE LOVES TO BE ALONE

The first thing that strikes you about Goldie Gilmartin (46) is her smile — it may have been perfected at the hands of the country's leading cosmetic dentist, but the sentiment behind it is contagious. Goldie, as those of you who are devoted fans of her morning show will know, is pure sunshine. Her eyes are bright, she radiates health, and if you could bottle happiness this ebullient star would be its source.

So just what is the secret of Goldie's physical and spiritual glow? The answer might surprise you. "I've discovered that for me the most important thing at this stage of my life is to nurture my mind, body and soul," Goldie tells me when we meet at her elegant West London home. "It's important to keep life simple," she continues. "Gone are those stressful days of my twenties and thirties when I was intent on having the perfect relationship, the perfect career and the perfect lifestyle. Now I know what works for me, and that's living alone and dedicating myself to work, friends and health. I read, I eat well, I exercise and I avoid late nights."

So, no handsome beau to share those long winter evenings by her romantic log fire?

"It's difficult to find the right person," admits Goldie. "What's important to me in a relationship is that there is a deep emotional connection, that is a meeting of intellect and interests. I'm sure that person will come along one day, but in the meantime I'm happy with just my cat to keep me company.

"To be honest with you," she reveals, flashing those pearly whites, "these days I much prefer an early night with a good book and perhaps a small glass of my favourite red wine. In my job it's important to put the viewers first, and by taking good care of myself I'm ensuring that they get the very best performance out of me every morning on the very best show. And, forgive me if I sound too boring, but it's all worth it to be given the privilege of doing what I truly think is the best job in the world."

And one final question — surely she must have one little vice?

After a few moments of consideration, Goldie flicks back those glorious copper locks and prepares to confess all. "I do," she admits. "Every now and then I have a little nibble at something I shouldn't. Sometimes it's chocolate, sometimes perhaps a tiny taste of caviar. But then, wouldn't life be terribly boring if one didn't have a secret indulgence?"

Well, I'm sold! As Goldie and I part I can't help but reflect that if moderation, self-control and celibacy are the key to looking as great as she does, maybe we should all give it a try!

CHAPTER
EIGHTEEN

I Got You, Babe

Ginny. Day 21, Saturday, 1p.m.

The hammering on the front door was incessant. Ginny opened one eye and squinted against the sun that was squeezing in around the perimeter of the window blind. The door-knocker was rapped again.

Ginny swore under her breath. If this was the postman again she was reporting him to his supervisor. Sure, he was young, sure, he was gorgeous, and sure, Roxy had once snogged him in a fit of petulance during one of her many fallouts with Felix, but that didn't give the guy the right to bang on their door every morning in the hope of a replay.

She staggered to her feet and checked her pyjamas to make sure she was decent. That's when she realised she wasn't wearing any. The tingle started at her toes, rose to her lurching stomach and turned her face scarlet when it reached the top.

Oh. Lord. Oh good Lord. Her hand flew to her mouth, embarrassment paralysing her. What had she done? All right, she knew exactly what she'd done, but ... *What had she done?* Or, rather, *who* had she done?

She closed her eyes. *Mortified!* Her heart was racing, her toes were curling and she'd gladly faint only she didn't want to get carpet burns when her buttocks hit the floor.

She had had sex with Goldie Gilmartin. And Jude. Together. At the same time.

Was twenty-seven too young to have a stroke, because she could swear her peripheral vision was going and she felt a sudden need to hyperventilate into a paper bag.

Sex. Goldie. Jude. Together.

Breathe, breathe . . .

And this was the girl who used to think a ménage à trois was a triple-fruit yoghurt.

Well, so much for the detox of her mind, body and lady bits. As far as she knew there wasn't a spa in the world that could offer a night of shagging one of the country's national treasures as a therapeutic escape from the stresses and strains of everyday life.

The knocking stopped. Fabulous, the postman had obviously given up and gone on to solicit intimate relations from another household. Okay, so what next? Ginny stood absolutely still, unsure of whether she wanted to go back to bed, go into the kitchen in search of intravenous caffeine, or just wait and hope that the shag-pile would part like the Red Sea and the ground would indeed ingest her whole.

She listened for a second — no sound. Did that mean Jude and Goldie had gone out? It was Saturday morning so Goldie didn't have a live show but she did sometimes pre-record features over the weekend.

338

She was so glad they hadn't slept in her room.

During that couple of hours of naked acrobatics she'd done things that were fairly unremarkable . . . if you worked as a full-time porn star. In Ginny's case, they were remarkable. *Definitely* remarkable.

And when it was over and they'd all collapsed on the floor, exhausted, spent, euphoric, she'd been overcome with a huge wave of . . . giggles. Yep, giggles. Snot coming down her nose, sides splitting, jaw aching, tears-streaming giggles.

It was another moment of indignity. But then considering she'd sat on the face of a major TV star while said TV star's boyfriend's cock was tickling her tonsils, she supposed dignity had probably already left the building.

The mirth had been contagious. The other two had joined in and it was a good ten minutes before any semblance of normal conversation could take place. And even then, that's only if the banner of "normal conversation" encompassed, "Ginny, babe, you were sooooo good."

And her own personal favourite from Goldie. "Fuck, honey, I could just lick you all over again. With cream on top."

It was Jude who'd eventually moved proceedings on. They'd lain in silence for a few moments, Jude in the middle, Goldie snuggled into one side of him, Ginny lying perpendicular with her head on his abs, when he'd whispered, "Do you want us to sleep here with you?"

Ginny had shaken her head. "No . . . er . . . thanks. I'm fine. But thanks anyway."

They'd peeled off each other, and Jude had kissed her softly on the lips. "See you tomorrow, babe. You really were amazing."

"Erm, right then. Thanks."

Then Goldie had repeated his actions, finishing with, "Incredible. Goodnight, my darling."

"Er, 'night then."

As she'd pushed herself off the shag-pile — nope, the irony wasn't lost — she'd listened to their feet padding through to Jude's bedroom. Still in some kind of post-bliss euphoric trance, she'd wandered into the bathroom, slipped into the now cool bath, and closed her eyes. It had been so surreal. It almost felt like she had been detached from the whole thing, the perfectly behaved, boring Ginny levitating somewhere up above Porn Ginny, watching the action in utter astonishment. After a five-minute soak, she'd dried off and slipped between the sheets, the prospect of looking for pyjamas and putting them on seeming like bolting the door after the slapper horse had bolted.

She should have stared at the ceiling for hours. She should have tossed and turned. She should have spent what was left of the night fretting about the consequences of what had just happened.

But she hadn't.

She'd slipped into a blissful, dreamless sleep. Right up until Postman Pat had almost battered her door down.

"Ginny! Ginny!"

340

She gasped, as her surreal existence moved on to a whole new level of absurdity. Had someone slipped something in her drink last night? Only, she was standing in the middle of her room, utterly naked, and all she could hear was her mother's voice.

"Ginny! Ginny! Open the door!"

Ginny grabbed a robe from the back of the door, threw it on and dashed into the hall. And there, in a definitely non-hallucinatory scene, were her mother's eyes, clearly visible through the letterbox.

"Sorry, Mum, sorry!" She dived to the door and threw it open, revealing her mother and Auntie Vera, both radiant in coordinating boot-leg jeans, polo-neck jumpers (Vera's blue, Violet's pink), fake fur gilets (Vera's pink, Violet's blue), huge grins and sparkling eyes.

"Sweetheart!" her mother screeched, falling on her and enveloping her in a hug so tight she could floss her teeth on the gilet. "It's so lovely to see you — oh, we've missed you, haven't we, Vera?"

Vera joined in, turning the scene from a tender embrace into a team hug.

Two threesomes in one morning, Ginny reflected.

"I've missed you too! Come in, come in. I'm sorry I'm not dressed, I was having a bit of a lie-in — late night last night." She gave her mother another squeeze, realising for the first time just how much she had actually missed her. Life just wasn't the same without her mother's eccentricities, her overwhelming affection and her . . .

"Right, love, let's get the kettle on, shall we?"

Yep, her beverages.

Ginny held the door open as they paraded in past her, carrying an assortment of plastic and canvas bags, then slammed it shut before the fashion police SWAT team could storm the flat.

"Mum, how long are you here for?"

"Oh, we're not staying, love. We're on the eleven o'clock train home tonight — just popped in on a theatre break. Our Roxy arranged it for us. We just thought we'd come to see you for a couple of hours, and then we're off for afternoon tea at the Ritz and on to the theatre."

"*Evita?*" she asked, knowing that her mother had a particular fondness for singing "Don't Cry for Me, Argentina" at ASBO level while in the shower.

"No, love, *Vagina Monologues*. Now here's a ginger slice — brought them specially because I know they're your favourites."

In an artfully constructed sequence, Violet filled the kettle, flicked it on, located three mugs, popped a teabag in each, added milk and sugar, found a plate for the cakes, set them in a perfect circle, poured the water into the cups, stirred them, removed and dumped the teabags, handed a cup to everyone and, on the third attempt, managed to lever herself up onto one of the barstools next to the kitchen island.

Vera followed suit, taking five attempts to mount the stool and breathing deeply, face flushed by the time she conquered it.

"Right then, love, come on," she gestured excitedly to Ginny. "We want to hear about everything you've been up to since you got here — and don't miss out a single thing! I bet you've been up to all sorts! Have you been to a disco yet? Ooh, I hear they get up to all sorts in the clubs here. Thank goodness Roxy's not one for going out much. I was always worried she'd fall in with a wild crowd. She's easily led, you know, easily led."

Ginny took a sip of tea in the fervent hope that it would reach the parts of her that were still aching after last night's activities.

"How is Roxy doing?" Ginny asked, managing to keep the venom out of her voice.

"Oh, she's great, just great, isn't she, Violet?" Violet nodded. "You know she's moved out?"

Ginny shook her head, dumbfounded. She's *what?* Dear God, no — if that bitch had somehow managed not only to get her evil fangs into Darren again but to move in with him, she'd have to kill her.

"Yes, moved in with young Juliet. Mother's away — didn't say why, but I'm thinking hysterectomy, very common these days, you know — and she's asked Roxy to look after Juliet for her. Isn't that lovely?"

Ginny hoped she was nodding. Either that or her brain was still swimming in champagne and adrenaline and sliding back and forwards. Her mother took over the story. Jesus, they were like Richard and Judy, but with four breasts and a high-grade Primark habit.

"Especially now that she's found love." Violet nudged Vera and they both exchanged beaming grins and winks.

"Found love?" *Love? Already?* Darren had only dumped her a few weeks before and already he was in love. Mean, cowardly dickhead — why hadn't he had the courage to tell her all this to her face? He'd definitely given her the impression that Roxy was a one-time thing, not a candidate for meetings with the vicar and a rousing chorus of "Here Comes the Slut". Okay, she might have made that last bit up but that's what *she* would be singing, through a megaphone, at the back of the church.

"Yes!" Vera was near giddy with glee now. "Her and that nice Mitch have been inseparable, *inseparable*, since the minute they met. Of course, they haven't announced it officially yet, but then you know how shy our Roxy is about these things."

Ginny's mug was frozen in thin air as she wondered if Vera had two daughters with the same name: Nice Roxy, and her evil twin, Satan Roxy, the one that Ginny had had to suffer since childhood.

How could a mother know so little about her own flesh and blood? Vera wasn't wearing rose-tinted spectacles; she was wearing a balaclava backwards.

But . . . *Roxy and Mitch*? Where the hell had that come from? And what about Darren, then? She presumed that Roxy had actually left Mitch's side when she was sucking off her ex-best friend's ex-boyfriend. Unless of course they'd gone to the Goldie Gilmartin School of Conjugal Behaviour.

None of this made sense, and now her head was starting to really, really hurt.

She took a huge gulp of tea as she psyched herself up to attempt to unravel the threads of the story. "So let me get this straight: Roxy is going out with Mitch . . ."

"Unofficially," interjected her mother, with a simultaneous tap to the side of her nose and a wink.

"And she's living at Juliet's, in the role of babysitter, because Juliet's mum is away for a hysterectomy."

"Correct."

"Oh." Unclear as to the appropriate response to any of these revelations, Ginny took the sensible approach and drank more tea.

"Anyway, we want to hear all about you, dear. Have you enjoyed working at Roxy's office? What are all the staff like? I bet they're dead posh. And have you met any celebrities on the tube or anything?"

"It's been fine. Roxy's workmates are all really nice and, yes, very posh. But no celebrities yet — although I'm still keeping my fingers crossed for Daniel Craig on the District Line."

Vera and Violet chortled. "Maybe we'll meet a celebrity at the Fanny Show tonight, Vera," said Violet with a nudge.

"Mum! I hate that word — don't say that!"

Ginny's face was burning. How provincial was she? Apparently it was fine to have intimate relations with that part of the female anatomy, but actually saying the word invoked deep embarrassment and moral outrage.

The older women ignored her, too enraptured at the prospect of rubbing shoulders with the glitterati. "I read somewhere that Sharon Osbourne goes all the time," Vera revealed conspiratorially.

"I love her hair. Do you think I'd suit those burgundy highlights, Vera?"

"You would! I can just see it — it would really bring out your eyes. Although I'm not sure it would go with your green mohair jumper — might have to donate that to the Cancer Research shop."

And off they went, veering off on a tangent, their conversation gliding along on a plane of mutual affection, joint interest and dual fixations on life's little irrelevancies. Ginny had absolutely no idea what they were on about, cared even less, yet could think of nothing nicer than sitting here all afternoon, drinking tea, listening to the familiar burr of their voices in the background.

This living a cosmopolitan life was all very well, but there was no denying that she missed the warmth and comfort of these two eccentric creatures.

She wondered if this was what she and Roxy would have been like in thirty years if neither of them had ever left the village. She doubted it — Roxy would be on her seventh unsuspecting husband by now, having shagged and drained the bank accounts of every man with competent bodily functions within a ten-mile radius. Meanwhile Ginny would probably be married to Darren and would have slipped into a boredom-induced coma that resulted in twenty-four-hour medical care and a serious gin addiction.

Either that or she'd be in jail after catching Roxy sucking Darren's dick behind the tombola stall at the annual summer fair and beating them to death with Mrs Robinson-Smith's prize-winning marrow.

Actually, right now that could still be a viable option.

Roxy. And Mitch. She'd no idea why but the prospect of that happy coupling had her hackles in a vertical position. At the risk of sounding like Ginny Wallis aged eight and three quarters, why did Roxy have to take *everything*? Mitch was *her* friend. He was the person *she* spent most mornings with, chatting over the newspapers and setting the world to rights. He didn't belong with Roxy, he was too nice. Roxy should be with . . . with . . . There was never a serial killer around when you needed one.

Vera's shrieks of hilarity cut through her thoughts. "Could you imagine! It would be like throwing a sausage up the Dartford Tunnel."

Both women were near purple with giddiness, her mother reaching for a re-infusion of tea to calm herself down. Ginny didn't even contemplate working the joke back from that punch line — there were some things in life she could live without knowing.

And, she mused, there were some things that she could definitely live without her mother knowing.

She had to bite her bottom lip to stop a smile forming as she imagined what Vera and Violet would think if they'd seen her just a few hours before. She was guessing there'd be shock, surprise, and an emergency call to Father Murphy requesting urgent Catholic intervention. Nah, they'd never believe it. If they thought Roxy was so angelic then they must think that Ginny was barely a step or two away from canonisation.

"Well, I wouldn't mind hearing the rest of *that* story," came an amused voice from the doorway.

Ginny's last thought before the chaos started was, "Oh dear God, here we go." Because there, in the doorway, wearing a thigh-skimming, cleavage-bearing purple silk robe, ruffled hair, and the unmistakable general messiness of someone who'd been ravished in recent hours, was Goldie Gilmartin, the woman Ginny's mother revered to such an extent that she had, on several occasions, called the *Great Morning TV* show to demand that Goldie run for prime minister.

"Vera! Vera! It's . . ."

"I can see, Vi, I can see, it's . . ."

"Morning, ladies, I'm Goldie," sang the sunny voice. Which would have been fine in itself if Goldie hadn't followed it by strolling across the room, kissing Ginny on the cheek and murmuring, "Morning, babe, how're you this morning?" in a very friendly manner.

Many times in life Ginny had read stories in the papers about people who reached adulthood only to die suddenly from a genetic heart defect that had been laying dormant waiting for some kind of extreme exertion or shock to deal a fatal blow. She had a feeling that if the same applied to her she was just seconds away from mourners and an extended chorus of "Ave Maria."

Shock Number One: she'd had no idea that Jude and Goldie were still here.

Shock Number Two: Goldie was half-naked and clearly just out of bed.

Shock Number Three: Her mother's mouth had been open for a good ten seconds, yet for the first time in, well, ever, she was apparently mute.

Shock Number Four: Her mother's tea was spilling down her faux-fur gilet and she hadn't noticed.

Ginny blustered the introductions then watched in awe as Goldie broke the ice like a pro, completely put her two biggest fans at ease and managed to sign their handbags with a hastily conjured-up marker pen while drinking fresh orange juice, slicing bananas, toasting two bagels and gracefully refusing an invitation to join them at "The Fanny Show". By the time she retreated back into the bedroom, Violet and Vera considered her family and had wangled an invitation to tour the studios on their next visit to London. Their lives were officially complete.

Ginny's was officially flashing before her eyes. What if they suspected? Did they know? Could they sense something?

Then she remembered that when it came to their daughters, these women had the insight and awareness of the average houseplant.

"Jude's girlfriend," Ginny explained as nonchalantly as possible.

"Is that right? You know what I think, don't you, Vera?"

"What's that, Vi?"

"That woman should be prime minister."

"Right, Vera, let's get going then."

"Are you sure you don't want to come back and stay here tonight, Mum? You two can have Roxy's bed and I'll sleep on the couch. I promise it's not a bother."

"Not at all, love, we need to get back. We're on a course tomorrow at the sports centre — something to do with cleansing your chapras."

"Chakras, mum, chakras," Ginny laughed.

"Exactly, dear. So . . ." she enveloped her daughter in a huge hug, "we'll see you next week then. And Ginny, honey, we're really sorry about Darren. You know if you want to chat about it just call us . . . or give Roxy a bell — it's always been such a blessing that you two are so close."

Ginny chose not to disillusion her. She'd deal with Roxy in her own way and in her own time.

She'd been so moved by their concern when she'd given them the sanitised version of her break-up — going out with each other for too long, grown apart, wanted to try other things, no one else involved, amicable on both sides, part as friends, etc., etc. They were surprised that neither Darren nor Roxy hadn't let the news slip, but she'd told them that was at her request. After all, if Violet was losing her reason for living, aka The Wedding Plan, then she thought it only fair that she break the tragedy personally.

Violet had given her a long, tight hug.

"That's okay, sweetheart, we just want you to be happy."

Ginny knew her mother was only saying that to console her — there was no way that a woman who'd sent the personalised napkin prototype back to the printers eleven times for adjustment, booked seven bands in case an outbreak of bird flu decimated the country's "Hi Ho Silver Lining"-singing musician pool, and visited every bridalwear shop south of Manchester could be this un-bothered.

They were in the hallway when Ginny realised that her eyes were welling up. This was ridiculous! She'd see them again in a week, yet she suddenly had the urge to throw her arms around her mother and beg her to stay. They could lie on the sofas watching old movies the way they used to do on a rainy Saturday afternoon before her mother and Vera decided that they were going to venture down the path to spiritual enlightenment and inner calm.

"Hang on, Vi, hang on, did you give her the parcel?"

"I thought you had it."

"No, you had it."

"Didn't you have it?"

They dropped their array of bags and started to rummage.

"You're right, Vera, I've got it. Here you go, love."

Ginny looked apprehensively at the brown square package. It was about twelve inches long, ten inches wide, two inches thick, and tied up with string. She leaned closer in a bid to ascertain whether or not it was ticking.

"Who sent it?"

"It was Mitch, love — dropped it in this morning for you."

"Oh." She took it, then lurched as she realised how heavy it was. Why would Mitch send her a present? Hold on, it could be a ploy — maybe Roxy had asked him to deliver it. She held it up to her ear. Nope, still no ticking, so she was probably safe.

351

"And this one's from us." Vi handed over a small square box tied with a bright pink ribbon. "Happy birthday for tomorrow, love."

Ginny was momentarily speechless. Her birthday. She'd forgotten all about it. Well, how about that? Serial shagging could obviously induce temporary amnesia. Who knew?

And since it was *her* birthday, that also meant it was Roxy's birthday too. Before she could stop it, a pang of sadness engulfed her. This would be the first birthday they'd ever spent apart. And somehow, given that they were on the same volatility level as, say, the average civil war, she didn't think it would be the last.

As soon as Vera and her mother were out of sight, she closed the door and then headed back to the kitchen for coffee. She'd only been in there a few minutes when Jude appeared, clutching two empty mugs.

"Hey."

"Hey," she replied warmly.

"Freaked out about last night?"

That was the thing about Jude — he always knew how to cut straight to the important stuff and say the right thing.

"You know, I probably should be but I'm not. Although, incidentally, I can't promise that my mother won't climb on stage tonight and announce that she's sending round a petition for Goldie to enter politics. What about you?"

He was obviously thinking through what he was going to say. "Ginny, I just don't want you to get hurt.

352

If you're okay with all of this then that's great, but I just
don't . . ."

"What?"

"I just don't want you to feel uncomfortable here, or
want anything to spoil our friendship, because I . . . er
. . . like that bit. *Really* like it. Will you tell me if it all
gets too weird?"

"Jude, I think we passed weird about a fortnight ago."

Her quip lightened the reflective mood. He gave her
a huge squeeze, then grabbed the refilled coffee cups.
"We're just going to hang out here today, watch a
couple of movies. Do you want to join us?"

Ginny laughed. "Tempting, but if you don't mind I'll
pass. Feel like a lazy afternoon just chilling out by myself."

"Okay, but if you get bored . . ."

Aaaah, the man was gorgeous. Gorgeous. Even now
as he wandered out of the room, her eyes automatically
fixated on his buttocks.

But not today. Today she wanted another couple of
hours' sleep then she was going to find a bookshop and
a bakery. Nothing but nothing was going to spoil that
or tempt her to do otherwise. Nothing. Absolutely —

"Jude, you and Goldie aren't planning on taking a
bath today, are you?"

He turned at the doorway, shaking his head while his
face cracked into a cheeky grin. "Wasn't in the plans
. . . unless . . ."

"No! No baths! Deal?" she jested.

"Deal."

She grabbed her coffee and both parcels and headed
back to the bedroom, where she swapped her robe for a

pair of fleecy tartan pyjamas then crawled back into bed. Mitch and Roxy. Aaargh! She shook off the irritation and diverted her attention to the present from her mother. She pulled the ribbon and opened the box, emitting a small gasp as she pulled out an exquisite gold chain. It took her a few seconds before she realised what the pendant hanging from it was — one perfectly crafted half of a heart, engraved on one side with her name.

As she clipped it around her neck she resisted the urge to phone her mum's mobile to thank her and tell her just how much she loved her. She'd do it later — her mum had a tendency to shout on the mobile phone, and if they were in a crowded place it could cause mass panic.

Next, Mitch's parcel. Chocolates? Nope, too heavy. Okay, she was stumped.

She peeled off the brown paper, astonishment overwhelming her when she reached the contents.

Crossing the Line, by Mitch O'Malley.

Underneath the title on the front page he'd written a note.

Hi Ginny,
Happy birthday! Hope you're doing great in the city. You said that you wanted to read this when it was finished, so here it is. Hope you enjoy. And if not, please lie to me because I prefer to be humoured. Give me a call sometime . . .
Love, Mitch. Xxx

He'd done it. He'd actually done it. And she'd . . . oh, shit, she'd spilled her coffee on it. She quickly brushed the brown stains off the page with Roxy's 800-thread-count Egyptian-cotton pillowcase. Sod her, she'd got the guy so she'd just have to get over the bedding.

She picked up the first page and started to read, defiantly ignoring the two big fat tears that splodged onto the page. The lack of sleep was obviously playing havoc with her emotions. Yep, that had to be it.

Eight hours, four toilet breaks, three sandwich runs and a couple more teary outbursts later she reached *THE END*.

And it was . . . it was . . . it was Mitch. It was honest, it was funny, it was clumsy, it was messy. There were bits that made absolutely no sense and there were little snippets of brilliance that had made her laugh until she cried. It was warm, it was adorable. It was . . . She missed him.

She missed him.

Thump. Thump. Thump.

She reached over to the knob beside her bed and flicked on the music system, turning it up just loud enough so that her moment of abject mournfulness wasn't played out to the backdrop of her flatmate's headboard banging against the wall. It was a wonder that six-foot slab of oak wasn't kindling by now.

She missed him. Hang on, was this some kind of reverse, petulant psychology at play because he was now the other half of her evil arch nemesis?

Or was it because she was lying here at midnight, on her own, while the shagging Olympics took place next door?

She could always go and join them, but somehow the idea didn't appeal. She realised that she suddenly felt exactly the same way as she did when she knew she should go out for a jog, but, quite frankly, couldn't be arsed.

Was that what sex had become? Relegated to the category of "physical exercise", somewhere in between pilates and a run around the village, stopping only when her thighs began to chafe?

She didn't want a workout, she wanted good company. She wanted to talk. She wanted conversations that didn't include the words *dick, cock* or *clitoris*.

She wanted . . . She had absolutely no idea what she wanted. But she knew, definitely knew, that she never wanted to spend another Saturday night lying in bed alone listening to a screeching, "Come on, baby, fuck me till I break."

She turned the music up a little louder. "Come on baby . . . harder!"

Louder.

"Oh, Jude . . ."

Louder.

"Oh, Jude . . ."

Louder.

Oh . . . crap.

The realisation made her tremble like a shelf in Ann Summers.

All this time she'd been so sure she was in control. So sure that she could handle what she was doing, so sure that coming here was the right thing to do.

But now, she knew. She knew. Because Ginny Wallis, for the first time in her life, was feeling a rising, thundering, all-encompassing wave of sheer, bitter, spitting jealousy.

Aaaargh! She wanted to stick her head out of a window and scream. She wanted to rage. She wanted to throw things against the wall.

Laidback, accepting, mild-mannered, che-sara-fucking-sara Ginny was gone, chased out of town by a big green monster — albeit one with an open-minded, experimental view of sexual relations.

She pushed herself out of bed and wandered through to the kitchen, her cheeks burning with indignation.

Fuck it. Fuck it. And she didn't ever say that word. But . . . Fuck it.

She was sitting at the kitchen island, her frothy cappuccino almost finished, when she heard the front door close and there he was, standing in the doorway, just a towel around his waist, with only the moonlight illuminating him.

"Hey."

"Hey."

"Was that Goldie leaving?"

"Yeah, she's got an early flight. She's gone home to pack."

He opened the fridge and, yep, right on cue she got that tingle in the pit of her stomach.

He pulled out a beer and popped the top of the bottle, then climbed on the stool next to her. Another unusual threesome: Ginny, Jude and Silence.

"So, do you want to hear something really weird?"

"Sure."

"You know earlier you asked if I was okay with all of this? Well . . . I don't think I am."

Silence.

And it lasted until Ginny absorbed and processed what he'd just said. And then a little bit longer than that, because the emotions that were tumbling inside of her had her vocal cords in a siege situation. Jude reached over and touched her face.

"I'm not okay with it. I was lying next door with Goldie . . ."

"Yep, I heard."

He had the decency to look bashful. "Sorry about that. But that's my point. I was lying there with Goldie and all I could think about was you. And not in the same kind of way as last night."

Her face took flushed to a whole new level.

"Just you. Ginny, I've never felt this way before and it's freaking me out. And I . . . I . . ."

"Hold on, I just need to check something," she interrupted, as she leaned towards him and slowly, tenderly, her lips touched his.

Her hands automatically came up and lost themselves in the thickness of his hair. Her lips parted now, her tongue meeting his as their breathing became deeper, deeper . . .

The doorbell sounded so loud it could be announcing the imminence of Armageddon.

Jude jumped off his seat first. "Shit, Goldie must have forgotten something."

As soon as he'd left, her head flopped down onto the granite counter and she pressed her wrists against the cold stone too. She'd heard somewhere that if you chill your pulse points your heart rate will slow down, and right now anything was worth a try.

She knew. Her instincts finally kicked in and they'd been right, and this was all going to be so complicated and so emotional and so weird, and she was going to have to change everything — her life, her job, her home . . . And, breathe, breathe . . . How could this happen? How could this happen?

"Ginny?"

How could this . . .

She bolted upright, the shock making her wobble.

"Mitch! What are you doing here?"

"I've come to get you."

She didn't understand. How did he —

"It's Vera. I'm really sorry, Ginny, but she's had a heart attack. They've rushed her to a hospital near the theatre, and I know things aren't great with you and Roxy but she's gone straight to the hospital and she needs you there. And so does your mum. We need to move fast, Gin, because it's, it's not good, Ginny — they don't know how long she's got."

St Joseph's Chapel, Farnham Hills

Dear Mam,

Thanks very much for the package. The gloves and scarf are great and, no, you'd never know they weren't bought from a shop. That knitting machine is the best thing you ever bought.

Uncle Niall is doing well — working day and night and he's not been to the dog track this month at all. Mrs Dodds is taking good care of him, although her hip has been giving her jip again and she's not one for hiding her pain.

And yes, I do know I don't write enough, but to be honest, Mam, it's all been a bit frantic lately. We've got a new visitor to the village — a girl called Roxy who is the cousin of Ginny. She's really nice and we've been having a great craic.

Ginny has gone off to London for a couple of weeks and it's not the same here without her. The only change there is that she's not going out with that fitness bloke any more. Mam, stop dancing before you do yourself an injury.

I still can't believe Uncle Niall told you how I felt about her . . . I was under the impression that anything told to a priest was confidential.

Anyway, I know what you're thinking, and yes, I am going to ask her out now that there's no risk of her boyfriend killing me. If you saw him you'd realise that was a genuine possibility.

360

Don't go buying the big hat and the new frock just yet though, because she hasn't said yes. But keep your fingers crossed that she does. A few prayers in the right direction probably wouldn't do any harm — you must have a few favours owed there after everything you do for the convent!

You take care of yourself now, and remember to keep watching the cholesterol like Doctor Flynn said.

Much love,
Mitch

CHAPTER
NINETEEN

If You Leave Me Now

Ginny and Roxy. Day 22, Sunday, noon
Through the large, oblong window, Roxy and Ginny watched Vera, still lying in the bed that had transported her back from surgery, with a spaghetti-bowl of wires coming from different parts of her body and connecting her to machines that beeped, ticked, swooshed, pumped and made mathematical graphs on a little screen.

A nurse bustled back and forward between the room and reception, eyeing the girls suspiciously every time she passed. Roxy wasn't surprised. After all, Ginny's arrival the night before had been relatively low-key . . . compared to, say, a fifty-strong SWAT team storming a foreign embassy.

Mitch had been first through the door and Roxy had jumped up and leapt into his arms. "Mitch, she's sick, she's really, really . . ." Then Roxy had spotted the other face right behind him. She'd wondered where Mitch had disappeared to — he'd been gone far too long just to be nipping out for coffees and fresh air.

And then Ginny was coming towards her, arms outstretched, tears streaming down her face. Closer, closer, she was almost right in front of her when . . .

"Noooooo, don't touch me, you traitorous bitch!"

Roxy had started flailing, her hands lashing out, swiping at every bit of hurt and anger and loathing that had been growing inside her for weeks.

"I don't want you here, I DON'T WANT YOU . . ."

Ginny's hands were around Roxy's arms, holding them tightly, desperately trying to stem the blows. "Roxy, don't do this. Babe, please! Don't do this!" she'd sobbed.

Roxy had wailed and pushed her away, propelling Ginny backwards until she hit the corridor wall. And that's when she'd seen it. It was hanging over Ginny's T-shirt, a mirror image of her own. The surprise had stopped her in her tracks and she'd stared at it. The other half of her heart.

Her tears had been silent by then, flowing down her face faster than her sleeve could absorb them. "My heart," she'd whispered.

Ginny's expression had changed from horror to puzzlement, then to understanding as she'd realised what Roxy had seen. Of course . . . Hadn't Vera and Vi given them the same birthday present every year of their lives? Twenty-seven years of joint parties, joint presents, joint lives. And now their mothers had just given them a gift that proved what they'd always known — they were two halves that belonged together.

Even if one of those halves wanted to kick the crap out of the other.

"Don't, Roxy, please," Ginny had whispered. That was when Roxy had slumped backwards, all her aggression gone, allowing Ginny to move forwards and take her in her arms, where she'd stayed, her face nestled into Ginny's hair, until Mitch had gently guided them back to the row of orange plastic seats.

And that's where they still sat, watching Vera through the window. Just watching. And waiting.

Sitting to Vera's left, clutching the hand that didn't have three probes dangling from it, was Violet, tears streaming down her face, her lips moving, talking incessantly to her unconscious friend, while a doctor made notes in a chart beside her.

Roxy stood up, crossed to the window pulled the sleeve of her hoodie down over her hand and then used it to wipe away another shower of tears that were coursing down her cheeks. She leaned against the wall, then slid down it until she was in the foetal position, her hands clasped round her knees.

"She can't die, Ginny. She can't die. She can't. It's like, like I'm only just getting to know her and if she dies then . . ." Her whole body was racked with convulsions as the sobs stopped the oxygen from reaching her lungs.

"She's not going to die, honey, she won't. The doctors said the surgery went okay . . ."

"But that the next few hours will be crucial!" Roxy cried. "Why didn't they say she was going to be fine, Ginny? She can't leave me. She can't."

Ginny crouched down beside Roxy and pulled her towards her.

"Ssssh, Rox, sssssshhh, it's going to be okay. I promise it'll be okay. Do you want to go back in there again?"

364

Roxy wiped away more snot as she shook her head and whispered, "No, s'okay. Let your mum stay for a while, it's time she got her turn. Fucking stupid rules. One person to a bed. Are they worried we'll break out the cocktails and have a party?" Ginny squeezed Roxy a little tighter, aware that Roxy's way of dealing with this alternated between distraught, overwhelmed, needy and angry, interspersed with very occasional moments of poignant sweetness.

The door opened, and as the consultant doctor came out, Roxy and Ginny jumped to their feet. He was tall, late fifties, with very distinguished grey hair and the kind of upright reserved manner that sat somewhere between confidence, arrogance and delusions of omnipresence.

"Miss Galloway?"

"Yes," Roxy replied fearfully.

"We've switched your mother's ventilator off . . ."

The wail was so loud that the relatives of several coma patients on the same floor would later swear that their loved ones had twitched.

"Miss Galloway. MISS GALLOWAY! She's breathing on her own."

Roxy stopped abruptly. "You mean . . . she's not dead?"

"She's not dead. The next few hours are still very important, but so far she's doing as well as can be expected."

He marched off down the corridor to traumatise some other poor, unsuspecting family.

"Come on, hon, why don't we go down to the canteen and get some tea? She's stable now and you're worn out. We'll ask the nurse to buzz straight down for us if anything changes or she needs you," Ginny coaxed gently.

Roxy thought about it for a few seconds then touched her hand to the window.

"I won't be long, Mum," she whispered. "Don't go dying on me."

They took the elevator down to the floor below and followed signs for the restaurant. It was something of an exaggeration — twenty oblong Formica tables, orange plastic chairs, a few vending machines and one small serving hatch with a large half-empty fruit basket, a tea urn, a coffee machine and three glass domes covering an array of rolls and sandwiches.

"Aw, look at him," Roxy whispered, pointing to a corner table.

There, his head cushioned by a rolled-up jacket on the table, was Mitch, sleeping soundly.

"Shall we wake him?"

"No, just leave him, he's been up all night and he must be knackered. I told him to go home when we got here but he wouldn't have it," Ginny revealed.

For the first time that day, Roxy smiled. "He's a good man. Stubborn, but good."

The knot in Ginny's stomach tightened. Everything had changed now. Only a few hours before she'd been so sure of what she wanted. She'd had to kiss Jude that last time just to be sure and it had proved her right —

she was still thinking about Mitch. (Okay, and maybe she'd just wanted to snog that delicious mouth again, but come on, who could blame her?) That's when she'd decided that she had to tell him, and to hell with how Roxy felt. After all, Roxy had slid off the moral high ground while clutching Darren's penis. But now . . . now everything was different.

They served themselves some tea and put a few pound coins in the honesty box, then sat at the table next to Mitch, both of them silent at first. The passing of the first wave of trauma had left them drained and displaced, and now they weren't sure how long they'd have to hold their breaths before the next one came.

Ginny caved first. "It's good that they've got each other, isn't it? . . . Our mothers," she replied to Roxy's questioning look. "I wonder what my mum was saying to her up there."

"I'm sorry."

"What's my mother got to be sorry about?" Ginny replied, puzzled.

"No, *I'm* sorry. I've been hating you, really hating you lately, and — although I had good reason — I'm sorry. I'm glad you're here."

Even if Jude had just walked in, dressed as a doctor, and proceeded to strip while singing the *Holby City* theme tune, Ginny wouldn't have been more surprised.

Roxy was apologising?

They sat in silence for a few moments. "Okay, I can't stand it any more," Roxy said eventually. "If we're going to be here for hours then we need to talk, so you go first."

"I'm sorry, Rox, it's just that, you know, under the circumstances, nothing seems appropriate."

"Ginny, my mother just keeled over during the opening act of *The Vagina Monologues* so I think we can safely say 'fuck appropriate'. I'm going to go crazy if I have to sit here in silence, so can we just be us? Talk about anything. Anything. Tell me what's been happening at the Seismic, tell me about Jude, tell me about anything."

"Tell me about Darren," Ginny blurted. Shit, she hadn't meant to do that. It was the last thing she wanted to bring up now.

Roxy sighed, then, after a few moments of pondering the question, matched Ginny's gaze.

"I gave him a blow job."

"I know."

"How?"

"He told me."

"Yeah, well you deserved it for fucking Felix."

Ginny groaned. "I did not sleep with Felix!"

Roxy took a deep breath, ready to launch into a nuclear offensive.

"He thought I was you, you daft cow!" Ginny blurted.

Nuclear mission aborted.

"*What?*"

"I was in your bed, I was sleeping, he let himself in with his key, stripped off, climbed into bed, felt me up, then he realised it was me and freaked out — which was not only very unfortunate, but also very unflattering."

368

Roxy's eyes were the size of side-plates. "You are kidding me! And what happened next?"

"Jude kicked him out." Ginny melted just a little. Jude. He'd been so sweet that night.

"So you didn't . . .?"

"No penetration. Zilch. No sex, no exchange of fluids, and no big, dramatic affair."

"And you haven't seen him since?"

"Rox, what part of all that didn't you get? He ambushed me, it was a huge mistake, and he was as horrified as me. When he was with you he was a twat, when he did that to me he was a twat, and it's a pretty safe bet that he's still a twat. I could quite happily pop my clogs without ever setting eyes on him again."

Ginny realised what she'd said just a fraction too late as Roxy tensed and looked upwards, as if some cosmic power could allow her to see into the room above her.

Ginny reached over and held her hand. "I'm so sorry, hon, that was a really tactless thing to say."

"S'okay — I gave your boyfriend a blow job."

The insuppressible burst of laughter almost woke up Mitch, and it took a few seconds for sobriety to regain control.

Both women stared at their clasped hands in the middle of the table, acutely aware that the scene was replicated upstairs.

"Do you think I should go back up now?" Roxy asked.

Ginny reflexively checked her watch. "Why not give my mum another ten minutes while you finish your tea. She and your mum always did have a lot to talk about."

369

"Do you think they ever get sick of each other?" Roxy asked.

"I don't know. If they do they hide it well."

"Unlike us."

"Unlike us."

"So. How's my life been? Did you hate it or have you started telling people you're me and stealing my Prada bags?"

Momentary surprise caused Ginny to stutter.

"Oh, you know, it's . . . erm . . . fine."

"Fine? Ginny, my life has never been fine, my life is *fabulous*. Okay, what's happened? Don't tell me you went out with the girls from work? Oh, you did! I can see it in your face! Don't tell me that you got pissed and then you snogged some random bloke and haven't been able to sleep since."

Ginny flushed. Was that what Roxy really thought of her? Did she think Ginny was so boring, so unadventurous that something as trifling as a snog would upset the equilibrium of her life?

"Look, just forget it. This isn't the time or the place."

"Oh my God, you slept with someone! You did! Apart from Felix, that is!"

"I did NOT sleep with Felix!"

"Yeah, yeah, I got that, but I can't promise not to throw it in every now and then just to rile you."

Roxy suddenly sat back and appraised Ginny from head to toe.

'Oh. My. God. I've just realised how different you are. You've had your hair done. You're not wearing man-made fibres. And don't think I didn't notice that about two minutes ago you said 'penetration' without turning purple in mortification. It's like you're a whole new you. But you're still a crap liar so out with it — who was it?'

"Nobody."

"Who was it?"

"NOBODY."

"Ginny, imagine I'm on my deathbed and you're baring your soul and you have to tell me everything. And don't refuse because it's my mum who's lying upstairs and you can't upset me at a time like this."

Ginny couldn't believe what she was hearing. "Don't you *dare* try to use emotional blackmail on me at a time like this!"

Roxy shrugged. "Look, I might have forgiven your indiscretion with Felix but that doesn't mean I'm perfect."

Ginny was incredulous. Crazy, incorrigible, shallow, inappropriate Roxy — oh, how she loved her.

"Okay, it was Jude. I slept with Jude."

Roxy's head fell into her hands. "Oh, honey, I'm so sorry. I should have warned you. I know he's so lovely and so perfect and so utterly fucking shaggable, but he's . . . he's Jude. Are you crushed?"

Indignation was setting in again. "Why would I be crushed?"

"Because," Roxy began, bewildered by Ginny's reaction, "wasn't it a one-night stand in between his dates with the rest of his harem? He's so not for you, Ginny. He'll break your heart."

371

"What makes you think I'd let him? Roxy, I'm a grown-up. Here's a newsflash — I can handle my life, I can handle men, and I can handle Jude — in fact, I did so many times!" Ginny was spitting the words out now.

"Oh yeah? And what about Chcska and Goldie?"

"Oh, trust me, Roxy, I can definitely, *definitely* handle Goldie."

It was all Ginny could do not to purse her lips and click her fingers after that last statement. Note to self, she thought — must stop watching the Tyra Banks show.

Roxy picked up the innuendo immediately and her chin almost hit the table. "You slept with Goldie? Behind Jude's back?" she gasped.

Ginny was biting her tongue now, horribly aware that she'd said far too much. After a lifetime of bickering you'd have thought she would have developed better coping strategies and stored them in her brain under "To Be Used When Roxy's Fingers Are On My Buttons".

"You gave my boyfriend a blow job!"

"Piss off, you're not using that to get out of this! I can't believe you went behind his back."

Ginny wasn't sure what to say. Was this one of those times where honesty was more important, or where secrecy prevailed? Honesty? Secrecy? Honesty? Secrecy? Honesty . . .

"Only about six inches. Actually, sometimes there was no distance at all." Her eyes squeezed shut with mortification as she confessed all.

Cue uncomprehending pause number 453 of the conversation so far, followed by astounding realisation number 676.

"You had a threesome! Holy fuck, I hope they've got one of those heart-machine shocky thingies on this floor!"

"A defibrillator."

"Don't you dare go all MENSA on me at a time like this!"

Thankfully, Roxy's attention was diverted by Sam and Destiny, who at that very moment burst into the room, Sam clutching a huge bouquet of flowers and Destiny looking slightly out of place in full make-up, a tight, belted mac and six-inch silver glittery platforms. She might have got away with it if it weren't for the three-foot tail dangling under the back of the coat.

Sam embraced Roxy, sounding uncharacteristically nervous. "I hope it's okay that we came. Jude called to say Ginny wouldn't be in today and told us what happened."

Roxy, reaching yet another twist on her emotional roller coaster, burst into tears.

"It's — [sob] — so — [sob] — good — [sob] — to see you!"

Ginny headed off to the urn for reinforcements while Roxy gave the newcomers the medical update. Ginny threw some biscuits on the tray too — well, she was Violet's daughter.

They were down to the last HobNob when Roxy, having re-calmed herself, had a moment of realisation.

"Sam, who's running the Seismic if you are both here?"

"Actually, I don't work at the Seismic any more. I was just there clearing out my desk when Jude called this morning."

Ginny nearly had a fatal tea-choking incident. "You got fired! Hold on, you can't get fired, you own the place. Oh, no, Sam — the bailiffs? I thought the club was doing really well."

"It is, but I don't — own it, I mean. My mother owns the Seismic. But the day before it opened she buggered off with some count to Monte Carlo, and all our money was in the club so I had no choice but to take over and run it until she came back. You met her, Ginny — the other night, remember? Tall, black hair, the whole hugging-in-reception thing?"

"That was your mother? She's gorgeous!"

Sam made a rueful grimace. "And unreliable, and irresponsible, and flighty, and self-centred . . . but hey, sometimes she's adorable too. So anyway, it's all over with the count and she's back to reclaim the club."

"Are you devastated?" Ginny asked, oozing concern.

"Devastated? I'm thrilled. I hated every day of working there — no offence, Destiny, but it wasn't for me. I'm thinking I might set up in business on my own — something that doesn't come with a vibrating cupboard. But it depends on . . . stuff."

Was it Ginny's imagination or was Sam staring a bit too intensely at Roxy when he said that? Was Sam . . .? Did Sam . . .? Was that the reason for all the questions? All the little chats that, now she came to think about it, were all in some way related to . . . *Roxy*. No! The poor guy was going to be so crushed when he found out about Mitch.

Mitch. Ginny glanced over at him, still sleeping soundly, his neck at an angle that was going to cause days of discomfort. Why? Why had it taken her this long to realise how she felt about him? Why had she let her relationship with Darren numb her to everything that was going on around her and inside her? And why, why did he have to be going out with the one person that she knew she could never, ever intentionally hurt?

Even if that person had given her ex-boyfriend a blow job.

"Roxy, sweetheart . . ." Violet had joined them and everyone spun to greet her, her arrival a stomach-churning reminder — not that they needed one — of why they were there.

Violet's shining eyes and ecstatic smile answered their questions immediately.

"She's woken up and the doctor has just been in again and he thinks she'll be okay!" The tears were flowing again. "And she's talking, Roxy — she's asking for you."

Roxy leapt out of her seat, but Violet stopped her. "Hold on, love, you can help me take up some tea. She's asking for it, and the doctor says it's fine to let her have some. The nurse offered but your mother does love my tea." And off she bustled in the direction of the counter.

Sam caught Destiny's eye and they both stood up. "We'd better go — we just wanted to drop these off and make sure you're okay. And your mum too," he blustered. "Make sure your mum was — you know . . . And she is. And . . . and that's great."

Ginny's heart went out to the poor, stuttering bloke. For the first time in living memory, Roxy was puffy-eyed, red-nosed, and so dishevelled she bore a faint resemblance to the bag lady outside Superdrug, yet Sam still couldn't take his eyes off her.

Eventually, Destiny gently nudged him out of the way so that she could give Roxy a huge kiss and a long hug.

"I don't suppose you've changed your mind about coming back?"

Roxy shook her head. "Nope — I reached the 'Y's in the career book . . ."

"You read a book?" Ginny joked.

"Cover to cover. And I had an epiphany."

"Is that something I should be offering as a service?" Destiny giggled.

"A youth worker. I'm going to be a youth worker. It's a long story, but I've found my calling," she announced proudly.

"Well, that's the future of the country screwed then," Destiny replied tartly. She turned her attention and hugs on Ginny. "And what about you, my darling — will you be back?"

Ginny shook her head. "I'm sorry, D, I don't think so. I only had another week to go anyway — but I think I'll head back home to help Mum and Vera."

Destiny answered by kissing her full on the lips then clutching her heart as she wailed dramatically, "But baby, how can you leave me — I was the best shag you ever had!"

Unfortunately for Roxy, this was said just as she was pushing herself to her feet. She immediately slumped back down in her chair.

"I hope there's a space in that bed next to mum."

Brick Farm, Co. Galway, Ireland

Dear Mitchell,
Here is the jumper and socks I promised, to match the scarf and gloves. I'm fair welling up at the thought of you looking so handsome — red has always been your colour. The knitting machine is kaput at the moment. The manufacturer is claiming someone damaged the workings. Can you imagine the cheek? As if anyone would want to sabotage a perfectly good knitting machine.

My cholesterol is only two points above normal now, but I'm still suffering terribly with the other thing. Only God knows why the fibre isn't working.

Finally, son, if you don't tell that lass how you feel then I'll be over myself. Aer Lingus has some great offers on the telly at the moment, and since the knitting machine is down I'm at a loose end.

Much love to you,
Mam

CHAPTER
TWENTY

Unbreak My Heart

Ginny. Day 22, Sunday, 8p.m.

She could sense that there were lights up above and she vaguely registered voices in the background. She tried to open her eyes but they wouldn't move. Her whole body felt like a dead weight — every bone hurt, every muscle cramped.

The voices — no, just one voice — was getting louder now, more insistent.

"Ginny, wake up. Wake up. It's time to go."

Ginny struggled to open her eyes, her confusion and disorientation battling for supremacy.

Where was she? Jude? Was that Jude?

"Ginny, wake up," the voice continued. The soft Irish voice.

"Mitch, what . . .?" She managed to get one eye open, then squeezed it tight shut again as the light attacked her pupils.

"Aunt Vera? Is she okay?"

"She's fine — she's sleeping again. And the doctors have capitulated and let Roxy and your mum stay overnight with her. Roxy said she'd accuse the grey-haired one of touching her up if he didn't."

"Ya gotta love her," Ginny quipped, her brain slowly recovering its powers of cohesion.

"Yep, you do," he agreed. Ouch, talk about rubbing salt in the wound. She felt her bottom lip start to tremble and bit down hard on it. She had to pull herself together. This wasn't the end of the world. Nobody had died. Some things were just meant to be. What was for her wouldn't go by her. She had to give peace a chance.

And now she'd run out of stupid bloody sayings that people came out with in a crisis despite the fact that they never bloody made anyone feel sodding better.

Meanwhile, Mitch was still in front of her and he was looking all rumpled and gorgeous, and *he was still Roxy's!*

"How long have I been sleeping?" she asked, her voice belying none of her inner turmoil.

"About six hours. I woke up and you were already lying here, zonked out. I've booked a room in the hotel next door so I can get showered and get some proper sleep and then come back in the morning. There's nothing more we can do here and I don't fancy driving back to Farnham Hills tonight. The journey here was scary enough — Roxy insisted on driving and I think we broke a couple of land-speed records."

"I've seen her driving. I can only put your survival down to your uncle having a direct line to God."

She loved the way his eyes creased up when he smiled.

"It's good to see you," he told her, his voice warm with affection.

"And you. Seems a lot has happened in the last few weeks in the village where nothing ever happens. I hear Roxy moved in with Juliet . . ."

Mitch shook his head. "She did, but she's moving back out again."

"But why?" Ginny couldn't hide her cynicism — this was vintage Roxy, changing her mind every five minutes, barging in, disrupting people's lives then leaving on a whim. But hold on — her brain was catching up with the latest developments — hadn't the Roxy who was here this afternoon been the new, improved version, the one who wanted to be a youth worker and was capable of doing radical things like listening to reason and apologising?

But then . . . she was still Roxy. A sudden thought entered Ginny's head and expanded rapidly. She was still inherently Roxy. Roxy who loved her glamour, loved her bling, and could live without food and water but wouldn't survive without her Gucci. Mitch, however, was the exact opposite. Roxy was a city girl; Mitch loved the country. They had nothing in common at all. Not a single thing. Except . . . that was it! Perhaps Roxy and Mitch were just two single people passing the time by having a fling, and if the last few weeks had taught her nothing it was that a fling absolutely did not have to constitute a lifelong commitment. So all she had to do was wait it out — stay patient until their relationship fizzled out and then she could tell him how she felt.

But not when he had a frown on his face like the one he had right now.

"Bugger, I thought she'd have told you," he said with distinct discomfort.

"Told me what?"

"About the pregnancy . . ."

"ROXY'S PREGNANT?" Ginny shrieked.

"I am," said a voice from the doorway. "And Mitch intends to bring the baby up as his own. You will be the godmother, Ginny, won't you?"

New Baby Shopping List

6 Babygros
3 blankets
5 white cotton hats
10 sleepsuits
10 pairs of socks
10 gloves
10 bibs
10 packets
   Pampers/Huggies
2 × 4 pack baby wipes
Vaseline
cotton wool pads
baby lotion
nail scissors
baby soap
car seat
nappy rash cream
thermometer
changing bag
changing mat
baby monitor
6 washcloths
3 towels
10 bottles
bottle brush
steriliser

cot
mattress
3 bedding sets (cot)
musical mobile
Moses basket
3 bedding sets (basket)
pram
2 bedding sets (pram)
breast pads
4 maternity bras
breast pump
2 breast-feeding T-shirts
rattle
bottle warmer
misc. toys
papoose
night light
baby seat
big pants (mine)

CHAPTER
TWENTY-ONE

Signed, Sealed, Delivered, I'm Yours

Everyone. Six months later.

It was the perfect day for a wedding — a crisp April morning, ripe with the aroma of the blooming daffodils and carpets of sweet peas that bordered the garden of Mrs Robinson-Smith's grand home. It was so kind of her to let them use her house while she was on her annual Buddhist retreat.

Out by the rose-decked gazebo, guests were already starting to mill around, chatting politely to strangers and wondering if they should mention that someone's child had grabbed the bandleader's cello and was making a dash for the pond.

In the back room, surrounded by a mille-feuille of white tulle, empty hatboxes and plates of sandwiches that were curling up at the edges, Roxy stared at her reflection in the ornate, gilt-edged mirror. She swivelled her body round to check her profile.

"How do I look?"

"Fat," replied Ginny.

"Remind me again why we're friends?" Roxy asked, and not for the first time. "I can't believe that on today of all days you can't say anything nice to me."

"Okay, I'll say something nice . . ." Ginny adopted a pensive expression.

"Sometime soon!" Roxy yelled.

"Okay, okay, I'm thinking!" Through the window Ginny spotted a familiar face. And large bump. "Got one — you're not as fat as Saffron!"

They both watched as Saffron tried to manoeuvre her nine-month-pregnant frame into a swinging garden seat. "If she falls off that the tremors will be felt for miles," Roxy observed.

"Don't worry, Juliet's keeping an eye on her."

There had been so many times over the last few months when the two women had marvelled at Juliet's maturity, intelligence and sense of responsibility.

When Mitch had confronted Juliet and Roxy, it was Juliet who had realised straight away who the pregnancy test belonged to.

"It's Saffron's! She skived off school yesterday afternoon, asked me if she could come here, and when I asked why she went all weird."

"And that was before the whole Alamo thing at the library?" Roxy had asked.

"The Ala — what?"

"Forget it — do they teach you lot nothing in history these days? The showdown. The big confrontation!"

"Yes! Oh my God, that's why she made Ben tell me. It's Ben's baby!"

Actually, as it transpired, it possibly wasn't Ben's baby as there were several other candidates whose sperm were in the frame. Turns out that Saffron wasn't exactly reserved with her favours.

Juliet and Roxy had arrived at Saffron's house half an hour later, a three-bedroom flat above the chippy that was straining under the occupancy of Saffron's mother, father, and five younger brothers and sisters. At Juliet's insistence, Saffron had moved in with her that afternoon and had never left.

"We've been best friends since we were babies," Juliet had explained with a pragmatic shrug. "I can't leave her now, she needs me."

Back in the present, the memory gave Roxy a sudden thought.

"Hey, do you remember in the hospital when I pretended it was *me* who was pregnant? I thought we were going to have to get Mum's doctor down to revive you."

Following a lifetime of tradition, Ginny tutted, rolled her eyes and assumed the approximate expression of someone who has just discovered that she is chewing a wasp.

"Yeah, well, God got you back, you evil cow. Just keep looking in the mirror."

Roxy tried to smooth her dress over her three-month bump. Nope, still visible. She couldn't believe he'd knocked her up so quickly — only weeks into her "Youth Key Worker" training course and she was throwing up in the college toilets every morning. Two of her fellow students had already slipped her leaflets on help for bulimics.

There was a soft rap on the door and Mitch popped his head in.

"Ah, my two favourite ladies," he teased. "Your public awaits you!"

"I warn you, I'm feeling particularly hormonal today, and overuse of smarmy crap may result in a fatal injury. Anyway, you're not supposed to be here. Bugger off."

He was yards down the hallway before the sound of his laughter subsided.

Roxy turned to Ginny, and held out her hand. "Ready?"

Ginny rose up, smoothed down her own dress and took her best friend's hand.

"You look gorgeous," she whispered.

Roxy's eyes filled and she fanned her face with her hands, determined to prevent the downpour. "Don't make me cry because this make-up cost me a fortune."

"Tell me you didn't buy it with Felix's credit card."

"Nope, it finally expired. It felt like losing a limb."

They hugged each other tightly. "I love you, you know that, don't you?" Roxy whispered.

Ginny nodded. "And I love you. Oh no, there goes the make-up."

Hand in hand, they made their way out to the garden, where the guests were all seated in dozens of rows, big hats and blooms everywhere. As they paused at the end of the aisle, waiting for the rest of the wedding party to assemble, Ginny cast a glance at the people in front of her.

In the back row of the right-hand section, Mrs Baxter from the village shop sat holding hands with one of the old blokes from the pub darts team.

Just in front of them was the whole of the fifth-year study group, an edgy Ben sitting next to Saffron, who had been placed nearest the aisle in case her waters broke and she had to make a run for it. Make that a waddle.

Over on the left sat Jude, with Goldie on one side and Cheska on the other. His crush on Ginny had lasted until Cheska's court case had finished unexpectedly early, whereupon she had surprised him with an unannounced visit, discovered him with Goldie, and realised that three had much more fun than two. Six months later it was still working for them.

The rest of the wedding party joined them at the end of the aisle.

"You look beautiful."

"Piss off, I feel like a tank."

Sam took Roxy's hand, then leaned over and kissed her on the cheek.

Juliet pressed a button on the CD player and the first bars of "Here Comes the Bride" boomed out.

As Ginny slowly marched up the red carpet, trying to avoid the holes that had been made by Mrs Robinson-Smith's over-enthusiastic Yorkshire terriers, Ginny watched the couple in front of her.

Sam and Roxy. They'd only been together six months. His catering business was still in a start-up situation, he was relatively poor and he didn't have a red American Express card. He was wrong for Roxy in every way. She'd never been happier. Or fatter.

"Am I supposed to tell you that you look beautiful too?" Mitch leaned over and whispered in her ear, a gargantuan task, considering he was trying to grin, walk in time to the music and avoid stepping on Roxy's dress all at the same time.

"Definitely," Ginny replied.

"Hey, watch the dress, dumwit!" Roxy spat, as the pull on her gown caused her to stumble.

Ginny and Mitch. They were on their six-month anniversary too. Six months since Roxy's dumb prank and the subsequent hilarity at Ginny's reaction had revealed that Roxy and Mitch were definitely *not* together. Six months since they'd spent the night together in the Travel Inn next door to the hospital. Six months since he'd finally found the courage to tell her that he'd been in love with her for months. And six months since she'd told him she loved him back. Oh, and that she'd recently shagged a stripper and his celebrity girlfriend. Well, it was only fair that he knew.

He hadn't been upset and the story had now become the central plot for his third novel — it was about a small-time girl who went to London, got a job in a brothel, shared a flat with a male exotic dancer and had a love affair with a very high-profile female television star. His publisher was worried that it was too unrealistic.

The music faded out now as they reached the marble podium at the end of the carpet. The attendants parted to allow the happy couple to take their places.

The Reverend Stewart puffed out his chest, wiped a tear from his eye, and held up his arms in a gesture of embrace.

"Dearly beloved, we are gathered here this morning to bless the union of a very special couple. A couple whose love for each other has weathered storms, touched hearts and leaves not a shadow of a doubt that these two special people will spend the rest of their lives by each other's sides."

Someone in the audience sniffed so loudly that several people turned to stare. Old Mrs Baxter from the village shop blushed furiously and buried her face in her lilac handkerchief. The reverend waited for quiet before proceeding.

"Do you, Vera Ethel Galloway, take Violet Emily Wallis to be your lawfully wedded wife . . ."

THE END